RADIO ROMANCE

Garrison Keillor is the bestselling author of *Lake Wobegon Days*, *Happy to be Here*, *Leaving Home* and *We Are Still Married*. He was born in Minnesota in 1942 and graduated from the University of Minnesota in 1966. He is married to Ulla Skaerved and they have four children. From 1974 to 1987 he was host of the popular live radio show *A Prairie Home Companion*. He lives in New York City.

by the same author

HAPPY TO BE HERE
LAKE WOBEGON DAYS
LEAVING HOME
WE ARE STILL MARRIED

GARRISON

KEILLOR

Radio Romance

faber and faber

LONDON · BOSTON

First published in the USA in 1991 by Viking Penguin,
a division of Penguin Books USA Inc.
First published in Great Britain in 1992
by Faber and Faber Limited
3 Queen Square London WC1N 3AU
This open market paperback edition first published in 1992

Printed in Great Britain by Clays Ltd, St Ives plc

Garrison Keillor is hereby identified as author of this work
in accordance with Section 77 of the Copyright,
Designs and Patents Act 1988.

A CIP record for this book is
available from the British Library

ISBN 0-571-16684-9

2 4 6 8 10 9 7 5 3 1

to Bill and Judy and Russ and

all the musicians on

the bus

Author's Note

Parts of this book first appeared in the *New Yorker* and *The Gettysburg Review*. Some early traces of it appeared in three *New Yorker* stories entitled 'WLT (The Edgar Era),' 'Friendly Neighbor,' and 'The Slim Graves Show,' and I stole a few lines from 'The Tip-Top Club,' which was first published in the *Atlantic Monthly*. All four stories later appeared in the Penguin edition of *Happy to be Here*.

I am grateful to Peter Stitt for his invaluable help with the manuscript and to Kathryn Court, who edited it, and to Caroline White, who assisted her. For the Ole and Lena jokes, I am indebted to the *Ole and Lena* jokebooks by Red Stangland (Norse Press, Sioux Falls, S.D.).   G.K.

Contents

A Radio
Romance

CHAPTER 1

Studio B

Studio B was the snakebite studio at WLT, the tomb of the radio mummy, and bad things happened to people who went in there. It was a big triangular room on the second floor of the Hotel Ogden, where WLT was located, at 12th and LaSalle in downtown Minneapolis. Dad Benson said it felt like a vacuum chamber—once, he gasped for breath during *Friendly Neighbor* and two huge flies dove into his throat and almost choked him. The Rev. Irving James Knox claimed he couldn't hear himself talk in there when he did *Hope for Tomorrow*. He was used to sanctuaries where his words rolled off the walls like ocean surf; in Studio B, the waves hit a big sponge. Reed Seymour once got the hiccups so bad in there his partial plate came off and he had to gum the news. And a week later, three of the Shepherd Boys, a gospel quartet, slipped in and quietly de-pantsed him during a long account of a tragic house fire leaving 6 Persons Dead in St. Paul. He kept reading but he yipped twice when they pulled off his shorts. Every other day or so, the Shepherds snuck in

1

during *The Noontime News* to play their little tricks: they put spit in his water glass and pelted him with food and poured mucilage in his shoes and one day they lit the script on fire and he had to read very *fast*—it was an obituary and he never got to the *Survived by* part—so the next day, Reed locked the studio door. Then, after the newscast was safely delivered, *the door wouldn't unlock,* and they kept him in there, frantic, whanging on the walls, until the pee ran down his legs. That was the sort of thing that happened in Studio B.

So none of the announcers liked to use B, they would rather go in A, the big studio, even with the musicians lounging around and smirking and smoking, or sit in C, a room covered with green acoustic tile and known as the Gas Chamber because Leo LaValley did *Reflections* in there and left it full of sour green farts. Once he had to go in B to record a couple dozen Minnesota Dairy Council commercials and he ducked out to see a man about a dog and when he returned, the remaining scripts were for Murray's Meats in Minneapolis. "Oh well," he thought, and recorded them, including a line that the copywriter swore wasn't his, "Yes, folks, nobody beats Murray's meat," a line that almost got Leo fired. "How could you read that and not see what it says?" said his boss Ray Soderbjerg. Leo hadn't spotted it because he was busy trying not to laugh at an announcer named Phil Sax standing in the door with his finger poking out of his fly, waggling. A typical Studio B story.

A red and green neon WLT sign hung over the hotel marquee, flashing, "W . . . L . . . T . . . WLT . . . WLT . . . The. . . . Friendly. . . . Neighbor. . . . Station. . . ." Then the "Friendly" turned bright red, and a cartoon man's face appeared, in blue, with a red derby hat, and his mouth line suddenly flashed a big toothsome grin and his eyes became sparkly white and the hat tipped, and when the eyes sparkled, the lights in Studio B dimmed. Only in B. Nowhere else. Gene the Chief Engineer checked the wiring. Nothing. It was a snakepit, that was all.

———

The curse of Studio B began in 1936, during a January blizzard, when a young disc jockey named Price Waterman, who emceed *Afternoon Ballroom* in Studio B, had to read school closings and road reports for two hours and ran out of water. His mouth got dry and his big meaty voice became a whisper and he couldn't get his breath. He talked without breathing for as long as possible and blacked out and when he came to, his voice was gone. He gargled and rinsed, he tried hot packs and cold, he rubbed his throat with goose grease, he dosed himself with hot gin and Moxie, with chili peppers, with birchbark tea, but his voice didn't come back. He could only hum or make a soft strangling sound like a pigeon. So he had to get a job. Through an uncle in the potato business, he found employment as a sorter in a warehouse in Minot, culling wounded spuds from a conveyor chute, and was killed in August, crushed in a massive potato slide when a truck gate opened and he was unable to cry out and warn the driver.

It was felt by his old colleagues that the ghost of Price stood behind the drapes of Studio B, restless, shifting from foot to foot, clearing its ghostly throat, waiting for The Last Sign-off. Shadows moved in the velvet folds when Price was stirring. Newscasts troubled him, so did drama shows, but he seemed calmer when musicians were around. On Saturday nights, the *Old WLT Barn Dance* broadcast from the Star of the North Ballroom one floor below, on a stage festooned with pine log posts and a big red barn backdrop anchored with hay bales, and the *Barn Dance* announcer, George Akers (Old Iron Pants), liked to slip up to B with a couple of the Buckle Busters and enjoy a bump of bourbon and a few hands of Between the Sheets during the gospel portion of the program.

He and the boys would play for ten minutes, jump up and leave the cards on the table and run down for a station break ("Thank you so much, Shepherd Boys! More Barn Dance coming up—this is WLT, your Friendly Neighbor Station, seven-seventy ay-em, studios at the Hotel Ogden, Minneapolis") and then return to the game upstairs.

One Saturday night, George returned to find his handful of aces gone—disappeared!—and in its place a variety of less meaningful cards. "Boys," he said, "the days of radio are numbered. Old Price is trying to tell us."

The boys laughed. Radio? In decline? This was 1937. When you were in radio, you owned the world. Men moved aside for you, beautiful women smiled up at you, doors opened, and as you slipped through, you heard people whisper your name.

"We're on the way out," said George. "We're going to go the way of the Ubangis. We're going to walk in the moccasins of the Sioux Indians. It's the last roundup, boys. We're sitting pretty now but it'll soon be over."

The boys gathered up the cards and redealt. Old Iron Pants got a pair of twos, a jack, a six, and a three.

"Yes, the handwriting is on the wall, boys. Fate has us in its cross-hairs. The iceberg is dead ahead. It won't be long now. The little bastard has our name in his hand."

"What's gonna take the place of radio, you figure?" asked Doc, the banjo player, playing his royal flush.

Old Iron Pants laid down his cards. "They will invent something," he said. "It'll have the same effect as bourbon but it won't give you headaches or upset the stomach, so it'll be used even by the kiddos. It'll earn gazillions. And boys, they are not going to deal us in on that hand."

Doc picked up the dimes. "Where'd you ever get such a load of B.S.?"

"Doc, I got it from old Price himself, and it's the level truth. Ain't that right, Price?" The boys looked up, and the drapes trembled.

———

In the salad days of the Ogden, before WLT moved in, B had been the Longue des Artistes, a ritzy little bar where, in 1910, the insurance playboy Howell Helmsdorf drank gin fizzes with his mistress Donna Donaldson. One night her husband strode in, a derringer in his trembling hand, and shot Howell in the ear and hauled the weeping woman home. She went on to found the Poets League of Minneapolis and the Well Baby Clinic and the Finding Society, and Howell, his ear shot off, went to Texas and was never seen again, except perhaps by people in Texas. The Longue featured luxurious frescoes of naked goddesses twined in misty wreaths of celestial bombazine—the walls later were covered over with green wallpaper, until one day an announcer peeled off a swipe of paper and revealed a woman's face, and other announcers in their spare time undressed her of wallpaper down to her waist and then to her golden thighs. They named her Donna LaDonna. She was serenely beautiful, on the west wall, behind the announcer chair. Turn around and there she lay, eyes averted, smiling faintly, inviting you to dip down into life's beautiful essence. It was considered good luck to pat her on the privates.

———

On October 14, 1937, Vince Upton did his *Story Hour with Grandpa Sam* in B, when C was closed for repairs after somebody punched out part of the wall. He plopped down in the "old porch chair" and read off the names of the Happy Birthday club and picked the lucky winner of an all-day trip to Excelsior Amusement Park and said, "Well, you young whippersnappers, how about you gather round for a good old-fashioned yarn?" and picked up his script and began to read. It didn't take him ten seconds to realize that he was in trouble. He had glanced at the script minutes before, and it looked okay, but now, instead of riding away to the Pecos to locate Sally and Skipper, Cowboy Chuck poured himself a stiff drink of—Vince made it root beer—and spat on the barroom floor and muttered, "I come from St. Paul, Minnesota, a city full of angry maudlin Irishmen and flabby chinless men with limp moustaches waving their shrivelled dicks at the cruel blue sky—and as soon as I was lucky enough to get in trouble there, I left town and started to see what life was all about," though of course Vince left off the part about penises. "Well, Cowboy Chuck is sure upset, isn't he," Vince ad-libbed, waving to the empty control room. He pointed toward the turntable up beyond the big control room window, made circular motions, gave the *cut* sign, but nothing happened. Where was Gene?

He swallowed hard and plowed forward. From St. Paul, Cowboy Chuck had earned vast wealth in the whiskey trade in Chicago and moved in with a dark Paraguayan beauty named Pabletta, whose breasts were pale and small and shivered at the thrill of his touch. Slowly, his voice shaking with the effort, Vince picked his way through the story, glancing ahead as he read and skirting most of the worst parts, but some things he didn't catch until he already had said them—"I slipped my pistol into her hot throbbing love nest"—and suddenly there were naked bodies slipping

6

around in the sheets moaning and pounding the mattress and he had to edit on the run, condense, mumble, beat his way out of the underbrush, and toss in an occasional "Of course, I knew I should not have done this," or "Something told me that someday I would be punished for that." Vince was a script man: the thought of speaking impromptu made him feel faint. Nonetheless, when Cowboy Chuck and Pabletta went swimming and Chuck stripped off the paper-thin white cotton shirt in which her taut nipples protruded like accusing fingers, Vince had to put down the script and improvise his way to shore. Cowboy Chuck ran out of the lake and put on his pants and rode to town and found a church. His mother was there, on her knees, scrubbing the floor. He knelt down and begged her forgiveness. He denounced the evil influence of modern novels. Word came, via a boy who rode up on his bicycle, that Pabletta had died beneath the wheels of a truck. Chuck called on all listeners, especially the kiddos, to obey their parents and attend church regularly, and then the big hand approached twelve, and the announcer said, "That's all for today. Be sure to join Grandpa Sam tomorrow at the same time for another exciting story." And it was over. Vince turned and glared at Donna LaDonna. "You're supposed to be lucky," he said, "and you're no different from all the others."

7

CHAPTER 2

Ray

Ray Soderbjerg, President of WLT, offered $50 for information leading to the author of Cowboy Chuck, and though he had no solid leads, he first suspected his younger brother, Roy, because Roy was mad at him. But Roy had been in Moorhead, on his farm, cutting alfalfa that week. Besides, the Cowboy Chuck script used sophisticated terms like *quim* and *rooty* and *pearl dive* and *the man in the boat* and *flushing the quail* and *table grade* and *plush run* and *bazoongies* and *zazzle*, words that Ray didn't think Roy had ever heard. Roy was an engineer, a deep thinker, not a quail flusher; his greatest pleasure in life, he himself had said, was the invention of an icebox so efficient it ran on one block per month. He was long and gangly, with big red wrists and thin sandy hair and wingflap ears and a large google in his throat, and he walked with a noticeable boing-boing gait and his breath was enough to stun a monkey. He was no pearl diver.

Ray was the diver. He was a looker, handsome in a

beefy way, smelling of *eau de lavande* and a heliotrope pomade, with a nice head of hair and dark, Charles Boyer eyes, a natty dresser who was made for the blue pinstripe suit and the red bow tie, and though built like a fireplug he had the nimble feet of a man who could find his way around a dance floor. Ray knew a number of friendly girls around town and in St. Paul and Duluth and a beauty named Mavis Feezer in Brainerd for when he went fishing and Sophie Sosnowski in Bemidji for deer-hunting season, also a Chippewa lady *outside* Bemidji named Bear Thighs. He didn't brag about his amours, being married to a fine woman, Vesta, but thanks to the mirrors in the Hotel Ogden coffee shop, which bounced entire conversations word for word to select spots, people at WLT were wise to him. Ray always came in at twelve-thirty for lunch and sat in the far corner, and the far corner could be heard perfectly by anyone sitting on one of the first six stools at the counter. That was where WLT people liked to sit and eat their sandwiches and hear him tell his nephew, Roy Jr., about women. Roy Jr. was the General Manager. He looked like his dad. He sat chewing, throat bobbing, not a word of moral admonition, just paying attention. "Holy cow, that Alma, she peeled me like a banana and threw me in the tub and we did it underwater and then in bed with her jumping around on me, dripping wet, barking like a golden retriever—holy cow, she was going to town like it was gym class. I still have marks on my chest," Ray said in a low voice, and along the counter, Reed Seymour and Leo and Gene and Art Finn sat chewing quietly, listening. *Alma. Alma Melting of* The Excelsior Bakery Show. *She certainly didn't* look *like that kind of woman, the kind who would bark.*

"I have wasted half my life in the company of boring and stupid and ofttimes treacherous men but I have yet to

9

regret a single moment I spent alone with a beautiful woman," said Ray. "And I've yet to meet one who isn't beautiful."

He couldn't help himself, Ray said. If there was a stylish woman nearby, he had to stand by her. And then he smelled something, and that wasn't his fault, was it? A lovely woman gave off a glow. He felt young and lively next to her, found himself telling stories and jokes, and if she didn't tell him absolutely no, to get away, he stayed stuck to her, and eventually, sometimes, he got lucky. "If I was your age, I wouldn't have time to come to work at all," said Ray. "I'd be bed dancing day and night."

Roy was disgusted with Ray's romantic ways, and told him so, but it was only envy, Ray could see that. Roy was a frustrated man, and his bad breath was a sure sign of sex deficiency. "Roy breathe on you yet today?" Ray would whisper to Laurel, the receptionist. "Ripe, huh? I tell you, he smells like the cemetery after the earthquake hit. No wonder he can't get his ashes hauled, huh?" Laurel Larpenteur had a creampuff mouth and big brown eyes and was one of Ray's favorites. Such a cutie. He loved to stand behind her and put his hands on her little shoulders and let his fingers tiptoe down the slope to her collarbone. He was saving her for a lucky day.

———

He told Laurel, "My brother Roy is one of the great original minds, but unfortunately he never wrote it down. But then, most of it was wrong, of course. Which is typical of brilliant men. Eighty percent of the time when they dip down into the font of wisdom they come up with a handful of horse hockey. You wouldn't believe the crap he's dreamt up. His very first major invention was the rear-drive horse-pushed wagon, which was a thrill to steer,

I assure you. Last week, he proposed a radio show based on *eavesdropping*—you'd hang a mike in a hole in the wall, and broadcast it. Once he designed a radio theater —it seats fifteen people and it has *sixty-four separate speakers* all around you so the sound moves around you. Brilliant. Unfortunately, you'd have to own sixty-four radio stations to run the thing. But if a genius like Roy happens to have a good manager like me, he can do okay, but unfortunately he can't bear to be contradicted. So he stays in Moorhead, on the farm, and spends days alone in his workshop. Little cot in the corner and a potbelly stove and his workbench and drawing table. Neat as a pin. His wife sends hot lunches to him in a bucket that winches out on a wire and he winches back his dirty laundry. Why would a man live like this? Alone on the godforsaken prairie surrounded by whispering cornfields and phlegmatic Swedes if instead you could go to picture shows and snazzy restaurants and dance with a beautiful woman with her head on your shoulder and her perfume driving you wild? I tell you, I have wasted half my life in the company of men and I have yet to regret a moment spent with a beautiful woman. Alone, that is. In groups, they're worse than Shriners."

Ray kept on the trail of Cowboy Chuck through the winter and spring of 1938. He hired a detective named Connors who traced the Cowboy Chuck script to an Underwood typewriter in the sales office, so Ray called in Art Finn, the sales manager.

"If it wasn't my brother, which it wasn't, then it was you, Art, and don't think I don't have a sense of humor, I do, but don't crap in the nest, doggone it."

Art just laughed. "If I were going to pull a fast one, would I use a typewriter in my own *office?* What kinda

11

squarehead do you think I am?" Art said he thought it
might be Reed Seymour. "Seymour's had a snaky look
about him for weeks. Ask him. I dare you. Sneak up
behind him and yell 'You're the asshole behind Cowboy
Chuck!' and see if he doesn't flinch."

So Ray called in Reed Seymour. The young man arrived, moist and quivering, eyes dilated, and Ray hadn't
the heart to accuse him. "How's everything going then?"
he asked. "People treating you okay? You getting a chance
to write any scripts for Grandpa Sam these days?"

"Things are swell, Mr. Soderbjerg," he said in a voice
so much thinner and higher than the big deep one he used
in introducing *Friendly Neighbor*. "Do you want me to
start writing scripts?"

"Mr. Seymour, I just want you to keep on doing good
work. You're one of the premier announcers in radio in
Minneapolis. You just keep on setting a high standard for
the others."

"Thank you, sir."

Seymour was too young to know words like *quim*. It
was Art all right. *Okay*, thought Ray, *there's one for Art.
Let him laugh. One is all he gets. Next one is my laugh.*

Cowboy Chuck stuck in Ray's craw for months. "Anyone who wants to could walk in and put us on the rocks
in a minute," he told Roy. "Walk up to that microphone
and say *Shit piss pecker* and we can kiss it all goodbye."
He leaned forward to whisper this, and leaned back. His
brother's breath reeked of Lucky cigarettes and oranges.

So Roy paid Leo LaValley $10 to tell a raw one on the
Noontime Jubilee, to get a rise out of Ray. Roy sat by Ray's
big oak desk with the souvenir coconuts and the *Queen
Mary* and the portrait of Vesta that lifted to reveal a naked
French girl lounging in a wing chair, and Roy cranked
up the volume as Leo said, "So Knute told Inga he loved
her so much he wanted to buy her a fancy new bed—he

said, I want one with that big cloth thing up over it? She said, a canopy! He said, no, that's *under* the bed and we're going to *keep* it down there."

Just as Roy had hoped, Ray hit the roof. He jumped to his feet and yelled, *"That's* it!" He fired Leo and drew up a WLT code covering all aspects of broadcasting ("The Principles of Radiation"), including a list of subjects to be avoided—sexual matters, bodily excretions, things that could be considered sacrilegious—and a dress code—jackets and ties at all times, trousers clean and pressed—and tips on music—No "hot" playing. No Jungle Rhythms. No showboating. Play the notes. No Crooning or Moaning. The Principles concluded: "Just follow these instructions. Don't ask why or by God I'll show you why, and this applies to everyone. Put a little starch into the performance, don't whisper. Most importantly, don't get big ideas about yourself. Just because you're 'On The Air' doesn't make you somebody. You're not. By the grace of God, it is given to us to cast our bread on distant waters. 'See then that ye walk circumspectly, not as fools, but as wise.' Eph. 5:15. No exceptions to this policy. *Management.*"

———

Leo was hired back the next day, of course, but Ray told the engineers to keep an eye out for people in the *Barn Dance* audience who seemed agitated and to be ready to throw the switch—there were plots, Ray believed, at a certain fraternity at the U and also in the city room of the Minneapolis *Tribune* to smuggle a person onto a WLT show to make a smutty remark. He hired two ushers named Stan and Gus Ekroos, big sturdy fellows, who could remove a person from anywhere in the ballroom in less than twelve seconds, using hand signals and a two-man fireman's carry. Ray made a new hiring policy: no fraternity boys, no college grads, nobody with a newspaper background. He could imagine a person like that running into a studio and yelling, "Suck off!" He could imagine a new announcer reading the livestock report: "Nos. 1, 2, and 3 220–330-pound barrows and gilts sold at 21.50 to 22.75, and No. 1 pig shit, 15–25 cents." He could imagine the duo-pianists Elmer and Walt playing merrily away as Alma Melting sang,

> Slip your hand up my dress
> Yes, yes, yes!
> Take off my pants and make me dance
> Ride me like a pony.

Or Avis Burnette, Small Town Librarian, going to work weekends in a tavern, and Dad Benson of *Friendly Neighbor* unbuttoning her bodice and drinking sloe gin. "Your breasts are as firm as a tabletop," he would exclaim as thousands of families across Minnesota and Wisconsin leaned forward. "Oh boy! and look at those pert nipples!" Ray imagined LaWella Wells stopping in the middle of *Adventures in Homemaking* to tell how he had had his way with her for a year. She was so sweet and her breasts like little apples but you didn't need to say so on the radio. "He took my clothes off me and lay on top of me," she would say. "He put his thing in me. He pressed against me. He made me. It was him, not me. A cheap, vulgar, rancid old man. I hated it. Fortunately, it was over before I knew it."

CHAPTER 3

1926

WLT (With Lettuce and Tomato) was founded by the Soderbjergs in 1926 to promote their new restaurant in the old Pillsbury mansion on Nicollet Avenue near the ballpark. Two years before, they had sold the family ice business on Medicine Lake, seeing refrigeration on the horizon, and bought the house, hoping to become the sandwich kings of south Minneapolis. The mansion had been the seat of the famous old flour family, later becoming the Portland Mortuary where two generations of well-heeled Lutherans had been carried out of this world in gloomy opulence, shined on by a French chandelier. Slender, semidressed maidens cavorted over the fireplace.

Dropping the Soderbjerg *j*, Ray and Roy opened Soderberg's Court with six sandwiches on the menu: egg salad, onion and cucumber, toasted cheese, chicken salad, ham and Swiss, and the Hamburg. *Best Quick Lunch in Town at Any Price*, said the sign. The egg salad was tops, four inches thick at the middle and served on wheat bread with a good hard crust, but their first year was grim, long days spent looking at empty tables. They lost a bundle—so they brought in their aunts, Ingrid and Grete, to run the kitchen. The ladies expanded into hot dishes such as Liver Loaf and Salmon Puffs and Tuna Mousse and Baked Baloney, and salads (Confetti Coleslaw, Kraut Rounders) and desserts, which many considered their best feature. The Chocolate Gotcha Cake was fabulous, the Tomato Soup Cake too, the Apple Pie in a Bag, the Cherry Stackups. But Soderberg's still was going nowhere.

The aunts thought the missing *j* might be why. "If you're ashamed of your own name and turn your back on your own heritage, then you're in trouble from the start," they said, but Ray pointed out that, in Norway, the family name was Molde, taken from the ancestral village near Trondhjem. When his dad, Mads Molde, came over in 1881, he went into ice, that being what he knew best, and started the Molde Ice Company. After he learned English well enough to understand that the name Molde is like a lampshade on your head, he changed it to Beneficial Ice and invented for himself the name Soderbjerg—*bjerg*, meaning "mountain," and *soder* from Minnesoder—and he immediately felt a surge of prosperity, which he celebrated by changing his first name to Eugene. No, dropping the *j* was small beer compared to Dad. Dad had thrown out as much of his heritage as he could get his hands on. And Americans, Ray said, cannot pronounce "-bjerg" and rather than make a fluff would eat elsewhere. Which, it appeared, they were doing anyway.

Roy thought the problem was poor location: a former mortuary. "Too many customers have been here once before, to bury a loved one. You sit down and spot the ferns or you hear the clink of ice cubes and you think about somebody pumping formaldehyde through a tube in your ankle. It puts a crimp in your appetite. We should've built a new place, out on the River Road." Their sister Lottie refused to set foot in the restaurant—or set wheel, since she was in a wheelchair, crippled since childhood from polio. She thought that opening a restaurant in a mortuary was morbid beyond words, the next thing to cannibalism itself. Ray was glad she felt that way: getting her up steps was a major undertaking, heavy as she was. It was like hauling a coffin, except you didn't have the nice long handles and the five other guys to help.

Roy thought another problem was the newspaper ads. A murky etching of two men in dinner clothing descending from a carriage under a lamppost against a weeping willow, and underneath: *The establishment to which gentlemen repair for refreshment.* "People will take us for a whorehouse," said Roy. "Especially if they know you personally." The ad was Ray's work. Ray said, "If we did as well as most Minneapolis whorehouses, we'd be cleaning up."

The real problem with Soderberg's wasn't the building, said Ray, but that, among your better families—the Pillsburys, the MacMillans, the Daytons, the Denhams— sandwiches are looked down on as something served free in taverns and eaten by a big bruiser in coveralls with his other hand wrapped around a beer glass. "People hear sandwich and they think saloon," he said. "They imagine a joint full of Polacks with cheese dribbling down their shirts and Bavarians in funny hats, people yodelling, big-boned girls in dirndls, dogs barking, big mutts. Music might help." A string quartet playing Brahms and Schubert would tone up the place, sprays of flowers—"No flowers, please," said Roy, "but music might help. What about radio? *Radio.*"

In later years, they disagreed over who had said what, whose great idea it had been: whether Roy had said they should purchase a radio *receiver* and mount it in the lobby as a curio and it had been Ray who said, "Why buy *one* radio when we could start a whole station!" or whether Roy had cried "Eureka! Radio!" and Ray had held back and dithered until Roy had grabbed him by the lapels and talked him into it. They agreed that it was the middle of a Friday afternoon on a cold February day, and Roy had his plaid shirt on and his warm boots and the trunk of the Packard loaded for a trip to Lake Mille Lacs for ice fishing, and that he had gotten a cup of coffee and sat down. "Radio," he said. "Think about it." (Or "What do you think about it?")

"It's how to make this business click! Radio. We have to grab it. Radio is going to change everything!" (One of them had said this.) When the brothers got excited, they tended to walk away from a conversation, still talking, and pace into the next room and shout from there, and at the crucial point, they remembered, they were in opposite wings of the dining room yelling, "Radio! Absolutely! Radio!"—"This only happens once in a lifetime. There are good ideas and then there are revolutions and by gosh radio is one of them, it's going to be a Radio Age, and if we get on board early, we can go as far as we want to," they each remembered saying.

Radio would take Soderberg's right into people's homes and they'd hear for themselves what sort of fine place it was. Roy's boy, Roy Jr., was studying engineering at the University, but radio was his real love. He built receivers from bicycle parts, and he'd jump at the chance to quit school and run a radio station. (Said Roy.)

According to Roy, Ray had been afraid of the cost, the danger of electrocution—a man had been fried at WLB while plucking "Camptown Races" on the banjo—but according to Ray, he (Ray) instantly saw the potential of it and could imagine the Pillsburys seated around a radio receiver in their new mansion, Fair Oaks, enjoying the fine music from Soderberg's Court, and commenting on those Soderbjergs and their wonderful taste in things, and him running into old John S. at the Minikahda Club who would actually pronounce his name right: "Soderbjerg! Aren't you the one with the wonderful radio station?" Him and Vesta dolled up and sipping champagne and hobnobbing with the plush crowd. Pillsburys and Heffelfingers and Denhams and Powells, that whole bunch of swells, the regatta element in their clean pressed whites.

"I don't know," he told Roy that fateful Friday afternoon, according to Roy. "I just don't know."

I don't know was Ray's form of the affirmative, so the next week, Roy obtained a license for $25, and Roy Jr. found a 500-watt transmitter, and on April 6, 1926, patrons came to lunch to find the windows draped with velvet, the tables arranged in a semicircle, and in the center a bastion of broad-leaved plants from which rose a black iron stand adorned with a golden eagle, the Stars and Stripes, and a microphone. Next to it, said Ray, was a pitcher of water, laced with aquavit.

———

Station WLT went on the air at noon that day with the Tuxedoans Quartet and pianist Patrice Duval Paulsen. Ray's lodge brother, the ever hearty Leo LaValley, was master of ceremonies ("Sure is good to be with you today, folks. We have a darned nice audience here for the broadcast, though they sure are quiet. Reminds me of the fellow who was driving along and his wife fell out of the car . . ."). Roy Jr. stood at the controls back in the linen closet. The Quartet sang "Whispering Hope" and "Take Me Back to My Little Grass Shack in Minneapolis," and Leo told the joke about the Norwegian mother who bought three shoes for her boy Olaf because he had grown a foot and the one about the farmer whose cow wouldn't give milk so he sold him, and the secretary of the Y.M.C.A. recited the poem "Let me live in a house by the side of the road and be a friend to man"—and then, though it was the first broadcast, Leo said, "And here's a number that so many of you friends and neighbors out there have written in and asked to hear, and of course we're only too happy to accommodate your desires, so the Quartet will do it for you now—'Hälsa dem dar Hemma.' " Finally, Ray was brought up for a few words. He planted both feet firmly, grasped the microphone with both hands, pressed it to his lips, and said in a loud voice that he and his brother Roy looked on this as a great day in their lives and he hoped all would work out for the best. Mayor Huffner spoke. "It is an honor to be given this opportunity," he said gravely, "and I sincerely thank you for it." Miss Corinne and Her Accordion played the state song and "By the Waters of Minnehaha (I Will Wait Tonight for You)." The broadcast lasted forty-five minutes, and afterwards there was a reception. Forty people milled around, excited—something big had happened—but what, exactly? They had seen a show that flew out invisibly as far as Anoka, Stillwater, and Hastings, a miracle, but how could you know it was true?

Roy Jr. switched off the transmitter. It sighed, expelling a faint breath that smelled of vacuum tubes and electrodes. Ray leaned against the doorway, feeling faint. His speech had exhausted him.

"Did anybody hear it, do you think?"

"Guess so."

"Anybody ring up and say so?"

"Nope. Maybe they were too busy listening."

Ray went home and found Vesta asleep on the sofa, snoring. Their brand-new Rivard receiver sat on the sideboard, whispering static. He switched it off, and she woke up. "Vesta," he said, "did it come through?" She said,

"It came in loud and clear. Clear as a bell, like you were in the next room."

He said, "Was it good?" She said, no. It was *radio* and that was exciting, but no, it was not good. Leo LaValley? Good? No, she was thinking that maybe she would have to go down to WLT herself and lend a hand. Go on the air and read something *good*, like "Thanatopsis" or "Invictus." Ray winced. No, she said, she thought maybe he was onto something after all.

CHAPTER 4

Lunch with
Lottie

The next morning, in the *Tribune*'s "Radio Log" column: "WLT 770 kilocycles. 12:00 Sign-On & Piano Prelude 12:15 Radio Program 1:00 WLT Noontime Jubilee 1:30 Postlude & Sign-Off"—the schedule had gone from forty-five minutes to ninety minutes in just twenty-four hours! The 12:15 program was Vesta reading "Intimations of Immortality" and "Thanatopsis," and the 1:00 was Leo and the Tuxedoans and Miss Corinne. Ray did not give another talk. He had said everything he had to say the day before.

That morning, four persons approached him and expressed an interest in sharing their talents via radio, including two more of his pals from the Sons of Knute lodge—a realtor and former Grand Oya named Walter "Dad" Benson and his brother Wilmer, who did impressions of people and barnyard imitations. He did a cow, a horse, a cat, a dog, a cowboy, a Jewish man, a colored man and an airplane for Ray. "Okay, it sounds good, we'll find a spot for you," said Ray, the voices were so realistic. The next day, more than thirty people dropped by and asked for the Radio Manager. Some of them held song sheets and seemed prepared to sing. Ray pointed them to Roy Jr. and said, "He handles the singers, the young guy in the white jacket with the fountain pens in his pocket. See him." So they put the arm on Roy Jr. "To whom should I talk about getting on the radio?" they asked him. "He's the boss," he said, pointing to Ray, but Ray had grabbed his hat and ducked out.

The third day, Ray had to close the restaurant. The lobby was full of people asking about radio, and they were too excited to eat. Their talent was on the verge of being discovered and they could hadly wait to start broadcasting.

He told Leo, "I heard a ladies' quartet yesterday who sounded like the night the orphanage burned down. How do you tell somebody they can't sing?" Leo said, "You say that you'll call them in a few days and then don't." But what if they think you only forgot to call, and they call to remind you? A person wants to admire persistence, but who has time to listen to it?

"Maybe," said Leo, "they would be satisfied with a speaking role. A small one."

The fourth day, it was clear that Minneapolis was wild about radio. The whole town had heard that Soderberg's was *the* place to go to "get on the air." Every day, a line began to form at 9 a.m. for the *Noontime Jubilee* and its popular "Meet Your Neighbors" feature, where Leo LaValley would come through the ferns with the big carbon-ribbon microphone in hand, hop down off the stage, and stroll from table to table, putting the mike down for folks to speak into. It was a real innovation— the voice of an ordinary person, such as the listener, carried to countless unseen homes as if he or she were the Governor! Miraculous! Whole families waited in line outside

Soderberg's for hours who had journeyed from distant towns, having alerted neighbors and friends to listen to their broadcast. People offered to pay money for the privilege.

To speak through the air on the radio! It was so wonderful—and so awful. Many a man who had rehearsed the golden words in his mind found himself tongue-tied at the crucial moment, and sat down in shame and wept bitterly and had to be comforted. Many a man who had thought to tell a joke chucked it at the last moment in favor of a religious or patriotic sentiment befitting the occasion. ("This is Albert M. of Waseca. Hello. For all have sinned and come short of the glory of God. My dear listener, if I can only persuade you of the truth of this verse, then I will have accomplished a great deal. Thank you very much.") Some people stood up and requested prayers for their mother who had been ill and who was listening at home. Respect for the flag was expressed, and the need for vigilance, the superiority of Minnesota cheese and butter, the beauty of her lakes and rivers, the belief in democracy, the hope for a better future through scientific methods of agriculture. Bracing their hand on a chair, they spoke of hardship and its lessons—the value of good friends and a close family—you learn these things when times are hard. Spoken on the radio, carried to distant places *instantly*, these truths seemed even more permanent, like the light of the sun.

Even the WLT regulars considered the idea of broadcasting pretty amazing. They could not quite believe it. They never got used to it. To think that their voices were heard by thousands all over Minnesota! Leo LaValley would tell his wife Leola in the evening about a particularly good joke he had told on the radio that day, "You should have heard it!"

"I did hear it, as clear as day," she would say. Of course

Leo knew this, and yet, never having heard it himself, he couldn't be sure.

One day, unable to bear the mystery, he backed away from the microphone as he was telling the story about Ole Torvaldson's horse. Ole got drunk as a skunk one night and his friends turned the saddle backwards on his faithful horse Henrik and Ole climbed on board and rode away home to Lena and burst in the door, weeping—Leo edged toward the door to the linen closet as he told the joke, the microphone in hand, and he cracked open the door just as he came to the punchline—Ole said, "They cut Henrik's head off but I stuck my finger in his windpipe and he ran faster than ever"—and recognized his own voice on Roy Jr.'s receiver inside, and cried, "I have heard it!" Sensing that the home audience might not grasp the meaning of his remark, he quickly added, "I am on the radio!" Ray was not tuned in for the windpipe joke. He was on Whitefish Lake, with Mavis Feezer, fishing, splashing water on her long brown legs.

———

By June, the broadcast schedule reached six hours daily, and by November, they were up to twelve, 7 a.m. to 7 p.m. Mornings were *Organ Reflections* with Patrice Duval Paulsen, *The Rise and Shine Show* with Buddy and Bob and The Lonesome Ramblers, *Dad Benson's Almanac*, *Elsie and Johnny*, *Adventures in Homemaking*, *Current Events* with Vesta (who returned in the afternoon with *The Poetry Corner*), *Morning Musicale*, *Scripture Nuggets* with the buttery voice of the Rev. Irving James Knox ("May the good Lord hold you in His loving hands and keep you until we meet again—and remember: keep looking up, friends!"), *The Classroom of the Air*, and *Let's Sing!* with the Hamburg Quartet,

It's the one, it's the one,
it's the one with the fun in the bun.
When you eat a Hamburg, you always clamor
for just another doggone one.

And *Today's Good Citizen*, and *Your Health and Hygiene*
with Dr. Dan Jensen discussing measles or back pain or
blood in the urine, followed by *In Memoriam* ("As we
make our earthly journey, / Let us take some time each
day / To remember friends and neighbors / Who have
helped along the way"), and the *Jubilee* and Leo and his
dreadful jokes and all the amateur acts, Miss Stephanie
and Her All-Boy Autoharp Band and Lance and Marilyn,
the Sweethearts of Song, and The Jolly Chums and Little
Kathryn and Her Court of Canaries and Ray's Uncle Albert
reciting "Under the spreading chestnut tree, the village
smithy stands," and one day they even had a dog named
Freckles singing "Indian Love Call." And there was *Avis
Burnette, Small Town Librarian*, an actual *show* with *actors*,
starring Marcia Rowles as the ever-patient Avis, the
woman who sacrifices her own happiness in the service of
others.

Radio leaped the miles and came to every home with a
bounty of cheerful information—what a boon! said Roy
—radio was the remedy for isolation, which was the curse
of the farmer. Now he had a friendly neighbor to sit down
with at any hour of the day and tell him interesting things.
Roy set up a farm bureau, and sign-on crept forward to
6 a.m. and then 5 for *The Farm Hour*, and he plumped
for a late sign-off, but Ray opposed broadcasting at night.
And even after he gave in and WLT stayed on the air until
8:30 and then 10 p.m., he was dead set against a Saturday night barn-dance show. Saturday night was a family's
one night together and radio shouldn't go barging in and
spoil it.

"All week long, we used to look forward to this," he told Leo. "My dad came home from the ice plant and played pick-up-sticks with us kids while Mother made spaghetti and meatballs. We did the dishes together and sang all the Norwegian hymns we knew, all three of them, and then we lay around the living room and Mother and Dad told us stories. He was caught in a blizzard once and would've died but he heard a bull bellow and he headed that way and walked headfirst into a haystack and crawled in and survived the night. That was our favorite story. It used to scare the bejabbers out of me. Then Mother played the piano. She played songs that could make you bawl your eyes out, like *Backward, turn backward, O Time in thy flight, make me a child again just for tonight*, which made me weep even though I was a child. Then we started the round of baths. I was the oldest and I went last, so I'd sit and read *Horatio Hornblower* or *David Copperfield* or *Robinson Crusoe*. Best night of the week. Why should we ruin this by putting some show on the air that makes people sit around like morons at the state asylum?"

"You chase every skirt in town and now you stand here and talk about the sanctity of the family?" cried Roy.

Ray held up his hand. "Every sinner has high ideals," he said. "Just because you can't reach the summit doesn't mean you can't see it."

But there was always a way around Ray, and Leo talked him into it.

Leo said, "Think of the people who are far away from their families on Saturday night, people who are lonely, people who need a little laughter, a little companionship. Our radio family will be their family. No, it's not like having your loved ones close, but it's better than looking at the wallpaper."

Ray agreed to a nighttime show on one condition, that WLT would sign off for five minutes to give families a chance to turn off their radios. Five minutes of precious silence, then the chimes and—"WLT now resumes its broadcast day, transmitting at 770 kilocycles from studios in Minneapolis. The correct local time is 7:05 p.m." Then the band would strike up the *Old WLT Barn Dance* theme song:

Hello, hello. It's time for the show.
We're all dressed up and raring to go.
Hello to our friends and our neighbors out there,
Won't you come in and pull up a chair?
Don't bother to change to your good shirt and pants,
We're only the Old Barn Dance.

Howdy, friends and neighbors, from the Old WLT Barn Dance here at our old stomping grounds, with some of the home folks here to sing and play your favorite tunes for you—starting off with a bang as we bring up Uncle Lester and his old squeezebox to play you the Yes She Does Polka!

"I hope people aren't actually listening to this," said Ray, meaning the Pillsburys. He hated polkas. Accordions depressed him. Uncle Lester pounding out a rollicking polka and crying "Hoo! hoo! hoo!" was all Ray needed to feel down in the dumps all day.

━━━

Every day, Ray posted himself by Soderberg's front door under the arch of plaster lilies, decked out in a natty blue suit with a polka-dot bow tie, checking the patrons filing in the big oak doors. Not the captains of industry he had hoped for, but a crowd of honyockers and wahoos and lady shoppers and old galoots with an afternoon to kill. Soderberg's had reopened as a hamburger restaurant, thanks to the tremendous effect of the Lettuce & Tomato station on sales: five hundred were sold daily, Roy invented a Rotary Fryer and Grete and Ingrid slapped the patties on the wheel, the grease floated in the air, the kitchen stank. Radio! A dazzling success! But so dreadful!

When his Sons of Knute congratulated him on WLT, Ray grimaced and shook his head. She was a bitch. Call it Norwegian negativity, but, boys, it was a dubious invention. He had been alarmed by it from the very beginning. He slowly came to despise it. Radio was too successful to be killed. But how awful!

The sheer bulk of it! After a year they had broadcast more words than Shakespeare ever wrote, most of it small talk, chatter, rat droppings. Radio personalities nattering about their pets, their vacations, their children. Dreadful. The thought that normal healthy people didn't have better things to do than sit idly absorbing it all—the daily doings of Avis and her cheery friends and Little Corinne warbling "My North Dakota Home" and LaWella's recipes for oatmeal cookies, the cowboy bands, the Norsky Orchestra, Grandpa Sam telling the story of Squeaky the Squirrel, and Vesta droning on earnestly, plowing through Louisa May Alcott—it was *eminently* dreadful, he thought—*I hope to high heaven people don't listen to all this!*

Radio invaded the home and distracted the family with its chatter and its gabble. It only made sense as a service for the elderly, the sick, the crippled, the shut-ins, the feeble-minded. That was why Ray told Leo to be careful to avoid references to people *going* somewhere—e.g. "Dress warmly when you go to work tomorrow . . ."— it would make the bedridden feel bad.

But the audience grew and grew, and it wasn't all cripples—persons apparently sound of mind and body sat enthralled by this trash.

Every day brought more people hoping to audition, a long snaky line of mouse-faced women in cloches and pimply men in shabby dinner jackets clutching retouched photographs of themselves, clippings from hometown papers, letters from their friends. A man in a *cape*, for crying out loud. There were dialect comedians, elocutionists, yodellers, mandolin bands, church sopranos, novelty trombonists, gospel-singing families, people who did train imitations on the harmonica, eephers, Autoharpists, a regular Pandora's box of talent, everybody and his cousin trying to worm their way onto the airwaves. They stood shuffling in the vestibule and around the cashier's cage, they lurked in the back hall between the kitchen and the scullery, they waited patiently, silently, ready to burst into great terrible grins at the approach of Management. A man even accosted Ray in the men's room. "I'd be glad to help around the place—wash dishes, peel potatoes," he said softly, "if you could get my girl on the radio. She sings. She's fourteen. She's waiting in the car." Pleadingly, he put his hand on Ray's shoulder as Ray took a leak—Ray jumped two inches.

The ambition to get on the radio puzzled Ray, who thought of performers as children, idiots, idiots who happen to enjoy being watched, and then he had an alarming thought. If all these people wanted to get on the radio, chances were that one of them was a nut. Somewhere in this mob of talent was some screwball who wanted to ruin him by getting on WLT and doing something so repulsive and vile as to make his name Mud in thousands of homes, including the Pillsburys'. Someone who'd burst into a joke about humping a sheep, or launch into the one about the young man from Antietam who loved horse turds so well he could eat 'em. Or the beautiful girl from the Keys who said to her lover, "Oh, please! It will heighten my bliss if you do more with this and pay less attention to these."

So, as WLT approached the end of its first year, he decided to sell it.

He told Roy, "So the restaurant is making money. Fine. But if I could sell the sonofabitch radio station, I'd do it tomorrow."

"Sell it to me and Roy Jr."

"Don't want to sell it to somebody in the family."

"Why not? We'll buy you out," said Roy.

"Don't," said Ray. "If I sold it to you, I'd worry about it more than if I ran it myself."

Ray owned a forty-percent interest, same as Roy, and their sister Lottie owned twenty percent, and she and Roy weren't speaking to each other, so Ray was sure he had her proxy. She had told Roy her great dream of pursuing a singing career on the radio, a good medium for a girl in a wheelchair. He rolled his eyes and snorted. "Forget it, Lottie. You couldn't carry a tune in a gunny sack. Don't waste your life." Communications between them had broken off at that point.

Ray invited her to lunch. He drove her downtown to the Young-Quinlan Tea Room, her favorite spot, and wheeled her up in the elevator and there at the table was a big vase of tulips, her favorite. "Oh Ray, you are my shining knight!" she cried, and bit back the tears. During dessert, he told her he didn't care for radio anymore. "It's trashy business. It brings down our family name to be associated with it. I'm just glad Mother never knew."

Lottie's big eyes watered up at the mention of Mother. Of the three Soderbjergs, Lottie was the one who looked most like their father Mads, with a big head and a lump of a nose and a face like a shovel. It was Mother who she wanted to be like—beautiful, cheerful Mother—but when Lottie looked in a mirror, there was Dad: poor old Daddy.

She blew her nose. He continued: "Radio is all flame

and no heat. The minute it's done, it's all gone, and believe me that's a mercy because there isn't a *minute* of it you'd ever want to be permanent. It's a dump."

He told her he wanted to sell WLT. It had accomplished its purpose and the restaurant was booming and they all had enough money so let somebody else have the headache. The announcers talked too much and never gave you the time of day, the singers were too loud—Dad Benson was all right, down to earth, he got the job done, he didn't waste your time—but the announcers acted like they were big stars, they sounded moody, they didn't speak up, they mumbled their words, as if it were enough that they were there, it didn't matter if they made sense. *Announcer.* An odd word for a paying job (What do you do? *I announce.*)—all it was was a donkey who could read words off the paper without knocking over the water glass. Anybody could do the job, but here you had letters from fans saying that this announcer or that was their favorite—like having a favorite elevator operator and admiring him because he stops at the right floor!

Ridiculous.

Why would sensible people sit and listen to a boxful of noise? and when all was said and done, what did you have to show for it? Silence. You could've had silence in the first place.

"If your mind is made up, I can't talk you out of it, I know you well enough to know that," she said.

He said his mind was made up. "I'm going to go to New York next week and see if I can't get a good price for it."

She didn't know that a radio station could be bought and sold. "What do you sell? The transmitting apparatus?"

"No, the license. The space on the spectrum."

"But it just goes through the air, doesn't it?"

Anyway, she agreed that he could sell it if he wanted to, whatever it was you sold.

CHAPTER 5

CBS

Every spring and fall, Ray went to New York aboard the Broadway Limited, either with Vesta or, more often, with an Other Woman. If he was with Vesta, they put up in a dinky room at the Mayflower, and if he was with an O.W., they camped in the Salad Suite at the Waldorf, with a living room as big as a handball court. He went to the city to eat oysters and steak tartare, buy socks and cigars, to dance to hot music and order the best scotch and wash the taste of boiled vegetables out of his mouth and enjoy a vacation from earnestness. The cigars were Cuban, *Questo de Floro*s, and the socks were silk, either yellow or pale green or white, patterned with seahorses. With Vesta along, it was all High Purpose: they made the rounds of bookstores and toured the sacred sites (Cooper Union, the Public Library, the Museum of Natural History). But with an O.W. he reclined in bed in gorgeous yellow pajamas and was waited on by the dear thing as he perused the newspapers and smoked and ate fruit and took shower baths.

About a week after his lunch with Lottie, he entrained east with a lady from Anoka named Gertie Berg, and one evening at 11 p.m., well-rested, well-informed, freshly bathed, a pale glow of nectarines on his tongue, Ray was treating her to a sirloin steak at the Cafe Angell when he heard the word "radio" twice, and then again. He traced the voice to a young man at a nearby table and stuck out his hand. "Soderbjerg's the name, radio's the game, and Minnesota's where I hang my shingle," he said.

The young man's name was William S. Paley, and he peered at Ray's business card: "Says *restaurant* here." He sniffed. "I don't believe I know you." He smiled. He blinked.

Ray said: "You're a busy man and so am I. I won't waste your time with false modesty. I and my brother, an authority on radiation, are the owners of station W.L.T. operating at seven-hundred-seventy kilocycles, a year old and already the preeminent station in the Upper Mississippi Valley and Great Lakes region. Thanks to the solid layer of Laurentian limestone that underlies Minneapolis, the signal is clearer than any in America and can be received easily from the Alleghenies all the way to the Great Salt Lake, and from the Mississippi Delta to the beginning of the great Canadian tundra, a region of vast untapped economic potential. With the construction of a one-thousand-foot tower, which we will undertake in the spring, this will be the preeminent radio station in America. All of this information you can verify with one phone call to Secretary Hoover in Washington. This station is now being offered for sale to selected buyers, in which connection we would welcome your interest, but I have taken enough of your time. Good evening."

Paley gave Ray a cigar. He said he was forming a radio network, to be called either the Columbia or the Princeton Broadcasting System. "Columbia would be my recommendation," said Ray. "Princeton sounds effeminate. You won't regret it if you go with Columbia." Paley thanked him and lit Ray's cigar. Ray thought it tasted like damp cornstalk.

———

Three weeks later, the Columbia Broadcasting System sent a man named Stanford McAfee out from New York. He wore two-toned shoes and a mustard-colored suit and plopped down and grabbed Ray's elbow and after twenty minutes of idle chatter about Victor Herbert and the dirigible and other things Ray didn't give a fig about, leaned across the table and told Ray that WLT ought to become a CBS affiliate.

To become the owner of a CBS-affiliated station, McAfee suggested, was the greatest thing that could happen to a man. "CBS is the greatest broadcast entity in America, and CBS artists have earned top favor in every city in the land," he said. "We are moving forward every day, signing people of the caliber of Smith Ballew, Lannie Ross, Louella Parsons, Marjorie O'Blennis, and Mary Margaret McBride."

"We have excellent singers and comedians right here in the Midwest," Ray said, disgusted. He wanted to sell, not join. "This is a mecca of talent here. No need to tie ourselves to some outfit in New York."

McAfee smiled as if correcting a child. "Hnnn. Local talent of local interest is all well and good, but the public demands the best, you know, and the best is not here, believe me, it's in New York. The stars of Broadway and the great recording artists—that's what the public seeks in radio! the allure of bright lights! the glamor and elegance and sophistication of the metropolis—that's what folks out here in the small towns want."

"Minneapolis? A small town? You must be joking. I know what people around here want, Mr. Manatee, and it's not a lot of lazy, overpaid, overaged New York prima donnas, no thank you. All those two-hundred-pound chanteusies and those matinee idols with the dyed hair—no sir, we don't need 'em. We've got something better here, we've got spunk and talent and the old get up and go. No, sir. You picked the wrong man for your particular sell, mister. I don't go for that brand of ballyhoo. I'm what you might call a small-town kind of guy." And Ray reached over and snapped on the radio.

He was hoping to get Miss Patrice, First Lady of the Keyboard, and a rippling rendition of "Liebestraum," but he was ten minutes too late. It was the *Jubilee* and none other than the Norsk Nightingale singing, "Ven vas da last time yew saw Inga?"

The New York man smiled. "Sounds like my butcher," he said.

"For your information, it's an old Dutchman who was wounded in the World War," said Ray. "Mustard gas. He was terribly disfigured while crossing no-man's-land to rescue a chaplain of another faith and so he sings with a mask. I suppose he's not a great singer but we're a loyal people here in the Midwest, Manitowoc. We don't knock a doughboy just because he's no Caruso."

"Hnnn. Well, here's the card. Contact me by tomorrow evening if you change your mind."

"Here's your hat and what's your hurry," said Ray.

It was the "Hnnn" that burned Ray's bacon. Waiting for the man to arrive, Ray had hoped, wildly, that CBS was going to offer him a price, he would propose twice that, and they'd settle somewhere around $60,000, money he would have been thrilled to accept and invest in a fish hatchery in Aitkin. Soderberg's would drop hamburgers from the menu and feature walleye and lake trout, "Choose

Your Own from Our Tank." But the "Hnnn" was so supercilious, so *smug*, so indubitably *East Coast*, Ray had no choice.

He was going to have to stay in radio for sure. By George, he was going to show the arrogant little bastard how hay is made. "You wanted to get my back up, okay, it's up," thought Ray. The man was a lowdown, lamebrain, sharp-eyed, three-piece, high-hat, hot-shit, numero-uno New Yorker. You leave the country in the hands of these people and it won't be worth living in. That was what William Jennings Bryan said and *he was right, boys*. The same afternoon, Ray borrowed $20,000 to boost WLT's power from five-hundred to fifty-thousand watts, and he told Roy Jr. that WLT needed some new shows and to pay people to do them, and then he did what he had told Roy they would never ever do—he said to Roy Jr., "Let's go ahead and sell commercials. For six weeks. On a trial basis."

Though there were frequent mentions of Soderberg's Court on the air, Ray and Roy had felt that out-and-out selling on the radio would offend people. Radio was sacred, mysterious, and people talked about it in hushed tones ("Got WJZ in Newark and KDKA in Pittsburgh last night, clear as anything, and last week I got WSM in Nashville," you'd hear men murmur on the streetcar), and ministers preached on its enormous potential for good, its power to bridge great distances and reach great multitudes and promote mutual understanding and world peace. Newspapers printed editorials about "The Responsibility of Radio" and urged the new industry to follow a path of sober adherence to solemn duty. To use such a gift and a godsend to peddle soap—would people stand for it?

Vesta would not, not for a minute—she said, "Introduce paid advertising into broadcasting and you will carry us down a road from which we will never return." She advised the high path, but then she always had. She was a Methodist, the daughter of a minister who kept a box of discussion topics at the dinner table. The box was passed around before the food, and you took a card, and when it came your turn, you were supposed to sit and expound on, say, the Role of Women or the Prospects of Amity among Nations. Vesta took to radio like it was her church. After her debut, reading William Cullen Bryant, and then her success with *The Poetry Corner* (Vesta held to the If-I-can-help-but-one-person-out-there standard of success, a standard that leaves little room for failure), there was no stopping her. She took charge of *Current Events*, which leaned heavily on *The New Republic* and other gasbag magazines, and *The Classroom of the Air*, where University instructors she knew from Chautauqua gave lectures about The World and How I Would Save It If Only People Would Listen. Vesta thought WLT should stand for World Leadership Today. "If you introduce advertising," she said, "it will send a message to the audience that WLT is not to be trusted or believed."

Roy said, "Introduce advertising, and we'll be selling jars of Cholera Balm and liver pads and Sagwa Resurrection Tonic made from healing herbs and elm bark and sacred buffalo tallow. But we won't be able to get out of town like the medicine show does. We'll have to sit and be sued for every hair restorer that doesn't, every cake of soap that won't cure dandruff, every jar of Wizard Oil that doesn't cure rheumatism, dyspepsia, constipation, and sexual neurasthenia."

But advertisers were waiting, hat in hand, to get into the temple. People approached Ray at the Minneapolis Club, inquiring about sponsoring a show. One day, Mr.

Pillsbury spoke to him. Not one of the flour-mill Pillsburys but a second cousin named Paul Pillsbury who was in the pie business. He told Ray that many of the *other* Pillsburys got their ideas from him, that he was the forward thinker in the family, and that if Evelyn Pies (named for his wife) came to WLT and did well, then Pillsbury's Best XXXX would not be far behind.

At last! A Pillsbury! Ray accepted his check on the spot, and that week *Let's Sing* became *The Evelyn Pie Hour*—

> You can serve soup that spills in our laps
> And sirloin steak like old skate straps
> With sawdust sauce on a sautéed shirt—
> You can make it up to me with an Evelyn dessert.

―――――

And once the dam broke, the river poured in. There was a deluge of money.

Amicus Whole Bran Flakes and Hot Bran Beverage picked up *Organ Reflections*, and *The Rise and Shine Show* briefly became *The Blue Ribbon Shoe Polish Show* and then *The North Star Tooth Powder Program. Adventures in Homemaking* was picked up by Crystal Bottled Water ("When neighbors drop in . . . nothing shows you care more than a big cold glass of Crystal Spring Water"), and *Elsie and Johnny* were sponsored by Hummel Hardware and *The Noontime Jubilee* became *The Green Giant Pea Shelling Party* and then *The Wheaties Jamboree* and then *The Bisquick Whoopee* and finally *The Wadena Beanfeed Jubilee* sponsored by Wadena Canned Beans and Cabbage, with The Cornshuckers Quartet to sing:

> Everybody's here and gussied up,
> Yup!

We've all got a plate with beans and slaw,
Ja!
It's time for singin' so grab a seat,
Lots of songs and plenty to eat.
The boys are ready and the fun's begun—
And there's plenty of beans for everyone.

Today's Good Citizen was brought to you by Munsing-
wear Wool Work Socks ("One size for all makes a comfortable fit, / Three nice colors and they're hand-knit")
and there was *The Excelsior Bread Show* with sweet Alma
Melting and her Bakery Boys singing "Excelsior! Excelsior! It rises ever higher! It's white, you see, for pur-i-ty,
so join the Excelsior Choir." There was Edina Chewing
Tobacco ("It never offends") and DuraTop Desks and
VentriloTone ("Ever wish you could throw your voice like
this man here?" *Help. Let me out of this box.* "Amaze and
amuse your friends with VentriloTone!") and The Minneapolis Institute of Graphology and The Donna Marie
College of Charm and Ramon's Warm Cafe.

As for rates, Ray told Roy Jr. to charge what other
stations charged. So he did. The advertisers bought every
minute offered to them and begged for more. To discourage
them, Ray raised the rates in the fall, and again in the
spring, and six more times in the next three years, and
nobody complained. "A fool and his money are soon
parted," said Ray. "If they didn't give it to us, I guess
they'd throw it in a ditch."

But the plain fact was: if you were in retail sales and
you advertised on radio, you got rich, and if you didn't,
you went broke. There were ten big department stores in
Minneapolis and five of them turned up their noses at radio
and began their long steady decline toward extinction.
Newspapers were all well and good if the reader had his
eye out for an ad, but for planting the seeds of customer

loyalty, nothing beat friendly broadcasting. By 1931, WLT was netting a profit of about $10,000 a week.

———

The spring of 1931 was cold. There was a false thaw in March and then the blizzard hit. It dumped snow for three days and after that the thermometer froze. On March 15, Ray got his dividend check, and the next week he boarded the Super Chief to Los Angeles. Alma went with him. They stayed at the Gardens of Allah Hotel, gambled at the S.S. Rex in Santa Monica, ate dinner in a restaurant shaped like a hat, rode rickshaws around downtown, and snuck into the Paramount Studio and became extras, standing at the rail of a fake ocean liner and waving and waving as the Marx Brothers darted past, ducking behind them. Ray told Roy Jr. it was the heavenliest two weeks he ever spent in his life. It cost almost a thousand dollars and when he got home, on a cold wet April afternoon, and recalled California, he knew he was in radio to stay. It was the money. He wanted to earn that kind of dough. And it was nice to think that Stanford McAfee, the big man from Manhattan, wasn't earning a fraction of that.

That wasn't McAfee who took the beautiful Alma west on the Chief and made love to her in a cozy roomette as they rocketed through the night, no, and it wasn't McAfee plunking down C-notes and scooping up the chips at the roulette table, with the lady on his arm, and it wasn't McAfee who squired her to snazzy dives and bought her oysters and bootleg French champagne at fifty bucks a pop. It was Ray Soderbjerg, the iceman. "Good for me!" he thought.

He had founded a land-office business and he had firm control of it with Lottie on his side. She had put her twenty-percent in his hands. She told him to run the company and to consider her a silent partner. She said she hoped that she and Roy would reconcile someday, the big stoopnagel, but that she was with Ray when it came to WLT. He was the business head in the family and always had been. So that was that.

Lottie wasn't as bad a singer as a lot of people thought, he decided, and she was sure to improve with experience. So now she had her own show, as "Miss Lily Dale, the Lady With A Smile," and every morning at 10:45 a voice with a carnation in its lapel said, "And now . . . Gruco brings you Miss Lily Dale with more of your favorite songs—to bring a smile or a tear, but always . . . to lift the heart!" Gruco was a sort of plaster that made wet basements dry. "My basement was dark, damp, a place where I kept potatoes," said Lottie, who now was ensconced in an apartment at the Antwerp, a stately old pile next door to the Ogden, "but now, thanks to Gruco, it's as elegant as the rest of the home, light and dry and sweet-smelling, a place where one can entertain guests." She sang three songs, a big horse-faced lady in a wheelchair, and chirped "Goodbye everybody! See you tomorrow!" and then the voice said, "WLT, Your Home in the Air, originating from studios in downtown Minneapolis," pronouncing "Minneapolis" as if Minneapolis were Paris. *The next time you're downtown at the lunch hour, may we suggest a visit to the famous Soderberg's Court restaurant— home of Soderberg's delicious and handsomely prepared sandwich plates*—he went on, while underneath a piano softly played the "Meditation" from *Thaïs*. Then came *The Classroom of the Air*, when Ray lay down and took a deep snooze.

CHAPTER 6

Boom

The money kept rolling in.

Dutch Brand Coffee wanted a show in which coffee-drinking would be prominently featured, so Dad Benson came up with *Friendly Neighbor*, in which he and his radio family would sit down and eat lunch.

"And do what?" asked Ray.

"Converse," said Dad.

"Converse?"

"We'll sit and talk and say things back and forth, like families do."

"Who's going to pay to hear that?"

But it was a beautiful idea, so simple. The show opened as daughter Jo (played by Faith Snelling) was fixing lunch. Her husband Frank (played by various actors: Frank didn't say much, just "Uh-huh" and "Well that's for sure" and some chuckling) was drinking coffee, and Jo told the latest news in Elmville—about Mr. Lind the grocer and his

43

spendthrift wife Hazel, Pastor Tuomy who was new in town and something of a slow learner, the town drunk Walt, the next-door neighbor Bernadine Biggs and her helpless husband Lester, the mailman Mr. Tummler, and Florence Roney, Jo's girlhood chum, engaged for twenty years to the banker's son, Rupert Lemmon. Then Jo said, "There he is now!" and the door opened and in came Dad, to sit and reminisce about old times and quote a few adages and recite a poem and talk to the listeners in a voice as natural and homey as if they were right there, and of course to keep asking for another cup of that *good coffee.* The show thrived from the first instant, thanks to Dad's voice: that warm dry Minnesota voice with a slight burr, a little catch in it, a little hesitation that got the listener leaning forward. Mail poured in. It was the first WLT program to attract tourist traffic, people hoping to see what the performers looked like. They stood outside on the sidewalk, and when they spotted Dad, they whispered, "That's him."

Oddly, as its audience grew, Dutch Brand Coffee went downhill, a victim of the success of the similarly named Dutch Toilet Cleanser. Briefly, Dutch became Scotch Brand Coffee, but that name raised thoughts of glue in the customer's mind, so they changed the name to Mama's and the company collapsed six months later. The coffee was replaced by Miles Lumber, then by Anne-Marie Cream-Filled Candies, and finally by The Milton, King Seed Company, and every spring the Bensons put in a big garden, which always yielded tons of produce. Jo served very little meat for lunch, they were mostly vegetarians from then on. And Milton, King became a giant in the Midwest. When you thought about flowers and vegetables, you just naturally thought about Milton, King. Thanks to radio and Dad Benson, when Minnesota children read the Song of Solomon, they assumed that all those plants were Milton, King products.

———

It had happened so fast! *A few months!* In the beginning, people gave speeches, played songs, told jokes, and then suddenly there were *radio* shows, like *Up in a Balloon* with Vince Upton and his wife, Sheridan Thomas, playing the parts of Bud and Bessie, a wealthy Minnetonka couple who, weary of the coal business, decide to sail with the wind in a helium balloon, *The Minnesota Clipper*, and together they drift in the stratosphere, describing the lands far below as Homer Jessie the sound effects man cranks the wind machine and makes geese cries and dribbles pop-corn (popped) onto a newspaper for the sound of rain. Homer was a true magician. The brave couple descended to the coast of Greenland to see a glacier break up (a cookie tin loaded with rock salt), landed in the Sahara Desert (a boxful of crushed corn flakes), plunged into the Amazon rain forest (a deck of cards, birdseed, and a C-clamp), and in Hawaii were almost struck by a wave of molten lava (mayonnaise, balsa sticks, and a box of gravel). With a teacup, an ice-cream stick, and a twopenny nail, he could make the firebell ring and the horses dash from the barn and the burning house slowly collapse as the pumpers throbbed and the neighbors screamed—nobody knew how he did it.

———

There was *Avis Burnette*, recommending good books to the ladies of town and fending off the men, and there was *Sunnyvale*, starring the dour young Dale Snelling as an auto mechanic named Al and various women as his wife Esther, including his real wife Faith (Jo on *Friendly Neighbor*, a real looker). Every day, Al handled a different problem, a tough clutch job or faulty plugs, and the dialogue was mostly Al talking to himself. In addition to the car problem, each owner had some personal problem that Al had to deal with: Doc Winters drank too much, and Lulu Strand couldn't get along with her mother, and Rufus Zeeveld lost his temper, and so, as Al bent over the engine block, he'd offer a word of advice. "When angry, count to ten," he said. "When very angry, go fishing." And the car started right up, and Rufus gulped and said, "Thanks, Al," and Al said, "The advice is for free, Ruf. But that fuel pump is going to cost you." That was it. Theme and out.

Sunnyvale and *Friendly Neighbor* were the shows Ray cited to Vesta when she told him WLT needed a program of great ideas, called *Philosophers Forum*. "More people have heard more great ideas on *Friendly Neighbor* than in all the philosophy courses taught at the University. It's a fact!" he said. "People have been helped by that show! There isn't a word said on that show that isn't in some way educational!"

"Yes, there is," she said. "The commercials." She despised them. Commercials were aimed at women, to tie them down in the hopeless quest for better bread and cleaner kitchens, to distract them from their real work, which was to change the world. She wouldn't allow a commercial near any of her shows.

"How about a bank or an insurance company? something dignified?" asked Ray. "Your philanthropy is burning a hole in my pocket."

She said, "If you put a commercial on those shows, then I'm leaving."

Well, it was a thought, he thought.

The non-commercial nature of those shows was, to her mind, a measure of their worth. *Classroom of the Air* and *Current Events* were an alternative; their job was to challenge and inform, so if listeners complained about them, that was fine with Vesta. She wasn't there to please everybody, she was there to do the right thing—spend a week on the subject of municipal charter reform, devote a couple hours to "Challenge and Change in New Zealand," give *Poetry Corner* over for a look at unjustly neglected poets of England. If someone complained that charter reform was almost as tedious as real estate law, and that New Zealand was a nation in which nothing of importance had happened since the invention of the sheep, and as for unjustly neglected English poets, well, sheer oblivion would be too good for most of them—the more complaints, the more Vesta felt she was doing her job. Programs of quality will *always* draw fire from Philistines, and if she got a postcard that said, "You can take your Current Events and sit on it and spin," it brightened her day. At least she had challenged that person and given his tiny squalid mind a few rays of information. Otherwise, why would he be so upset? Why—if not because she had helped change him and change is painful?

She told Ray, "Why couldn't we teach *Spanish?* It's a beautiful language! We could sign up students and send out lesson books and they could listen during dinner—people could use their mealtimes to *learn*, instead of just feeding their faces."

She stood, poised, waiting for a rebuttal so she could pounce on it and whip it to death. The way to fight her was to throw her off-balance with statistics, but Ray couldn't think of any about Spanish.

"People don't *want* to learn Spanish during dinnertime," he murmured.

"Ha! People don't know what they want until you offer

them a choice! If all you give them is pap and pablum, then that's all they'll want. Whatever happened to the ideals you professed when I married you?"

She wheeled and marched to the door and as she went, she said, "This discussion is not ended."

Out she went and in came Roy, with an idea that radio transmission might be useful in assisting plant growth, particularly flowers, and would he care to invest in a radio agronomy research project at the University?

"Sure," said Ray. "Might as well do some good in the world."

CHAPTER 7

The Hotel Ogden

The fifth anniversary of WLT passed, and the sixth and seventh. The stock market crashed but it didn't fall on radio. Radio was golden. Roy bought a 400-acre farm in Clay County, near Moorhead, where Dad Soderbjerg had spent a miserable three years as a farmhand, and Roy turned his mind toward the invention of a more perfect plow. He was gone for months at a time. When Roy showed up in Minneapolis, Ray bitched about radio. He complained to his lady friends. He harangued Dad Benson. Radio was a gold mine, and it was a plague. Over thousands of years, man had won a measure of privacy, graduating from tent to hut to a home with a lock, and now, with the purchase of a radio, man could return to cave-dwelling days when you were easy prey to every bore in the tribe, every toothless jojo who wanted to deposit his life story all over you. Ray tried not to listen to radio. And then he would forget and tune in and listen, and get miserable again. He fired off memos to Roy Jr.

49

Tell Sheridan to speak up. I can't understand a word she says. Is she sick or what? There's no reason to whisper. She is supposed to be heard, for heaven's sake, this is radio, not eurythmics.

Today Dad commented that Jo's crocuses aren't blooming. Yesterday it was hyacinths. Be consistent. Have somebody keep notes on these things so you don't contradict yourself.

This morning I woke up at 6 a.m. and heard somebody talking about fishing. He talked for ten minutes and nothing he said was of any interest whatsoever. He had two or three fellows in the studio who sat and guffawed though it was not humorous. Don't let these people do that sort of thing. I am not paying for that and I won't put up with it.

The sheer trashiness of radio! the tedium and garbage and fruity pomposity and Mr. Hennesy's maundering about the Emerald Isle in that warbly voice ("O sweet Mary, me proud beauty—lying there in the green hills of heaven, dear Galway!"), the false bonhomie of fatheads like Leo ("Hey, have we got a barn-burner for you tonight, folks, and here's a little girl you're gonna love—"), the pompous balloon-like baritone of Phil Sax drifting moon-like through the news, the fake warmth of radio stars. *Evenin', folks, and welcome to The Best Is Yet to Be and I just want to say how much it means to us to know that you're there.* Bullshit. But that's what radio was all about! *False friendship.* That was radio in a nutshell. Announcers laying on the charm to sell you hair tonic.

———

"Why can't we have a little more humor around here?" he told Roy Jr. "Is there a law against jokes?"

And an hour later: "I want shows that are useful shows, not just a poof of glamor, shows that leave you with something."

Then: "Why does everything have to sound so *earnest?* What's wrong with a little piss and vinegar?"

———

Radio had destroyed the world of his youth, beautiful Minnesota hail to thee—who cared about that now with radio coming in from everywhere? No local pride, no hometown heroes except crooners and comedians and all-around numbskulls. Radio gave so much power to advertising and now advertising was everything. The businesses that poured money into radio got rich and the ones that didn't went nowhere, *it was as simple as that*. All those wonderful little dairies and meat markets on the North Side were gone, Ehrenreich's and Mahovlich's and Kaetterhenry's, and all their business went to the big boys, all because a cheery voice on radio could sell more wieners than quality could, so now the Scottish Rite was run by big shots and blowhards, the solid element was fading, the old fellows who told stories about their adventures in the North Woods in logging days and how they shipped out on an ore boat when they were seventeen and went to Brazil, the guys who had *lived* were fading away, gone broke, replaced by the big shirts created by advertising. Simple as that. Al's Breakfast was a hole in the wall when it was opened by Al, a Swedish novelist who emigrated in 1921 and never got the hang of English but could scramble eggs and make pancakes, then it boomed when Al bought time on *The Hubba Hooley Show* and every night after the *Ten O'Clock News*, drowsy listeners heard the Hooligans sing:

I'll pick you up in a taxi, honey.
Try to be ready 'bout half past eight.
Now honey don't be late,
We're going to go to Al's and have some breakfast.
Our romance bloomed at late-night dances;
It's time our love saw the light of day.
You'll see how sweet I am
Over scrambled eggs and ham.
We'll be true pals at Al's Breakfast Cafe.

And six months later, the Cafe moved to a building half a block long, with turrets and stained-glass windows, packed day and night. It was bigger than Soderberg's Court, which was packed with radio folks and throngs of fans. "Time to move," said Ray. "We'll drop the restaurant. I'm sick of hamburger grease. Let Al sell burgers, and we'll sell Al."

Driving north of Minneapolis, cruising the back roads through the orchards and truck farms along the Mississippi, Roy found a potato farm for sale in Brooklyn Park, and took a sixty-day option and worked up a blueprint and made a small perfect scale model out of balsa wood, with sponge trees and a glass pond and an American flag on a pin and a blue paper-maché river splashing over the rapids. On a hill above the pond, reflected in it, stood the WLT building ("The Air Castle of the North"), a Gothic pile with a bell tower, patterned after the Chatfield College chapel, set in a park of perfectly conical pines surrounded by a hundred tiny white houses. *Radio Acres.* They'd borrow the money and build the station, wait a few years for land values to rise, then build the houses and sell them —at wonderful prices, thanks to the magic of radio. *Radio Acres.* The stars would have homes there, and for $6000, anybody could become their neighbor. Who wouldn't pay a little extra to be a neighbor of the Benson Family or Bud and Bessie? Five hundred homes, at $6000, yielding $2000 pure profit apiece, would make them rich men.

"Would make us paupers for life, and our children," said Ray. "We'd be sitting in doorways on Skid Row in our old overcoats, and people'd drive by and say, *Look. It's the Soderbjergs. They started with a restaurant and went into radio and then they tried to clean up in real estate.* Old men sleeping on broken glass. No, sir. No thank you."

"Think about it. Take your time. It's a good idea."

"If that's a good idea, then I'm a full-blooded Chippewa Indian." They argued for a few days, and then Roy's attention wavered—that was his way—the flame flickered and he drifted along to something else—the windmill, the lithograph, the ball-float toilet. Perfecting the arm-action ball-type reciprocating flexer. The search for the y-joint grouter. He drifted back to his workshop.

The "Air Castle of the North" was wrapped in tissue paper and packed away in a box, and one day Ray shot billiards at the Athletic Club with John S. Pillsbury's brother-in-law Bud. "If you're looking for quarters, Jack's got two floors to rent in his hotel," he said. And that night, Ray signed a ten-year lease on the second and third floors of the Hotel Ogden on 12th and LaSalle, across the street from the MacPhail School of Music. It was a narrow, six-story, two-toned building, tan on the bottom floors and the top floor, red brick in the middle, like a Soderberg sandwich. He spread the papers in front of Roy, as if showing a winning hand. "Right close to the source of supply. Tuba players, trombonists, violins, you name it. Singers by the hundred. We can audition them in July when the windows are open. You want a park with a pond? Loring Park is a stone's throw away. They even have horseshoe pits. The Auditorium is walking distance, and the Physicians & Surgeons Building. The Foshay Tower is right there."

"You can't go off and sign a lease without talking to me about it," said Roy. "I'm your partner."

"We discussed it last week. You talked about buying a potato farm, you made a little toy town out of balsa wood, you wanted to build a church. It was crazy talk. Somebody has to take care of business here. So I took care of it. Nice building, the Ogden. Fireproof. And I found a buyer for the restaurant. He takes over on Tuesday."

———

And that was that. Roy was deeply wounded, of course, but then he often was. He retreated to Moorhead and didn't come back until spring. A cartage company hauled WLT out of the Court in one truckload and Roy Jr. wired up the studios and a control room in rooms 215, 217, and 219 of the Ogden, and they were in business. Ray hired a woman named Ethel Glen to manage the place. She was six feet tall, a bookkeeper, and she could play the piano and the marimba, which might come in handy. Ethel brought in The Bergen Brothers, Carpenters, and they tore out walls and installed a waiting room, two big studios, a practice room, dressing rooms, a Green Room. Fresh pine, fresh paint, new carpets, and the waiting room was lined with seven rose-petal wing chairs and sofas and walnut side tables with tall brass lamps with lavender linen shades and a bookcase with leatherbound sets of Shakespeare, Milton, Dickens, Thackeray, Trollope, the Brontës. Upstairs, on the third floor, six offices, including two big ones for Roy and Ray, adjoining, identical, except Ray's looked toward Nicollet Avenue and the Foshay and City Hall, and Roy's looked at MacPhail and he got to hear the sopranos. Ray's was six feet shorter, due to the stairwell being on his side.

"You take the big one," he told Roy. "You're the brains of the outfit, you need more room to pace up and down and think up your great ideas."

Roy didn't notice, until years later, that Ray had an extra office for himself, a bedroom actually, up the stairs, on the fourth floor. Ray told Miss Glen it was for naps, and she almost believed him until she noticed one day that when Alma Melting arrived for *The Excelsior Bakery Show*, the elevator was coming down, not up.

He couldn't help himself. There was Alma and there was a lady from the paper and for awhile there was a Nordic goddess from the Ice Follies who was willing to hang up her skates if he wanted to marry her. *No thanks.* A schoolteacher lady who brought her class in for a tour and wound up sending them home unaccompanied on the streetcar and she ended up in room 434 with Ray.

"I somehow knew she was going to go to bed with me the moment I looked in her eyes," said Ray over lunch the next day. "Of course I've been wrong sometimes in the past, and here she was with thirty twelve-year-old kids, but still, I had a notion. On the tour, I kept touching her on the back, on the shoulder, and she didn't jump, and then we posed for a photograph and she put her arm around me and pulled me closer and turned toward me so that her breast was halfway into my shirt pocket. That was when I asked her to dinner. She said yes with only a moment's hesitation. We had wine at dinner and the wine made her frisky. I told her that we might never meet again, that tonight was our night, and that I would like to make it beautiful for her, and we got right on the elevator. She was so lovely. She stood on a chair and I undressed her in full light and I believe nobody had ever looked at her before. She was voluptuous in that Swedish way, those mild eyes and that pale golden hair, and breasts like ripe pears."

Dad Benson, sitting at the coffeeshop counter, held a spoonful of split-pea soup in midair. The voice sounded just like Ray's.

"She smelled of chalk dust and laundry starch, like all those teachers, but she smelled a lot better when I got the clothes off her, and then when we'd worked up a little sweat, she smelled the best of all," Ray said. "There is nothing smells so sweet as a sweaty woman, especially if some of the sweat on her is your own."

The third-floor quarters spread to include the fourth, and Ray's bedroom moved to the sixth, the top floor. On the third floor were the executive offices, Accounting, Continuity, and Sales. Ray had hired another Sons of Knute brother, Art Finn, to run Sales, and Art kept hiring new men every month, sales were so good, phenomenal in fact. Art said, "Ray, we've got so many people on the waiting list, we could start charging them rent." Accounting started as a man named Loran Groner, and the next time Ray stuck his head in, three men in green eyeshades looked up, blinking, from the balance sheets.

On the second floor, the two studios became four, behind a double-door marked *ABSOLUTELY NO ADMIT-TANCE*, and beyond was another, marked *Keep This Door Closed At All Times*. Ray avoided the circus in the studios, but once, lost, looking for Roy Jr., Ray blundered into the Green Room and there were the Dakota Gypsy Yod-ellers tuning up for the *Jubilee* and arguing about who was in key. Leo was trying to keep them from socking each other.

"Please settle this somewhere else," said Leo.

"Well, there's no point telling *me* that," said a Yodeller.

"Go talk to him. He's the one who's mad. He's mad because he can't tune his damn mandolin. I'm not mad. Anytime he wants to apologize to me, I'd be more than happy to hear it."

Elsie and Johnny stood to the side unstrapping their big blonde Bueno Vox piano accordions, a big red-headed bruiser and her forlorn husband—she had had him on a strict potato diet and he lost sixty pounds (because he didn't like potatoes) and his skin hung on him like waxed bags. "You keep jumping the beat," she muttered. She rolled her eyes: he was a lousy musician but she was married to him so what could she do? A scraggly guitar player sat noodling, a burning cigarette tucked under the strings, looked up at Ray, and said, "Clint?" Ray knew of no Clint at WLT. Out in the hall, the Norsk Nightingale was huddled with his Norsky Orchestra over a bottle of Rock 'n Rye, and Sister Nell and Brother Reuben slouched by in full hillbilly regalia, sunflower bonnet and bib overalls and all—*Why do they bother? it's only radio*—and script girls, engineers, the children of sponsors, the cleaning ladies, and The Shepherd Boys Quartet. He could tell they were gospel singers by their deadly cologne and their fatuous smiles. "Morning, Mr. Soderberg," said Wendell —or was it Elmer? or Rudy? He almost genuflected as Ray hurried past, looking for the exit. That was the problem with paying your employees so little—the dreadful bootlicking and brown-nosing, the ingratiating smiles, the cringing and groveling.

"Where The Door Is Always Open," the motto of WLT, appeared on the elevator doors, with the smiling face tipping the hat, and the point was not lost on the employees: no matter what, you were always welcome to leave.

The tenth anniversary came, April, 1936, and when

Roy Jr. proposed a celebration, Ray said, "Celebrate what?"
He didn't intend to hobnob with the help and pat their
backs and make a speech about how wonderful it all was,
because it wasn't. So Roy Jr. bought a big chocolate cake
and set it out in the Green Room, and by noon it was all
eaten.

CHAPTER 8

Patsy

WLT kept growing and growing, and one day Ray spotted a door marked "Artists Bureau." He had never heard of such a thing. He opened the door and there were six women around a table typing like blazes and a man in a green silk vest jabbering on the phone. "What do *you* do?" asked Ray. The man told him the Bureau had been in operation for six months, booking WLT artists on tours of the Midwest. "Last month, we did more than $8,000 worth of business," he said. Slim Jim and His Bunkhouse Gang with Miss Ginny and Her Radio Cowgirls were the No. 1 draw. "They're packing them in like sliced bread," he said. Ray had never heard of Slim or the Cowgirls. "Oh, yes," the man said, "they're hotter than biscuits."

WLT's quarters were so spacious that Ray heard rumors that musicians lived on the premises undetected, sleeping on couches, bathing in the men's room, cooking their meals on hot plates they kept in desk drawers, hanging their damp undies on radiators to dry, and Ethel told Ray that one of the Radio Cowgirls and the fiddle player in the Rise and Shine Band had moved into Studio B and lived there for six weeks, conducting wild parties where gospel singers high on benzedrine played strip poker and naked ladies waltzed through Accounting at midnight. The Radio Cowgirls, she said, wore short skirts and a lot of fringe and tassels, telltale signs of prostitution, but they couldn't hold a candle to the gospel singers. The Shepherd Boys could kill a quart like it was lemonade and then they would jump in the sack with anything in high heels, hop out and sing "The Old Rugged Cross," and feel so good, they'd jump right back in.

"I don't want you to lose a moment's sleep over this," Ray told Ethel. "I will handle it."

So Ray got to know the Cowgirls, Patsy Konopka in particular. She was slender and lovely and sang alto and favored silk blouses and wore her hair tossed in a short bob. In the Cowgirl photographs, it was her face that your eyes rested on, her vibrancy, the light in her face—he asked her to dinner and invited her up to the sixth floor for a drink.

"You have a look in your eyes that no woman I ever knew ever had," he observed, edging closer to her on the couch, and she explained that the light in her eyes was due to theosophy and positivism. She had been a theosophist for more than eight months and studied with a Gnostic master in Sioux Falls who could telepathically open a can of coffee. She had learned there the secret of The Oval of Life and the Four Powers (Ability, Capacity, Facility, Vitality) and the Seven Doorways of Celestial Selection. These are brief openings in the cosmos, when a great leap of spiritual knowledge is attainable. Now she was turning her attention more toward ethereology and the science of electivism with its vast lore on the determining power of radiation. Radiation was Patsy's true passion, the study of the nimbus of light around the body. The practiced eye could read it like a book.

"What do you see in me?" he whispered.

She studied his nimbus and frowned and read his palm and then she asked him to take his shoes off so she could read the lifeline on his soles.

She held his bare foot and thought long and hard. "You are a man of a generous soul but starved for truth. You lie to yourself. You are swift of intuition, but you lack depth. But you are seeking to improve. You know your time is not long. You try to penetrate the darkness. And you are trying to get me to take my clothes off."

He agreed that this was true and inquired if it were possible.

She said that there is a hand of inevitability that guides these matters and it can only be perceived with time.

They shared a glass of sherry, and then he drank another. They sat cheek to cheek and he told her about New York, how majestic it was in the fall, the rattle of the trains and the deep-carpeted hush of the big hotels and the golden light at dusk on the avenues and the happy throngs pouring into the theaters and afterward the cafes, and he kissed her. He told her that for all her knowledge of electivism, he knew something about pleasure, pure simple enjoyment, which is the main advantage of adulthood: the freedom to amuse ourselves as we like. He kissed all her fingers, then her lips and her ears, and along her neck, and then he opened her blouse. The buttons were like butter.

"I need to know your sense of the emanations of this moment," she said, softly. "Do you sense the fields of light?" Yes, he did. Her shoulders were so young. He slipped off her blouse—how lightly it slid on her skin—

and opened the straps of her light blue chemise. It fell like a leaf to her waist, revealing the two dazzling white emanations of her brassiere.

She said the pulsation of energies was very strong, he should almost be able to feel it. He did. He reached behind her, his left cheek touching her little ear and a delicious wisp of her black hair brushing by, and unclasped the Three Hooks of Advancement and gently removed the garment. He set it on the couch and lightly touched her dark nipples, big as half dollars.

"Now," she said. "Turn out the light and tell me what color is the nimbus. Around my body you may see a spectrum of shades, shadows tinged with color, called the antinodes and antipodes, but one light is strongest, the parhelion, do you see it?"

"I see so many colors——"

"Which color is strongest to you?"

"White."

She grimaced. "I thought you might be my true opposite, but I don't think you see any pulsations at all," she said. She put her blouse on. "You weren't even close," she said.

"Let me try again."

She smiled. "I am psychic, I know what's on your mind."

"I want to know more. You've shown me so much I was not aware of and I want to go farther."

"All you want is to get on top of me and shove it in," she said. "I want to have sexual concord with your totality."

He said he was *not* only interested in that, that he was interested in *her*, that sex was his way of getting to know her, that he admired her as an artist, that he could get the Cowgirls their own radio show, perhaps a Saturday night spot.

"I'm so sick of yodelling, I could spit," she said. She told him she wanted to be a writer. Her dream was to write plays and movies and stories that would help people understand the principles of theosophy—not the tangled thickets of exegesis that emerged from the disputes and polemics of the recent past but the simple beautiful spirit of the Theosophist Golden Age in Baltimore in the late 18th century, writers such as Carleton Phipps and Jane Delton Phipps, his daughter. The Phippses were able to say great things in a few words that seemed to have a nimbus of their own.

"Jane Phipps was the one who said, *It is always too late for grief.* That is a sentence that I keep coming back to and keep finding something new in. Or *Patience expects joy.* Or *First content, then wisdom.* Or *Fate smiles on the one it fools.* Most people think of theosophy as reams of dusty tomes, and some of it is, but so much of it is so simple and *pure.*"

Ray wished he had guessed blue instead of white. Blue might've gotten him a long way. But he couldn't help himself. He told Patsy that maybe he couldn't read a nimbus as fast as some people but he could see talent and intelligence, and he offered her a job as a writer at forty dollars a week. She accepted with pleasure.

———

Patsy Konopka got a desk in the Women's Bureau, run by Miss Hatch, where two home economists sat and wrote answers to all the questions listeners wrote in, such as how to remove stains from spills on carpets and couches. *Service.* It was Vesta's idea. Patsy sat at a big Royal upright and banged away at scripts, practicing the discipline she had learned from the positivists, who believed in automatic writing, allowing one's innate sense and intelligence free flow and then *trusting what you write* and not editing it. That was the hard part.

She created *Golden Years* (1937), about Elmer and Edna Hubbard, who, dissatisfied with the frenzied pace of life in the big city and the emptiness of material success, move to the little town of Nowthen and open a coffee shop and do big favors with an unseen hand. They also become vegetarians and devotees of sunshine. But behind the counter of The Golden Rule Cafe, they seem like an ordinary old couple, patiently attending to customers, especially the blowhards who park on a stool and squawk all afternoon, and only the listener knows that the Hubbards are multi-millionaires who regularly bestow anonymous gifts through the mail. A squawker would enter and plant himself at a corner table and squawk ("Whatsa matter widdis java here? You people clean yer pot widda grease rag or what? Nobody cares ennamore. That's da problim. Nob'dy cares.") and then a good person would come in and perch on a stool and bless his lucky stars ("Oh my but life is good! Doggone it! My crop failed and the cow went dry and I need a back operation, but praise the Lord, I'm a lucky guy"), and then maybe you'd get a discouraged good person who sees a world of suffering and wonders why God doesn't do something about it. Then there was a commercial for DeFlore's Florists ("Hi, I'm Betty and I'm a DeFlore florist trained to come up with exactly the right floral gift for that special person you want to please") and then back to Nowthen, the next day: the bewildered and grateful recipient drops in to tell the Hubbards—"A trip to Florida! And another check to cover the cost of Sheila's teeth! Who in the world could've done this?" And Elmer murmurs, "More coffee?"

It was so good, Patsy came up with another one just like it, *Love's Old Sweet Song* (1938), the story of Folwell Hollister, wealthy New York executive, who moves back to his hometown of Hollister Corner after doctors tell him that he has six months to live. Folwell buys the farm he had always wanted, the old Reddin place, and stocks it with prize Orpington hens and blackface Highland sheep and he cuts kindling and hoes the tomatoes and observes the slow graceful turning of the seasons, and then falls in love with Jane Maxwell, his boyhood sweetheart and the woman he should have wed instead of chasing off East, who is married to Thomas Reddin, a louse. To relieve the pain of "a love that cannot be," Hollister does good for others in small, anonymous ways. It was hard, week after week, to compose rhapsodies to falling leaves and snowy fields, even for a positivist, so one week Mr. Reddin was killed in a gold-mine explosion and Folwell swiftly married Jane, who called him Folly, and the show took a sharp turn. Jane was quite a looker, even at sixty, and Hollister Corner was a place she'd been wanting to escape since she was eleven, and so the Hollisters purchased a large home in Golden Valley, a stone's throw from Minneapolis, and they founded The Metropolitan National Advertising Agency and became tycoons and only visited the farm on weekends. They travelled to New York twice a year to see the opera and ballet.

"We could go to New York and see the sights and you could be inspired even further," Ray suggested to Patsy, but when he guessed her color that day (red), he was not even close (white).

Patsy took over *Avis Burnette* and turned her toward Eastern philosophy. "People of other countries have much to teach us," she told Craig, who was anxious to marry her. "Have you ever heard of Tsu Li who said that some men's absence is good company?" He had not.

She created *The Hills of Home* and *The Best Is Yet to Be* (1942), further variations on the theme of weary-striver-finds-contentment-in-simplicity, and she even took over

Friendly Neighbor when Dad Benson hit a dry spell and was unable to write Jo's lines. "Don't know what a woman'd say in that situation," he said, and for a few days poor Faith Snelling found blanks on her script:

DAD: Looks like your apple tree is going to bear this year.
JO: (Something about the tree)
DAD: Good point. Maybe I should.
JO: (More about tree.)
DAD: Well, you know what they say. Never talk about rope to a man whose father was hanged. Yessir.

Patsy created *Arthur Fox, Detective* and *Another World* and *The Lazy W Gang* and many more, writing a hundred pages a day, automatically, without trying to make it shine. It just came out. One of the Phippses had said that the way to get something done is to do it, and that helped, and so did the old positivist idea that "Nothing comes from nothing," which Patsy interpreted to mean that you should take what you can wherever it's available, a story from the newspaper, from novels, from other radio shows, but her main stimulus was time. The approach of a deadline inspired her. The clock ticked, and she wrote, and the big hand crept toward airtime, and the pages came faster and faster. She believed in the power of threes, based on an old theosophist concept of virtue as triangular, and always looked for threes in a story, trios of characters, trilateral story lines, beginning-middle-end, thesis-antithesis-synthesis, quest-defeat-redemption. She believed in the morning, as her father had taught her ("Some work in the morning may neatly be done that all the day after may hardly be won"), and rose early and went straight to work at her typewriter. She believed that friends steal away months and families steal years, so she stayed single and she kept friends at bay by working day and night. She moved into the Antwerp Apartments, next door to the Ogden. She left the Women's Bureau when she found that references to household spills were creeping into the scripts—Forrest dropping his glass of cranberry juice when Jane tells him that perhaps Thomas may have survived the mine explosion after all, and Babs dropping her platter of Tuna Ting A Ling and prune whip when General Mills announces that he and Fritz have brought home a pet elk on *The Hills of Home*. Babs wept for the waste of good food and the elk gobbled the fallen casserole right up. "A little disgusting, the sound of elk's lunch," Ray told her. "Couldn't Babs have cleaned it up?" She explained to Ray that she didn't want the women in her scripts on their knees scrubbing floors. "You should meet my wife," he said.

CHAPTER 9

Dad

Friendly Neighbor with Dad Benson, the Ole Lunch-time Philosopher, came on the air at noon, and in a good many towns around the Midwest, the noon whistle was blown a couple of minutes early to give people time to get their radios warmed up. The announcer said, "WLT, seven-seventy, The Air Castle of the North, from studios at the Hotel Ogden, Minneapolis" and the WLT chimes struck twelve, the organ played "Whispering Hope," and the announcer said, "And now we take you down the road a ways to the home of Dad Benson, his daughter Jo, and her husband Frank, for a visit with the Friendly Neighbor, brought to you by Milton, King Seeds, the best friend your garden ever had. As we join them today, the family is sitting around the kitchen table, where Jo is fixing lunch . . ." and wherever you were back then, everything stopped.

Dad Benson ran a feed store in Elmville and he was like a real person who sat down next to you, he just talked and said the things you had always thought yourself. The

68

show might start with Jo saying, "I don't know why I can't make this egg salad as good as what I used to," and Dad saying, "Oh, your egg salad is the best in town and you know it," and Frank saying, "Sure looks like we might get some snow tonight," and then Dad would remember the big blizzard of '09 and how dangerous it was, you couldn't see two feet in front of your face, and how it taught everybody to keep a weather eye out and use the sense that God gave geese and take care of each other. Dad preached a pretty simple philosophy: the Golden Rule mostly, with plain common sense tossed in. Smile and you'll feel better. East or west, home is best. There's no summer without winter. What can't be cured must be endured. Hunger makes the beans taste better. We must work in the heat or starve in the cold. Nobody is born smart. Do your best and leave the rest.

When she took over writing the show, Patsy made the Bensons a little less perfect, to make it more interesting for herself. Jo and Frank started bickering over money— Jo sent off for some youth-giving face cream made from bee hormones and ground antlers, and Frank hit the ceiling. "Three dollars! Three *dollars?*" Frank was liable to drop work at any time and take the *Christina Marie* out fishing for walleyes, though he always came back empty-handed—"Three hours!" cried Jo. "Three *hours!*"—and Dad was a terrible sucker for a hard-luck story. "So who'd you give away money to today?" Jo'd ask. "Well, you know Mrs. Chubb has been down with the neuralgia," he'd murmur, and of course the listeners knew Mrs. Chubb from way back, she hadn't had a well day in her life and wouldn't have one if she could help it.

Patsy made Dad into a ladies' man. A man who appreciated women, whose voice softened when he spoke of women and their troubles and their bravery and goodness. It was sad that he was alone in the world. Mom Benson had been struck by a car two years before and lay in the old-folks home with a coma, and Dad could not bring himself to cut loose. When Jo told him he should take Miss Judy the schoolteacher to the Volunteer Firemen's Ball, he said no. She said, "Dad, it's time you started thinking about your own happiness," but Dad said, "I'm married to Mom, Jo. I married her in summer sunshine and I won't leave her in the dead of winter. What if she suddenly woke up and found me with another woman? I couldn't bear to cause her more pain."

"You could invite Miss Judy for lunch," Frank pointed out, but Dad explained, sadly, "There's no sense starting what you can't finish," and you could hear his frustration, but there was no way around it and the subject was closed. He was a wise and good and lonely man.

One day a man in a blue tuxedo strolled into Dad's feed and seed in Elmville and demanded directions to the Moonlight Bay Supper Club. He was accompanied by a little girl in a pink prom dress and a tall buxom bejeweled woman named Ginger and you knew the moment she said, "Pleased ta make yer acquaintance, I'm shur," that she and the man were not married.

Dad tried to direct him, but the club was fifteen miles away and could only be reached by back roads through the bird refuge and along the banks of the whispering Willow River. It was a real hideaway where the well-to-do cavorted with their paramours, not on the main road, so the directions were complicated. And so, when Dad said, "And then turn left at the farm with the red barn with the Chaska Chick Starter billboard," the man blew up—he threw his cane and his kid gloves and his top hat on the counter next to a sack of sweet-corn seeds and said, "Boy, isn't this the rotten luck! Go away for a swell weekend and you wind up stuck in a stupid little burg where people can't even give you directions out of town! Boy, that takes the cake!"

He stalked around and fumed for a few minutes; meanwhile Dad struck up a conversation with the little girl. "My name is Rebecca," she said, very sweetly. "I'm almost ten. If we get to Moonlight Bay, my dad is going to take me *swimming*." Dad said, "Oh?"

"Yes! And if I'm real good, we'll go fishing too."

"Well, if ifs and ands were pots and pans, there'd be no trade for tinkers," remarked Dad.

They chatted away and she asked him what he sold in this store and he gave her a tour. "This is our most popular tomato seed, the Milton, King Big Red Beefeater," he said. She'd never seen tomato seeds, didn't know tomatoes came from seeds. She'd never had a garden in her life, living as she did in a big suite on the thirtieth floor of the Waldorf Towers in New York, and she skipped along from bin to bin, scooping up handfuls of seeds as if they were jewels, sniffing their sweet dry seedy essence, as her father groused and grumped in the background and demanded a telephone and tried to call his lawyer and Ginger smoked a cigarette and whined, "You *promised* me a nice *weekend*, Bobbsie. *You* said we'd go *swimming* and *dancing* and we'd do a little ootchie-cootchie-coo—you didn't say *nothing* about hanging around in no *feed* store," and meanwhile Dad and Becky were getting to be fast friends. She had never ridden a bicycle or thrown a ball or had her own dog or cat, either. "No bike? Oh, you should come and visit us sometime," said Dad.

"*Ohhhhhhh*," the little girl said. "I wish I could," she whispered.

"My daughter and I have a big dog, Buster, and a cat

named Tuna. We've got an old bicycle just about your size. Maybe your daddy could bring you back someday for a visit."

"My daddy doesn't like to go on trips with me. Is your daughter my age?"

"Jo? No, no, she's—old enough to be your mother." Dad gulped at the thought: a grandchild.

"Oh. My mama is home with a headache so my dad decided to bring Ginger. Sometimes he goes to Europe with my mama. Then I stay home with Françoise. She's our maid."

"Oh. That's nice. Well—"

"And you never said word one about bringing the brat along neither," Ginger hissed not far away. She blew a big cloud of smoke, and her heels went *rapraprap* like a tack hammer. "Quit foolin around, Bobbsie, and let's get there and start having some fun, honey. C'mon. Puhleeze?"

Becky began to weep softly. "Oh, that's just great!" said her dad. "Bring you along and you bawl like a baby. Look at you!" He took Dad aside. "Lissen," he said, "sorry I talked so rough before, I've been under a lotta pressure. Here's a hundred bucks. Think you could look after my little girl for a few days until I get back? You and her seem to get along. Whaddaya say?"

There was a short, sweet pause, where you could hear Dad loathe the man, then he said, "It would be my privilege. She is as welcome here as if she were my own."

———

So in she came, Little Becky, played by Marjery Moore. Marjery Moore was fourteen but Dad thought she could play a little girl just fine. She was the daughter of Dr.

W. Murray Moore, the physician who was treating Dad's hemorrhoids, and Dad had known her since she was tiny. "Let's give her a chance," he told Roy Jr.

Dr. Moore was a big hearty man and more of a kidder than you'd want a doctor to be. He'd look at your piles and grab a pair of pliers and call out, "Hang on to your hat!" His daughter took after him. She was a handful. She smoked Camels, half a pack a day, and swore like a cowboy. Her mother brought her from school at eleven-thirty and dropped her off at the WLT entrance and she smoked a cigarette in the elevator and another one in the studio before the broadcast. Dad told her, "Honey, those coffin nails are going to hurt your voice," but she just made a face. "It's my business if I do. You're not the boss of me, ya old dodo."

It dawned on Marjery within days of coming on *Friendly Neighbor* that she could get a big rise out of the radio folks by saying things in her Little Becky voice, such as "Hi, mister, want to see my panties?" She could make Dad levitate an inch by tiptoeing up behind him in the hall and crying, "Look at me! I'm naked as a jaybird!"

"Honey," he said, "it's not funny. We got sponsors back here, sponsors' kids, employees' families. Don't ruin it for them."

"Well, don't have a shit fit about it."

"Honey, what you do drunk you pay for sober. Sin in haste and repent at leisure. Think about it."

"Stuff it, Pops."

She liked to goose people, and she was quick and had strong hands. She'd cry *"Whoooo"* and grab up into your hinder and make you flap your arms and fly. Ray saw her creep up behind Reed Seymour one day and give him a good hard one and poor Reed jumped so high his glasses fell off. He tried to kick her but she squirted away and sneered at him, "Missed me! Ha ha! You fairy!"

———

A few days after Becky's arrival in Elmville, Ray took Patsy for lunch to Richards Treat and told her to get rid of the kid. "I hate kid actors and this one is worse than most. She talks like her shoes are too tight. She's as bad as Little Buddy. In fact, she makes him sound almost reasonable." Little Buddy was the son of Dad's friend Slim Graves, who came on *Friendly Neighbor* from time to time to sing maudlin ballads about dying children. "Ditch her," said Ray. "Have her dad come back from New York and pick her up. Have her die and have Little Buddy sing at her funeral. Do any damn thing, but get rid of the kid."

Patsy ordered lima beans and rye bread and a pot of tea. Ray ordered a steak, medium-rare, with a beer.

"How's Roy these days?" asked Patsy. "What's he up to?"

"Crazy as always. Inventing junk."

"What sort of junk?"

"The useless kind. A radio couch with loudspeakers in the cushions. Something called a cocking gun, whatever that may be, God only knows. And a radiophone, so you can call up your brother from anywhere and pound his ear for awhile."

"Interesting."

"So?" said Ray. "The kid. Let's dump her."

"Ray, we got five hundred letters about that show. Most popular we've ever done. Milton, King called and said they want to put her picture on their spring catalogue. They want to put out a Little Becky Scrapbook in the fall, give it away for three empty seed packets. Our contract with them comes up in two months. Little Becky is a money-maker, Ray. And I want a raise."

Ray still didn't like it. He didn't like the premise of it. You take a child away from her own father and what's next? You want all the kiddoes to hate their dads? Compared to Dad Benson, maybe *their* dads aren't so nice either, maybe they belch and walk around in their underwear, so what? Kids should run away from home so life can be like it is on the radio?

"Ray, people have been reading novels for years. They go to plays, they see movies."

"There's a difference. You go to a play, you have to *go* someplace. When it's over, you come home. You read a book, you hold it in your hand, you can see it's only writing. Radio, it's right in the home. You turn it on and everybody else has to shut up. A movie is just a picture, but people think that radio is real. They think that it's *real*. Look at your damn *coats*."

Real
People

The friends and neighbors in radioland thought of the Bensons as real people, as Patsy discovered after Frank complained about Jo's bee-hormone compound costing three dollars and the show received $440.28 in three days, grimy dollar bills clipped to letters that said, "Honey, you go buy any kind of bee compound you want. We love you."

Anytime the Benson family suffered misfortune, contributions poured in to WLT, even when Dad dropped a piece of glass fruit:

(SFX: GLASS BREAKAGE)

DAD: Oh gosh. What a butterfingers I am. And that was Aunt Molly's good one. Did I ever tell you, Jo, about the time she and I went sugar-mapling and treed a skunk?

JO (chuckling): I don't believe I ever heard that yarn, Dad. Did you, Frank?

FRANK: Nope, not me.

The next day, dozens of glass apples, oranges, pears, and bananas arrived, cases of them, and from then on, Patsy designed the Bensons' troubles for charitable purposes. Once, for the Ebenezer Home's annual spring rummage sale, Dad went walking down to the widow's house one Sunday with a pan of Jo's fresh oatmeal cookies and tore his best suit jumping over a fence when a dog chased him, and the station received more than a hundred good suits in four days. In the fall when the Salvation Army needed warm coats, Dad would do an episode in which, for example, he and Little Becky went to Minneapolis and had lunch at The Forum and somebody stole Dad's coat, and Becky said, "Someday, I'm going to become a *lawyer* and put those men in jail," and Dad said, "No, Beeper, most people are good at heart. That man must've needed it more than me, that's all." And within a few days, the coats would be piling up in the WLT lobby by the hundreds, and Dad shipped them over to the mission. Of course, the coats were mostly size 48 and larger, because people thought of Dad as a big fellow, but as Dad said, beggars can't be choosers.

For the Home's drive to build a recreation hall, there were several financial crises—a sudden hailstorm that wiped out the corn, a stolen wallet, a dishonest stockbroker, a needed operation for the dog Buster—and the money rolled in.

To Ray, whatever good the show did wasn't worth the price of having Marjery on the premises. One day she tripped along behind him and said, in her Little Becky voice, "How come your pants are so big in front, mister? Can I see?" He beat a fast retreat to his office and closed the door and wrote Patsy a note: "For the last time, ditch the kid. She's a burr in the butt. Give her malaria or something. She could die of an infected tooth like F. W. Woolworth. That would encourage listeners to go to the dentist. Myself, I would prefer she died of an infected hemorrhoid, like James J. Hill, but perhaps Dad would be sensitive to that."

For a few weeks, Dad and Jo and Frank sat in the big sunny kitchen and talked, and Little Becky stayed away —off at school, presumably—and Jo, as she fixed soup and sandwiches, would relate some pithy comment the child had made during breakfast. "She's a smart little tyke," noted Frank. "Can't put much past that one, you can't. Wonder if her father will ever come back, that no-good—" and Dad cut him off. "There's a lot of human nature in everybody, Frank," he said. "And that man is more to be pitied than envied. It's like my father used to say: the angry man drinks his own poison." Well, Frank couldn't disagree with that. Soon it was time for the noon-time hymn. And then, gathered around the lunch table in the little white cottage under the big oak tree at the end of the lane, their humble home, a place like no other, Dad said a little prayer and tossed in a word of thanks for sending Becky their way. "Amen," said Frank. "I shouldn't say it, but I wish that man would never return," said Jo.

But Ray did not soften. He wanted the child out. Children, he explained to Patsy, are inherently unreliable people, and when you make a child into the star of a show, you are building on quicksand. Children have mercurial moods, are immature, easily spoiled by attention, and they quickly grow up and become unattractive. "Child performers are monsters, every last one," he said. "You're going to turn this kid into another Skipper." David ("Skipper") Drake was a six-year-old tapdancer from St. Paul who was discovered by Marguerite Montez and taken to

Hollywood and became a cocaine addict and threw his mother off the Santa Monica pier.

So the next week, Little Becky got terribly sick, and Dad was in something of a panic, what with Jo and Frank away on a car trip to Michigan and no money on hand for a specialist—and finally she was knocking at death's door, 105° fever, babbling about angels and bright heavenly emanations—"Uncle Dad, Uncle Dad, they have such beautiful faces." Marjery talked through a bath towel to get the faint voice of the dying child, and Dad said, all choked up, "Lord, I never doubted You until now, but —how can You let this child suffer? Lord, take her home or work a miracle, but please, Lord, do it soon." The switchboard was jammed with sobbing fans—more than $20,000 was raised in one week for the children's wing of Abbott Hospital. Becky's fever continued. She babbled about nimbuses and auras and wholeness and purity. A few days later, Ray relented and gave Marjery a six-month contract, and the next day Dr. Jim burst in the door with a brand-new serum flown in from the city. Buster barked for joy and Jo and Frank came back with a tidy sum inherited from a Michigan uncle they never knew they had, and Becky said, "Uncle Dad, why are you crying?" "Oh, don't mind me," he muttered. "I'm just a foolish old man, that's all. And sometimes I wish I were smarter. It seems like life is half over before we know what it is. But you close your eyes and get some sleep now."

BECKY: Why is Dr. Jim here?
JIM: Just came to make sure my girl is all right.
DAD: You rest now, honey.
BECKY: Uncle Dad?
DAD: Yes?
BECKY: Heaven is the beautifulest place I ever saw. It was all bright and starry and full of music, like a car-

nival except the rides were free, and Jesus was there, and jillions of angels, and there was no sadness there, no crying, or nothing, just happiness, but still, I'm glad they sent me back to be with you, Uncle Dad.

DAD: I'm glad, too, little Beeper. You rest now, honey. I'll just sit here beside your bed and hold your hand.

BECKY: Oh, and there was a nice lady who said to say hello to you. Her name was Benson too. Florence Benson.

DAD: Mom!

He rang up the Home and found out Mom had passed peacefully from this life a few minutes before. The first person to come bearing condolences was Miss Judy, who brought a pan of fresh banana bread and Becky's geography lesson (South America) and fixed a pot of coffee and told Dad that he should always feel free to count on her.

━━━━

WLT got a ton of letters, and Patsy got a note from Ray: "You win, but no more deathbeds for awhile. I'm not as young as I used to be." And Ray got a note from Katherine Doud (Mom) who was angry that her character had dropped dead and told Ray that Dad had promised her that Mom would stay in the Home until she, Katherine, was off the bottle. "He is a dirty rotten liar and a cheat and maybe it's time you know that he is having an affair with Faith Snelling, Dale's wife," she wrote. Dad? In the sack with Jo? Ray sent Katherine some money and told her that when she got on the wagon for good she could return for one episode as Becky's New York mom, visiting Elmville to take the wretched child home. He would pay her handsomely for it.

If the fans loved Little Becky before, they were even

crazier about her after her terrible illness. They baked pies and cakes for her by the hundreds, enough to keep the oldsters at the Ebenezer Home stuffed for weeks, and they wrote her bags and bags of mail.

Most of the letters expressed thanks to God, advised her to dress warmly, and said that she was their favorite radio performer, but a different letter arrived one day from Mindren, North Dakota. It said:

August 16, 1939

Dear Becky,

My name is Francis With, I am almost eleven years of age, and I reside in Mindren with my mother and daddy, my sister Jodie, and my Grampa. We all listen to your program every day while we have our lunch and we think that it is quite agreeable. My uncle Art works for WLT. Perhaps you have made his acquaintance. His name is Art Finn.

I think it would be remarkable if you and Dad made a trip to New York City and spent a week there. You could have a delightful time, and it would be elucidating for the rest of us. I hear that New York is a thrilling location.

My Grampa is Danish, born in Aalborg, and if Mr. Benson wished to relate the story of Grampa's journey here and how he met my grandmother (dead now, alas) on the program, I would be pleased to send you the story. Please let me or Mr. Art Finn know if this would be suitable. (It's a good story.)

Yours very sincerely,
Francis With

The letter arrived at WLT in the pocket of the writer. It was his first trip to Minneapolis, his first trip anywhere alone, and he wore a blue jacket and a red tie in honor of the occasion, and a tie tack with a rhinestone. Uncle Art

81

and Aunt Clare met him at the Great Northern Depot and took him home with them, and the next day he and Art went to the top of the Foshay Tower, thirty-one stories high, and stood on the observation deck buffeted by winds and gazed out over the green wooded city to Lakes Calhoun and Harriet and Nokomis and beyond to the farms of Hopkins and Richfield, and then they came to WLT.

"Here's my radio station here, Franny. That's where I work. I run that. That's what I do," Art said, wheeling into the parking lot behind the Hotel Ogden, waving to the attendant.

"I know," said Francis.

They took the back stairs up past the Ballroom, the big log stage empty, a thousand empty seats, and up to the third floor to watch *Friendly Neighbor* from the control room.

"Don't be too shocked," Art said. "Little Becky ain't so little."

But Francis was dazzled by everything—*This was where it all came from*—the engineers at the control board, three of them, one to man the big black volume knobs, one to run the turntables and cue the commercials, and a big fat man behind a podium with a green gooseneck lamp on it, who talked over a microphone mounted on a brass ring around his neck to the sound effects man in the studio. The studio was small, with green walls like a lavatory and the actors had to squeeze around each other to get to the microphone, where they made terrific faces, reading their lines, and then stepped back, went slack, yawned, drank coffee, glanced at the morning paper. Jo and Dad looked about like he had imagined, but Frank was much younger, and Becky, of course, was not little. She was an ungainly teenage girl with big feet, smoking a Camel and rolling her eyes. But she looked like fun and he still intended to give her the letter.

"Do you know Little Buddy?" he asked Art during a commercial for Milton, King medicated mulch. Sure, of course he did. Little Buddy was eight, he and his dad Slim Graves sang on *Friendly Neighbor*, they lived next door to the Bensons. Jo and Frank and Dad—Art knew all those people. "Dad and I play cribbage every Friday night," he said. *Really?*

"Yep. Dad even had me on the show once playing the town cop, Rudy. Didn't you hear that one? Where Dad's dog Buster gets into the Jensens' garbage and finds Mrs. Jensen's wedding ring in the coffee grounds?" *Really? That was you?*

"Yep. And that man there—that's Dad's brother Wilmer who plays his old Negro fishing buddy Tiny." *Really?* The sad-faced man in the little brown fedora and the brown suit?

And a minute later, they were back on the air, and the sad-faced man grinned and said, *De nevah help to worry much, Mistah Dad. Ain't no use. Dat's what I sez. I say, just do de best you kin do, dat's all. An' fine you a real good gal. And don't nevah fo'git to go fishin'. Hee hee hee hee.*

"Yep, that's Dad's brother who plays Tiny. Even Dad's wife Beatrice, she's on sometimes, she plays Mildred, Dr. Goodrich's nurse."

"I thought Dad's wife was named Katherine."

"Nope. You're thinking of Katherine Doud. She's the actress who plays Mom, or used to, but then she turned into a lush. Just lies around her apartment at the Antwerp, fried to the gills. Good looker but a real stewball."

The show was ending. Francis wrote "lush" and "stewball" in the notebook where he kept new words. He was trying to learn five a day. "Let's go in and say hi," said Uncle Art, his hand on the studio door. "No," said Francis, stricken with unbearable shyness. "Please, no." So Art went in alone. Francis heard them laughing in there, and

Art came out. They took the elevator down to the lobby, which was full of *Friendly Neighbor* fans. "Look at the deer flies," Art muttered. "Place is full of them." The people were waiting, twenty or thirty, standing modestly behind a rope, quiet, smiling, hopeful, like job-seekers, or orphans. Some of them held gifts, hand-knit socks or bags of vegetables. They waited, almost motionless, as the minutes ticked by, and then suddenly the elevator opened and there was Dad. They all clapped, and he ducked under the rope and walked into the midst of them. *Hi Dad.* "Hi. How you doing?" *Fine. Real good.* "That's good." *Mighty good show today.* "Thanks." *You got a minute?* "Of course. I've always got a minute."

"How is your back doing?" a woman asked.

Dad looked puzzled. She said, "You strained it last week pushing Pops Simpson's car out of the snow."

"*Oh*," he said. "My *back*. Yes, it's fine. Just a strain. Thought you said my 'bag' and I was trying to think what you meant."

An old man shook Dad's hand gravely, looking deep into his eyes. "Don't you think Eunice is ever going to come back? We sure miss her."

"Oh, I'm sure she will. Nice to see you," he murmured. "But which niece is that you're asking about?"

"You think Eunice *will* come back?"

"Eunice! Well, we'll just have to wait and see." He was signing all the pieces of paper they held out to him. He put his arm around an old lady and said, "This is the best part about the radio business, is getting to meet beautiful women close up." She blushed. He pressed the flesh with her husband and nodded and beamed and squeezed elbows and patted heads and chummed around. He signed an autograph book, posed for a snapshot.

"Is Becky going to come down? Sure be nice to see her."

Dad smiled and shook his head. "She's kind of shy, you know. And she was in a hurry to get back to school. But she told me to say hello to you and to say thank you for your letters."

"What about Carl——?" a woman said. "Carl Farnsworth? At the Mercantile?"

"Right," said Dad. "Carl."

"He was married to Myrt. You know? She worked at the beauty parlor a while back?"

"Right. Myrt."

"But today you mentioned Carl going to Little Rock with Margaret. He didn't get a divorce, did he?"

"No, of course not. No, they've never been happier. No, that's just me being forgetful. I must've been thinking of Margaret Donohue at the bank."

"Donovan," said a woman in back.

"Of course. Quite a gal."

"We haven't heard her in a long time. She didn't leave town, did she?"

No, Dad said, she was fine. Everybody was fine. "How are you?" he asked the kids who were pushed forward to say hello to him, and they murmured, "Fine." And he bent down and said, "Now, I'm sorry but I keep forgetting your name," to a girl with Shirley Temple curls—she squirmed with pleasure. "Peggy," she whispered. *Peggy. What a beautiful name. How lucky you are.* He worked his way through the crowd and finally came to Francis, who looked straight into Dad's big red tie with the sunflowers on it. Dad looked down at him. "Let me guess your age," he said, and squinted hard and squeezed Francis's skinny shoulders and said, "Thirteen years old! Seventh grade! No?"

"I'm almost eleven. Is Becky still upstairs?" he asked.

"She's gone, son." Dad squinted. "Weren't you up in the control room?"

"Yes," whispered Francis. "Could you give her this?" He handed Dad the envelope, and the minute Francis gave it over, he started to think of more things he wanted to tell her and tell Dad. He wanted them to know everything about him. He wanted to invite them up to Mindren to meet Daddy and Mother and to show them his room and introduce them to his school. Everyone would clap and Dad would stand up, beaming, and say, "Thank you, boys and girls, and thanks to our good friend Francis With for inviting us." *Our good friend Francis With.*

C H A P T E R 1 1

Mindren

Francis With rode the Empire Builder back to Jamestown on Sunday, where Daddy picked him up. They
were back in Mindren at 10 p.m., and the next
morning Francis was in school. He told everyone that he
had visited WLT and seen Dad Benson but nobody believed
him. As usual, he left school at eleven-fifty on the dot
with his sister Jodie and slid into the kitchen chair at one
minute of twelve, just in time for the WLT chimes that
signaled *Friendly Neighbor*. The chimes sounded exactly
like Mother's big wall clock that bonged in the hall, and
so he had always imagined that the Benson family lived
in an old dark house like theirs and that the Bensons'
kitchen table had a blue checked oilcloth on it and sat by
the window looking at the muddy backyard and the Bensons' linoleum was faded green too, and their steep stairs
smelled of pine disinfectant, and the wallpaper was forget-
me-nots, and they used a white enameled thunder jug to
pee in at night. Now that he had seen into the studio and
knew that none of this was true, it made the show more

exciting. And he refused to tell Jodie what Little Becky looked like. That was his secret now.

Francis was ten years and four months old. He was smart, thanks to his regular reading of *The Children's Hour* magazine and his membership in its Word Club. The words rolled around in his head: *brazen, genial, splendrous, succulent.* For lunch, he ate a baloney sandwich, two slices on white bread, lightly buttered, a bowl of Campbell's chicken noodle soup, and a glass of milk; he could stomach nothing else. He could listen to no other station but WLT.

At noon, Daddy set his big railroad watch to the WLT chimes, snapped the case shut, and put it back in his vest pocket. Mother put the sandwiches and soup on the table, Daddy said grace, and they all ate quietly, listening, except Grampa, who was not in his right mind and also deaf. Grampa called them to the table by shouting, "Vootsie vootsie vootsie!" and then sat in his wicker rocker and talked to himself in Danish as Francis used his new words.

"Pass the salt, please," said Jodie.

"I am very *amenable* to passing you the salt with *alacrity*," said Francis.

"So pass it."

"Are you sure you're not being *mendacious?*"

"You are so impossible."

"You are very *perceptive*," said Francis.

It was not such a good show that day. Becky wasn't on and neither was Jo. Mostly, Dad and Frank swapped fishing stories. Dad burned the soup. "There's no feast for the miser," he remarked. After he and Frank said "Bye now, bye everybody," there was an Evelyn Pie commercial and then a high husky voice hollered, "Come and get it!" and Excelsior Bread brought them *The WLT Noontime Jubilee* with Whistling Jim Wheeler and His All-Boy Band, Elsie and Johnny, "Ice Cream" Cohen, Norma Neilsen and Fargo Bill, the Olson Sisters, Jens Hansen the Norsk Nightingale, and your host, Leo ("Buy 'em by the Dozen") LaValley. "Oh boy," he yelled, "have we got a good one for you today, folks! It reminds me of the old Swede, one time he heard a joke so good he almost laughed. Let's kick 'er off with 'Pat Him on the Popo, Let's Watch Him Laugh,' okay? Whaddaya say, boys!" The All-Boy Band yelled, "Go get 'em!" and Jim cranked up his fiddle, and they played the popo song and then the Norsk Nightingale sang:

Ja, yew shur are mine, Tina, and yure so bewtiful,
Ay vant to die, ja, ven yure not near.
Ja, ay yust ban missing yew, by golly, since Nowember
Val, yee whiz, ven ay ban tenk of yu
Vat gude skol visky be?

That perked Grampa right up. On Grampa's bad days, he thought he was back in Aalborg as a young man, and on his good days, he was in Aalborg as a boy. The Norsk Nightingale somewhat penetrated Grampa's deafness and he leaned forward over his zwieback and muttered, "Hvad laver de? Hvad siger de?" *What are they doing? What are they saying?* Relax, said Daddy, and he put his hand on Grampa's. If Norma and Bill sang "Red River Valley" or "Beautiful Brown Eyes" or another song he knew, Daddy turned up the radio and sang, and if Whistling Jim played a square dance number, Daddy waltzed around the kitchen with Jodie or Francis standing on his shoes. Grampa said, "Ja ja ja," and smiled down into his soup. Mother liked Leo and his jokes. "I can never remember a joke one minute after I've heard it," she said, wiping her eyes from the last one, and sure enough she had already forgotten the punchline, and Francis had to remind her: "The lady says to Lena after church, you look like Helen Brown, and Lena says, I don't look that good in blue either."

89

At twelve-thirty, Dad Benson came back and read the news, and Daddy sat and sharpened his pocketknife on a stone, and then more *Jubilee*, and at one o'clock, it was *Up in a Balloon*, a boring show but better than school, and at one-fifteen *Love's Old Sweet Song*, which Mother listened to, and Daddy if he was home. Daddy was an engineer for the Great Northern Railroad and worked the doghouse shift and ate his breakfast at noon.

Francis and Jodie got to hear those shows only if school was out or they were sick; they went back to school at one. It took a minute and a half if you ran. By the time the announcer said, "Don't go away, friends! We'll be right back!" Francis was already heading out the door, but of course the radio stayed tuned to 770, as nobody needed to remind Francis. Their dial was locked tight on WLT because of Uncle Art. WLT was their family's radio station.

Uncle Art was his favorite uncle. He drove a brand-new Chrysler, two-toned. He wore a blue suit with a hanky in the pocket and smoked cheroots. He blew smoke rings that turned either clockwise or counterclockwise and some-times turned both directions and folded into a figure-8, and he could make smoke come out of his ears. He shot billiards and bet on horse races. He could flip cards into a hat at twenty feet, one after the other, either face-up or face-down, and if you said "What card?" he would tell you as it flew, "Nine of clubs!" and it usually was. Art knew where every card in the deck was: he shuffled cards the way a postman sorts mail. He taught Franny gin rummy, whist, lowball poker and firehouse poker and German poker, and cribbage. He didn't work as hard as Daddy. "Never put off until tomorrow what you can put off until the day after tomorrow," was Art's motto. He knew magic and made coins vanish and then come out of your ear and he made his hanky disappear and then turn

90

up in your own pocket and when you pulled his pinky finger, he cut a soft little fart. You could count on this. Art did not miss a trick.

Uncle Art had had a chance to go to New York with Jack Benny who Art met when Art was the house manager at the Shubert Theater, but he stayed in Minnesota out of loyalty to his pals and missed his chance. "He could have had his own show in New York," said Aunt Clare.

"No shows for schmoes," said Art.

She said, "He has *such* a good personality and sense of humor and a nice singing voice—he coulda been up there with Jack Benny."

"Jack Benny was not looking for a mandolin player," said Art.

Knowing the Benson family personally as he did, Art knew what their homes looked like and what they did for fun, and Francis meant to ask him about this someday. Francis also wanted to know, "Can other families get on the air?" Once Art was Bessie's brother Clyde on *Up in a Balloon*, the one who cast off the lines when the balloon ascended and called out, "Happy landings! Don't take any wooden nickels!" and Francis imagined Bud and Bessie getting out of that balloon and the With family getting into it, but if they had their own show, what would they do about Grampa? He would have to be on the show with them but who could understand Grampa except his own family? A family with Grampa in it was going to have a hard time breaking into radio.

Upstairs, off the dark hall from the three bedrooms, was the sewing room, where Francis had his desk and sat and did his homework. Out the big window was the Sheyenne River, the Mindren Public School, St. Bonifacius Church, and the main line of the Great Northern. The Withs didn't attend St. Bonny, Mother being Lutheran, otherwise the window contained most of the known world, the house and the black asphalt roofs of the stores in downtown Mindren, the chimneys poking up, and the hundred little houses around it. The population of Mindren was 439, and none of them were rich like Bud and Bessie or Mr. Hollister. So many rich people on WLT, like the heiress Mrs. Aldrich Bryant Colfax, who turned up in Johnson Corners on *The Darkest Hour* one January day suffering from amnesia caused by a terrible experience, her baby having been strangled to death when its little wool scarf was caught in the wheels of the baby carriage as Mrs. Colfax, oblivious, wheeled it along fashionable Fifth Avenue, window-shopping. Now she was incoherent, weeping, half-frozen, torn by grief over *something*, she couldn't remember what, and had to be nursed back to health by Mildred, the minister's wife, who knew the terrible story from a scrap of newspaper that fell from Mrs. Colfax's purse. Finally, after weeks, Mrs. Colfax *did* recover, and she left a large legacy to the library, which stupid Mr. Hooley dropped in a snowbank the same day her playboy pal Emerson Dupont arrived to fetch her in a long black Packard, his nose full of vowels—and away they sped, and the money was lost, and nothing to do but wait until spring and hope for the best.

What if a rich man came to Mindren? Francis often imagined this. It would be very gaudy like the circus, and bands would play, and the man would laugh and hand out money on the schoolhouse steps, a hundred dollars for each person, and Francis would save his for college. But in fact the only rich man to come through Mindren was Myron Mindren himself, the man who arrived in North Dakota in 1884, bought a section of land from the railroad, platted the town and sold the lots for a tidy fortune, and hot-footed it to San Francisco.

If it were *him*, Francis thought, he would take his fortune to Minneapolis and use it to do good.

Mindren. The name was a mumble, impossible to say with any grandeur. It was said of Myron Mindren that he mumbled so badly, his buyers misunderstood the price of the lots and the terms of the deal: they thought Mindren had said that *he* would pay for the school and the park and the opera house, and there was talk of sending a posse to California to bring him back. But then came word that the fortune was gone, lost in the sinking of the *Mary Jane* in a hurricane, and that Mindren himself, having seen the bank men lock up his nineteen-room stone mansion on Nob Hill, had disappeared on foot, aiming for Alaska, leaving his immortality sitting on the North Dakota prairie, broiling in the summer sun, covered with dust, sitting out the long dark bitter winter. The opera house became Mindren Trucking & Transfer, the big Mack truck parked nose-first under what was left of the proscenium arch, a border of plaster leaves and fruit and a dusty angel and a shadow of Norwegian inscription: "Ej Blot Til Lyst." *Not Only for Pleasure.*

If he were rich, Francis would buy a mansion in Minneapolis for the five of them, and a piano, and a pony. But they would stay good people, not become snooty like the rich people on WLT. The radio shows took place in small towns like Elmville, Lakeville, Park Rapids, Parkerville, but rich people often came there and got their comeuppance. A hard-hearted millionaire was stranded in Forestville by a flood that washed out the highway and swept away his roadster like it was a toy, and he learned the value of patience, on *The Hills of Home*, and learned that pain, when past, is a sweet pleasure. He sat in Mother Sundberg's kitchen, wet and cold, wrapped in a blanket and drinking hot coffee, and took a deep breath and said, "Life was never so good to me as it is right now at this moment, good people." And he meant it. Bumbling nobility like the Duke of Worthington arrived in the middle of the night, in agony, suffering from terrible gout from stuffing himself with goose liver, and was helped over to Doc Winegar's office and treated to a good talk about Tomorrow Is Another Day and how helping others helps to take your mind off your own troubles. "I reckon we don't look like much to you, Your Lordship, a one-horse town with a passel of folks who don't know much about books or plays or paintings, but people here sure know a few things about living," and the Duke harrumphed and said, "I am deeply obliged, my good man." Bigwigs were always taught a lesson by the good people, and usually they responded well, like the tycoon who learned the true meaning of Christmas and gave Fritz and Frieda a diamond as big as her knuckle. Then Babs dropped it on the ice as she crossed Lake Marcia and though they scraped the ice again and again, it was never found, and it sank in the spring melt.

"Oh, it was never meant to be!" Frieda cried. "We were never meant to be anything other than what we are." The other folks arrived at the same conclusion. Better to be happy with what you have than to aim high and become vain and miserable. The highest branch is not the safest roost. As Dad said, "It's awful hard to carry a full cup."

CHAPTER 12

Daddy

On *The Parkers of Parkerville*, the Highball Express derailed in a howling blizzard and slid into a ditch, and the famous Hollywood producer Mel DeMille was awakened in his baby-blue Pullman bedroom by snow drifting across his face and was hauled out by pig farmers and dumped in a haywagon and covered with gunnysacks and carried to town. He stood shivering next to the stove in the General Store, griping and groaning —"Get me out of here! Call my office! Tell them to rent a plane, a car, I'll pay anything, but I'm getting out and I'm getting out *tonight!* I'm not going to be stuck in this lousy two-bit tank town! I've got movies to make! I'm supposed to be in Louis B. Mayer's office in *eight hours!* Mr. Mayer himself! Eight hours!"—"Shur," said Mr. Ingebretsen, the mayor, "and it's only a block from here, so take it easy, there's plenty of time!" when in walked Dorothy, Pop Watkins's lovely daughter.

"There's a room for you at the hotel, sir," she said,

smiling in a way that made Mel DeMille's eyes go out of focus. "Come, I'll show you the way. It's a nice big room. I made it up myself."

"My dear girl," Mel DeMille whispered, "who made *you* up?"

"I must have you for my next picture!" he cried. He took her little hands in his big paws. "A twist of fate has led me to you, to offer you a new life—no, not I—the *American people* are offering it to you, for they need the sunshine in your face, the laughter in your soul—Miss, whoever you are, wherever you come from, paradise or the planet Venus, you're no hotel chambermaid anymore, you're—a *star*."

———

So when the storm stopped and the Highball was back on the tracks, ready to head for Hollywood, Dorothy was set to go. She had sewn herself a new dress and said goodbye to Bob, Ma, Pop, Spot, and her night job at the Hob Nob Bakery. They were all proud as punch, and she promised to never never forget them. "I owe it all to the people of Parkerville. You believed in me! And now my dream has come true. And now I go forth. But I carry you in my heart and in my prayers," she told the crowd in the high-school gym on Dorothy Day. But the next morning Pop woke up sick with the grippe and took a bad turn and lay feverish, hallucinating, clinging to a pillow and moaning "Dorothy. . . . Dorothy . . . Dorothy," and she realized how much they needed her and she tore up her movie contract. "No! No!" cried Mel as the train started to chugga-chugga-chugga. He stood in the Pullman door, pleading, "Dorothy, think of the American people!" as the train glided away, chooga-chooga-chooga, and he watched the platform where she stood, so lovely, so pure, waving, getting smaller and smaller. "Don't cry," she told her bedridden pop after the fever broke and he begged her to go and seek stardom.

"The Bible says to comfort the sick, not to go off and be a big shot. And I'd rather stay here with you and Ma than live in the biggest mansion on Wilshire Boulevard."

All the Withs heard the Dorothy episodes except Daddy, who was working the overnight run to Bismarck. Jodie sat on the couch and wept when the Parkerville folks came and shook Dorothy's hand and muttered that, gosh, it was good to have her back, and Dorothy said, "Be it ever so humble, there's nobody worth being except exactly who you are." But Francis thought it was dumb. When the bell rang and the steam hissed as the Highball pulled away, Francis knew that he would've gotten on that train with Mel right then. *"Last call for the Highball Express, with stops in Riverside, Hill City, Big Lake, Lakeville, Center City, Wheatville, River Falls, Littleton, Parksburg, Green Rapids, Park Rapids, Greenville, and Hollywood. . . . Board!"* Then the train pulled away, and soon the whistle blew away far away in the distance as it raced west. You were dumb not to go if you had a chance to. If you didn't like it there, you could always come back.

———

Francis's daddy died a few weeks later. *October 5, 1939.* He was killed in the crash of Engine No. 9, on a straight dry stretch of track near Tyler after he was called at 2 a.m. to go out and sub for Mr. Ratliff. He must've fallen asleep at the throttle and the engine jumped a switch and went down into a ravine and rolled over, bursting a boiler, and the crew was cooked in the hot steam so that the flesh fell off their bones. At school, a few days later, the children made up a song about it:

Francis, Francis, your daddy died.
He was boiled, he was fried.
They poured water on him, a ton,
And now there's soup for everyone.
Ya ya ya.

The news about Daddy came at dawn, via Cliff the night man at the depot who burst in the front door and stood at the foot of the stairs yelling, "Missus! Missus! Your husband's dead!" Even when Mother ran out on the landing, Cliff yelled. "They're all dead, missus, the train burned up! It's horrible! Gene and J.L. went and looked, it's just frightful. Your mister's dead and all of them!"

The boy lay in his warm bed and listened to the bad dream. A person's daddy did not just go off to work and die, it didn't happen like that.

His mother shrieked. "Where is he! Where is Benny?"

"You can't go there, missus. The district superintendent is driving over himself from Fargo. His name is Flynn, I think, or Finnegan, but anyway, he'll see to it. You stay put. Dave just sent me down here to make sure you're okay. Dave and me, we got the news about an hour ago from a farmer name of Pisek? the Piseks out around Tyler? He said he heard an explosion and looked down the hill, there was a fire on the tracks, and he heard voices screaming. He run down there and he said you could tell by the smell there were people in there, but it was so hot it burned his eyebrows off. So there's no point you going over there. They'll take care of it. You got any coffee, missus?"

The boy lay waiting for his dad to come clumping upstairs and end the dream. Francis'd close his eyes and his dad'd say, "You're not asleep, you're playing possum, you little skeezix," and sit on the bed and Francis'd screw his eyes closed tight and wait for the first little poke in the ribs. His dad leaned down and he smelled of smoke and coffee. "You little squirt," said the voice by Francis's ear, "you bugger, you." The boy started giggling even before the poke. Poke, poke. Then his dad gave him a hawkeye on the kneecap, put his arms around him, and gave him a big fat buzzer on the neck. "There. That'll teach you to play possum with your old man, you skeezix. You gonna get up for breakfast now?" *Yes,* the boy cried, *yes, yes, yes.* "Oh no you won't," said Daddy and gave him another buzzer. Then he lay down beside him as the sky got light and told him about Grampa riding the train down from Winnipeg with his new bride, Mathilde, who he had met the day before. Grampa came on the boat from Aalborg many years ago. Grampa went to Mathilde's father's store to buy groceries, and Mathilde thought he was a Polack. She said to her father, "Han lugter lige som et stykke gammel ost, men for søren, hvor er han flot," *He smells just like a piece of old cheese but damn he is handsome*—and Grampa smiled and said, "Synes du det?" *Do you think so?* She was so embarrassed she ran out the back door and Grampa chased her, trying to comfort her. He stayed for dinner, and the next morning they got married. Grampa lived in his own room now and he only came out for breakfast and supper, he didn't recognize anybody, he thought he was eight years old, living upstairs from his dad's bakery.

Francis was not afraid, even when his mother called to him in a strange voice, it wasn't real, it could still be changed, but then Jodie stood in the door, holding a kerosene lamp. She whispered, "Franny, Daddy is dead." And that did it. That made it true. Her saying it, and the smell of kerosene.

Grampa came out and saw them in the kitchen, Jodie and Franny sitting with tight faces, their hot red eyes, waiting for Mother to come down and tell them something, and he said, "Hvor er Benny?" He knew something was up. He sat down and asked for a beer and Franny got him one, and a glass, and set it on the table in front of him. He motioned to wipe his mouth and Franny brought him a napkin. Even though he was crazy, Grampa still liked things to be just so. He poured the beer, which Daddy brewed in the basement for him, and drank half of it and carefully wiped his gray moustache. He folded the napkin and set it down, and put the glass on it, and set his big hands palms-down on the table, waiting.

"Daddy is dead, Grampa," Jodie said. "He died on the train." But Grampa couldn't hear her, of course. Grampa said, "Vaer sa venlig at give mig et stort stykke ost," so Franny brought him a big piece of cheese. "Tallerken," Grampa said. *Plate.*

Mother came down the stairs slowly and stepped into the kitchen as if she wasn't sure where it was, and said that she was going to get somebody to drive her to Tyler to see to their poor father. "I don't want them to leave him lie out there all night," she said, "and that's exactly what they'll do if it's left up to them."

She turned to reach for the telephone on the wall and knocked the sugar bowl off the shelf and it smashed on the floor.

When Grampa saw it shatter and saw the broken pieces of crystal glittering in the sugar, he finally understood that everything had fallen apart once and for all. He cried without hiding his face. He cried hard, his handsome old face turned toward her.

Benny, Benny.

She said, "Grampa, you go to bed and get your sleep, we're taking you to Fargo tomorrow. I got all I can do to take care of myself and the children."

CHAPTER 13

Uncle
Art

Aunt Emma and Uncle Charles arrived a few hours later from Brainerd and Mother went to bed. That was on Friday. She made an attempt to get up on Sunday and again on Monday, for the children's sake, but she was too weak to stand so she lay on her side and sobbed with abandon. He was a good man, the only one she ever loved, her life was over now, she had nothing left. "Might as well bury me next to him, Emma! Might as well!" Francis's words that day were *reprehensible, pallor, niggardly, lickspittle,* and *coax.* He asked Uncle Charles if "niggardly" comes from "nigger" and Charles frowned. He was a slight, sad man with his brown wool suit and galluses, his moon face and his pale puffy hands, who had a delicate stomach and couldn't eat certain foods, such as tomatoes or beans, and had to have his meals come precisely on time. "This is a great tragedy," he told Francis, "it's no time to talk about things like that."

Aunt Clare and Uncle Art arrived Friday evening from Minneapolis. Francis was in his room, cutting ribs and struts out of balsa wood for a model plane, which Daddy had shown him how. When Art walked in, Art did his vaudeville shuffle ("Hell-o tootsie, hell-o"), and said, "Hey, Franny, did you hear the one about Lena after Ole died, she said to her friend Tina, 'Oh Tina, he didn't leave me a penny of insurance, the old coot.' So Tina says, 'But Lena, where'd you get that diamond ring then?' And Lena says, 'Oh, he left $100 for his funeral and $400 for a big stone and this is the big stone.' " *Ker-bang. Tingaling.*

Clare made a pot of spaghetti—you need to eat, she said, so they ate. "I need no *coaxing*," said Francis. After supper they all sat in the living room, except Mother and Emma, and Art had a couple beers and they listened to Wingo Beals and the Shoe Shine Boys on the radio, except Charles, who read *Popular Science.*

Emma and Charles returned to Brainerd in the morning. His stomach was acting up. Art and Clare stayed for a week. Clare sat with Mother in the dark bedroom and fixed meals and cleaned, and Art cracked jokes and had a ball. There was nobody like Art, he was like a big bald kid with a moustache. Nothing was serious, everything was a game to him. "Bet you I can throw this pea in your mouth," he'd say at dinner and then do it, when Clare was in the kitchen. Art hated peas. He hated all vegetables except sweet corn and seldom got up before ten in the morning and tried to get out of chores. If Clare asked him to run to the store or fix the kitchen faucet, Art would say, "I've got to take care of that furnace first, something's wrong with the air intake," and give Francis a big wink and slip down the basement and lie around and read *National Geographic.* He had his own copy with nothing but naked women in it, neatly pasted together, which he enjoyed looking at every day. "Catch the hooters on that one," he'd say, passing the book to Franny. "Boy, she's

got a pair of bazongas you could eat off of." One night
he got down his mandolin and sang a song about a girl
who ran away with a sailor. Clare told him it was in poor
taste to sing such a song so soon after—and she nodded
at the children, but Art said it was one of Benny's favorites.
And then he sang another:

> I was brought up to
> Work hard every day.
> Eight hours of labor for eight hours of pay.
> But then I discovered
> This great mystery:
> When I ask for money, people give it to me.
> I sell them swampland
> And snake oil, too.
> I tell them stories,
> I've got one for you.
> I'm a thief and a gambler,
> And I just want to say:
> Everything's going my way.
>
> Now I drink the best whiskey
> And always eat steak.
> I own a big mansion
> Sits down by the lake.
> Got rings on my fingers
> And gas in my tank,
> And about half a million
> Keeping cool in the bank.
> I'm a thief and a gambler,
> I get drunk every day.
> Everything's going my way.

Mother was unable to attend the funeral. She knew she
should but she couldn't. She lay in bed and wept for this
terrible failure, her faithlessness to Benny, her unworthi-

ness. He was burned to death and now his wife couldn't even get out of bed to bury him, poor man. She was too weak to get up. "I might as well be dead myself," she told Francis. The copper coffin sat in a parlor of the undertaker's house. It looked too small to Francis, like a child's coffin. The six of them sat and the minister read from the Bible and smiled reassuringly. There were twenty-six chairs, but the Withs had only lived eight years in Mindren and nobody knew them. Hamburgers sizzled in the kitchen. Francis thought of the train crash song. He touched the coffin, which was cool. Then they drove three blocks in a drizzle to Resurrection Cemetery and put him in the deep black hole. Art took Francis's hand and they walked home. At the cemetery gate, Art stopped and lit up a stogie and said, "That's one less here and one more there, they laid him in the ground. Rest in peace, and now there's more beer for the rest of us." It was cold and gray and the next day Francis had to go to school. He didn't want to go but Clare said he had to do it for his father's sake.

So he did. After the Pledge of Allegiance, Miss Theisen said, "I am sure that we all extend our heartfelt sympathies to Francis With, whose father was killed in that terrible train wreck," and she passed around a sympathy card and everyone signed it, including Francis, and then they gave it to him. Later, at recess, the children sang:

> The engine crashed and broke in two,
> Burst into flames and cooked the crew.
> The superintendent said, "Hee-hee!
> We'll feed the public school for free,
> And we'll just call it wieners."
> Ya ya ya.
>
> Teacher, teacher, come and see.
> Hairs in the hot dogs, one-two-three.

Big black hairs and a big tattoo
Saying "Evalina I love you"
And sixteen warts and a dirty goatee
And bloodshot eyes looking up at me.
He must've worked on the railroad.
Ya ya ya.

Golly gee this lunch is fine,
I just found a note in mine.
"A pound of liver, a loaf of bread,
A barrel of beer," is what it said.
Guess he was a German.
Ya ya ya.

You will know he was a Hun
If your nose begins to run
And your throat is hot and sore
And you puke your guts out on the floor.
Must be Benny With.
Ya ya ya.

Poor Francis. Children pranced around and sang this ditty in his face while the big boys pinned his arms and squashed him down on the sharp cinders and the girls hollered, "That's about yer faw-ther!"

"He *wasn't* a Hun, he was Danish!" Francis yelled. *B.S.*, said David and Darrell the dogfaced twins. They sang,

Big black hairs and a big tattoo
Saying "Hello Francis, how are you?"
And ashes in the overalls
From one little wiener and two black balls.
Ya ya ya.

He had no brothers to stick up for him, and Jodie was scared of her shadow. She preferred to remain in the school library during recess and read picture books about the lives of rich people in New York City. Jodie cried and the school cook Mrs. Grebe supplied her with extra tapioca pudding with raisins in it, but Francis couldn't cry. He was too scared to cry. Daddy was dead and now Grampa was gone and what would happen to them? A man with a red face had come in a car for Grampa and Grampa trembled as the man put Grampa's hat and coat on him. Then the man held Grampa's arm tight and steered him out the door. This could happen to anybody. And now Mother stayed in bed having a nervous breakdown. Clare waited on her, bringing bowls of soup, which sat getting cold. She had no friends, Mother wailed. Her only friends were on the radio. She listened to the radio from morning to night. And Francis kept up with the Word Club, trying to improve himself. *Arrant, confrere, agape, barbaric, eclipse.*

The only good part was Uncle Art, who passed him the copy of the *Geographic* and taught him the fine points about women. Art was a connoisseur of women and to pass muster with him they had to score high in the Bosom Division, which he divided into: nice titties, torpedoes, real knockers, a pair of headlights, major bazongas, and a shirtful of hooters. If Clare marched through on her way upstairs, Art would suddenly say, loudly, "So how's school coming?" and if Jodie came in and flopped down, he'd have to flip cards for awhile or remove quarters from her nose, but then she had to help Clare with supper, and the men returned to their favorite topic.

"Aw, you're too young, kid, I shouldn't be leading you down the garden path like this," Art muttered. Franny assured him that he was not too young, that he knew a lot already and was interested in hearing more man-to-man information about women, and that he wouldn't tell anybody where he heard it.

"Well," Art said, glancing around. "For fooling around with, the girls with the flat chests are your hot babes. The ones with the melons, they get a little old on the hoof, and you have to throw a flag over them feedsacks so they don't bang you on the head, so you want a woman with nice little titties. And a talker. You always want a woman with good chops on her. She'll give you a lot of yap but she'll give you a lot of hubba-hubba too."

Franny wanted to know more—what is hubba-hubba, for example—but he didn't want to betray ignorance.

"Your daddy was a real ladies' man, now there was a man who knew his way to the bedroom. Not that he two-timed your mom, I'm not saying that, I don't know that, but back in his bachelor days, you never saw anybody could rustle up a nooner like Benny could. He had a cock like a ballpeen hammer. We used to go around north Minneapolis, we knew where all the hot babes were. He was a pistol, your old man. And now he's gone, there's more for you and me, kid. Just remember that. When you're dead, you'll be dead a long long time, so you might as well live when you're alive. Your daddy did."

"I'm hoping to move to Minneapolis someday," said Francis, matter-of-factly. "I'm planning to attend the University of Minnesota."

"You do that, Franny. What'll you study?"

"I want to study to go into radio."

Art laughed. "Nobody studies radio, kid. They don't teach it in school because it's too much fun. People go to school to be a teacher or a dentist. Radio is just a bunch of guys having a ball. It's incredible. I tell ya, I don't know anybody in radio who works more'n about fifteen minutes a day. It's a gravy train! You want to get into radio, you come and see your uncle Art, I'll put you right up at the head of the parade."

CHAPTER 14

Poor Children

When Art and Clare got in their big Chrysler to drive back home to Minneapolis, Clare was sniffling and dabbing at her eyes. Jodie and Franny stood by the car and she put her hands on their heads. "You poor children," she said. "We are *undaunted*," said Francis, thinking of his other words, *global* and *delinquent* and *archaic* and *erode*. Art took two quarters out of Jodie's nose and found a matchbook behind Franny's ear. Art said, "You oughta come with us to Minneapolis, kiddoes. You'd have a ball there. Go to shows and stay up late and have ice cream for breakfast." He said to Franny, "I could get you a job at the radio station. You could work for me there." Clare sighed. "Come on, big shot, time to hit the road."

After Art and Clare left, the house was silent except for the radio. Mother mooned around, daunted, day after day, her face pale and damp, *global*, in Daddy's old brown bathrobe, her dark eyes hollow and her tangled hair hanging down on her shoulders. She *eroded*. She stayed upstairs and slipped around like a tattered shadow. She lay in bed day after day and held Benny's big brass railroad watch, scorched black, the glass half-melted and the face crumpled. Every day when Francis came home from school she called out in a shaky voice, "Come here to Mother," and burst into tears when she saw him. She seemed to sing when she cried, her mouth twisted agape, she shook, her eyes shut, and Francis put his arm around her. And then sometimes he was *delinquent*. He and Jodie sat at the table and tuned in their shows and ate their soup and Francis studied his vocabulary. They still set a place for Daddy at the end. Though he was *archaic*.

"He is happier now, in heaven," said Jodie.

Francis said, "There's no such place. It's all a *fabrication*." He wasn't sure he thought this but it felt good to say it. And it was a word on yesterday's list. But Jodie wouldn't talk to him then, because he was evil.

"Daddy is with Jesus in heaven," she said, "and you are the evilest person in the world and you will go straight to everlasting hellfire."

"You don't scare me."

"Good." Jodie smiled. "I'm glad. Because I want you to go."

With Jodie not talking and Mother sick in bed, radio was the only friendly voice in the house, especially Francis's good friends, the Bensons. He wondered about Little Becky: was she a real-life friend of Dad's too, or just an actress? He guessed she was real and just as sweet as on the show. She sure added a lot to *Friendly Neighbor*. Her father had given her expensive clothes but never much love, and she was happy as a clam with Dad and Jo and Frank, and Dad had always wanted a grandkid, so it was a good deal for everybody. They got along without a cross word between them. Becky learned to ride a bike one day, she learned to dry dishes, she learned hymns, and one night Tuna gave birth to six kittens at the foot of Becky's bed. They enrolled her at Elmville School, where Miss Judy, Frank's mom, became her teacher, the wonderful widow-lady who had made the cake for Dad's birthday every year since Mom Benson died from the coma, so Francis could imagine that Miss Judy would be dropping by more often and might bring her nephew Little Buddy, who yodelled.

One day, Jodie wrote a long tearful letter to Aunt Emma and Uncle Charles in Brainerd and asked to come live with them, and they took her, the little traitor. Francis asked her why she was going away and she said, "Because you're not Christian. I'm going to live with a Christian family."

Francis couldn't believe she really would go away and leave her own mother and brother in their darkest hour, but the day came and Emma and Charles arrived and Jodie smiled and said goodbye and even kissed him—she had never kissed him before, but she gave him a dreadful dry little peck on the cheek. *You lied,* he thought. Emma told him to be good and take care of his mother. Charles looked ill, as always.

Becky loved it at the Bensons', and her dad and Ginger never did stop on their way back from Moonlight Bay to get her, of course: they needed to go to Morocco first, and then something came up at his ranch in Montana and then he was off to London on a business trip, and by then she was enrolled in school so he decided to let her be. "It's a good place for you," he said, and considering what a vile father he was, he was right. He dropped in to see her a couple times a year for a minute or two and offered Dad money which Dad always refused.

"Uncle Dad," Becky asked once, "why doesn't my daddy ever write to me?" "He's a busy man, Beeper," Dad answered. "Humph," said Jo.

Jodie almost never wrote to Francis but it was nice to think that she was listening to the radio at the same time he was, that they had something in common, and Francis sent in her name to the *Jubilee* and Leo read it on the Happy Birthday Club.

"Happy birthday to Jodie Marie, the most splendrous sister a boy could ever have—well, isn't that sweet, Jens?"

"Ja, aye tink dat boy, he is a real sewper-dewper kid dere. By yiminy yes."

After *Friendly Neighbor*, Mother sent him to Kohler's Drugstore for more cough syrup. He stayed out as long as possible, playing in the ditch, digging snow caves until it was dark, then he snuck in the house and dawdled around in the kitchen, as she called again and again, "Francis? Francis?" When he slouched in by her bed, she bawled and held him tight to her bosom and said that he was all she had left in the world now, everything else was meaningless. She reeked of camphor and eucalyptus. The radio was on all day, chattering away beside her bed. She followed all the shows: the Benson family of course and *Up in a Balloon* and *Down in the Valley*. The house sat soaking in grief. Emma came every week, bringing hot meals in covered dishes wrapped with towels, taking away dirty laundry. It was rich food, which made Mother gassy, and when she pulled back the blankets, a cloud of farts flew out. Emma taught Francis to wash clothes and to use plenty of blueing and wring them out and hang them outside. It was scary in the basement, pumping water into the tub. The kerosene lantern cast a flickering light and sometimes shadows moved and Francis jumped. Maybe Daddy was mad at him for making him go on the train and get burned up, and maybe Daddy told Emma to send Francis down in the basement, down to where Daddy could punish him.

Mother kept the radio on even when the minister called. He perched on the side of her bed and patted her hand and listened to her shows with her. The church sent a stale chocolate cake and a box of old clothes. Once when Francis clomped home after school the minister rushed out of Mother's room pale and distraught and said, "Oh! It's you! Good! You're home!" and jumped around buttoning his collar.

The next day Francis listened through the furnace vent, how the minister told her to lie still and close her eyes for the healing ministry and murmured about the efficacy of skin contact. On the radio, people jumped around on the *Jubilee* and hooted and told jokes and the Norsky Orchestra played and a man whistled like birds and tapped out tunes on his teeth. "Touch her, Lord, and make her whole," the minister moaned. "Her body is open *unto* Thee. Our sister places her trust in Thee. Lord, she is entirely Thine. Touch her now, touch her and heal her." There was rustling and murmuring. Francis crept away downstairs and dropped a casserole dish on the floor. The man came to the head of the stairs. "Are you all right?" he said. He was very tall up there and dark with the light behind him. Francis whispered: "Go away."

———

He told Emma on Saturday that he was afraid of the minister and she said, "Don't be silly." He thought of writing to Dad Benson about it. Mother wrote in to the radio all the time. She wrote a get-well letter to Dad and another one to Dad's sister Hannah, who was down sick with a brain inflammation brought on by worry. The name Hannah proved to Mother that the Bensons were Danes too, or at worst, Norwegians. She wrote to Hannah that she herself knew how hard it was to be sick and urged her to have faith in God, though faith had not worked thus far in her own case. She stayed in bed. Christmas passed, a dark gloomy day. Lily Dale sang "Beautiful Jesus" with a choir and the Bensons welcomed carollers to their kitchen and gave them cocoa, but Francis and Mother spent a quiet tearful day. She tried to go to the kitchen and cook a goose and she fell down the stairs and had to be helped to the couch. The doctor came and scolded her for feeling so sorry for herself, and that threw her into a state of collapse.

"Benny, you come back here," she screamed. "You can't get out of it as easy as that! Benny! I want you back *now!*"

There were more presents than ever, all from Art and Clare and Emma and Charles, and none that he wanted except the lampshade from Art with a Hawaiian girl on it. When you turned out the light, her clothes disappeared and her body glowed in the dark.

Jodie wrote that she sure loved her new school in Brainerd and she got all *A*s except for one *B +* and she got a red Schwinn bike for Christmas and would come visit in the spring. She didn't come with Emma on the food visits—she was too busy with her schoolwork, Emma said, and it was better for her not to get upset. "Jodie is more high-strung than you are," said Emma. "She has an artistic temperament." Emma was Daddy's older sister. She was beautiful in a fussy sort of way and was proud of her singing, which was ridiculous. When she sang, she whinnied like a horse. The tragedy was hard on her nerves, which were bad to begin with. She was so broken inside, she said, that she could never sing or play the piano again, and Francis hoped she would be true to her word.

His only hope was Art. From those few words, "You ought to come with us to Minneapolis," spoken between blue clouds of cigar, Francis imagined a happy life in the future, riding the trolleys, going to the ballpark, listening to the radio. Uncle Art was a big man at WLT, The Friendly Home in the Air. He knew all the stars. He sent Francis a copy of the WLT Family Album. It showed Bud & Bessie and Leo and Dad Benson and Little Becky visiting an orphanage and giving a wheelchair to a crippled boy, and it made Francis feel that if he could make it to Minneapolis, he would be all right.

CHAPTER 15

Showman

Francis wrote Little Becky a second letter:

Dear Becky,
I know you miss your dad because you talk about him
sometimes, well I do too and my dad is deceased (dead).
Would you correspond with me? Or if you are too busy
(which surely may be the case), just send me a card
with your name on it. It surely would be a comfort.
Could you sign it, "Your Own Personal Friend," or
"Your Friend" (if you prefer)? I would be very very
very extremely grateful.

The kids in Mindren might see him in a new light if a
radio star were his friend, but then weeks went by with
no reply, and he could see that a letter from Little Becky
would make no difference at all. None. These people were
not *Friendly Neighbor* people. Obviously. One cold day,

they had him pinned and were singing the song about Daddy and Darrell put his ugly dogface down next to Francis's and said with his dog's breath, "Sing it!" and Francis did, loud. This amazed them and they let him up. So he sang it again, *louder*. He stood, grinning, arms out, and sang all their verses including:

My daddy got drunk on nigger gin,
Pickled his brains and cooked his skin,
So we had him cleaned and sliced.
Is he tasty? Jesus Christ,
He's better than a meat loaf.

They all gawked like he had eaten a toad, it was **THRILLING,** and some girls tattled to Miss Theisen and reported that Francis used bad language and he was made to sit in the corner and face the blackboard, which made him a true hero, and afterward several boys became his best friend.

Francis was the only one who knew all the verses of the Daddy song and he sang it for them again. They nicknamed him Showman. He got to come in the boys' clubhouse, a Chevy truck sitting on rusted rims by the railroad siding behind the lumberyard, and they all lay in the back of the truck and smoked and argued about ballplayers and looked at each other's wieners and told dirty secrets. Darrell said his sister Sally had a lot of boyfriends and when one of them drove in the yard and honked, she would go out and pull up her skirt and lay in the back seat with him on top of her, his hairy butt bumping like a sonofagun, and her howling like a barnyard dog.

Francis made up a story about Jodie, that she liked to take off her clothes and do backflips and crabwalk up and down the stairs. She had tiny breasts with big brown nipples like Hershey's chocolate kisses. She had thin curly hair between her legs.

Tell more, they said. So he said she had her a boyfriend in Brainerd named James. They went swimming stark naked in the crick and she held his wiener in her hand until it was big as a loaf of bread and then he poked her with it. Tell more. So she had a tiny baby that was born in the middle of the night with a big red mark on its head. They gave it to the fat hairy junkman as he rode along on the junkwagon behind Big Ben clop-clop-clopping down the alley early in the morning. He was singing *Bring me your iron, your copper and iron, bring me your stee-el* and Jodie dashed out and handed up the new baby.

She gave the baby to the Jew? Yes, the baby went to Jake the Jew, went to the junkyard, and the Jew sold him to other Jews in Minneapolis. He was mailed there in a box. Sold him for fifty dollars and the postage cost 35 cents and the Jew packed a sugar teat for him to suck on. Now Jodie's baby was a Jew. His name was Isaac and his mother and daddy were rich, lived in a house with twenty-seven rooms and seven servants and Isaac had his room, his own car and chauffeur to drive him around to the zoo, to movies, to the ballpark. He was the boy who got to throw out a new ball when the Millers hit a homer. He had seventy pairs of shoes and two hundred pairs of pants and three hundred shirts and six dozen sweaters. Argyll socks and saddle shoes. Leather jackets. Caps and hats, a closetful. And though Isaac was only a kid, he got to sleep every night with a beautiful Spanish woman, her dark hot skin lay next to him, her big ripe breasts, her long legs wrapped around him, holding his little pecker in her hand, singing Bing Crosby songs.

"How do you know?" Because it's true, that's how.

"What if they find out he's not a Jew? They'll kill him."

"It's worth that chance," said Francis, "to live in Minneapolis."

He tried to write Daddy a letter to explain why he had said these dreadful things, but then he thought, "You died. What do you care? You're not my dad anymore. You're only a body in the ground. You're lying in a box with the rain leaking in and you're rotten to the bone and worms are crawling in your ears and eating your brains. Maggots in your nose. Your eyeballs are gone. You got enough problems without thinking about me."

━━━━━━

That summer Mother wanted to go to a sanitarium in Fargo where there was a specialist who treated nervous breakdowns with electrical waves. The nervous system, she explained to Francis, works on electricity, and her currents were irregular and needed to be regulated by the use of a Tremular Calibrator, a large machine like a culvert in which she would lie for four hours a day wrapped in a protective magnetic field and slowly come to feel more and more like herself. The ordinary treatment was for a month but because she had deteriorated so badly, she would need six weeks. The thought of being well again made her happy for one whole evening. She got out of bed and brushed her hair and talked about how, when she came back, they would go to Minneapolis and see the sights. "We'll sing the night away! Champagne and oysters!" she said. "We'll dance on the restaurant tables!"

Francis was sent off to Camp Wigwam, north of Minot. Daddy had been a member of the Brotherhood of Buffaloes and they gave Francis two weeks free of charge at their camp, and Emma paid for four more. The camp was run by six Buffaloes who stayed in a tarpaper shack by the

lake and played poker, seldom coming out into sunshine
except to tell kids to shut up. It was wonderful. The boys
and girls slept on straw beds in old boxcars in the woods,
and Francis met a girl named Annie and she slept next to
him. The children took off their clothes and played Indian
all day. They wore a little breechcloth, or then sometimes
they didn't. Francis knew about Indian ways from *Boys'
Life* so he was the chief, married to Annie, whose Indian
name was White Clouds and who was the doctor who
examined the Indians when their bodies bothered them.
The two weeks when Annie was there were pure shining
happiness untroubled by the weary dogfaced world except
when the Buffaloes came out and made them play softball
or go swimming in the murky water. Francis hated softball. The ball burned his hands. You had to stand around
in the sun and be bitten by flies while the other team beat
the crap out of you and hooted and sneered. He was terrified
of the lake, weedy, teeming with turtles and gator gars,
and the moment the Buffaloes went back to their poker
game, he led the Indians out of the water and back into
the woods. They danced in the grass, naked, and they
sang songs that he made up—

> O woods and trees,
> O skies and clouds,
> O blue and green,
> O shining sun

And they lay in rows on the grass and Annie came along
and touched them and they got over their smallpox. Then
he and she retired to their home in a pool of tall grass in
a clump of bramble bushes and lay down next to each
other and hugged and talked. This seemed to him the
happiest conclusion that he possibly could come to. He
put his arms around her. She touched him. She said, what

is this? He flung his leg over her and they lay a while longer, him running his hand along her skinny back, feeling her spine, her ribs, her wings, the golden down, kissing her. "Lie on top of me," he said. She stretched out on him, her lips touching his, her belly, her knees, her toes. Then a twig cracked and he looked up and a woman with long black hair peered down at him as if she were going to stamp on them like bugs. "Stand up," she said.

She wore a long dress and carried a switch; she said, "You're going straight to hell, sonny boy, and when you get there, you won't have this anymore"—and she whipped at his pecker twice—"it'll burn off in the fire." She told them to come with her and when they picked up their clothes to get dressed, she flung the clothes into a tree. "What you need clothes for? You already showed everybody your bare ass." She led them along a winding dirt path that went up over the rise and skirted the slough and around up to the county road where a green Model A Ford was parked, covered with dust. She told them to get in. The backseat was torn out, replaced with boards specked with white droppings and feathers and blood. They drove a little way to a road that went far back into the cottonwood trees, to a little white tumbledown house. She locked them in the cellar, in the dark, on a cold dirt floor, naked, with no blanket. "You can study each other down there," she said. "Sit down there and fool with each other all you like. When you're ready to accept Jesus, knock on the floorboards and you can come right up." They found three old potato sacks to put over them and he put his arms around Annie and they sat, shivering, looking up at the crack of light around the trapdoor.

"Will she hurt us do you think?" He said he didn't think so. She said she had to whiz. She went into the corner and a moment later he heard her water falling on the dirt. So delicate and musical. When she tiptoed back and stood by him, he took her in his arms again.

"We could go up and accept Jesus," he said.

"Jesus doesn't go for liars."

"She's got nothing to do with Jesus. So how can it be a lie?"

Annie didn't have an answer for that. She looked him in the face. "You are my best friend, Franny," she said after awhile. "I would lie for you anytime."

———

He banged on the door. A chair scraped overhead and the woman scuffed across the floor and opened the trap— "Took you long enough," she said. She hoisted them up and made them kneel right there and accept Jesus, and that seemed to satisfy her. "Now you are newborn children in Christ, fully redeemed and members of the Kingdom," she announced. She gave them clean sacks to wear and fixed them pancakes for breakfast. "You see, the pleasures of the flesh are the works of the devil, but the joys of the spirit are lasting and true for they come of the Lord. I am so thankful to be the vessel of your redemption. Praise God," she said, and she kissed them both goodbye and gave them each a Bible verse torn from a calendar.

They hiked back to Camp Wigwam, where the Buffaloes were getting ready to organize a party to search for them. "Oh boy, what a sight for sore eyes," said one Buffalo, with a mosquito net pinned to his hat. "You damn kids had us worried sick. What are you doing running around in sacks?" He looked away in disgust and went back into the shack and opened a beer.

That night, Annie cried herself to sleep and the next night she wouldn't sleep next to him. She said she was afraid and that nice people didn't do that.

"But you are *indispensable*," he cried. "Please. Be *magnanimous*."

His words did not touch her. She moved to a boxcar where only girls stayed, and she went swimming, and when Francis walked out to her, she swam into deep water, out to the diving dock. He walked in up to his waist, the point of fear, and beyond, to his armpits, and sweetly, despite terrible trembling, he called her name, *Annie, Annie*, but she turned her back, and he didn't dare swim to her. She went home when the two weeks were up. The rest of the summer was endless. Francis was so bored, he sat all afternoon on the Buffaloes' porch and read their newspaper. He walked to the southeastern corner of Camp Wigwam, where the fence met a tree that they called The Woodtick Tree, and he climbed up it, despite the ticks, and could see a brilliant light far away, the reflection of the sun on a distant silo roof, and thought, "Minneapolis."

CHAPTER 16

Radio Sex

Mother came back from Fargo exhausted. "Nothing goes right for me," she said. The treatments had failed and the failure discouraged her. She was discouraged by how discouraged she was. "Other people are braver than me, Francis. I'm not the only one who ever lost a husband. Other women keep going and I don't know why I can't. You've got yourself a rotten mother, that's all. I'm so sorry." She cried whenever she looked at him now. "You ought to have a happy home like other kids and look at you. You got an old hag of a mother who sits here bawling like a calf. A big baby. That's all I am." Her day was regulated by the radio. It was the only life she had. She woke early for the Shepherd Boys Quartet singing gospel songs on *The Rise and Shine Show* and she went to bed after *The Calhoun Club Ballroom* and the sweet music of Tommy Leonard and His Lake Serenaders and the dancers slipping quietly around the breezy terrace overlooking Excelsior Boulevard. And in between she followed all her shows faithfully, listening, writing in. She told

Dad to beware those man-hunting women and she com-
mended Tiny for always being cheerful (and got back a
postcard: "Yo sho' keeps a-makin' me Happy!"). She wrote
letters to Little Benny ("I have a boy not much older than
you, and when I hear you sing, I like to imagine it's him
singing to me") and she became a member of *The WLT
Tip Top Club*—"Whenever you feel blue, think of something nice to do. Don't let it get you down; wear a smile,
not a frown. And you'll be feeling tip-top too!" She wrote
in regularly to Smilin' Bud Swenson and once received
$3 for her poem, "Trees," which was read on the show.

> When I see a tree, it inspires me
> For a tree from a tiny seed grew.
> If something so small can grow that tall,
> Then there's hope for me and you.

She subscribed to the *Tip Top* philosophy, to concentrate
on the good things and forget the bad, to smile and look
forward to tomorrow and do good for others, but, as she
explained to Francis, it didn't work for her because she
was too weak. She couldn't bear to face the neighbors
because they all talked about her and how messy her house
was. She couldn't move to Minneapolis because it cost too
much and what would she do there? She could only listen
to the radio.
That Christmas, 1940, Little Buddy sang "Christmas
in the Depot," about a boy named Little Jim whose daddy
had been a railroad engineer and died in a crash—Mother
reached over and turned up the radio, and Francis got up
off the floor where he was studying Art's special *Geographic*
and sat by her on the couch and held her hand—and now
Little Jim was lost in the crowded train station on Christmas Eve trying to get back to his dying mother on the
Evening Mail—

"All board," cried the voice on the platform,
As all of the people got on.
And Jim he looked in his jacket
And the precious ticket was gone.

He looked in the old cardboard satchel,
And his pockets, the left and the right.
He had lost his ticket to see her,
And Mother was dying tonight.

He whispered, "Please, Mister Conductor,
The Evening Mail I must ride,
For Mother is dying in Pittsburgh,
And I need to be there at her side."

The conductor looked down at him gravely.
He said, "There is naught I can do.
There are rules by which railroads are managed,
And we make no exception for you."

So Jim found a gentleman standing
Beside the first-class sleeping car,
And he wore a fine suit and a top hat
And smoked a three-dollar cigar.

And Jim said, "Please, sir, can you spare me
Two dollars to pay for my fare?
For I must tonight get to Pittsburgh.
My mother is perishing there."

And the gentleman sneered at him cruelly,
"Be gone or I'll call the police.
I'm tired of beggars and chisellers!
Be gone, you're disturbing the peace!"

So Jim found a place in the station,
A corner behind the front door,

And he felt so cold and so sleepy
As he lay on the cold marble floor.

And he dreamed he saw angels in heaven.
How sweet were the anthems they sung,
And there in the middle was Mother,
So happy and lovely and young.

And she said to him, "Jim, you're a good boy,
A child of sunshine and love,
And tonight you will join me in heaven
And live with your mother above."

And Jim put his hand out to touch her
And the heavens resounded with joy
To know he would have no more suffering,
That ragged and poor little boy.

A janitor found him at daybreak,
And they covered him up with a sheet,
And they sent round a hearse in an hour,
And they carried him up the main street.

And O how the sidewalks were crowded,
'Twas Christmas for young and for old,
And nobody saw the black wagon
With its cargo so tiny and cold.

They were busily worshipping Jesus.
They sang halleluias to Him.
But Jesus looked down with a smile
And He said, "Welcome home, Little Jim."

Mother was radiant. It was the loveliest song she had
ever heard. So sad, but she couldn't cry, it was too beau-

tiful. "Things will turn out for us, I know it," she said. "It's just like the song says."

"But why does he have to die to be happy?" Francis thought it was the worst song in the history of radio.

"Don't you think Daddy is happy?" she asked. Her upper lip trembled. "I know he is. He says he is. He tells me every day that he is." She turned off the radio. "Dying is the easy part," she said softly. "It's the waiting that's unbearable." Francis turned the radio back on. Little Buddy's dad, Slim, was talking about corn flakes. It would be nice to have a dad, Francis thought, especially one who could play the guitar.

The next summer, Francis moved to Minneapolis to live with Art and Clare for awhile because Mother had to go back to the hospital. She had dreams, terrible ones, and now the dark figures from her dreams were coming to her during the day. "Do I seem crazy to you?" she asked him. He said no. "But I am," she said.

She came to his room late at night and sat on the edge of his bed. "My life is gone, Francis. Gone up in smoke. We were happy once and then Daddy died. He burned up, Francis. He was a good man and God let him die in the flames. We were so happy. I don't know why this happened to us. You're my little boy and I love you more than anything else and my wish is that you could have had a happy life but there's nothing to be done. I'm sending you away but it breaks my heart to do it. Just do one thing for me, Francis, because I don't know if we'll ever be together again. It's all I ask. Remember your mother, Francis. Just remember me. That's all I ask. Will you promise me that? Will you? Promise that no matter what happens, you'll always remember your mother, who brought you into the world. I love you. Goodbye, darling boy. Remember your promise. Remember."

Art was waiting at the Great Northern Depot and they drove up to Art's cousin's plumbing shop on Plymouth Avenue. "You hear that Ole and Lena moved away too?" said Art. "Yeah, they moved away because Ole read in the paper that most accidents occur at home." Ed the cousin locked up the shop and took off with them and they all had hamburgers at a gleaming steel diner where the dishwasher had a dark green eyeball—"Zez Hoover. Usedta catch for the Millers long time ago, got hit by a pitch," said Ed—and then they dropped in at the fire station for a hand of cribbage. Art had a silver flask and passed it around. "Gotta go check out a babe," he told Francis. "You stick with Ed. I'll be back in a shake."

Francis and Ed shot pool with a couple firemen, then the two of them walked back to the shop. "That Art. Quite a guy," said Ed. "Quite a guy. I sure envy him. Plumbing is nothing, you're dealing with nobodies. I tell you, one thing about radio is that a man can get laid faster than anywhere else. They're all doing it. Those firemen you just met? Lily Dale goes there once a week and does half the guys in the department, that's why she has so much tremolo."

Lily Dale? said Francis. Oh yes, she drove down to Engine Co. 1 after her show, pulled the big Caddy into the barn next to the pumper and the firemen lined up at the rear door. All those radio people were banging away as fast as they could. That Leo LaValley, they say he's a real pussy hound. That minister who's on Sunday mornings, him too, and that Shepherd Boys Quartet, that bass singer, they say his balls hang down to his knees.

Leo a *what* kind of hound?

"Oh, he's hot for that woman who's on in the morning. That LaWella."

LaWella Wells? The homemaker?

"That's the one. They say she does that whole damn show in her undies and sometimes she takes them off and sits there naked as a jaybird. Not a stitch. A real knock-out, too."

LaWella Wells? The peanut butter cookie recipes and how to get cranberry juice out of a wool sweater?

"Sits there in her little brassiere and panties, and whenever the recipe calls for milk, she unhooks the top and whenever the recipe calls for sugar, off comes the bottom. I heard that from a guy who worked there. He said the control room was so crowded during that homemaker show, you couldn't take a deep breath."

That sweet woman with the cheery "Good morning everybody! It's a beautiful day and it's so good to have you here in my kitchen!"—naked?

"She's got breasts as firm as a McIntosh apple. Real nice little breasts with big pale-brown nipples. Nice long legs. Real nice. Soft red hair. Beautiful woman. Sits there at a table covered with soft green felt and she's talking real smooth and sweet about making bread pudding, in those lace panties and that pretty little black brassiere, and she talks about breaking up them bread crumbs and adding a cup of milk, and she reaches back and unhooks and suddenly her two little breasts are there, covered with goose-bumps, and the nipples sticking out a half an inch, and then she comes to the half cup of sugar and she gets up and lies down on the table, under the microphone, and she eases out of those panties, first one long leg, then the other, and she's talking along just so cool and sweet about putting that pudding in the oven, and she's moving her little hinder around and around and holding those little boobies, and she touches herself down there and when she says goodbye, she points at one guy in the control room and he gets to come down and bang her right there. Just one guy. She chooses a different one every day. That's the truth. That's what he told me."

"Bang her?"

"Yeah, those radio guys got it made. Plumbing is nothin'. It's like sled dogs. Unless you're the lead dog, the scenery never changes."

On the way home, Art drove downtown and parked and took Francis into Dayton's Department Store, and they rode the elevator up to the twelfth floor. Twelve floors of goods to buy, a palace of underwear, a cathedral of socks. Great high pillars and arches and below, aisles and aisles of sweet new pajamas and suits and, on the third floor, dozens of naked dummies in corsets and slips. Art bought a slip.

"For Aunt Clare?"

"It's for her birthday. Don't mention it to her, okay?"

"Does LaWella Wells really do her show in her underwear?"

"I don't know. I've never seen her show. Want me to check it out for you?"

Francis nodded. Yes. He would like to know this.

———

Mother was in the hospital for June and July, and got out, and went back in for most of August. Clare took Francis up to Fargo to see her and she didn't recognize him. She called him Chester and thought he was pretty funny, or strange—she laughed and screwed up her face at him and gave him a friendly shove. Clare kept saying, Ruby, Ruby, it's Franny. They stayed for only a few minutes and when Mother got too worked up they left. She kept pointing at the radio and laughing at him. Maybe she thought he was Leo, from the radio. Anyway, Mother certainly enjoyed seeing him. It was the happiest he had seen her in years.

———

Art was not as much fun to live with as he had been when he visited. He didn't do card tricks or tell many jokes, he preferred to sit in his big easy chair in the dark and smoke and drink Manhattans. The ice clinked and the red coal got brighter and dimmer.

"Mind if I sit with you, Uncle Art?"

"No."

"Care for a little light on the subject?" (One of Art's lines.)

"No thanks."

"Anything I can bring you?"

"Francis?"

"Yes?"

"If you're going to fidget, go fidget somewhere else." And he'd peel off a dollar bill and give it to him to go buy comic books. Francis soon had the largest collection of comics on Blaisdell Avenue, and even though he'd trade them three-for-one to other boys, trying to win friends, his pile grew and grew. He bought the Doctor Dolittle books, he bought Richard Halliburton and novels about men sailing away on tramp steamers to the Orient and detectives and Gene Autry's adventures in the Golden West. Like the good doctor from Puddleby-on-Marsh, Francis learned to find company outside of the human race. Instead of animals, Francis collected books.

CHAPTER 17

Minneapolis

Francis attended West High School for six years and lived with Art and Clare except when they felt under the weather. Then he'd live with Clare's brother James and his wife Alta for a few weeks, or with Alta's aunt Rosamond. Clare sold cosmetics at Dayton's and the crowds exhausted her and she'd come home and lie down on the sofa and when Art got home she would whisper to him and he'd call for Francis and send him away. Or sometimes Art sent him away for reasons of his own. Art's limit seemed to be a month, and after that, he got tired of having Francis around, no matter how nice Francis tried to be.

Francis learned how to be extremely nice, even invisible. He sat in his little room in the attic, which he kept neat and clean, and he made no noise, treading around in stocking feet, and never bothered anybody, washed and dried the dishes, did all his own laundry, darned his socks, sewed on his buttons, earned his own money delivering the *Tribune*, shoveled Art's snow, listened to Art, was agreeable, and still Art would say, "Maybe it's time you went with James and Alta for awhile, okay?" and off he'd go. James and Alta had four little kids and no spare room, and Francis slept on a couch in the basement that otherwise was their dog's. Rex resented Francis and growled at him. The little kids stole his stuff. He woke in the morning with dog hair in his mouth. His clothes were full of it. He smelled of Rex at school. After a week, he'd creep back to Art and Clare, humiliated. They didn't give him a key to the house but he was able to jigger the basement window open and slither through and climb onto the laundry tub and tiptoe upstairs to his room and lie in bed and hope they wouldn't be too upset that he was back.

Art didn't do his magic tricks or tell his jokes, except if James's little boy William came over. He ran straight for Art's pant leg and hung on and squealed, and then Art was the old happy-go-lucky Art. Otherwise, he read the paper and worried about the war. Art was sure that Hitler would be in Minneapolis before next Christmas, the Panzer divisions of the Wehrmacht speeding west across the plains to meet the Japs in California, the Luftwaffe settled in at Wold-Chamberlain Field, and a Heinie as mayor of Minneapolis. Art told Francis that if the Germans came, he would sell the house and they would move to Canada and Francis would have to go back to Mindren. Art said that we had made a big mistake sending ships and planes to England and that Hitler's wrath would be all the worse for our sending weapons to kill German boys. Roosevelt had betrayed America by getting us into this war. American cities would be laid to rubble, Americans would die by the tens of thousands, all because the President was an Ivy League cookie pusher with a weak spot for the Brits.

After school, Francis liked to ride the Como-Xerxes streetcar downtown, spend an hour at the main library, and walk to the Hotel Ogden and hang around WLT and then ride home with Art. It was scary the first time: he approached the desk in the lobby and said, "I'm Francis With, I'm Arthur Finn's nephew, I'd like to be able to go up and see him if I may, please," fully expecting the tall woman with bright red fingernails to laugh cruelly and call a cop and have Francis pitched out into the street. But she only smiled and said, "Fourth floor," and after that he didn't need to ask, she only smiled. And then he didn't go to the fourth floor, where Art wasn't so happy to see him; he went to Three and wandered near the studios.

He had a story ready in case somebody asked him what he was doing there. He was Arthur Finn's nephew and he was writing a term paper for school on the subject "Radio Goes to War," about the vital importance of radio entertainment in keeping morale high on the home front. But nobody ever asked him. Men stood and smoked in the halls, men charged past and dove into studios a moment before the *On Air* light flashed, men in cowboy clothes sat and read the newspaper, Homer Jessie studied his scripts and practiced woofing or whinnying or chuckling or sobbing, and once a trained seal flapped past on its way to play "Silent Night" on the *Jubilee*, and nobody asked Francis anything. He walked off the elevator, turned left, walked through the double doors and past Studio B and into the Green Room, got a Coke out of the cooler, and sat and listened to the radio. And after a moment, the people he had just heard on the radio would walk into the room, pour themselves a cup of coffee, plop down, and shoot the breeze. Francis sat, polite and invisible, a fly on the wall.

One day, Leo was on the radio talking bravely about the value of determination and how many impossible deeds had been achieved by people simply because they refused to quit, and a moment later he was flopped on the couch and complaining to Gene the engineer that Little Buddy had spit seeds in the studio and they stuck to Leo's pants.

"The little shit, somebody ought to drop a rock on him," said Leo. "He's spoiled rotten. The kid sits and eats grapes by the bagful and sprays the seeds in all directions. Then he gets the runs and goes fills up the toilet and doesn't even flush it! What you gonna do with a kid like that? I'd say, drop him off the roof and be done with it."

"Kinda sours a person on children in general," said the engineer.

"Even his own father hates him," said Leo.

Francis did not know Little Buddy Graves personally, only as a voice on *Friendly Neighbor* with his father Slim, singing "I Heard My Mother Call from Heaven" and "Little Bob the Newsboy," and then later on their own show on Monday nights at 7:30. Slim strummed guitar and sang along, but Little Buddy, of course, was the star. He sang songs about sickly children with drunken fathers who lay dying in the snow. The show closed with Little Buddy kneeling at his radio bedside in prayer, asking God to bless his dad and his mother and his brothers Bobby and Billy and "all of the dear children listening tonight," and when he chirped "Good-night, Daddy," it made Francis think about his own daddy coming in to kiss him good night.

"I'm not kidding," said Leo, lowering his voice. "I believe the kid is a midget. Check him out sometime. Follow him into the men's room and stand next to him and take a glance at his gonads. I bet you'll find that he's in his twenties and a little small for his age. Yank his hair while you're at it, five bucks says it's a rug."

Francis had seen Little Buddy's picture, of course, in the souvenir songbook: he was short and plump and had long dangly golden ringlets.

"Naw, he's a kid," said the engineer. "You can tell by the way he's scared of his old man. I've never seen a man rag on a kid like Slim does, he's on that little bugger about every little damn thing. Other day, he yells, 'Don't look at me so dumb, ya look just like yer photographs, ya cheesehead.' He stands over him and makes him sign the autographs and makes sure the kid writes big and loopy. The kid gets so spooked, he starts forgetting the words or singing off-key and then—you never saw anybody chew out a kid like Slim does." The engineer stiffened and glared and hissed, "Shape up ya little dipshit—ya keep slowing down, yer gonna put everbody to sleep—so quit farting around and *stay on the beat* or I'll kick your fanny out of here and get somebody else and nobody'll know the difference except it'll be better!" And then the engineer smiled warmly and said, "Welcome back, friends and neighbors, and now it's hymn time. Isn't it, Buddy? Yes, Buddy asked me last night, after he said his prayers, if we couldn't do 'What a Friend We Have in Jesus' on the broadcast today, so here it is. Son?" And the engineer whispered in a little high-pitched voice, "This is for all the little children, especially the ones who don't have enough food to eat." And the engineer sang, in Little Buddy's voice,

> What a friend we have in Jesus,
> All our sins and griefs to bear.
> What a privilege to carry
> Everything to God in prayer.

And then he piped, "Bye, everybody, and see you reeeaal soon!"

Leo laughed. "By God, Gene, if it wasn't for the gin on your breath, I'd've thought it was the little shit himself."

Gene smiled. "I've got him down pretty good."

"That Christmas song? The one about the kid in the

depot? They stole that song off a drunk in a dive on Hennepin Avenue."

"I thought Slim wrote that."

"Hell he did. He rolled a drunk for that song. Some poor guy, the bartender told him that Slim was on the radio, the guy comes up and says, I got this song, do you think it's any good? Slim read it, he said, Naw, that's nothin', but here, I'll give you a quart of Four Roses for it, so he wound up with the song and the guy winds up dead in the gutter and Slim takes the song and has the little shit record it and they earned *four thousand dollars* off it! That's right! Four grand!"

The engineer shook his head. "That's pretty dirty."

"And those lyrics—that was a true story. The drunken guy was the little kid."

"Little Jim?"

"Himself. He'd scrawled out the lyrics with carpenter's pencil on the back of an envelope. Slim had to ask Lily Dale to decipher the last verse. He told her the whole story. The guy's name was Jim, he was the kid, and the story was all true except that he hadn't gotten to heaven yet. He needed the Four Roses to put him over the top. He gave Slim his song and drank the whiskey and collapsed on the floor and Slim left him lying there and brought the song over to the studio and never even bothered getting the man's last name or his address."

"His lucky day, I guess."

Leo got up and poured another cup of coffee. He was getting warmed up to the subject. He didn't notice Francis sitting behind the Coke. Francis was studying the holes in the ceiling, counting them.

"Christmas in the Depot," the song Slim stole from the drunken Jim, was what got Buddy and Slim the *Cottage Home Show*, six days a week, at $350 a week, said Leo. Mr. Dameron, the president of Cottage Home Cottage

Cheese, heard Little Buddy sing it and had to pull his car over to the side of Highway 12 and sit and weep. He didn't know Slim had swiped it off a dying man. Mr. Dameron's mother was ill in Des Moines. He had just turned fifty. Cottage Home stock was down to 2.28, due to lagging sales. He had had harsh words with an employee that morning and had fired the man on the spot. He had left work early, feeling depressed, to return to his mansion, Brearley, on Lake Minnetonka and there perhaps to take his own life. To Mr. Dameron, "Christmas in the Depot" was a call to action. He rehired the man, visited his mother, hired Little Buddy and Slim, and sales of Cottage Home almost doubled. Mr. Dameron said, "Nothing sold more cottage cheese than when Little Buddy said, *oh boy.*"

Francis had heard the Cottage Home commercials, of course. Everybody knew them. Kids at West High would say, "Oh boy!" in a high-pitched voice and everybody laughed.

SLIM: I'll tell you one thing Buddy loves more than ice cream, and that's a big helping of Cottage Home cottage cheese.
BUDDY: Oh boy.
SLIM: Yes, Cottage Home is chock full of vitamins and protein and all the good stuff that helps little skeeters like Buddy grow up to be straight-shooters and real go-ahead guys, but best of all, Cottage Home is the cottage cheese with that mmmmmm-good real honest-to-goodness homemade flavor. You just ask Little Buddy.
BUDDY: Oh *boy*.
SLIM: That's right. That's Cottage Home. Sing it, son.
BUDDY: I'm a good boy, ain't I, dad,
So can I have more, please?
That real good—makes me feel good—
Cottage Home Cottage Cheese.
Oh boy!

Leo said the commercial took away his appetite for cottage cheese forever, but what could you do? They were a big hit. The little shit's face appeared on the front of the carton, "Little Buddy's Cottage Home Songbook" was published and then a storybook and then a coloring book, and Dameron paid WLT a bonus to expand the show to a half-hour and then signed a two-year contract at double the existing rate—evidently, the little shit was going over big with the friends and neighbors.

"The man must be a pederast to pay $350 a week for a so-called child to mince around like that. So what does that make us—pimps, I guess," said Leo. Francis did not know what a pederast and a pimp were, but he could guess. Leo snorted. "If that kid's a kid, then I'm Greta Garbo. I keep seeing razor nicks on the little nipper's cheeks, don't you?"

Gene said he thought that Little Buddy was no more than ten years old.

"Some hermaphrodites do not experience the change of voice until their late twenties," said Leo. "They have only one gonad, like John Wilkes Booth. A famous case. Booth had a piping soprano voice and played women's roles until he was thirty. Had no lead in his pencil. That's why he shot Lincoln. Another was Typhoid Harry, the Georgia farm boy who milked his father's cows day and night and spread the deadly disease that almost wiped out Atlanta. Another hermaphrodite. An accident of nature, but the pattern for these little fellas is not cheery." Leo put two cubes of sugar in his coffee. "Think about it. Little Buddy going berserk with a handgun. Don't laugh. A child is more than capable of handling firearms, especially if he's in his early twenties and a freak of nature. Even herma-phrodites *want* a woman, you know. The desire is even more pronounced with the lack of apparatus. That's why the little shit is such a winner with the women, they can hear that sob in his voice." Leo sipped his coffee. "A real man's man can no more sing than a dog can read books. Singing, *any* kind of performance: it's pure frustration that causes it. Blue balls. Yes. It's true. Men who can get it up don't need to prance around and lay it on like show people do, that's a fact. All that la-di-da and the costumes and the big grins, that's hermaphrodism talking. The same, by the way, is not true of women." He leaned forward and pointed a finger into his own chest. "I," he said, "have no talent for performance whatsoever, nor any desire to have any. I am quite happy to be normal."

CHAPTER 18

Søren Blak

All the radio stars trooped through the Green Room; Francis saw them all—kindly Dad Benson and sweet Alma Melting and Miss Lily Dale in her wheelchair, the Norsk Nightingale who (surprise) didn't talk with an accent at all and his name wasn't Jens but Jon, a big rangy bald fellow who sang like Gene Austin when he donned a black mask and became The Masked Balladeer on *The Calhoun Club,* and Faith and Dale Snelling, a husband and wife who hardly acknowledged each other, and Little Becky. She was the only one who noticed Francis.

"You waiting for somebody?" she said once. Yes, he was waiting to talk to certain people. He was writing a term paper about radio's role in the war.

"You sure you're not just hanging around hoping to see my tits?"

No, he assured her that he was not.

She snorted and leaned over him. "But you wouldn't mind seeing them."

He didn't know how to answer this. He didn't want to insult her, but on the other hand, she looked to him like one of those persons whose tits he definitely would *not* care to see.

"Well, maybe someday I'll let you have a little peek," she said. She turned away and knocked an ashtray off the table and a hundred butts shot all over the room, ashes drifting down like snow. "Oh shit!" she said. Francis immediately started gathering butts off the rug but then suddenly sprang forward head-first into the wall when she goosed him. It was a deep goose, a serious grab with her thumb up his bunghole, and he banged his face on the wall molding and landed on his head and shoulder, scrunched up by the couch. She shrieked with joy. "What a clyde you are!" Just then a kid in short pants and a Navy jumper rushed into the room, a boy with golden ringlets bouncing—Francis recognized Little Buddy, though the boy looked glum. "Didja get him?" he cried. "You promised I could see!"

"You're too late. I already drilled him." She looked at Francis. "Didn't I?"

Francis shook his head. "I don't know what she's talking about," he told the boy. Little Buddy looked up at Little Becky. "You didn't goose him, you big fat liar!" He kicked her in the ankle and ran and hid behind the couch, chuckling to himself. But Little Becky was after Francis. She approached him, eyes narrowed, and shoved him. He shoved back.

"I did so goose you and I'm gonna take your pants down and prove it to you," she sneered. "C'mere, Buddy, and have a look at his rosy-red rectum." She made a ferocious dive for Francis's good corduroys and he stepped back and brought up his knee and cracked her a good one. She plopped down, hands to her face, and moaned. Her hands came away bright red with blood.

"You asswipe," she muttered, rising slowly to her feet. Little Buddy snickered as she reached for the ashtray. Francis grabbed her wrist, and they struggled, her spitting in his face and trying to butt him, but he threw her down, just as Dad and Leo and Gene strolled in.

Little Becky burst into tears. "He punched me!" she cried, running to Leo with open arms, but Leo side-stepped her. "It's about time," he said. "I wish it had been me."

Dad told her to go wash her face and she turned and glared at Francis and fled from the room. Little Buddy came out from behind the couch. "She didn't goose him," he said, gravely. "He hit her in the nose."

"Look out or he'll do it to you," said Leo.

The child shook his little ringlets. "If he does, I'll shoot him with a gun."

"If you do," said Leo, "you'll go to the electric chair and they'll fry you until your hair turns straight and your eyes fall out."

"Leo——" said Dad, but all three of them were laughing. Leo turned to Francis.

"I'm sorry," said Francis. "I didn't mean to hurt her."

Leo said it was nothing to apologize for. "You ought to get a medal," he said. And the next day, he gave Francis a coffee cup of his own, on which he had written, "The Man Who Handled the Monster." Leo showed him where to hang it, over the sink, in the white cabinet where all the stars kept their coffee cups, and every day when Francis came around he got down his cup. After awhile he even developed a taste for coffee.

———

Up on the farm in Moorhead, meanwhile, lying on his Sound Couch, Roy thought Little Buddy was a comer. He called Ray on the Radiophone and told him that the boy had a preternatural instinct for radio, to ditch Slim and to give the boy free rein. "You're making that old mistake again," he shouted through the static. "You're full of beans, as usual," said Ray, happily. Unfortunately, the Radiophone went on the fritz and Roy's voice came out of the big desk speaker in broken shards, little blips of words, such as "savant," "ideation," "ritual," "ether," "efficacy," and "positivism"—"Have you been talking to Patsy Konopka?" yelled Ray, but that didn't affect the voice of Roy, which babbled on—"sequential" came through and "predate."

Roy had been reading a Norwegian philosopher named Søren Blak and sent Ray a copy of Blak's big book, *The Experience of Innocence* (*Uskyldigheds Oplevelse*), with a note: "I know you won't read this but am sending it anyway so you can't say you didn't know about it." Ray summoned Ethel. "Read this for me," he said.

Søren Blak raised goats in the mountains above Glomfjord and wrote poetry and thought about civilization, which he felt had mostly come to the end of the road, except for radio. In his small stone hut, far from the corruption and urban despair of Oslo, Blak's one connection to the world was a small Atwater-Kent radio, over which, through the propitious combination of sunspots and high clouds and the crazy bounce of the airwaves and the altitude of his hut, he occasionally received *Fibber McGee and Molly*. Blak had taught himself English years before by reading John Greenleaf Whittier, the only English book in the Glomfjord Library, and he kept fluent by speaking to his goats—"Ay, my tattered legions, goats of Glomfjord! / Shake off thy rooky torpor now and leave / The cloistered warmth of this thy straw-paved bower / And follow close the well-tripped path of horned flocks / Vexed by pebbly pains and by a scourge of flies / Yet daily drawn by hunger that cannot be shut / Forth to yon dewy-beaded meadow / Bent upon the cause of mastication"—and so, to him, the English of Fibber and Molly came as a distinct innovation, almost a new language, lean, angular, more allusive, more contrapuntal than the Quaker Bard's windy speeches. In his mountain fastness, surrounded by rocky splendor, he lived for Monday nights and the half-hour with the folks from Peoria. The state radio signal from Oslo was a pipeline of triviality, rat crap, a monument to the invincible smallmindedness of the Norwegian people, but Fibber and Molly were a fresh breeze from the New World, a work of art that enlarged and extended radio just as he, Søren, had taken clunky Norwegian and made something sensuous of it in his *Oplevelse,* not that the Norwegian people had ever noticed; no, they had not.

The boastful Fibber was, to Blak, a paradigm of western man, and the famous loaded closet, of course, represented civilization and all its flotsam and loose baggage, while the childlike voice of Molly, bringing the man back to reality, cheering him up in his moments of inevitable defeat, seemed to Blak the voice of culture in its deepest and most profound incarnation, that of the adored Mother, the Goddess of Goodness, the great Herself. Molly's trademark line, "Tain't funny, McGee," expressed Blak's mood exactly. Radio was a Great Mother (*Stor Moder*) that reached out through the ether to gather its farflung herd of goats and bring them temporarily back into one dark warm barn. Only when *Fibber McGee and Molly* came faintly into his dark little hut did Søren Blak feel truly connected to the human race. His long letter to the world was dedicated to them and their home at 79 Wistful Vista.

Radio, Roy believed after reading Blak and going on to Carl Jung (whose work may have been based on some transcriptions of *Inner Sanctum* and the Cliquot Club Eskimos), was a raw primitive gorgeous device that unfortunately had been discovered too late. In the proper order of things, it should have come somewhere between the wheel and the printing press. It belonged to the age of bards and storytellers who squatted by the fire, when all news and knowledge was transmitted by telling. Coming at the wrong time, radio was inhibited by prior developments, such as literature. It was as if the ball had preceded the bat, so that when the bat finally was discovered, it was relegated to the ninth inning, when players would throw bats in the air and try to hit them with balls. In the same way, literature, which was alien to radio, prevented it from reaching full flower.

If only radio had come first, it would have kept poetry and drama and stories in the happy old oral tradition and poets would simply be genial hosts who chant odes and lays instead of a bunch of nervous jerks like T.S. Eliot. Radio could have *saved* literature, but instead, literature had imprisoned radio in literature's own disease, like an editor who asks the writer to take out all the funny parts. Literature had taken radio and hung scripts around its neck, choking the free flow of expression that alone could give radio life. Scripts made radio cautious, formal, tight, devoted to lines. But radio is not lines—radio is air! said Roy. Literary principles of form mean nothing—radio has no linear context whatsoever. It is dreamlike, precognitive, primitive, intimate. It has less to do with politics or society than with sex, nature, and religion.

———

Ray read one of Roy's letters out loud to Ethel: "Radio travels at the speed of light, 187,000 miles per second. Instantaneous, and the signal is reproduced *by the recipient*—an unlimited number of them, at no additional cost per unit. By comparison, the printed word is produced one copy at a time, at additional per unit expense. It is a *possession*. The printed word is much more rapidly perceived, or read, than the spoken word can be heard, due to the fact that speaking involves a much higher level of complexity than writing. Writing is spelling and grammar; it stops there. Speaking involves tone, pitch, inflection, volume, rate of speech and changes of rate of speech— factors that, each productive of slight variations of the other, increase the expressive power of speech geometrically. Unfortunately, the radio speaking voice is restricted by the speaker's aural memory of *how radio people should speak*—which results in a certain similarity among speakers as to inflection and rate, which may also be due to the old limitations of microphones, primitive instruments requiring the human voice to accommodate existing technology. As the technology improves, we must teach the voice *not* to accommodate itself to the technology of yesterday. We must show announcers how *not* to speak so clearly."

"It goes on," said Ray.

"Do you want me to deal with it?" she asked. She had written for Ray a three-page summary of the Blak book. Ethel was ever businesslike.

"He is my brother and he cannot be dealt with. He must be endured."

━━━━

Roy's enthusiasm for Little Buddy was based on his belief that only children could master radio, it was too simple a medium for adults. Spontaneity was what the doctor ordered for radio—and the more mistakes, the better! Goofs were better than anything you could plan. "Innocence must instruct experience!" he wrote Ray. "The child is father of the man!" Ray wrote back: "You better have your well

147

water checked. I believe you are absorbing some sort of minerals in the brain that have short-circuited your Down button. How is the Mrs.?"

Then Little Buddy hurt his voice. Leo told Francis the doctors weren't just sure how but that some of the WLT people thought he had been choked by his dad. "Throttled the little booger and squeezed his vocal cords and now he sounds like the wind in the outhouse." Leo said that Slim couldn't keep the show going for two minutes without Little Buddy. "Isn't that the hell of it? Here's a darn good guitar player and he needs this brat to put him across with an audience. Makes you think twice about being in this business."

Slim played on *Friendly Neighbor* the next day and sat around after in the Green Room. Francis had skipped school. Slim was a sawed-off guy with a weathered face and a sad smile. He was a lot smaller than on the radio, Francis thought. Slim rolled a cigarette on his knee and lit it. He told Leo, "I think it got to be too much for the kid, all that acclaim and attention, and he fretted about losing it, and it tightened up his voice box, and when he craned his neck, it strained him. A few days rest and he'll be good as new."

―――――

But a few days rest did not help. Buddy lay in bed and if anybody suggested that he get up and go to WLT, he moaned and wept and hugged the pillow and said his throat was burning.

Slim did the *Cottage Home Show* alone the next week, and according to Leo, WLT got a thousand calls and letters asking, *Where's Buddy?* Even the *Tribune* printed a story about it: Child Star Home Sick, But Show Goes On.

The next day, Leo was waiting for Francis when he

arrived. "Grab a glass of water and follow me," he said. Slim was waiting in Studio B, tuning his guitar. He glanced up and smiled. "Leo says you can sing real good," he said softly. Francis shook his head. "Let's give it a try, pardner. What you say? You know 'Red River Valley'?" He strummed the old guitar. "Key of C ought to work for you," he said. "Try it. Come and sit by my side if you love me, do not hasten to bid me adieu." Francis looked for Leo but he had disappeared up into the control room, where he and Gene were laughing about something.

"I can't sing," Francis whispered.

"Try," said Slim. So Francis did. He closed his eyes and sang as much of "Red River Valley" as he knew. And Slim said, "You're right. You can't sing. But that's okay. I can't stand on my head."

"I'm very sorry. Maybe if I took the music home and practiced—"

Slim smiled. "I don't believe that's gonna help, pardner."

Francis was about to say again that he was very sorry, and then Slim shook his head. "I don't believe that anything is going to help me now," he said softly. And Francis could see that was true. The broken brown teeth, the scaly white hands, the lost eyes: this man was on his way to the crash, about to become Daddy.

CHAPTER 19

Bryan

Ray's wife Vesta appeared at WLT every morning at ten, a pair of sensible brown shoes, big legs in a long brown tweed skirt, a thick torso in a brown silk blouse, and Vesta's large head and short brown hair. She was nearly six feet tall. She carried a lit cigarette and a black leather briefcase and her feet clomped as she headed west along the back hall. There was a flash of lipstick and a turban with a green plume, but brown was her trademark. She disappeared into her office in the Women's Bureau, emerged at five minutes before eleven, strode into Studio B to introduce the *Classroom of the Air* speaker and tell why his or her topic ("Meeting the Needs of the Cities" or "The Future of Architecture" or "Women in Broadcasting") was of vital interest to all of us, and then disappeared for the rest of the day to clip out articles from *The New Republic* and *The Women's Precepts Weekly* and to compose a memorandum to Ray, reminding him why he should fire Leo ("a fool"), why they should broadcast the Metropolitan Opera ("to inculcate a love of opera in young children").

"A child who has learned to love Wagner is a child who could learn to enjoy a pig slaughter," replied Ray, who was no fan of pig slaughters.

Vesta did not mingle, except at Christmas, and then only because it was Christmas and people expected it. At the WLT party, she stood in a corner of the Star of the North Ballroom and sipped sherry for a few minutes and escaped before the entertainment began. She loathed the sight of smiley people on stage laying on the charm and telling jokes and showing off. To her it was embarrassing that people should be so dishonest in public, but of course that was the point of entertainment, so she preferred to stay away. The terrifying prospect was that Santa (Leo) would see her and call her up to the stage and she would have to stand and grin like an idiot and give away trashy gifts. She fled before Santa arrived.

The worst part of radio was the comedy, and after that came the commercials. Whenever she heard one, she reached for the knob. Disgusting, vile, repulsive things. Someone paid you money to say what they wanted you to say and you said it. "Here's ten dollars. Say *shit*," so you took the money and said it. You said it ten times, as many as they wanted, and you said it with a grin, or whatever they wanted. A horrible truth in America: *money talks*. Not truth, not society, not art, but money, and when money talks, it doesn't tell the truth, it talks money. No wonder the Republic was in the hands of midgets like Harding and Coolidge, when the greatest educational innovation of all time—the permanent invisible universal classroom of the air—is given over to dumbheads to use to sell toilet bowl cleaner. Throw out the professor, bring in the janitor to teach the class.

151

"This could have been the Acropolis," she told Ray bitterly, "and you made it a bazaar."

"It's only Minneapolis," he said, "and what's bazaar about that?" He grinned. She did not feel the slightest impulse to laugh.

Patsy Konopka and Vesta Soderbjerg met in the halls of WLT once, when Patsy took a wrong turn en route to the Ladies' room, and they circled one another with the poisoned courtesy of wasps in the arborvitae. Patsy considered Vesta an old snoot and Vesta thought Patsy was one of those women Ray took to New York. A whore, in other words.

"Mrs. Soderbjerg—an unexpected pleasure!" said Patsy much too warmly.

Vesta winced. She peered at the girl. "My dear, you have a scrap of fruit in the corner of your mouth," she murmured, and sailed on.

Patsy dabbed at her mouth. Nothing.

"You have blood running down your stocking," she called, but the ship had gone around the corner.

The next day, Patsy introduced a family called the Plumbottoms to *Friendly Neighbor*, William Jennings Plumbottom and his wife Lester. Lester had a voice like a man's, except plummier and warblier. She talked up in her nose and came to borrow fresh vegetables from the Bensons and stand around as the Bensons picked and she yammered on about the beauty of opera. Lester adored opera, and sometimes she would get so enthused, she burst into a song, "Vesta la jujube," and she sang out the one line and the rooster crowed. "Well, *he* likes it," said Dad.

Vesta never heard the Plumbottoms, but Ray did and he was touched. William Jennings Bryan was his hero. "Patsy knows that, God bless her," he said. "And I don't take it amiss. By God, if Bryan had been on the radio, nobody would remember his name today anyway."

People looked around for the door anytime that Ray mentioned the Great Orator. They remembered urgent errands awaiting them, friends waiting on streetcorners, phones left off the hook.

Ray had seen Bryan in 1896 in Fargo, North Dakota. He remembered the crush of people under the blazing sun, the clouds of dust, and the faraway man in the black frock coat standing tall and motionless on a platform, the bunting and the banners, the crowd so still, straining to hear every word, and the man's voice rising and calling, crying out —Ray didn't remember the words, but the voice was clear as a bell. He had waited for Bryan to arrive, counted the days. "This is history," his father said. "This is something you will remember and tell your grandchildren." Ray had pressed forward in the crowd, tripped and was nearly trampled, his legs were stepped on, his father shoved through and cursed in Norwegian and people stepped back and he yanked Ray to his feet. He remembered his mother had lost a silver brooch in the crowd. It was hot. A team of horses bolted, it took six men to hold them. Somebody sold cups of cold water for two cents a cup and it was *cold*. Bryan's voice—so strong, so vibrant, so *beautiful*, and he spoke for more than an hour, and the crowd was so still, you could hear the banners flapping when a breeze came up. Bryan was too far away for him to hear, except for a word now and then, and yet it was so moving and memorable. The address was printed the next week in the newspaper. People bought it and read it and then placed it neatly in a trunk, or a box, or in a Bible, pressed like it was a leaf and, though seldom read, it was cherished.

Now it was all gone, Bryan and the Fargo of 1896 and his father and horses and the steam threshers on the farm, all gone, and what had killed it? Radio had.

"Nobody today would walk across the street to hear

Bryan speak," Ray said. "They just want to listen to the radio. You could put Bryan on the radio and there he'd be, the same as a comedian or the fellow who sells soap. Back then, that man could stand on a train platform and hold ten thousand people in the palm of his hand. Today, any jerk who can keep talking, you stick him behind a microphone and fifty-thousand will sit there and listen to him blabber about nothing."

The tragedy was that Bryan was *right*. Bryan lost in the 1896, 1900, and 1908 presidential elections, but he was right, boys.

Ray's voice warmed up. Roy Jr. slid glumly down into the chair. Dad looked out the window streaked with rain. Bryan was opposed to monetary policies that enriched the rich and impoverished the poor—he opposed bloody American imperialism and that jackass Theodore Roosevelt who wanted to out-England the English—he opposed America's entrance into World War I, the most worthless and ridiculous war ever known to mankind.

Ray stood up and came around the desk. Bryan lost on all these issues! and then he lost in the history books! Today, we mainly remember him as the tired old man who lost to Clarence Darrow in the Monkey Trial in Dayton, Tennessee, 1925. He died of a broken heart. A complete loser on all counts and yet—he was right!

"Remember that," Ray told Roy Jr.

1896, when Bryan lost to McKinley, was a watershed year. We will be paying for that a long time out here on the prairie. We had no interest in owning Cuba or the Philippines and damn little interest in fighting a crazy worthless European war, but we lost and over we went. Out here on the prairie, we wanted free trade, low tariffs, to keep prices of goods and machinery low, and we lost. We wanted the government to intervene, in behalf of the people, against the power of the railroads and large corporations, and we lost.

"That was the year we voted down the people and voted in Wall Street," said Ray. Bryan was the great champion of the prairie—but those New York bankers beat him down.

"They tried to buy me out in 1926, the year after Bryan died," said Ray. "I wouldn't sell. Those New York bastards tried to get WLT so they could spread their lies a little farther. But I wouldn't give in to them!" The phone rang. He picked it up. "Yes? Oh. All right." Roy Jr. could tell it was Vesta on the other end. He nodded to Dad. They stood up and slowly made for the door.

CHAPTER 20

Slim

With Little Buddy laid up with laryngitis, Slim was out of work. Cottage Home cancelled their show, and Slim took to living a life that he and Buddy hadn't sung about, staying out till 3 a.m., belting the grape and breathing hard on young women, and from the pals he found jamming in smoky clubs down around the switchyard, he formed a cowboy swing band called The Blue Moon Boys, which played the *WLT Barn Dance* on Saturday night—one song in the Sweetheart Chewing Gum segment, for $35, seven bucks per man, pretty pitiful. Slim tried to get a show of their own, telling Roy Jr. that their music was ten times better than the Cottage Home crap he'd done before, but unfortunately the public had liked that crap and didn't care so much for his new songs, which were about roaming around and finding women.

> Come with me, my pretty little miss,
> Come with me, my honey.

Come with me, my pretty little miss,
And I will do your laundry.

How old are you, my pretty little miss,
How old are you, my honey?
How old are you, my pretty little miss?
I'll be sixteen next Sunday.
I'll be sixteen on Sunday.

Would you forsake your husband dear
Would you forsake your baby?
Would you go for a ride with me
And be my honey maybe?

"Couldn't you have said she was eighteen?" asked Roy Jr.

This type of material simply did not draw listener mail like Little Buddy had. Too bad, but mail is mail, and if the folks don't write, then chances are they aren't out there listening very hard. Tough luck, said Roy Jr. Lots of performers improve their act and lose the public's favor, Roy Jr. explained, and that is exactly why the successful performers try so hard not to improve.

Leo said, "Little Buddy was big and you can't knock success. The kid was a crowd pleaser." Six months off the air and WLT *still* got so many inquiries about him, they had made up a mimeographed letter. He showed it to Francis.

Q. Why did Little Buddy leave WLT?
A. Buddy did not "leave" WLT. The little fellow suffered a sudden injury to his vocal cords that made singing painful and doctors advised that he take a long rest to avoid permanent damage. WLT fully concurred in the necessity of this, and will welcome Buddy back anytime the doctors allow it.

Q. Where is Buddy now?
A. Buddy lives with his daddy and mother and his baby brothers, and attends public school and church and is active in Boy Scouts. He misses his radio friends, but he is very busy and happy in the normal life of a 12-year-old boy.
Q. Will he ever return to the air?
A. Buddy's future plans remain uncertain but it can safely be said that a talent as true as his will not go untapped for long.

Buddy improved, but Slim was sick of all those weepy songs, and besides, the kid refused to come back.

"Make him do it. You're his father," said Leo one afternoon in the Green Room. "You got to stick with what works for you. The cornball songs are what put the pancakes on the table. Seven bucks? You can't live on seven bucks. Get that kid's butt back in the studio."

"The kid will not go back on the radio. Period. So what can I do?" Slim glanced at Francis and then looked away. "I tried to find somebody else and they weren't there to be found." *Sorry*, thought Francis. What a disappointment he was to everybody!

Art never looked him in the eye anymore. Clare only spoke to him through Art ("Tell him to put the newspaper back the way he found it! I keep finding the comics pulled out. And tell him to leave the crossword alone"). Mother and Jodie never wrote to him, except a few paltry sentences every other month. Jodie always said that everything was fine and she was enjoying school and how are you, and Mother said that she was having one of her bad days and was thinking of him, poor kid. She only wrote on bad days, it seemed, and she wrote on scraps of cereal boxes, the backs of old envelopes, candy wrappers, as if her letters didn't deserve their own paper.

She wrote on a piece of flour bag, "Today it is six years since your daddy died and I meant to go to the cemetery but did not have the strength. I still can't believe he's gone. Seems like a cruel joke to be alone and I am only 36 and I feel like 72. But there's no reason you should want to hear about this. You have your life. I sure wish I did."

———

Slim did his best with the Blue Moons and Dad Benson went to bat for him, Slim being his neighbor. Dad told Roy Jr., "They're a little lowdown, sure, but they're not *mean* anyway. They're all young fellas, they don't know what's what. Besides, Slim has another little boy, he's three. Cute little bugger. Give him a year and he'll be right up there where Buddy was."

So Slim got the 7:30 a.m. slot, right after the Shepherd Boys Gospel Quartet on *The Rise and Shine Show*, sponsored by Sunrise Waffles. Slim's sponsor was Prestige Tire & Muffler so he renamed his band The Blue Movers.

They replaced Wingo Beals and The Shoe Shine Boys, a fine band—twin fiddles, electric guitar, doghouse bass, and Wingo playing piano, a country swing band doing hot versions of old tunes, but after four years they were lighting no fires, and so the Artists Bureau sent them on a four-week tour.

That was how WLT killed off the lame and the halt: the Bureau put you on the road, in an old schoolbus, rattling from one end of the five-state area to the other playing $15 dates at high school assemblies and insane asylums and sleeping in your clothes on couches and eating slabs of grease and enduring the shame and the squalor until one day your mind snapped and they found you in your underwear crawling down a corn row in Kandiyohi

County with an empty in your hand whereupon they shovelled you back to Minneapolis and put you in a Home for the Wretched and that was it, you were done. And that was how they got rid of Wingo Beals.

Roy Jr. called him in and said, "Sunrise isn't happy, the audience seems a mite low for that time slot, so I think we need to get you out where the public can see you."

"Please don't do that," pleaded Wingo. His old brown eyes glistened, his old hairy hand trembled as he gripped Roy Jr.'s desk and looked the young executive in his steely blue eyes.

"Folks need to see you, meet you, get acquainted with the boys. That's how we build up a public following."

"Please. I'm begging you. Don't send us on tour."

"I know it's hard work but you're all young and you have your health—you see if touring doesn't make a *big* difference."

So the Bureau worked up a sixteen-page itinerary, and when Wingo looked at it, he saw it was their death sentence. Four weeks on the road, four shows a day, sometimes five, some of them a hundred or more miles apart. All told, he'd play a couple hundred different pianos, all of them out of tune and with missing keys, some so badly beat up they sounded like somebody banging on bedsprings. Wingo knew the road, he'd gone out with Courteous Carl Harper and the Pierce Sisters and four times a day had to hear the Sisters render "A Big Brass Bed, a Rocker, and a Range" and Carl sing slightly flatter than Ernest Tubb:

> Darlin', I can't live without you.
> I wouldn't know how to start.
> I can't help that my love is so strong
> For you have taken my heart.

The friends and neighbors looked up, spellbound, and swooned at this garbage, meanwhile you sat on stage exhausted, wrinkled, stiff, crusted, dirty, a little drunk, pissed-off at the drummer, and though you felt awful you had to *play music*, a wounded bird made to dance, and you had to endure the humiliation of grinning and playing in front of an *audience*. If one could use such a fancy word to describe this gang of lost souls who filled the seats (and some more than filled them). The poor emcee stood up front in his cheap suit and cried out, "Oh it's good to see you wonderful people," but from the stage, they looked like deceased walleyes, mouths agape, eyes glazed, gasping. And those were the better audiences—even worse was the 8 a.m. junior high crowd where hideous gap-toothed children wriggled and jeered at the feeble jokes of the poor dying artists on stage, or the old-folks home where rows of the senile and deranged sat rocking back and forth, chins on their chests, licking their lips, pools of urine at their feet, or the Kiwanis and Jaycee luncheons with the tables of big boomers and boosters hunkering over the hot beef sandwiches, or the ladies' luncheons, or the church socials, or the county fairs—they all melted into one massive wall of flesh, dreadful, immovable. After months of grace and ease playing in a quiet room at the radio station, it was hideous to think of facing The Folks of Radioland—pale, damp, rancid, quivering. Dead fish.

"Oh God, save me from this," Wingo cried, but he went out with The Shoe Shine Boys and soldiered on and almost made it through four weeks of pianos to the end. He came darn close. He did the next-to-last show, in Paynesville, and only a breakfast show in nearby Willmar remained, a cinch, but then Wingo made his fatal mistake and called the Bureau. "We're coming home," he whispered, his big hand shaking like a leaf, and the girl said,

"We've added two shows. Osseo and Braham. Both on your way home." Wingo wept. "It'll only take a few hours," she said. He asked to speak to Roy Jr. or Ray. They weren't in. So Wingo tried to go to Osseo. He got as far as the bed, and lay in it, and lost track of time. The Boys pounded on his door to rouse him but it was the wrong door. Wingo lay in bed for a day, hallucinating that he was riding in the box of a coal truck. Meanwhile The Shoe Shine Boys sped south to Osseo to the gig and the bus missed a curve on the West River Road and overturned in a shallow ravine and the Boys were killed, their necks broken by fifty-seven cartons of unsold record albums, and Wingo went to work at the post office, in parcel post. When he heard music on the radio, it made him flinch. Wingo preferred absolute silence.

Slim Graves and The Blue Movers dedicated their first show to Wingo. Like Wingo's shows, theirs consisted of the weather and livestock reports, fan mail and requests and dedications, and about four songs, of which one should be a hymn. The Movers had plenty of songs about losing women, drinking, losing their jobs, shooting people, riding freight trains, finding other kinds of women and then losing them too, but not many songs about Jesus, so Slim brought in a singer named Billie Ann Herschel, who had performed with the Shepherd Boys, to do the hymn segment. She was twenty-four. She stood at the microphone while Slim stood behind her, playing guitar and looking at her slim hips under the cotton dress. While singing hymns, she liked to shift her weight from side to side, and he found it hard to keep his mind off her, not that he tried to—her rear end was prettier than most people's faces.

162

Slim opened the show, whistling a few bars of "Only a Pal," then Swanny the announcer said, "Morning, friends and neighbors, it's time for Slim Graves and The Blue Movers for Sunrise Waffles—gosh! they're good—with more of that good old lonesome blues music, so pour yourself a cup of coffee and enjoy the show, there's DAYLIGHT IN THE SWAMPS!" and the band swung into "Locomotive Daddy." The next tune was a vocal, and then Slim said, "Well, what say we take a look in the ole mailbag here." The letters from listeners were written by Slim himself. ("Loved the way Ernie picked apart that Dill Pickle Rag. Man, it's hard to believe that's one person." "Sure enjoy all those two-steps, stomps, and shuffles. You boys are the best and I sincerely mean it. Please play Under the Double Eagle." "You are my favorite band and I look forward to hearing your show every morning. Keep up the good work. Especially love Billie Ann and her duets with Slim. P.S. This is the first fan letter I ever wrote.")

Billie Ann, though she was brought in for hymns, stayed around and sang more and more with Slim. Their voices were a natural blend. At first, they did songs like "Polly Wolly Doodle" and "Froggy Went A-Courtin'," but then they did a couple cheating songs and hit a groove and settled in. Cheating seemed to bring out their best vocal qualities.

Nobody had ever done cheating songs that early in the morning before, but for The Blue Movers, seven-thirty was a continuation of midnight: they were night owls, the show was their last stop before they hit the sack. Slim and Billie did famous old cheating songs like "On Top of Old Smoky" and "Foggy Foggy Dew" and "Black Jack Davy" and then they wrote their own. They wrote "A-D-U-L-T-E-R-Y (That's a Word That Makes Me Cry)" with Billie as the young wife with two little children (the truth)

163

who is attracted toward the old cowboy who comes to town with his band—"What is that word that begins with *A* that Daddy said to you?" "It's a word, LaVerne, that big folks say, that means I've been untrue"—and "She Gets Pleasure from Seeing Me Cry" with Slim as the husband with three children (the truth) whose wife is cold and enjoys seeing him miserable—and "Why Must the Show Go On?" in which Slim and Billie are singers in the same band and fall in love—

> We're just a couple of people
> In the show business,
> Doing a radio show,
> But deep in our hearts
> As we stand here singing,
> There's something that you folks don't know.
> We fell in love—there,
> I'm glad that I said it—
> And my love for another is gone.
> Why can't I break up this act I've been living?
> Why must the show go on?

You couldn't make it much clearer than that.

Billie Ann's husband, Tom Herschel, was a WLT engineer and worked the afternoon shift, but he certainly knew what was up between his wife and Slim, and so did the early-morning engineer, Harlan. Engineers were a tight brotherhood, united by a shining contempt for performers, and Harlan made trouble for Slim every way he could. When Slim needed to clear his throat and gave Harlan the "Cut" sign, Harlan left the microphone wide open, and Slim, after a long night of it, had a lot of phlegm to account for and had to honk and hawk pretty hard to bring it up, none of which endeared him to the listener at home who maybe had a headful himself and didn't care to hear Slim's sinuses so close up. Harlan also figured out ways to make Slim's voice sound thin and warbly and to give it a sibilant nelly-like texture. He could even bend the pitch, and on Slim's high note, his money note, the big note at the climax of the song, Harlan could bring Slim in a quarter-step high, with a flutter, a tone that made your front teeth hurt. Slim did "Down the Chisholm Trail" and on the long yodelling part, Harlan played with him like a puppet on a string, it sounded like the cowboy's horse was running away with him and he was bouncing on the high pommel.

This did not discourage the two lovebirds, however, and they carried on without an ounce of shame, grabbing each other, smooching during the waffle commercials, kissing during songs, and Slim sometimes liked, during Billie Ann's hymn, to run his hand inside the back of her dress and twitch her underwear. "I love her," he told The Blue Movers, "she's the most excitement I've had in twenty years, and boys, there is no substitute for excitement. No *sir*." The Movers, rascals though they were and quick to snatch up any cupcake loose on the great table of life, nevertheless were concerned about Slim's doing it on the job, in full view, with the husband nearby. "Don't jim the gig for us, boss," said Smiley the steel-guitarist. "Do your two-timin' in the tall grass like everybody else. Keep it under a bushel. Don't go wavin' it around like this."

But Slim didn't care. The Little Buddy years had taken a toll on him, all those mawkish ballads about children. "You boys have forgot how important love is," he said.

He and Billie sang "They're Only Two Dogs in Our Manger of Love"—"Her and him, they're only in the past / And what we have is better and will last. / There's nothing they can do, / They can't stop me and you. / You're mine and I am yours / And loyalty don't open many doors. / Though marriage is made in heaven above, / They're Only Two Dogs in Our Manger of Love," and Billie said, in the recitation part, "I didn't tell him about you because I didn't need to. He knows. He knows when he touches me that my heart doesn't jump like it used to. It can't because my heart is far away, with you,"—and a mile away, on Blaisdell Avenue, Francis heard it, waking up early and getting dressed to do his paper route.

He sat in the dark kitchen, his feet up on the green linoleum table, drinking coffee, waiting for the big bundle of *Tribune*s to hit the front porch, the little white radio turned down low so as not to wake Clare. Francis had liked Wingo okay but Slim and Billie Ann were really something. It was thrilling, so early in the morning, instead of farm reports and hymns, to get somebody singing about exactly what was on his mind, sex and misery. He had let Slim down, and a hundred times since, on his paper route, Francis had sung "Red River Valley" and gotten it to sound sweet (he thought), but now that Slim was in decline, drinking hard, stinking up the Green Room with his beer breath while he slept off a hangover, putting the bite on his WLT pals, a moocher and a four-flusher and a louse to his wife and kids, he became a better and better singer, Francis thought: the only really astonishing singer at WLT, the only one who sang so true and naked that you shivered to hear him. Sex and misery.

The others all warbled about Home, Home and Mother, Mother Waiting at Home, The Wandering Boy Coming Home, I Wandered Away But Now I'm Going Back, There's No Place Like Home, but Slim sang "Frankie and Johnny" about the lovers who swore to be true to each other and Johnny went out for the evening and Frankie went down to the corner to get her a bucket of beer and the bartender told her about Miss Nellie Bly and she took her big .44 and got in the cab and got off on South Clark

Street and rang the big brass bell and went upstairs and looked over the transom and there he was, on the bed making love, and the gun went Rooty-toot-toot, and they rolled him over easy and carried him to the graveyard in a rubber-tired hearse and they threw her in a dungeon cell and threw the key away. He was her man but he done her wrong. It was as simple as that. You love somebody and they break your heart and you break theirs. It was a *noble* song.

And then one day Slim said on the radio, "Here's a new song that my good friend, Harold Odom, wrote, and I want to do it for you now." There was some commotion in the background. "Well, boys," he said, "I apologize for that, but I drank a lot of coffee last night. Anyway, here's the number."

'Twas the ninth day of October,
The sky it looked like lead,
And Old Number 9 left Fargo.
In an hour they'd all be dead.

Once she had been a fast engine,
But her day had come and gone,
And now she was only for short runs
To Minot and Jamestown.

Benny With kissed his wife and his babies,
And they wept as their dad went away,
And now he cut loose with the whistle
To sing them to sleep where they lay.

And they gave him his orders at Fargo,
Saying, "Benny, we're way behind time,
You must get those empties to Minot,
It's all up to Old Number 9."

And Benny, he was the new man
And must prove himself to the rest,
And a good run might get him promoted,
This evening would be the big test.

If he came into Minot by morning,
He'd be put on the mighty Express
And his babies grow up in a nice house
And their lives would be crowned with success.

So he jumped on the green light and fired
The engine with bales of dry grass,
And he laid on the coals and in Erie
They'd ne'er seen a train move so fast.

Through Luverne and Sutton and Barlow,
Like a rocket whistled that train,
And her lights were a blur in the darkness
As she blazed cross Dakota's broad plain.

And he turned and said to his fireman,
"Jack, we must put on more coal,"
And the screech of her whistle in Heimdal
Was the cry of the engineer's soul.

And in Tyler, the long stretch of railroad
Suddenly curved by the town,
And Old Number 9 could not hold the tracks
And she jumped about half the way round.

And her whistle cried out in terror,
And her wheels on the track did scream,
And the men in the cab they prayed to God
And were scalded to death in the steam.

And the rain falls black as cinders
And the sky is dark as a grave,

And the children weep in the little white house,
The home of the engineer brave.

May God watch over their suffering souls
And guide them in love and light,
But never, no never, will they forget
Their daddy who died that night.

Francis listened, frozen, his hand on the cupboard door,
as if someone had knocked him senseless with a rock, and
then he put his head into the crook of his arm and he
cried.

CHAPTER 21

Frank

The most memorable part of West High was the worst: the first day, when his name was called on the loudspeaker and a boy said in a shrill, pansy voice, "Oh Franthith With! Mithter Franthith With!" and for a miserable month he wouldn't let up—"Oh you wicked *With*, you!" he'd squeal, and other boys laughed, and Francis shrank down inside his jacket.

In his freshman year, he gave up the Five Words a Day Plan: in the lunchroom, talking to his only good friend, Francis used the word "insidious" and sensed a coolness in the boy's eyes. He was different enough, he decided, without talking funny. He was small for his age and he had inherited the long Jensen face from Mother's side, the thin nose and the watery blue eyes, the thin lips, a man's face on a kid's body. In sophomore year, he experimented with parting his hair higher and lower and on the right, but it was no use. Though Uncle Art and Aunt Clare dressed him in nice corduroy pants and white shirts and sweaters, he was a queer duck. He avoided sports, lusted after girls, was avoided by girls. Everyone else believed in the war, and Francis secretly did not, a terrible secret. Churchill and his cigar and the V-sign, Roosevelt and his big grin riding in a convertible, Hitler with his little moustache dancing a jig in a French forest, Hirohito on his white horse, the Japs, the Krauts, it was all a story that he tried to have strong, pure feelings about and support the boys by saving scrap metal and buying war bonds and he couldn't. And then suddenly the war was over. Everyone else at West was jubilant and leaped out of their chairs and tore out of school and stood in the street yelling and honking horns and stopping cars and riding around on their running boards. Except Francis, who went home and wondered what was the matter with him.

He was voted Most Anonymous Person in the Class of 1947, and graduated on a hot May afternoon and went home and took a bath. Girls had hugged each other and wept at the ceremony. Two girls had even hugged him, but he had no idea why. School seemed predetermined to him, you went where you were told and you waited there for nothing to happen. Teachers told you so much that wasn't true—e.g. "These are years you will look back on as some of the best of your life"—that you gave up trying to believe them.

He wrote to Mother and said it would be nice if she came to his graduation, and she wrote back and said she couldn't, she could hardly leave the house to go to the drugstore, so how could she come to Minneapolis? "You don't really have a mother. All you have is this funny old lady in her dirty chemise who sits and listens to the radio. How come I don't hear you? Are you ashamed of me?"

One night, Uncle Art offered to send him to the University, but he seemed drunk, and Francis said no, so Art gave him a pearl gray '46 Chevy instead as a graduation present. That was Art's way. Ignore you and never want

171

to be with you and then dump some huge gift on you and expect you to grin and jump up and down. Francis walked around the car twice. "Nice," he said. "Thanks."

Art crouched down to inspect the grille. "Leo says you're thinking you want to come to work in radio," he said.

"I haven't decided," said Francis.

There was a polio epidemic in Minneapolis. A neighbor boy came down with it. Went swimming at Lake Calhoun and the next day was in the hospital, a cripple. Francis fled north to Mindren, at the wheel of his own car, afraid he might have polio already. North of the city, he saw a Sherwin-Williams billboard, the bucket of paint pouring over the globe, and thought of steering east instead and becoming a gypsy (We Cover the World), but the thought of Mother straightened him out. He drove home.

Mother was a little better but not much. She knew him all right but not much else. The insurance money was gone, she thought, and Mr. Mortenson at the bank had sold the house, she thought (but wasn't sure). The yard was overgrown with weeds, the garage full of trash. He shovelled it out and burned the debris, which gave off clouds of bitter acrid smoke. "I have a good job now," she said, but had forgotten where it was. She tried to remember and gave up. Oh, life is unfair, she said mournfully. One morning, Mortenson came in and took the clock. "Your mother has run up debts downtown and people are demanding payment, of course. Somebody is willing to settle for this old thing and best to accept before they change their mind." Francis asked if the house had been sold. The man was vague. It had been optioned, he said, and they would know more soon.

"Franny, I'm not ever going to get better, am I," she suddenly said at supper, a spoonful of chicken noodle soup midway to her mouth, and all his reassurances, so hollow, that yes, she *would*, he knew she would, of *course* she

172

would, only made clear her doom, and tears fell, and she was right. She was an invalid. She would always be looking toward the door, waiting for somebody to come through it and help her up.

"I'm sorry I'm such a mess. I can't even make a decent home for my own kids." And she wept more. He couldn't imagine where all the water came from.

Emma arrived for Memorial Day. Uncle Charles had migraine and kidney stones and could not bear the slightest motion or sound or ray of light, but Jodie was doing well at Wesleyan College in Ohio. "You wouldn't know her, she's so grown up." He asked why Jodie had not come home. Emma said, "Home? Her home is with us. We're the ones who took her in. Don't only think of yourself, Franny. Jodie has blossomed into a fine young lady. She couldn't have got that here. Look at your poor mother. I'm going to have to go sign papers on Tuesday and put her in a hospital. My dad used to say that nothing is so bad but what there's some good in it, but I don't see it in her case." Emma clucked. "Poor thing."

───

After Minneapolis, Mindren seemed like a ghost town. Men stood in the hardware store, looked out the window, as if waiting for something, then went back and sat on a nail keg and talked to Walt, who said what he'd been saying for years: *You never know. Only time will tell.* It was dry. There was dirt in the air. Men stood watering their lawns, their thumbs in the hose to make a fine spray, pissing away the evenings. The kids were sullen and logy. The minister passed him on the street without a hello. Little kids kept a safe distance, window curtains seemed to rustle when he walked by, blinds were pried open a crack, people whispered.

A letter came from the Great Northern, a W. L. Jamieson, Assistant Superintendent, to say that he, Francis With, as the son of the late Benny, qualified for a college scholarship under the terms of the Hill Trust for Railroad Orphans, left by the late Albert Hill, author of the song "The Wreck of the Fast Express," and thus he, the superintendent, was pleased to offer him a place in the freshman class at Carleton College in Northfield on September 8, please advise at the soonest.

As Francis thought about it, this offer did not resound with the clear ring of fate; it sat on the page, a vague invitation to go somewhere and read books and see if something stuck. He sat down to make a list, "What I Want to Do Before I'm Twenty."

1. Have sexual intercourse with a beautiful woman
2. Earn money

Were there beautiful women at Carleton College? Probably, but they would belong to someone else. Tall cool women in blue plaid skirts and knee socks, their books pressed to their left breasts, matched up with men who moved in their circles. Not him. Men like Frank Fairmount on *The Hills of Home* who quarterbacked the Center City Wildcats and went away to Yale and broke Babs's heart, but of course you knew somebody like Frank would *never* wind up with a Babs. Bluebirds don't marry sparrows. He'd match up with a college girl in a blue plaid skirt.

And then he turned the paper over and wrote:

Frank With. Frank With. Frank With.

It was a better name, no doubt about it. He wrote: Frank B. With.

The problem was the soft last name. It died at the end. *With*. You said it and people always said, *"Who?"* He made a list of names: Benson, Burgess, Fox, Upton, Autry. *Frank Autry. Frank Rogers. Frank Mix. Frank Armstrong.* It was a shameful thing to turn your back on your own name. Especially with your father lying in the ground without a stone over his head. But he had no family left, not to speak of. And then he saw that by adding an *e* to *With* he could get *White*.

Frank White.

The names made a nice click like closing the bolt on a .22.

The night before Emma drove Mother to the state hospital for the insane, he wrote a letter to his father.

Dear Daddy,
It is hard, but you know that. Mother is sick. I have been to Dr. and he doesn't know what's wrong with her or else he won't tell me because it's too terrible. Maybe she will be better when she gets out of Mindren. This is an awful bad place. I know you liked it but without you it isn't so nice. Daddy, our family has no true friends in this town. They can all go to hell. Grampa is in The Danish Home in Spirit Lake, Iowa. We visited him there and he does not know us anymore, but I do not think he is angry. Daddy, I am going to Minneapolis and get a job from Uncle Art. I want you to be proud of me. I wish we were all here together. I think of you every time I hear a train, and at other times. I will do everything to make you proud of me. I love you very much always and always,

Sincerely,
Your son,
FRANK WHITE

He stuffed the note in a clean bottle and buried it late that night in the long low mound over Benny's grave. Mother and Emma left early in the morning, suddenly. Frank dreaded saying goodbye and hung back but Mother seemed cheerful, as if going off to a movie. "Bye!" she called, "See you later!" Emma was coming back with Charles to close up the house as soon as his migraine let up. She said, "Franny, take what you want, of course, and the rest goes to the poor, I guess." He took his father's straw hat and Army blanket, a Danish Bible, Grampa's glasses and slippers, a box of old picture books, and the engine of his Lionel train. He locked the door behind him, dropped the key in the flowerpot, dumped the stuff in the back seat, pulled out of the alley, and the town slipped away in an instant, like dropping your pants.

WLT came in loud and clear as he drove south. It was like the Bensons were in the car with him. Jo was feeling sorry for Mr. Lassen, whose boy Leon was living a sad profligate life in Chicago and driving his poor father to distraction. The boy was sullen and careless, ran up bills he didn't pay, wasted the gifts his father generously sent him, and took up with bad companions who meant him no good. "Nothing costs so much as what we get for free. An abundance of things engenders disdain," said Dad. "A thrifty father makes for a prodigal son." Frank thought, "Was Daddy thrifty?" He didn't think so. Anyway, Daddy was dead and in his grave. Maybe a dead father makes for a lively son. He gave her the gas and pulled around a cattle truck and held her right at seventy-five, barrelling through the hazy sunshine as the radio signal got stronger and stronger.

CHAPTER 22

The
Antwerp

He moved back in with Art and Clare. He slept for eighteen hours, woke up, and went around the corner to the Rialto for a triple feature. He dug dandelions out of the lawn. He tried to stay out of the way. And then, in one black day, three terrible things happened —he lost the car, they kicked him out, and a girl laughed at him. The pearl gray Chevy was parked in front of the house and, *bang*, somebody took it during the night. The cops shrugged. Francis had left the keys in it. *Welcome to the city, boy-o*. There was no insurance, of course. Tough beans. "Looks like you're on foot now," said Art. Frank walked downtown to kill time in Dayton's and caught the eye of a beautiful girl with long black hair as she bent down to re-arrange the ties in the men's tie counter, and she looked away and snickered, a withering laugh, like she had seen something in his nose. And then Art took him to the Pascal for a big lunch, duck soup, porterhouse steak, mince pie, the works, and two bottles of beer. Art had a double bourbon. He was not slow getting to the point. Clare was feeling poorly, he said, and he thought it best if Francis got a room at the Antwerp. It was convenient, right next to the Ogden, a nice old brick apartment building that Ray Soderbjerg owned. "A lotta the radio folks put up there, it's clean and cheap. I'll take care of your rent until you're on your feet. I got an appointment for you to see Roy Jr. about a job. You're in, so don't worry about it." Art looked older and wearier than Francis remembered him being a few weeks ago.

"Are you okay, Uncle Art? You look peaked." In fact, Art looked worse than peaked, he looked to be at the end of his rope.

"That's Clare that's sick. I don't know what's wrong with her. But I'm fine," he said. To prove it, he pulled a quarter out of Frank's ear.

"By the way, I've changed my name to Frank White," said Frank.

"Okay," said Art. "I'll try to keep that in mind."

"And thank you for everything."

Art sighed. "I hope you make friends here," he said. "That's important. You're too much of a loner, Francis. And I can't be looking after you. You're on your own now, you understand?"

Frank nodded. He understood it by the fact that Art did not say that he hoped Frank would come have dinner with them often.

Art said, "I'll take you over to the Antwerp tomorrow. Introduce you to Mr. Odom."

"Why not today?"

So they drove home to collect his things. Some clothes, a red mackinaw, a couple hundred books, a "Minnesota's World-Famous Hull-Rust-Mahoning Open Pit Mine" poster (a gift from Art), a plaster bust of Abraham Lincoln, a few games, Pit, Rook, Authors—amazing to think that he lived here for all those years.

"Take the bedspread and a couple blankets," said Art, in an expansive mood. He peeled off ten twenty-dollar bills. *Here.*

When he pulled up in front of the Antwerp, Art didn't make a move to get out of the car. "See you at work," said Frank and opened the door.

"Did you hear Marjery Moore lost her boyfriend?" said Art, cheerily. "Robert Kellogg, that guy with the tweedly voice who played Vic. The nephew, the one with the dog. On *Love's Old Sweet Song.* I heard he knocked her up and kissed her goodnight, drove to the depot, abandoned his car, and took off for Chicago with Victoria Marshall."

"Peggy?" Peggy was the secretary on *Arthur Fox, Detective.*

"One and the same. So Monday afternoon both of them got killed. Vic's car crashed head-on into a lightpole and an hour later Peggy left the office suddenly, without a word, and her body was found in the lake. A dangerous business, radio. But Robert and Victoria are shacked up in Chicago. What a honey she was. Boy, you want to talk about tits, she had a pair of tits woulda made a man out of anybody. Don't tell the world, but I was the first one who ever had her. Late one night in my car. Good Lord. And I mean that sincerely. I didn't even say a *word.* Just slipped my hand down there and held it until she got hot and started to hum. Oh boy. I was driving her home. Pulled over at 38th Street and those panties came off like autumn leaves and she climbed aboard the old pistol and she went around the block a couple times and then I got on top and man, what a girl she was. Cars going by, people peeking in the window—I didn't *care,* I was on the stairway to stardom." Art looked pleased and flushed at the thought of her. "One or two nights like that one, Francis: what more can a man ask?"

Frank's room was 4-C at the Antwerp, but it was actually three rooms, kitchen, bedroom, living room, furnished with a brown sofa, a dark green table, and a double bed with two shallow troughs in it. His own telephone, GEneva 2014. "Rent is $30 a month," said Mr. Odom, the manager. "It's a nice building with plenty of friendly people, if that's what you're looking for. There's really only three rules around here and I forget two of them. The main rule is secrecy. If you're having a good time, don't let your neighbors know about it, especially after ten p.m. and before eight in the morning."

Frank had hoped his room would face the YWCA next door, and it did, but the windows opposite him were dark and he doubted that one of them would be the locker room. A locker room would surely be in the basement and have frosted windows. But if the YWCA burned and naked women fled into the street, he'd have a front row seat. Meanwhile, he could drop slips of paper down and maybe a ventilator would draw them into the locker room and a naked dripping beautiful girl would find it lying on her towel, GEneva 2014.

———

Art dropped him there on Wednesday, and by Thursday he had made a friend, a woman named Ginger who was folding clothes in the laundry room when Frank went down to wash a shirt. She had bleached hair and eyebrows redrawn in a look of permanent alarm and wore white pedal-pushers and a translucent blouse. She told him about her divorce and how much she liked being single again and how much she'd love to see Chicago sometime. She held up a brassiere. "What do you think of this?" she asked. "Too seductive?" She had been on WLT herself, she said. "I was an actress and then I was Ray Soderbjerg's little whore for five years. Now I work at a candy counter. At Kresge's. Stop in. I'll give you a Nut Goodie, or something." Friday morning, Frank would go in to WLT to see Roy Soderbjerg Jr., General Manager. "A cinch," said Art on the phone. "I got the fix in for you, Francis." *Frank*.

━━━

It took the lady in 3-C, directly below Frank, several days to find out his name. She had three rooms, too, each with a table and a typewriter in it, and mounds of old scripts in apple crates. Patsy Konopka heard him come in Wednesday night, but was frantically finishing *Friendly Neighbor* and didn't pay attention; on Thursday afternoon, when he clomped up the first flight of stairs, her ears perked up—his step told her he was young and slight of build—and when he ascended the second flight, she could hear modesty and purposefulness and decency in him. She was so tired of men: their breezy bullshit, the unbelievable lies they dished out. Lying so artless and bald-faced, you couldn't imagine why they bothered. She rose from her typewriter, and as he walked past her door on the landing and headed up to the fourth floor, she got a glimpse of him through the peephole. His brown corduroy trousers were two inches short and he carried an armload of groceries and a big hank of brown hair hung in his eyes. "A plain face reveals an honest disposition," she thought, and then she wondered if he might not be Jeanine's old lover, Mr. Devereaux, the one she had met in New Orleans, finally arrived to consummate the romance, unaware of Jeanine's embrace of the Baptist church and her marriage to Rev. Willetts and their joyful departure for the mission fields of the Belgian Congo. She braced herself for the task of filling him in.

"She's happy, Mr. Devereaux, and that's the important thing, isn't it. I don't think she's any more Baptist than she is a pumpkin, but we believe in what we wish for, and she wished for a husband. She waited for you and talked about you for three years and how many years does a person have? Finally she said to me, Patsy, I met somebody. And a month later she said, 'I wouldn't mind having his shoes under my bed.' And there you are."

She sat back down at the typewriter with a page of *Golden Years* in it, the dreadful Coopers and their lousy money that they kept dishing out anonymously as if it made a cent's worth of difference. Patsy wished they'd fall off a cliff. She wished she could write: *Pistol shots ring out and cries of pain and confusion.* She waited for Mr. Devereaux to dash out in the hall and lean over the landing and yell for Jeanine. *I told her I'd be back this summer! I only went back to France to see my old mother! It's true I'm three weeks late, but the freighter I shipped out on was blown off course west of the Canaries and capsized in the south Atlantic and we drifted in the lifeboat and finally were picked up by an Argentine frigate and taken to Buenos Aires and from there to here, hitch-hiking, it takes more than a couple of days. Why couldn't she have waited?* But Mr. Devereaux calmly walked into the kitchen overhead and put the grocery sacks on the table and started to stash the stuff. He whistled a tune she didn't recognize at first, and then he stopped and sighed. Why? He rustled among the bags and sighed a longer sigh.

He had forgotten something! Something simple and obvious, like sugar, or salt. She could take him up a jarful, as a welcome gift. His angel from below. *Mr. Devereaux, I'm Patsy Konopka, I live downstairs. Among my people, there is an ancient tradition of welcoming new neighbors with a sack of salt and a jar of sugar. May life be sweet and may life have savor.*

And then she remembered. She didn't have any salt or sugar, she ate all her meals at the coffeeshop.

———

That day, Little Becky returned to *Friendly Neighbor* after a few days' visit to some people in Littleton. Marjery seemed morose about her boyfriend running off. She gave Frank a listless look in the Green Room and didn't recognize him.

> BECKY: Dogs really care about you when it seems like nobody else does, don't they, Dad? (WOOF) If you're having a hard time, it doesn't change how they feel about you. When you just need someone to put your arms around, well, a dog is always there—(*Dog pants*)
> DAD: What's bothering you, honey?
> BECKY: I spent all the money from picking radishes on a box of chocolate lozenges and they weren't any good and they're all gone.

That evening, Ginger knocked on Frank's door. She had met him in the laundry, she explained, and wondered if he happened to be busy. If so, she could return later. Frank did not invite her in, not even when she said she was very upset and wouldn't mind a beer. He told her he was tired.

———

Downstairs, Patsy Konopka listened carefully. Ginger was moving fast. But the door closed and only one pair of feet came across the living-room floor, Mr. Devereaux's. He stopped overhead, and stood in the living room, read a letter, then walked into the bedroom. His footsteps sounded like on *The Other World* where a man awakes at midnight in his bed and gropes around for the lamp switch and touches a cold brick wall and finally finds a match and lights it and gasps, for of course it is a tomb. She hoped he wouldn't spot the big hole in his floor by the radiator. Sitting at her kitchen table, under the hole, she could hear him breathe up there. He tromped down the hall and stopped for a moment and then she heard his water, gallons of it, like a horse, hit the center of the bowl. And now Mr. Devereaux flushed, and headed to the bedroom. Patsy heard his clothes hit the floor. He lay on the bed. He was touching himself. She listened. She hoped he would not be alone for long. She wondered if he was sensitive to emanations or had any familiarity with the psychic realm.

She thought a clear thought about him and waited, listening, to hear if he was struck by it, but he continued, and then he gasped, and she returned to *Golden Years*. "Who is that out there on the street?" asked Edna. "Who?" said Elmer. They were in the cafe, coffee cups rattled, someone was griping about sore feet. "That handsome young man standing by the lamppost, his hands in his pockets, his red mackinaw pulled up around his ears, and his long black hair blowing," observed Edna. "Oh, him," said Elmer. Edna said, "Imagine being that young again, with the world laid out in front of you like the county fair. Imagine being twenty."

CHAPTER 2 3

Hired

T he next morning, despite a grievous headache, he landed the job at WLT. He had gotten the headache Thursday evening. He had been strolling around the block, past the Kenosha and Belfont and Arcola Apartments, none so nice as the Antwerp, and gazed down at the basement windows (frosted) of the YWCA and around past the big limestone Minneapolis Auto Club—he reminded himself to buy a car someday, a Studebaker—and studied the menu in the window of the Pot Pie and the faculty list in the window of MacPhail School of Music— a Maude Moore taught elocution, he should see about lessons so he could become an announcer—and then he retraced the trip in the other direction, planning his great radio career, and in front of the Auto Club he ran into Mr. Odom and accepted an invite to go for a bump at the Red Eye Lounge on Hennepin Avenue and there, in a dark booth, had tried various concoctions, including a bourbon and sour, a vodka sour, and something called a Bombaroo. Mr. Odom, he discovered, had known Daddy from when they attended commercial college in Park River and had been living in Minot when Daddy was en route there and they had planned to have breakfast together the very morning that Daddy died. Mr. Odom had written "The Ballad of Old No. 9" the same day. Frank told him that he didn't remember much about his dad. They drank a toast to his memory, a couple of Rusty Nails and a Galesburg Gearbox and then something called Molly in the Morning and—though Frank hardly remembered this—he dashed out the front door and deposited the entire evening over the curb and into the gutter. A woman in a sealskin coat stood nearby. She looked away, as if she'd seen this before and wasn't interested.

In the morning, Frank rolled out, took aspirin, and climbed into a tepid bath, and tried to think of a speech ("I want to get into broadcasting and apply myself and be useful, sir, and earn your confidence so you will let me go on and do bigger things, and whatever I lack in intelligence I will make up for in hard work") but the pain came and sat inside his left eyeball, like a long nail. So when he went into the Ogden Hotel, he was in a mood to be calm and not shake his head.

A sandy-haired red-faced man named Sloan interviewed him. He had a big beak and his hair was combed hard, in straight furrows. He snapped his gum and winked a lot. He glanced at the questionnaire Frank had filled out and said, "No college and no newspaper experience. Good. They don't go for that here." He picked his teeth thoughtfully and remarked that Frank's Uncle Art was probably the smartest man that he, Sloan, had ever met. Then he led Frank upstairs to Mr. Soderbjerg's office, opened the door, and said, "Go in."

There were two men in there, a younger one, lanky, in a nubbly brown wool suit and a portlier one, about sixty, with a mane of white hair and the younger one was

saying, "She can't even boil an egg! Can't boil an *egg!*"
Then he turned to Frank. "We're talking about my wife.
She can't boil an egg."

"I think it's easier to fix a *steak* than boil an egg," said
the older one. "First of all, you have no idea what's inside
that egg. Each egg is different. You can't tell by looking
at them. Some eggs, the shell is too thin. The chicken
didn't get enough milk in her diet. So you leave it boiling
for two minutes and fifteen seconds and it comes out like
an old tennis ball, and the day before, you did your egg
three minutes and it came like a bad cold. No, I'd
rather run a radio station than have to boil an egg. The
perfect egg is a myth, like the Northwest Passage. It's a
miracle anytime you get one that's edible." And he waved
at them to clear out. "Anyway, I don't want to hear about
it. I'm going upstairs to bed. I think I slept too fast last
night."

———

"Frank," Mr. Roy Soderbjerg, Jr., said, when they got
to his office and he sat down in the big chair and swivelled
around and faced out the window, "Frank, I hear from
your Uncle Art you're a good man, and I like the looks
of you myself, so as far as I'm concerned you're hired. I
must say I've had bad experiences with orphans like yourself, they tend to be treacherous, but you don't seem sneaky
yourself, so I'll just bring it to your attention. It's a ten-
dency to avoid. Trust is what we operate on here. We had
an orphan once who stole money out of people's desks, if
you can imagine that. He slid around here opening drawers
and lifting petty change and anything else he saw, stop-
watches, ladies' necklaces, and finally he tried to take a
revolver from my dad's desk and the gun went off and
nailed him in the knee. He lost his leg. Now he hawks

umbrellas on the streetcorner. So remember that radio is a great business and it's all about honesty and if we lose trust with each other, then we're out on our rear ends. Now go see Sloan and he'll find you some work to do."

Sloan was in the basement, yakking with the mail girls. Frank's job, Sloan told him, was to follow the Soderbjergs around and take care of things for them. "Just keep your eyes peeled and make sure they're happy and you'll be happy." He told Frank to go out and buy six pounds of Jamaican coffee, three boxes of White Owl cigars, and some greeting cards: twelve dozen Get Well and six dozen Happy Birthday and twelve dozen With Deepest Sympathy—an assortment, not too many floral ones and nothing Scriptural—and then to come back and walk Ray's dachshund Columbus. He referred to the Soderbjergs as The Sodajerks. "He likes to do his business around the front doors of taverns. When you get back, you can wait around in the lobby for Roy Sodajerk, Jr., to go out for lunch. Nobody likes to eat lunch with the poor bastard, so he may ask you, and if he asks you, go and God help you. Part of your job. He'll take you to the Pot Pie. Make sure you have a couple bucks with you in case he forgets. Let him sit with his back to the door and you take a seat facing the door. It's your job to identify incoming friends so when they say hi, he can say their name. Of course, you can't do that now, being new, but you'll catch on. The Sodajerks can't remember the names of their own children. Old Ray Sodajerk runs off to New York every fall with a different broad on his arm and two months later at the Christmas party he's asking you what her last name was. I tell you, they're a caution. And if he doesn't ask you to lunch, then come back here and I'll show you how to sign their names. We're a week behind on sympathy cards."

Then Sloan went back to discussing something with the

girls. Frank fetched the dog, who was old and fussy, and walked him to Woolworth's and bought the stuff and came back and delivered it. Ray was drowsy from his morning nap. He told Frank that he was out of cigars and Frank gave him the box of White Owls. Ray was impressed. He asked Frank if he played golf. Frank said, no, he was sorry but he didn't. Ray said, "Why be sorry? You'll never meet more boring men than on a golf course. A game for pygmies." Frank made a note to himself: *don't be apologetic unnecessarily*.

Down in the lobby, he hung around for fifteen minutes near a crowd of fans waiting to see Dad Benson come down from his show. *Friendly Neighbor* had just celebrated eighteen years on the air, the same age as Frank. The fans were holding signs from their home towns, Waseca, Marshall, Pine City, Menomonie, Decorah, Crosslake, Sanborn, and getting their Kodaks ready, lining up the shots. One woman had brought her six little children in red satin vests that appeared to be home-made and had their names sewn across the back: Marilyn, Merwin, Marianne, Meredith, Murray, and Miriam. Frank introduced himself to the receptionist, Laurel, who said, "Ray Soderbjerg I wouldn't trust as far as I could throw him but Roy Jr. I'd do anything for, believe me. That man is as decent as they come." Laurel was a peach, he could see that. He was going to invite her to the movies but before he could work in that direction, Mr. Odom came by, pushing a mop. He looked up and said hi.

"I thought you managed the Antwerp Apartments," said Frank.

"I do it all, son," said Mr. Odom. "I'm half janitor, half manager, and the rest of the time I do everything else. I hear you got the job. Congratulations."

Mr. Odom asked how he liked his room. Frank liked it fine. "Oh," said Laurel, "do you live at the Antwerp?"

"Yes," said Frank, and wanted to say, *Alone. I live alone at the Antwerp, Laurel. I am older than I look, twenty-three in fact, and I am affectionate and congenial and generous to a fault and have fantasies from here to Chicago,* but then Roy Jr. came out of the elevator and Mr. Odom melted away and Roy Jr. said, "You have your lunch yet? Good. We'll go around to the Pot Pie, they have a good sauerkraut soup there. Hello, Miss Larpenteur."

Roy Jr. talked all the way across the street and down to the lunchroom, about this, that, and the other thing, and ordered the soup and a plate of chipped beef and resumed talking. He said, "I've fired forty-one men in my life and six women and two children. Each one was memorable. Some of them begged for another chance and some of them cursed me with a passion and a resourcefulness they had never displayed before and one of them quietly went away and jumped off the Hennepin Avenue bridge. He hit the ice and it broke his back and he is somewhere today, a helpless cripple, working for a newspaper, I believe. I was his executioner.

"You're a young man and you don't know what it's like to take away someone's work, so I'll tell you. You have to do it quick. The moment his rear end touches the chair, in that exact instant you say it in one sentence: I'm sorry, Jack, but I have decided to let you go—your employment here is ended today. Then you say something for a minute—express sorrow, hope, reminiscence, commiseration—so he can recover, because no matter what kind of an idiot he was, he never thought it would come to this. Then you lean back and let him say his piece. Maybe it does him some good to cuss you out. Fine. Harvey Olson almost jumped over the desk and strangled me when I fired him. He said WLT was a dead end where his talents had gone unrecognized and in two days he'd

190

have a job at twice the pay with people who knew something about radio."

Harvey Olson had been fired. The popular breakfast newscaster who said, "Hello and good morning, and may your day be filled with good news!"

"Harvey invested heavily in Honeywell when they were trying to sell this solar hat, and he lost his shirt, and shoes, and went downhill rapidly. For two years he'd come to work drunk every morning and now the police had found him passed out in his car on University Avenue with his pants loaded—and it was the *third time*—and when I told him the obvious, he leaned over and screamed at me. Fine. Harvey found another job a year later picking up dead branches for the Park Department, but at least he could look back and know he had had *one* proud moment in his life, when he called me a dirty bastard. When I fired Dusty Eustis he called me disloyal, a backstabber, a rat, a leech, and probably some other things. Here was a man who tried to get a sixteen-year-old usherette to go upstairs to a room with him and he was angry that his many years of service hadn't entitled him to this. There is no limit to self-deceit, Frank. I keep looking for the limit and there is none. Not among people in show business there isn't.

"The performer I admired the most, I think, was Uncle Albert, actually my dad's uncle. We hired him about 1927 and he stayed for twelve years until he died. We hired him because he broke his leg and couldn't be a street preacher anymore with the Salvation Army, which he had been for forty years. He was one of General William Booth's old stalwarts, and when Booth came over from London, he and Uncle Albert would go nightclubbing in Chicago. Neither of them touched a drop, of course, but General Booth loved to dance. He was wild about the turkey trot, the foxtrot, and the Buffalo, but of course he couldn't dance with young women, lest it lead to carnal desire, so he danced with Uncle Albert. After a hard day among the down-and-out and a long evening service, the General'd lean over and whisper, 'How about a little hoofing?' and off they'd go. Around the hot spots of Chicago, two men dancing together was definitely eccentric. In fact, it was so eccentric that people who were as drunk as everybody in the clubs was didn't believe their eyes, and so the old gents, decked out in their somber Army regalia, flung themselves around the dance floor in happy abandon, and left refreshed, and woke up at dawn to resume the Lord's work.

"For us, Uncle Albert recited poems. By heart, of course. He recited on *Jubilee* and sometimes on *Friendly Neighbor*, whenever he happened to be around, and often on the *Afternoon Ballroom*, the announcer would say, 'Uncle Albert is in the studio now and I wonder if we couldn't get him to recite a poem for us. Uncle Albert?' And the old man, who had tremendous eyebrows, great thorny overgrowths with trailing vines and creepers, approached the microphone. Slashed on his neck was an ugly scar from when a Memphis woman had tried to slit his throat, a close call that led to his conversion. He had a voice like a trombone—he was unable to lower it very much from a volume that would have carried across rivers and stopped lynch mobs—and he had such burning vitality and magnetism in his youth, he was always able to draw big crowds, but he could never win them for the Lord because nobody wanted to come within a hundred feet of him. Too loud. Even when he was old, people braced themselves whenever Uncle Albert walked in the room so they wouldn't jump and hit the chandelier when he said hello.

"He was at WLT because he was family. He understood this, and understood that he was not to preach. We had other people who did the preaching. Albert recited poetry.

He was paid for this. He never read from a page, which he considered cheating, so his repertoire was limited. He never expanded it. He wasn't ambitious in any way. He only wanted to be useful.

"He knew fifty or so poems by heart, 'The Wreck of the Hesperus' and 'Curfew Shall Not Ring Tonight' and 'Excelsior' and 'Over the Hill to the Poorhouse,' and he appeared in the studio whenever the fancy struck, and the announcer had to work him in. Albert didn't like to sit and he would get to clearing his throat if made to wait too long, a powerful BRRAACH-HEM! like a lion letting other lions know he was here, a signal to announcers that he was ready to recite.

"When Albert recited, the engineer turned the volume gain down to a sliver, and his voice came through loud and clear.

BREATHES there a MAN? with soul . . . so DEAD?
Who NEVER to HIMSELF hath SAID?
THIS is MY OWN? my native LAND?
Whose HEART? hath ne'er within him BURNED?
As homeward his footsteps he hath TURNED?
From wandering on some FOREIGN STRAND?
If such there BREATHES . . . GO! MARK HIM WELL!

"Every year on April 15th, the anniversary of Lincoln's death, he did 'O Captain! My Captain!,' a poem that, in the hands of an amateur, can be rather flat, but, coming from Albert, was a clarion call, warning that the Republic is in constant danger, that any triumph is followed immediately by tragedy, heartbreak, treachery, and despair.

EXULT, O shores! . . . and RING, O bells!
But I . . . with mournful tread,

Walk the deck . . . my Captain. . . . lies,
FALLEN . . . cold . . . and dead.

"This performance never failed to move and captivate. You might expect a grown person in the 20th century to be pretty much immune to the fevers of 'O Captain! My Captain!,' but Uncle Albert was a powerhouse, and the radio stars dreaded him. His great moment was at the *WLT Barn Dance* Tenth Anniversary Show at Williams Arena where he preceded Bob Hope on the bill and gave the greatest recitation of 'O Captain! My Captain!' of his life. The old man stood before an audience of seventeen-thousand, which was approximately his lifetime total audience as a preacher, and he flexed his eyebrows and said the poem and killed the captain and wept and cried out and knelt and whispered and saved the Republic, and at the end, the seventeen-thousand had no choice but to stand and cheer—he had closed off the alternatives, such as polite applause—so they stood and wept and shouted until he came out and did 'Breathes there a man' and now the audience was beside itself, standing on the chairs, shouting themselves hoarse, throwing babies in the air, clapping till their hands bled, and Uncle Albert returned for a final selection, 'The Charge of the First Minnesota at Gettysburg,' and the people collapsed into one damp quivering heap. The show was now over, though it still had an hour to go, including Mr. Hope's twenty-minute monologue. The great man stood in the wings, his famous grin a bit taut, his famous ski-jump nose glittering with sweat, and he whispered to Leo, the emcee, who signalled the orchestra, and they played 'Columbia the Gem of the Ocean' and then Otto and His Trained Pig did the Leap From The Ladder Through A Flaming Hoop Into The Arms Of The Catcher and the Moonglows sang 'A Guy Seldom Sees a Gal Like Louise,' but eventually Hope had to go on stage, which he did, and found that everybody was still thinking about Uncle Albert and was disappointed that he was not him. After the death of Lincoln and the battle of Gettysburg, the rapid-fire gags about golf and dames and Bing and booze seemed pretty small potatoes, and he soon sensed, though blinded by the spotlight, a slow but widespread movement of bodies toward the Exit signs.

"Well, like most of the disasters of the great, this one went unreported. The press is always afraid to stray too far from what the reader expects, so they wrote about the event that *should* have taken place—Ole Bob laying them out in the aisles, a few local performers also on the bill —but Ole Bob knew what happened. Up until that night, he had been a Fabian Socialist and one of the Paramount Seven, the elite core of the Hollywood left wing, but Uncle Albert showed him the power of the flag and Ole Bob has been wearing it ever since. He became a Republican that very night, Tailgunner Bob, the fighting man's favorite. You care for dessert? No? Good. Check, please."

CHAPTER 24

Friend of
the Soderbjergs

So Frank moved into a cubicle on the fourth floor, around the corner from Ethel Glen, next to Roy Jr.'s office, with a table and a chair. He spent his first day carefully drawing a chart of WLT employees and a map of the station, all three floors, and always carried a notebook in his pocket in which he wrote every fact about WLT the moment he learned it—new words, names of wives and children, who did what, where they went afterward and with whom.

He learned the three Soderbjerg signatures and began sending out the cards for them, paid parking tickets, walked the dog, bought cakes on the birthdays of employees and assembled a choir to sing, took various clients and shirttail relatives on tours around the studio and brought them by Ray's or Roy's or Roy Jr.'s office and remembered to say the guest's name *loudly* and *clearly, twice,* because it was true, the Soderbjergs never remembered anybody. Frank was Fred for a few months, and then Frank, then

Stan, or Young Man, sometimes resurfacing as Fred for awhile.

"Fred," said Roy Jr., "go get me the last five weeks of *Sunnyvale* scripts. Do we keep those or throw them out, by the way?"

"We keep them, and my name is Frank, sir."

"Frank! Of course. Frank."

He returned with the scripts.

"I've got a feeling that Al has been working on brake linings for weeks and isn't Esther starting to repeat some jokes too?" So Frank sat down and read a pile of *Sunnyvale*s and reported that, no, brake linings weren't the problem, worn clutches were: six of them in the past two weeks. The joke, about Ole and Knute getting drunk and walking home on the train tracks and Ole saying "This is the longest stairway I ever climbed" and Knute adding, "It wouldn't be so bad if they hadn't put the bannisters so low," had been repeated twice in one month. And so had Wordsworth's lines, *When from our better selves we have too long / Been parted by the hurrying world, and droop, / Sick of its business, of its pleasures tired, / How gracious, how benign is solitude.*

"Is Patsy Konopka writing this?"

No, Dale Snelling was. When Frank asked Dale if there was a problem with *Sunnyvale* these days, Dale blanched. "Who wants to know?" he said. He was working on a play, "Launcelot and Guenevere, A Drama in Verse," for Vesta, who wanted to start a serious drama show, and he had farmed out *Sunnyvale* to a woman named Grace Marie Schein. "What's the problem?" he demanded. "Who sent you?" Frank said that the new writer didn't seem to have a broad knowledge of cars. Dale said, "You're snooping around for Roy Jr., aren't you?" He poked Frank in the chest. "Butt out, kid."

But Ray liked him. "Fred," he'd say, "where you going

so fast? Sit down. Don't try to do it all at once, Fred. Make haste slowly. *There is luck in leisure.* My dad used to say that. My wife wakes up in the morning with a list as long as your arm. She's out the door and gone before I'm half awake. The woman is possessed. She's on ten boards of directors of ten godforsaken organizations and sits through more meetings in one week and listens to more nonsense than I could do in a year and survive, and she does it because she's out to save the world. Endless meetings and nothing ever comes of it because these people are all crackpots but they're all cracked in different ways and they never agree on anything. Well, she can't save the world, and neither can you or I. Don't concern yourself with things you can't change, I say. It's more *important* to make a very good cup of coffee in the morning and a very good piece of toast than it is to worry about Josef Stalin, because I can do something about breakfast and I can't do *anything* about Stalin, and I'm sure he's having a *wonderful* breakfast. You know that coffee you bought me? From Jamaica? It's the best. Ever. My wife eats more bad food at these meetings. Rubber chicken and sweeping-compound gravy. You know why I married her—it was because when we were fourteen I saw her eat one hundred cinnamon caramel rolls in one day. I was a friend of her brother's. She ate ten rolls for breakfast and her mother said, 'Vesta, if you eat one more of those you'll get sick,' so she ate *ninety* more. About twenty of us were there to watch her at the end. She didn't look a bit sick, she was just out to show what sort of stuff she was made of, and she sure showed me. I said, that girl's for me. She never ate another one afterward. Now she eats burnt toast and cold hot dogs and spaghetti out of a can. Terrible. Have you had your lunch yet?"

What made all the Soderbjergs happy was to have Frank sit and listen to them, which Frank was glad to do and

Sloan was glad to be shut of: "Man oh man, that Roy Jr. can talk the ear off a barber. Lemme know if you hear any juicy gossip." He was helping one of the girls find an apartment, Lucy, who was nineteen. Frank went up and sat in the hall outside Roy Jr.'s office at eleven-thirty and Roy Jr. stuck his head out the door and said, "Oh. Say, are you busy for lunch?" and they'd go to the coffeeshop or over to the Pot Pie for a plate of wieners and baked beans, and Roy Jr. would talk. He trusted Frank with inside information. He told him that Patsy Konopka was crazy, that Ray and LaWella were friends, and so were Ray and Alma, and that Dad Benson was talking about retiring and ending *Friendly Neighbor*. He said, "Dad saved the station after Pearl Harbor. We still get mail about it. It was Sunday, you know, and a young guy named Babe Roeder was on duty when the news came over the wire and he hesitated to put it on the air right away because he'd gotten burned by a practical joke a few months before—somebody had handed him a bulletin in the middle of a newscast, which seemed to be about a flood that had wiped out downtown St. Paul, but then, in the second paragraph, there was a big ark and a lot of animals—so Roeder didn't want to get burned again. He sat and thought about it. Then he tried to call up the *Journal* to see what they thought. Their phone line was busy. Meanwhile, *Melody Hotel* was coming toward the station break, and Reed Seymour the announcer came out and got the weather forecast and Babe handed him the bulletin and said, 'We're at war. I think.' Reed didn't want to put something like that on the air without somebody's permission. It was December and Little Tommy and Pop and Betty and the Bellhops were singing Christmas songs in Studio A and I suppose Reed was reluctant to ruin their fun with a war against the Japs. So he called me at home, but he got my dad instead. My dad had just gotten up from a nap and was groggy. Now, my dad had soured on Roosevelt years before, considered him power-mad, a liar, a skirt-chaser, and a fraud who was in league with the Morgans and Rockefellers. My dad never got over the death of populism. He thought a world war was the worst disaster America could find for itself. So he gave young Reed Seymour a lecture on history. He told him that the only purpose of war is to give the goddamn government an even tighter grip on your nuts than it's got already and to make poor bastards die so the rich can get richer. He told him that war was a horrible nightmare that must never be repeated or it would mean the end of civilization.

"Young Reed interpreted this to mean, *Don't read the bulletin.* So the minutes passed and Reed did the station break and did the weather forecast and turned it back to Pop, who told a joke about a dog and brought in the Bellhops for a Bud's Salve jingle. There they were, at one of the most important moments in American history, a day that you look back on and remember exactly where you were when you heard the news, but there was no news on WLT, just a quartet of goofy guys singing

No matter if it's bunions, burns,
Or boils that you have,
Nothing else will do the job
Like Bud's Old-Fashioned Salve.

"The phone started to ring off the hook, irate people wondering how WLT could sit and fiddle and sell unguent while American boys were dying in Hawaii. I tried to call and couldn't get through, but Dad Benson was downtown and heard the news and ran to the station and took over. He told Babe to bring him every scrap of wire copy, and Dad sat in Studio B, the old mausoleum, and told people what was happening and talked in his quiet way about how awful war is but we can only live in peace if our neighbors are willing. But if Hitler and the Emperor wanted war, then they would have it, and though it would be a long hard struggle and there would be sacrifices, we would come through on top because Americans always pull together. Pop and the *Melody Hotel* gang worked up a version of 'There's a Star-Spangled Banner Flying over Home Sweet Home' and it was so tremendous and rousing that nobody remembered we were almost an hour late with the news. If Dad hadn't been there, we might've been shut down for high treason. You care for coffee? No? Where is the waiter?"

That evening, as Patsy listened to Mr. Devereaux take a shower, she almost wrote him into *Golden Years* as a French-Canadian hockey player torn with self-loathing when his slap shot kills an innocent passer-by and in terror he plunges naked out the door of the shower room and through the snow seeking absolution and meets Miss Leffwell, she of the lonely nights, who gasps at his nakedness, but offers him her coat, and then he gasps, for she is naked under the coat—*hmmm*, perhaps, *but does it make sense?*

She thought of inviting him down for dinner.

Frank's door banged the next morning, and he walked out the front of the Antwerp, no hat on his head, wild hair over the collar of his Navy peajacket, hands jammed in the pockets, and turned at the curb and stood and looked up at the roof. Maybe, she thought, he could be a young writer whose novel she might read, earthy and full of grunting and moaning, naked perspiring bodies writhing in the dark, and she would provide insights from the womanly point of view ("Here at the bottom of the page, where he cups her breasts, frankly don't you think the metaphor of young golden apples is trite? And the 'hard throbbing muscle of his manhood'—why don't we just call it a cock and be done with it?"). He headed east, past the YWCA, leaning into the wind. Au revoir, mon Philippe. It was the next day before she learned his name. It was printed on a pale pink letter stuck under his door. *Francis*, it said, *I can't believe that our home is gone and other people live in it and we have nothing, our family is gone. It is a beautiful day today and I hope you will come visit me soon. They hate me here but I don't care. Their hearts are full of hatred and mine is at peace. What a sad life it is.* That evening, Patsy heard him whistling, over the sink as he washed his dishes, "Red River Valley," the theme song of *Golden Years*. She rang Mr. Odom downstairs and asked, "Harold, who moved into 4-C?"

"Patsy, his name is Frank White. But the way he said it, it's probably something else. He works for Roy Jr. Ethel Glen says he's got Sloan's job."

"Sloan's leaving? For where?"

"He doesn't know it yet, but Sloan is bound for the big Out There. He got too smart-alecky. He had this way of every time he left Ray or Roy Jr.'s office, making a smart remark over his shoulder. I hope somebody takes this kid aside and tells him what the score is. He's Art's nephew, by the way."

"Harold, you are a doll."

And then suddenly one day Frank came clattering down the stairs at WLT as she headed up to bring LaWella the script for tomorrow's *Adventures in Homemaking*. He galloped past her and around the bend toward the studios. Vince was behind her. "Who's that?" he said. "Frank White," said Patsy, "and he's a comer."

A week later, Frank White finally had purchased a few kitchen utensils and was making himself breakfast and supper instead of running out to the luncheonette, but Patsy could hear that he was eating too much fried food. Perhaps a neighborly visit to 4-C: "Mr. White, I'm Patsy Konopka from downstairs, welcome, and here's a free

VegaRama—it peels, pares, slices, dices, minces, chops, hacks, and makes food preparation a pleasure—perfect cole slaw every time with no big hunks, no lumps, no snappers," but his apartment was a mess with all the clothes she'd heard him drop on the floor, he'd surely be embarrassed to see her. Odd, that he took his pants and shorts off first, then his shirt. An interesting man.

Hero

He did everything. He washed coffee cups and emptied ashtrays and gave his opinion when it was asked for. "What do you think of her?" Roy Jr. asked, after Faith Snelling left his office, upset that Dale was off *Sunnyvale*, hinting that her days on *Friendly Neighbor* might be numbered. "She's Jo," said Frank. "And Jo is what makes the show go. You couldn't do it without her." And so Roy Jr. smoothed things over with her.

When the annual "Little Becky Souvenir Scrapbook" came out, full of inspirational poems and songs and a dozen photos of a golden-haired child with unremitting smile (not Marjery Moore) in various lifelike poses (Little Becky Wakes Up, Little Becky's Breakfast, Enjoying A Chat With School Chums, Little Becky Spells The Word Correctly, Little Becky And Miss Judy, Home For A Nourishing Lunch, Little Becky And Dad Say Grace Together, Climbing A Tree, Practicing The Piano), Frank had to address hundreds of them and mail them out. More than

40,000 copies were sold or given away. The child drew about a hundred letters a week, several of which were written by Frank, who made sure that Marjery saw them. "You disgust me, you little wretch, and I wish you'd get the hell off the air and leave performing to people with talent," began one. They didn't bother Marjery at all. She thought of them as the work of some creep with a hair up his ass.

He arrived at the office at seven-thirty, made coffee, wiped the excess polish off the executive desks, and sharpened six pencils each for Ray and Roy Jr. Ray liked a fresh pencil, liked to smell the shaved wood and lead. When Ray arrived, Frank helped him off with his coat. "Thanks, Stan," said Ray. *Frank.* "Of course. Frank." Then he got their mail from the mailroom, where the girls were barely awake at eight. He had to rummage through the sacks and yank the Soderbjergs' letters and run them upstairs: the day didn't start for Roy Jr. until he had opened a letter. Then Frank waited for Roy to call him from Moorhead.

Roy was an early riser and by eight he had saved up a large load of conversation. Frank got to hear everything; he was new, he hadn't heard it before. "I don't know. I've been thinking," Roy'd start out. "Radio seems to me to be fading. What do you think?" Frank said he didn't think so. Roy continued: "I used to listen to the Barn Dance when I lived in St. Paul, and then one night I quit listening to it. It was still on, and I could hear it, but I was listening to next door. A couple lived there who fought a lot, and in warm weather, they left their windows open, and I sat and listened.

"They'd fight over money—he was a carpenter, a journeyman, and she worked at The Emporium—or they'd fight about sex. They'd start slow and then get to yelling and running from room to room and then she'd smash something and then it got very quiet. She cried and he comforted her and in a few minutes, you'd hear that bed thumping the wall. It must've been on loose rollers. They'd go at it for fifteen, twenty minutes. Ka-bam, ka-bam, ka-bam. And then they lay and talked and smoked.

"In broad daylight, this was a couple you wouldn't look at twice, but secretly, they were fascinating. She'd say, after they'd had sex, 'I can't figure us out.' And he'd promise that everything'd be better. And then they remembered how they met. It was at her dad's drainpipe warehouse, and she came in after school and around a corner and came face to face with a man's crotch. It was his. He was standing on a stool, measuring a doorpost. She was going to ask her old man for money to go to Europe and suddenly there was a fly and a bundle inside it. She looked up and he held up the measuring tape. Three and a half feet. And she didn't go to Europe.

"I thought to myself: this is what should be on radio." He meant it.

"Hank, the future of broadcasting is eavesdropping. We could use hypnotism. Ordinary people could be actors of the subconscious. Their dreams and all the night thoughts people think—put it on radio. Of course, it'd be obscene and against the law, but, you wouldn't try to change the law, just change radio. Put out a signal so a person needs a decoding machine to receive it. Put it beyond the law. Radio's fading fast, Hank."

Frank.

"And you know what could save radio, Frank? If you put a microphone in my brother's jacket pocket. My brother dogs around town like nobody's business. But maybe you know that. My brother could save radio single-handed. Not that he would ever use his hand, of course."

Frank did know that. He drove Ray one day to the Great Northern Depot to entrain him for New York and there was Erie Monroe, a young actress on *The Hills of Home*, a little green suitcase in hand. The old man beamed as he took her hand and kissed it. He turned to Frank. "Tell Vesta I took an extra berth for the Great Books," he said.

Erie took Ray's arm and Frank carried their bags down the stairs and up the platform alongside the Empire Builder to the Pullmans up front. "By the way, I am going to talk to a buyer and try to sell the station," said Ray, stopping to catch his breath. "Bing Crosby. That's between you and me. I've decided to sell. I'm not getting any younger. That's what my brother says." Erie squeezed Ray's arm and smooched him on the side of his head.

"My brother is up in Moorhead pondering the imponderable. And I am going to go to New York and screw the inscrutable." He squeezed Erie back. "Bye, kid."

The conductor hollered "Board!" Up went the stepstool and the Builder steamed away and across the Stone Bridge over the Mississippi, the cheery glow of the parlor car disappearing behind the NSP power plant. Frank drove the big Buick back, walked the dog, watered the lawn, closed the windows. Two weeks later, Ray returned. Bing had been in Tahiti, but never mind, Erie had been wonderful and Ray was feeling pink again. They had gone to Radio City Music Hall and seen Fibber McGee and Molly, Jack Benny and Fred Allen, Frances Langford and Don Ameche, Freeman Gosden and Charles Correll, Gene Austin, the Boswell Sisters, and Jesse Crawford at the Mighty White Wurlitzer, in a four-hour broadcast with not a minute of slack, not a single song or gag or line that didn't belong there, a glittering all-star revue.

"Radio," Ray declared, "it's here to stay, and we're going to stick with it."

The love of a beautiful woman seemed to be a real picker-upper. "New York is the ticket," he told Frank. "Terrible place to live. People lie to you. Perfectly nice people. They lie all the time. You buy a suit and the salesman promises it by tomorrow morning. Two days later you call him up and he pretends to be upset, says the tailor got the chalk marks mixed up, it'll be here Tuesday. Finally on Friday you start to get steamed, but now he's blaming it on a missing button, and Monday, he says Wednesday. Wednesday, it's Friday. Finally, you walk in and threaten to kill him with a screwdriver. You screech and rave until the spit is dripping off your chin. And you see, this is what he expected! He listens and when you're finally done screeching, in comes Sam with the pants. You have to yell at people to get things done. Terrible place to live. But my gosh, a good hotel, and a Broadway show and dinner and breakfast at noon in bed reading the newspaper. That's the life, Frank."

A few days after Ray returned, Frank became a hero. It was a Monday, and WLT went off the air. The transmitter shuddered and the air went dead about midway through the *Jubilee* during an Evelyn Pie commercial.

> I don't care if the meat is pale,
> If the soup is thin and the jokes are stale,
> If the gravy's lumpy and the spuds are dry,
> You can make it up to me with an—

And nothing happened for awhile. Bells didn't ring and lights didn't flash.

Reed Seymour, sitting in the Green Room, resting his eyes with a copy of *Peek*, reached up and switched the wall monitor from Program to On-Air and heard silence. He switched back to Program. He didn't want to be the one who brings in the bad news. What with Eleanor Grantham (Babs, on *The Hills of Home*) throwing him over for an engineer—the ultimate disgrace for any announcer—Reed had been through a lot and the thought of calling up an engineer and saying, "Something's wrong, Chuck," was too much. Let the engineers handle it. That's what they got paid for, the big dorks.

The engineer, Chuck, sat engrossed in the *Jubilee*, listening to Leo's joke about the man who wants to buy a new car for his girlfriend and the salesman asks, "Chevrolet?" and he says, "Well, we'll see once we get the car," which made Chuck chortle and wheeze and grab onto the console for support. He did not turn and look at the transmitter dial behind him, so he wasn't aware that the needle lay flat and that the WLT audience was now limited to him and a few other people on the premises.

The young man who sat in the transmitter shack at the foot of the WLT tower in Columbia Heights and read the meters was Ray's neighbor's boy, Wallace Tripp, and this quiet and tedious job suited him well, except that he was afraid to give bad news too. He was the only child of older parents who cared for him so well that Wallace could not bear the company of other children, who were all stupid, nor was he suited for the rough and tumble world of the office. The transmitter shack, clean and dry, furnished with a desk and a cot, on a hill behind a barbed-wire fence with "Danger: High Voltage" signs posted everywhere, was exactly right for him. He loved to be at the transmitter. He needed no days off. Work and recreation were one to Wallace. The monastic life appealed to his sense of mission. He was a baseball fan and an astrologer and kept elaborate zodiac statistics on the American Association, team and individual statistics, and could tell anyone, if anyone had been interested, how the Millers compared to the Toledo Mudhens, for example, in Batting Average (Full Moon), and had theories about which signs to favor in which situations, e.g., to steal with a Leo with a Libra at bat, to walk a Gemini if the next batter is a Cancer. When Wallace looked up and saw the transmitter meters lying as flat as beached fish, he figured it must be a mistake. The transmitter *must* be on. So he made up readings to indicate that it was on and wrote those in the log book. He didn't want to be the cause of trouble. He didn't want Ray to get mad and throw him out on the streets.

So WLT was off the air for a whole afternoon and evening. The switchboard lit up and the operators, Janice and Jo Ellen, took careful note of the many complaints and put them into a complaint basket, six hundred remarks from listeners that WLT was *gone*, which a messenger boy picked up a few hours later and carried downstairs to the Program Department, where a secretary began typing a letter of acknowledgement: "Thank you for your interest in our broadcasting service, recently expressed, and please know that we consider *all* comments from listeners and weigh them seriously in making our program decisions. . . ."

Roy Jr. called from his dentist's, where the nurse had mentioned something about WLT having been struck by a blast of lightning. "What's wrong?" he asked, a little loopy from the laughing gas. "Wrong?" asked Gene the Chief Engineer. So it was up to Frank to discover the problem when he returned from lunch. "We're off the air," he told Gene.

He and Gene drove out to Columbia Heights. Gene got lost on the way and then it took them awhile to breach Wallace's security system. Gene lobbed stones from the street onto the roof of the shack, but Wallace thought it was only some boys, and if he didn't do anything they'd go away. Finally, Frank climbed the fence, scaled the barbed wire, opened the gate, let Gene in, and Gene found the tube that had blown.

A couple hours later, back at the station, Frank asked

Gene how long before he could get the station back on. Gene wasn't sure. He was waiting to hear about a part he had ordered. "When did you order it?" asked Frank.

"Sent Chuck out with it an hour ago."

"Sent him where?"

"To mail the letter."

"A letter to whom?"

"The distributor in Chicago."

Frank told him to find a distributor in Minneapolis and to get a part right away. "Okay," said Gene, "but it's your fault if Roy Jr. gets mad. He gets mad and goes around here silent for weeks and don't look at a person. So when the shit hits the fan, that's your ass, mister."

So Frank became the whiz kid with his finger in the dike. Roy Jr. said, "Thanks." "It was nothing," said Frank. Roy Jr. asked Gene what the problem was with the distributor.

"I knew you were going to get mad. I just *knew* it," said Gene.

"Please, Gene. Let's not screw around when the signal's down."

"Sure. Right. I won't. But I want you to know why I did what I did. I knew you were gonna blame me. That's what makes it so hard to work here. I never know what you want. I never know if you're mad or what." Gene put his face in his hands and sobbed. Frank had never heard an engineer cry before. It was a hard rattly sort of weeping, more like gnashing, or the grinding of a gearbox when the clutch won't engage.

CHAPTER 26

Maria

When Roy, who was spending the summer in Moorhead, needed a trigger tube, an ignitron, a triode, and a damper, and wrote to Gene, the letter wound up with Frank, and Frank went and found the stuff and mailed it, which led to correspondence. Roy was beavering away in his workshop on the farm, working on something he called a Resonance Radio, which would let a listener hear the broadcast voice as resonantly as his own, to give *listening* the same sensation as *speaking*. The Radio was constructed as a chair with big padded speakers mounted in the back and the headrest and in the arms, conducting sound directly through the torso. "This will be to your ordinary tabletop receiver what the airplane was to the North Coast Limited, and we will be ready for mass production in the spring, soon as we iron out the kinks," Roy wrote on a postcard. But before it was perfected, he lost interest and moved on. He experimented with egg yolks as sound insulation and invented a microphone that could be thrown, to give a listener the sensation of flight.

He wandered briefly into the realm of dual microphones —coming within inches of becoming The Father of Stereo—but gave it up. "Music is too complicated to be reproduced," he concluded. "Too many different sounds: brass, reed, bowing, plucking, banging, strumming. Radio can no more reproduce music than a man can get pregnant." He invented a radio jacket with speakers sewn in front and back, but it was too bulky for comfort and the underarm speakers jammed into your ribs and a loud selection made your head hurt.

Discouraged, he locked up, left home, roamed around Europe until November, 1948. He mailed disconsolate postcards from Vienna and Venice and Paris and London, lamenting the waste of his talents—"Wherever I look, I see things that I could have done. If only I had had the discipline. I'm one of those men who goes out to shop and comes home without his pants. Oh well. If wishes were horses, beggars would ride, and the world be drowned in a sea of pride." He went to Glomfjord and found Søren Blak and was crushed to discover that the Plato of Radio, angered by poor reception, had hurled his Atwater-Kent into the fjord and now owned a Victrola and was an adherent of Patti Page. Søren felt that "The Tennessee Waltz" summed up life's essence.

"Only yew know how much I have lost," he told Roy.

Then, in his tiny cabin on the S.S. *Jostrup* steaming for New York, Roy hit on the idea of building a radio big enough for the listener to sit in.

"The power of radio is its intimacy and closeness to the listener. This is why the phonograph record on radio is such a disaster. Costwise, it made sense, but it removes the listener so far from the music, the music is lifeless. Too many steps in between: the recording, the pressing, the transmission, the reception—the music is translated five times before John Q. Radio hears it: six, if you include

213

his eardrum. It's straight out of Rube Goldberg! All the life of the music is dissipated in transporting it! Like a gasoline-tank truck made of lead. Like a picture of a picture of the Mona Lisa's reflection in a mud puddle. That's what playing a record on the air is like! The Radio Capsule will give the *reality* of sound!"

He spent the winter constructing it and in March he brought it down to Minneapolis in a potato truck. The Capsule was five feet high, six feet wide, and eight feet deep, resembled a deep-sea bathysphere, and you entered it through a hatch on the top, backwards, grasping the two steel handgrips and lowering yourself into the seat which lay at a 45-degree angle. It was dark inside, except for the dial overhead, and with the sound on, the contraption seemed to shrink skin-tight around you. The sound came from all directions. It bored right through a person. Most people who tried the Capsule found that, after one minute, they wanted to get out. It needed a little more room, and a little less volume.

Two Capsules were built, one more than the world seemed to require, and Roy moved on. He went on to cornsilk, which should be good for something, he reasoned, and if not for shirts, then rope, or parachutes, and by the time he had failed with cornsilk, he had already moved on in his mind to circularity. He woke up one morning and looked at his alarm clock. The circle! Of course! Why hadn't he done more with *that?* All the work he'd done with lines and rays and angles, he'd completely overlooked the realm of sphericity and curvature and rotundity, of circularity and convolution. He peered into his cereal bowl and he studied the toilet as it flushed and he walked around and around the yard thinking about the *Circle*. And then he took the afternoon off and went bowling. When he came home, though his thumb ached, he sat down and wrote a note to Frank. "Despite my crazy family, I have had a wonderful life. How lucky I am! Tonight I want to get back to the problem of resonation." That was the great thing about Roy. He never was able to concentrate long enough to become bitter. He kept moving. He forgot well.

———

Sloan heaped more and more work on Frank, which he was glad to get, and Sloan was glad to free up more of *his* time for the mail room and attend to the problems of lonely young women in the big city, particularly a girl named Annette, whom he was teaching how to give backrubs. Sloan had a sore back. But as he devoted himself to her, he failed to notice that Frank was now doing his entire job for him, and doing it quite well, and a few weeks later, Roy Jr. called Sloan in and fired him just as his rear end touched the seat.

Not long ago, he had been Employee of the Year and won a bronze statuette of Winged Victory inscribed "For Meritorious Service" and "Through Truth, We Prosper" and now he was de-horsed, eating dirt. He found Frank in the hall, waiting for lunch, and punched him in the nose. "To hell with you, you little opportunist," he said. He marched out the door and around the corner to the Red Eye Lounge, where the usual cloud of barflies, including most of the News Department, sat in the corner working on vodka slings. "To hell with it," Sloan said, tossing down a Bombaroo and chasing it with a Banshee. "Roy Sodajerk, Jr., is a liar, a tax cheat, a thief from his own family, a raging idiot, a bully, a fraud, and a buggerer of young men. He doesn't have a brain in his head. He is a greedy rapacious degenerate piece of trash and I am going to squash him like a bug. He will rue this day for years to come! I'll tell the world all about him and his vicious ways." Frank heard all this from a darkened doorway—Roy Jr. had sent him over, nose bleeding, with Sloan's last paycheck—and he thought to himself, *Don't stay in radio too long. Keep your eyes open. Something else will turn up.*

———

What turned up that spring was an actress from Milwaukee. Maria Antonio had black black hair and milk white skin and deep dark eyes, and looked like Donna LaDonna, the Girl of Studio B, must have looked in her bloom. Maria had been hired to play Corinne Archer on *Love's Old Sweet Song*, Forrest Hollister's first love's daughter who brings the lonely millionaire the news that Lally pines for him in Palm Springs. Then she became Doc Winegar's niece Dotty on *The Best Is Yet to Be*, the one who comes in from Chicago and breaks Bud's heart:

DOTTY: Frankly, we're not right for each other. Your speech embarrasses me. You talk funny, Bud.
BUD: But I've always talked like this.
DOTTY: I know. But I'm returning to Chicago in the fall. You'd never fit in there.
BUD: But I love you. Dotty, you're the sun, the moon, and the stars to me.
DOTTY: I know. I'm sorry, Bud.

Frank met her in the hallway one morning at nine o'clock. He was bounding up the back stairs two steps at a time with Roy Jr.'s mail, and saw her on the third floor landing, sitting on the concrete floor next to a bucket. "Don't mind me," she whimpered, "I'm only dying." He asked if he could help, and she said, "No. Please go. I have never thrown up with anyone except members of my immediate family." He asked what was wrong. She said, "I don't think I'm pregnant," and then looked up and grinned, to show it was a joke. The smile seemed to jar her insides, and she leaned her head over the pail and vomited three times. He put his hand on her shoulder, to show that he wasn't disgusted and that he supported her in this difficult moment. She cleared her throat and spat, *phthoo*. "That's the first time I've thrown up since I was six years old," she said thoughtfully.

Then she looked up. "Why, you're Frank White!" she said. "I know about you. You're the one who slugged Little Becky." She stood up. "Well done." Frank picked up the pail. "I'll take care of this," he said. "I hope you're feeling better. There's a couch in the Women's Bureau if you'd like—"

"Bye," she said. He studied her as she went through the door and down the hall. How perfectly she walked. A green plaid skirt.

For days, he kept running into her. He had worked at WLT for six months and never laid eyes on her and now every day, two or three times a day, there she was, black hair, big smile, and all.

They went to lunch at the Pot Pie. He learned that she was twenty and had had many boyfriends. *How many?* Lots. She said, "I like older men. They can sit and talk about themselves without demanding that you show complete interest. How old are you?" Frank told her, "Twenty." She seemed to recognize this as a lie, and to be touched by it. She put her hand on his knee. "That's nice," she said. His knee began to swell. He walked with a limp the rest of the afternoon.

He learned that she lived in two rooms upstairs in an old lady's house on Willow Street, by Loring Park, and that the old lady was deaf as a stone. "We used to dance up there at two in the morning."

"Who's we?"

"I used to have a roommate, named Jean."

"Gene?"

"Yes. Jean. She was my best friend for months but she smoked like a chimney. I tried hiding her cigarettes and it threw her into such a panic, she ripped her best jacket looking through the pockets. She smoked enough for two people, so I asked her to cut out my share, and she moved out in a huff. I tell you. You get no gratitude for trying to be a good influence on people."

The next day, he brought her a pot of weak tea with sugar and lemons before the show, and she had him massage her neck muscles to relax her. That afternoon, he was in the Green Room, reading a story in the paper about Milton Berle, when she sat down beside him. He said, "Did you know that more people see Milton Berle's television program in one night than have seen *Hamlet* in the past three-hundred-and-fifty years?" She said, "Who's your favorite movie star?"

"Katharine Hepburn." It was the correct answer, he could tell from Maria's face. "Me too," she said. "Katharine Hepburn is just exactly like how I remember my older sister when I was little. Tall and leggy and striding along and not letting anyone put one past her. When she got married, I came home from her wedding dance and bawled half the night. We shared a bedroom for all those years. I wore all her old clothes. I used her perfume. I tried to talk like her. At night we'd lie in bed and talk about how we'd go to Chicago someday and share an apartment and have jobs and go to swank nightclubs and meet men. That's where my imagination stopped: meeting men. I couldn't imagine who they'd be or why we'd want them. She married a sweet guy. They moved to Cincinatti and had two kids and then that was it for her. She gave up being interested in things. She became *dull*. I suppose he must've liked her that way. I think dullness is evil, I really do. I'm afraid of Minneapolis. I don't want to *be* like them." And then, as if she had said too much, she stood up, said goodbye, and strode out the door.

They went to a movie, about a detective who nabs a German spy in a small town in New Hampshire. When a vicious dog, fangs bared, suddenly tensed for the leap onto the detective's back, Maria squeezed against him.

He walked her home and then they walked around the park, the moon shining on the quiet pond, the empty tennis courts, the horseshoe pits with their upright posts reminding him of what he was all too aware of. "You're my lucky horseshoe," he said.

"Thanks," she said. "Frank, do you think I should change my name to Anderson?"

"Why give up a great name like Antonio?"

"People think Italian girls are loose."

Are you? he thought. "I'll tell you a secret. My real name is Francis With. It sounded so wispy. I changed it for good luck."

But the good luck was her. She wove her fingers into his and looked him deeply in the eye. "I want to know you," she said. *Well, okay, that can be arranged.* She turned her face up to be kissed, and he kissed her on the lips and felt a flick of her tongue. "Again," she said, so he kissed her again.

They ate lunch together in his little office, sandwiches that he made the night before. He stood in the control room during her shows. The massages moved into the shoulder region and along the spine and under the wings. When he moved forward, along the rib cage, she pressed her arms to her sides, but glanced back and smiled, as if to say, "Not now, but soon."

When Dotty returned to Chicago, having put a tremor in Bud's voice and glamored up the poky people of Green Corners, Maria moved to *Friendly Neighbor* where Dad felt a young actress might settle Marjery down. She was taking to whooping it up during commercial breaks—lighting a smoke and rolling her eyes and saying, "Boy, this bra itches," or "I wonder what folks would say if they knew Little Becky's on the rag." Dad had to ask Faith what that meant.

Worse yet, Marjery suffered from the giggles. The word "cheese" set her off once and once Dad said, "Hunger makes the beans taste better," and she almost blew a gasket. Faith clapped a hand over the girl's mouth and hauled her out of the studio—Dad was reminiscing about his late mother at the moment, and had just mentioned how hard she had had it with six children during a drought: hardly the time for Little Becky to shriek and guffaw—so they improvised for a few minutes, until Marjery got control of herself and came back into the studio, and her next line was "Pass the beans, Dad," and she dropped to the floor by the microphone, tears streaming down her cheeks, her face contorted in ugly helpless laughter. All because she remembered the lines:

> Order in the court—
> The judge is eating beans.
> His wife is in the bathtub,
> Counting submarines.

So Patsy had to remember never to put beans in another *Friendly Neighbor* script, which she added to a long list of forbidden Becky words, such as "chicken," "crabs," "prunes," "turkey," "spaghetti," "meatballs," and "pickle."

The next day, Dad, still thinking of his mother's sad life, remarked, "Well, everyone is the judge of their own luck," and Becky fell down foaming at the mouth again.

So Maria came into the story as beautiful Delores DuCharme, whose car broke down south of Elmville, near Round Lake, en route to Detroit. It was a sunny day and birds sang as she walked along and over the hill and saw Dad and Tiny in the skiff, fishing, about the same moment they spotted her.

TINY: Laws, Misteh Dad, but dey's a gal oveh dere who am jes' 'bout de purtiest lil gal dese ole peepers has evah peeped 'pon—an if'n she ain't lost, den mah name ain't Tiny.
DELORES (OFF): Yoo-hoo.

They brought her home for lunch, naturally, it being lunchtime, and she sat down with Dad and Jo and Becky and Frank, Tiny having excused himself ("I'se gots to go do sumpin' 'bout the Widda's terminites, boss. Dey's gettin' just fierce oveh dere"), and Jo gave Delores a bowl of tomato rice soup and a toasted cheese sandwich. "Sure is nice to have Frank back," said Dad. (Frank had been gone for six months, prospecting in Alaska, because Randolph Cleveland, who had been Frank for all those years, had upped and gone to Chicago, and the new Frank, Dale Snelling, Faith's husband, who had been playing gangsters and foreigners since the demise of *Sunnyvale*, didn't sound much like the old one. Six months, Patsy thought, should be long enough for the folks to forget.) "Thanks," said Dale. "So what do you do, Miss DuCharme?"

She was a dancer, she said, looking for work in a roadhouse near the Motor City and also looking for her boyfriend Bo, who'd gone there to seek employment in the manufacturing industry.

"What kind of dancer?" asked Becky.

"Hush, eat your lunch," said Jo.

"Exotic," said Delores.

The actors looked up. *What did she say?* They checked the script.

It said "exotic" all right.

On the fourth floor, Ray, rising from his chair to go upstairs for a nap, heard "exotic" and sat down again.

"Oh, that's interesting," said Dad. "My late mother loved to dance, but there wasn't much exotic about the polka, I guess. Not if you're from Windom."

"I dance on tabletops in smoky bars full of truck drivers who like to reach up and stick dollar bills in my clothes," said Delores, hesitantly.

"In your pockets?" asked Dale. "They put money in your pockets?"

"Sort of. And they like to put money up here. And down there."

WLT performers were strictly cold readers, one and all. The notion of rehearsals was foreign to them. It was a matter of pride to stroll into the studio in time to pour a cup of coffee, drink it, pick up the script, glance at it, and when the red light went on, do what the words said to do. You answered the door, you pulled the trigger, you leaped from the ledge, you walked to the mailbox or to the gallows or to the kitchen—you wept, you thundered, you murmured, you gasped, whatever it said, and when the light went off, you chucked the script into a wastebasket and got the hell out.

And now, drifting down the stream of dialogue that had suddenly become a rapids, the cast backpedalled, reading slowly . . . with long pauses . . . trying to read ahead. "My late mother used to earn money dancing, but only in polka contests there in Windom. She won $25 once," said Dad, saying each word separately as his eye scanned to the bottom of the page and the top of the next. *When would he need to abandon script and maybe tell a story about his mother—"Speaking of my mother reminds me of the time . . ." But what time did it remind him of? What mother stories had he told recently? And would Maria know enough to abandon script too? or when he finished the mother story would she pick up again with men stuffing dollar bills in her pants?*

"Sometimes you get $200 a night dancing on tables."

"Gosh," said Little Becky. "You get that much just to dance?"

"You can if you dance like men like to see you dance. You do the hootchi-koo and a little this and a little that and then you go sit with them for a few minutes. Have a drink. Talk. Hold their hand. Then maybe if they're nice—"

Dad swallowed. And then Tiny came back. "Misteh Dad, I'se finished wid dem terminites an' I'se wondrin' if'n you got sump'n fer me to do here. Uddawise I'll jes' mosey back to th' Lake."

It was Wilmer, Dad's brother, trying to be helpful and offer them an escape. The actors looked up. *What did he say?* There stood Wilmer—without a script. *Wilmer is winging it.* Maria looked to Dad. But Faith spoke first. "Maybe you could take a look at my—at my—clematis, Tiny."

"Yo cli—what?"

Now Homer the sound effects man perked up his ears. He had been clinking coffee cups, rattling silverware, slurping soup, all easy business, but what in blazes is a clematis and what sound does it make? He thought, *whirr.*

"My clematis. It's on the back porch."

Homer looked around behind him. *Shit, where's the*

screen door? It's summertime. All I've got here is a big heavy oak door and a creaking door and a car door and a jail cell door.

"No sense rushing out there to prune a *vine*—it'll wait," said Dad. Then he heard a body fall. It was Becky. The reference to prunes had felled her and she lay in a heap, her body racked with giggles.

"Sit down and have a cup of coffee," offered Dale. It was all he could think of to say, Faith having knelt down to stifle the child. But her sobbing could plainly be heard. "Little Becky's kind of allergic to that clematis. It makes her wheeze. That's why Jo wants it trimmed back, I guess," added Dale.

"That's right!" Faith called up from the floor.

Roy Jr. and Frank and Ray all arrived in the control room in time to hear Dad say, "Well, anyway, we're pleased you dropped in, Miss Douche."

"That's not her right name, is it?" whispered Ray.

Dad was perspiring. He held up two fingers. *Page 11,* he mouthed. *Last page.* They were on page 9. The others flipped ahead to page 11, except for Wilmer who misunderstood the signal and went back to page 2, the fishing scene. Wilmer arrived there first.

"Ah sho recommends you puts a new wum on dat hook, Misteh Dad. Ah blieves yo fust wum is near 'bout daid."

Dale didn't hear him. "Jo, this is the best coffee cake you've ever made, I swear," he said. "But I'd give anything to have a piece of your jelly roll."

"Miss DuCharme," said Dad, "let me show you to your bedroom."

And the organ came up with the closing theme, and Reed did the back-announce, and the studio was still. The actors stood stock still. "Jesus H. Christ," said Dale.

And that was what made Roy Jr. come striding red-faced into the studio. "Never say a word near a microphone that you wouldn't want to go out on the air. Never," he said. Itch the engineer had been so convulsed by "Miss Douche" he forgot to flip the mike switch and so "Jesus H. Christ" went out to the friends and neighbors in radioland and so did Faith's "Get your fat little butt off the floor and out the door," spoken to Marjery but, as Jo speaking in Elmville, it could only have been directed at Delores.

"Don't ever curse in a studio. Don't ever assume a microphone is off. You're professional radio people. You know that."

"Well," said Dad, mopping his face, "it could've been worse. At the moment, I don't see how, though."

And then Mr. Odom popped in to say that Patsy had called to apologize—some pages got left in the script by mistake. "Some mistake," said Roy Jr. He turned to Ray. "She's your problem. I can't do anything with her. You hired her and you're keeping her here, for reasons that have nothing to do with radio, if you ask me. Fine. Do what you like. But don't ask me to manage a situation that's unmanageable."

"Patsy Konopka is a *hell* of a writer," said Mr. Odom.

Roy Jr. turned and cocked his head and blinked. "I didn't ask for your advice, Mr. Odom."

"If you don't want my advice, then don't talk about Patsy Konopka in front of me."

"Patsy is fine," said Dad, "but she isn't writing for our audience. I don't know who she's writing for."

Ray said he would talk to Patsy, and Roy Jr. went off to call up Marjery's mother to tell her he was giving Marjery six weeks' notice.

Listening to the last minutes of *Friendly Neighbor* from the control room, Frank didn't find it funny. Not at all. The actors in the studio looked pale and helpless, and Maria trembled for ten minutes after it was over. He hugged her. She laughed and then she cried. "I'm going to get fired," she said. "They'll throw me out on the street because I played the bad woman. You wait and see."

"No, they won't," he said. "It's only a part in a play."

"I might as well pack up and go back to Milwaukee," she said. "Oh, Frank. Just when I was getting to like you!"

So Frank ran, three stairs at a bound, up to Roy Jr.'s office. He was still talking to Mrs. Moore.

"Marjery's a little old for ten. She's been ten for almost fifteen years and she was fourteen when she started," he said.

"Maybe Little Becky ought to grow up," said the mother, hopefully.

"I don't think she can grow that fast. So I think she ought to go back to her dad. All good things come to an end, and this is one of them. Anyway, I think that Jo and Frank are going to have a baby."

"I'd like to talk to Ray about this."

"Honestly, Ray doesn't deal with this anymore. He turned this all over to me, Mrs. Moore, and I don't like to be the one to have to tell you, but I am the one, and you just have to accept it."

"I think that if people knew—if the listeners out there were *aware*—that you are getting ready to dump Little Becky like she was a sack of potatoes—I think there'd be a real uproar out there if people knew."

"She's a popular girl, don't think I don't know it. But I think the listeners would be a little surprised if they knew that Marjery's twenty-nine years old."

"I know those people, Mr. Soderbjerg. I think they'd be behind us."

"I'm not taking a vote, Mrs. Moore. I've made up my mind."

"We'll see about that."

Roy Jr. hung up and said, "Had your lunch?" and he and Frank strolled over to the Pot Pie. Then Roy Jr. said, "Naw, let's splurge." And they walked downtown to Charley's. They ordered oysters and prime rib steaks. Frank had never eaten oysters before, and when the plates arrived, he thought of asking, "Is it *raw?*" and then thought, "Naw, of course not." And ate all six of his, doused in red sauce. He was in love with Maria. He could eat anything.

CHAPTER 27

Be There

The waitress at Charley's was one who believed in striking up meaningful conversations with customers and after she brought their steaks, they got to hear her thoughts about the criminals running loose in Minneapolis. She thought there were too many and that politicians were in cahoots with them and held back the police from making arrests. She said it was getting so that the streets were too dangerous for a girl to walk, even in broad daylight. She felt that a lack of religious faith was behind this trend. She said, "A person who goes to church on Sunday isn't going to come around and rob you on Monday."

"No," said Roy Jr. "If he is going to do it, he'll probably do it on Sunday."

"Well," she said, "it's been nice talking to you. Let me know if you care for dessert."

The moment she sidled away, Frank leaned forward and said, "Mr. Soderbjerg, I have to ask a favor of you. Maria Antonio, who was on the show today, she's a friend

of mine, and she's a wonderful person. I hope you're not
going to fire her because of that. It wasn't her fault——"

Roy Jr. stuck up his hand. "Don't give it another
thought. It wasn't that big a problem."

"She's worried that you'll cancel the show or something."

"Not a chance. It was an accident. Put it out of your
mind." Then he said, "Which one is your friend?" Frank
told him. "Oh," said Roy Jr. "The one Patsy Konopka
is trying to get me to fire." He laughed. "Poor Patsy
doesn't care for Catholics, I think. She told me your friend
is a gold-plated whore. Interesting terminology."

"Who is Patsy Konopka?"

The older man smiled and looked at the ceiling, as if
about to launch into a story, but then he thought better
of it and frowned. "She's our head writer. An old friend
of Ray's. Sits over at the Antwerp and cranks out six shows
a day, believe it or not. It certainly isn't Broadway material
but people like it. But she gets sloppy. Can't keep the
characters straight. Dad's had six different next-door neighbors in the last month."

Frank thought he would look up this Patsy Konopka
and see what he could do to change her mind about
Maria——but Roy Jr. was saying, "No, this episode today
——I tell you, all the worst things that happen in radio
aren't as bad as you think. The only unforgivable sin is
to not show up. Punctuality. The first law of radio: BE
THERE. Remember that. The corollary of that law is: a
radio man should own two alarm clocks and have a third
available. Not many people were ever fired for not being
brilliant, but the list of brilliant guys who wound up as
shoe salesmen because they came late for the shift is as
long as your leg.

"We had a fellow once named Burns L. Strout who
overslept one snowy morning and as a result *The Early*

Birds wasn't there at five a.m., not the theme song, 'Bugle Call Rag,' or the cheery voice saying, 'Morning, early birds! And a beeeeeyoootiful morning it is too!' The voice that was supposed to say this was in the sack, dead to the world, having been out until three a.m. climbing into a whiskey bottle. Burns had a problem of wanting to be two things at once: a responsible decent person who brings sunshine into the lives of thousands *and* a crazy man who feels the throb of the midnight tom-toms and goes coursing out into the crowded avenues of the great hairy metropolis to seek the woman of his dreams.

"On this particular night, I believe, he had had to hire a girlfriend, so he was absolutely broke and came home to his slough of an apartment and passed out in a pile of old clothes and woke up late with a hangover that felt like his head had melted and came high-tailing it into the studio at 5:07 with terror in his watery blue eyes and hurled himself into the chair like a sinking ship, a sheaf of weather reports and livestock summaries and news headlines in hand, and he looked at his engineer Itch—the guy you just met—his real name is Mitch but he was always a little late with the microphone, so we called him Itch—a joke he never got, by the way—and Burns hit the chair, landing on his hemorrhoids big as Concord grapes, and his brains sloshed, he moaned and said, "Jesus, this light is bright. Why in flaming hell can't I hear the music, you asshole?" The reason he couldn't, of course, was that the microphone was on. Itch had put him on the air the moment his butt hit leather.

"Well, as you can imagine, out in radioland, all the friends and neighbors woke up in a flash. There they were, dithering around the kitchen, when suddenly this deep horrible voice three feet away says *asshole*. It's like the escaped rapist is sitting by the toaster holding a shotgun on them. Then they heard this awful breathing, and a bout of throat-clearing, like a swamp being drained, big gobs of phlegm rattling—and then he retched, a big dry heave—and you can imagine out in the friends' and neighbors' kitchens, where the good folks are fixing breakfast, the sound of a man retching on the radio is pretty darn disgusting.

"Well, Itch leaped out of the chair and waved at Burns that *Your microphone is ON!* and Burns, who was operating in dim shadows, looked up and said, 'Oh fuck you.' The friends and neighbors looked up from their coffee. I happened to have just turned into the parking lot and I made it from the car to the control room in six seconds. Burns saw me the moment he realized what had happened. He didn't say a word, and neither did I. He got up and went out the door and became a shoe salesman.

"That was six years ago. He's still down at Thom McAn, kneeling and smelling the feet, and you're here in radio, Frank, which is preferable. Just remember the rule: **BE THERE.** And never curse around a microphone. Never."

"Did you get a lot of complaints that time?"

"If we'd apologized for it, we'd've gotten an avalanche, but without an apology, people couldn't be sure they had really heard what they thought they heard. It was five a.m. People don't exactly *hear* the radio at that hour. It's more like a warm thing that hums and reminds you of your mother."

"Did this happen to take place in Studio B?" asked Frank.

"Of course," said Roy, Jr.

———

Ray found Patsy at the Antwerp, banging away at the typewriter, her radio blaring, a band playing a polka—he had to pound hard on the door, ten heavy thumps, before she opened it.

"I'm sorry, Ray," she said. "I heard the show. Cripes, I'm embarrassed as I can be. Come in and have a drink." Ray sat down in a leather chair and accepted a shot of bourbon. (*Who do you keep bourbon around for?* he thought.)

"I am burning the candle at both ends trying to keep all these shows and all these small towns going," she said, "and—do you know how *taciturn* Midwesterners are? No, you don't unless you have to write scripts about them. Sometimes these buggers just plain *won't talk*. So you got to keep pushing them and poking them and sometimes it gets *so hard*, writing late at night and you don't feel like doing anything but going to a movie, and to keep yourself awake, you write a few pages of risqué stuff, and then, of course, you yank it out, but these pages in *Friendly Neighbor* weren't quite *bad* enough to catch my eye and I left them in by mistake. I feel dumber than dirt about it, but there you are. Care for another shot?" Yes, he said, another shot would be nice.

"What sort of risqué stuff do you write that *does* catch your eye?"

"A few weeks ago, I was starting to grind out another Hoho"—*Hoho* was short for *Hills of Home*—"and I looked down and I was already on page 12. I couldn't believe it. So I read back, and I'd written ten pages in my sleep! Frieda had murdered Fritz—sunk a hatchet in his head as he sat and mumbled over his fried eggs—and Babs had buried the body and gone out and shanghaied the grocery boy—walked up to him in produce and grabbed his head and put it between her breasts. Then they went in back and made love. Then Fritz walked in and so she shot him this time, the big lug, and stuffed him in the freezer and she and the stock boy hurried off to the dairy section and they humped some more. Then there was a commercial break, and then I woke up."

"Maybe you ought to take naps. You could come up to the Ogden—borrow my room—it's nice. On the sixth floor. You can see all downtown from there."

"You took me up there once, years ago. Remember?"

Ray grinned. "Of course. A man always remembers the girls who said no."

"You're a dirty old man, Ray. Funny you should come over here to complain about a script of mine. The dirtiest line in that script was a nursery rhyme compared to your life, Ray."

Ray smiled. "I have wasted half my life among boring men," he said, "but I have yet to regret a moment I have ever spent alone with a beautiful woman. All my life people kept telling me I'd be sorry but, hell, I haven't been, never, not for a moment, except I *was* sorry that you never would come to New York with me. That's all. I'm still sorry about that."

"You're too late," she said. "I am spending my nights alone with a beautiful man."

Ray winced. He shook his head. "I envy him. Don't tell me who he is or I'm liable to shoot him." He said that maybe he would like to have another shot of bourbon.

She went to get him one. "You didn't used to drink so much," she called from the kitchen.

"I'm scared. I don't think I'm going to be around a lot longer," he said.

She stood in the doorway, hands on her hips, studying him.

"No, I try not to look too far down the road because down the road doesn't look too good. I think I got something. I hurt a lot down in my gut. And I'm scared to go to a doctor."

She sat on the arm of the chair and put her hand on his cheek and pulled his head against her hip. "Baby," she said softly, "you have to go to a doctor."

He looked up, his eyes full of tears. "Before I die, I want to make love to you," he said. "That's all the doctor I need. Then I'll be glad to die. I'll die with a smile on my lips."

She shook her head. "Baby, I've got to get you to a doctor."

"Come to bed with me and afterward I'll do anything you like."

No, she said. She was sorry. She liked him. But she valued her self-respect and—

"You talk like a fourteen-year-old Methodist," he said.

She took her hand away from his cheek. She stood up and told him to get the hell out.

"I didn't mean to offend you," he said. She steered him toward the door and opened it for him. She said, "I didn't mean to *be* offended. But I am."

She was listening late that night when Frank came home. He drank two glasses of water, peed, took off his shoes, and put a sheet in his typewriter and pounded away for ten minutes. His typewriter sat on the kitchen table, whose legs sat on a beam, apparently, because his pounding made her silverware rattle.

Dear Daddy, he wrote, *I have learned four important things this week. One is the value of Trust. I want people to trust me. It's the only way for a person to do a job. Trust MUST be won. A man MUST be the same person to everybody, you can't swing with the breeze. No. 2: The WAY to win trust is to LISTEN and to let people know that you DO listen. The way to do that is: RESPOND exactly to what people actually say. NOT to be smart and make wisecracks. NOT to show off with big words. NEVER be sarcastic. I*

am determined that I WILL BE a good listener. No. 3:
Avoid profanity and smutty talk—it CHEAPENS your com-
pany and it KILLS TRUST. No. 4: Be CHEERFUL.
SMILE if possible. And I do. I have met a wonderful girl.
Love from your loyal son, Frank.

CHAPTER 28

Lily

Ray was glad to see 1950, he told Frank. The old decade had worn him out and the change would be a tonic. "We'll get rid of a few more old bastards and some more girls will become legal age," he said cheerily. For New Year's Eve, he opened his house, Villa Fred, and threw a WLT party—Vesta was in Florida, speaking at the Tampa Chautauqua on "What Radio Can Do to Change Minds." Slim and The Blue Movers played jitterbug music and even Dad Benson got tipsy. Late in the evening, he almost fell on Frank and Maria, who had scootched down behind a divan and were necking like a house afire. He gazed down at Maria, her top three buttons unbuttoned and Frank in a lather, and cried: "Good! Go to it! Stolen pleasures are the sustenance of life!" They dressed immediately.

It was 2 a.m. when Mr. Odom dropped them off at Maria's boarding house. "You go on," Frank told him. "I'll catch up." He guided her to the front door, and she stopped and put her arms around him and looked sleepily up at him. "What do you dream about?" she asked.

"You."

"Liar." She put her head on his shoulder. "I have such a good time in dreams. We sit around and laugh and eat plates and plates of spaghetti. I don't know any of the people but we have a wonderful time, and they understand me completely and they don't mind a bit."

"Can I come up with you?"

She kissed him. "I'm glad you want to," she said. "Good night."

<hr>

It was a big week. Vince Upton said he wanted to quit *Up in a Balloon* and Ray talked him out of it. "But I only meant to work here for a *summer*," said Vince. "That was twenty years ago. I wanted to earn a few bucks and take Sheridan to Mexico." He turned to Frank. "Twenty years I've been riding around in the damn balloon, Frank, and I've never been anywhere." Ray walked to the window, looked at the Foshay Tower, and gave him the Speech. Frank had heard it six times before. *These are hard times. Radio's in trouble. We're a family. We have to hold the ship together. We need you. It's your decision but remember that it affects each one of us. People here look up to you. I know it's hard. But if you give up, it makes it that much harder for the rest of us to keep on going.* Vince stayed.

<hr>

Ray bought a television the next day. He saw it in a store window on Harmon Place as he walked to work. His doctor was making him walk and Ray was trying to avoid it. "There is nothing between here and there that I want to see," he said, but then he came upon a crowd peering into the store window. *General Television & Tires* said the sign. There were six screens inside, and he stopped and watched. One screen showed the head of a blonde woman talking, then a chimpanzee drinking coffee, then a man pointing to a chart, then a car crashing into a wall, and the other five screens showed the crowd on the sidewalk. An immense camera on a tripod took the picture. A dozen people stood in close and watched themselves on the screen and another thirty squeezed in and looked over their shoulders. There was no microphone and nobody said a word. Ray went in and bought one from an old coot in a red checked suit. "You're lucky, that's the last one on the floor," he said. "We'll see about that. Have it sent to my office," said Ray.

The television was as big as an icebox and the screen was the size of a dessert plate. They trundled it in and set it against the window and pulled the shade. A pinpoint of light appeared in the center of the screen, which a minute later blew up into a fuzzy picture, a man behind a desk talking, but Ray couldn't get sound. He turned the volume all the way up and only got a loud hum. "Here, make this work," he said to Frank.

Roy Jr. was there and Ethel Glen and Uncle Art, and Dad Benson came in, and some people hung back in the doorway, as if the thing might explode. Frank swivelled the antenna and turned a knob that made the picture flip over and over, and he made it go black and then bleached white. Then he turned the channel knob a notch and BLAAAAAAUGHHH—the thing blared so loud he jumped and the people in the door ducked away. He turned it down. "There," he said. "Just a matter of adjusting it."

Ray sat behind his desk and Roy Jr. perched on the desk, his arms folded, and Art and Dad took the couch and Ethel leaned against the wall, then sat on the floor, and the people in the doorway edged into the room, a few and then more and then about ten. Everyone was quiet. The man on the screen was reading the news, apparently. He looked up as he finished each sentence. He was young, wore a dark sportcoat, had a crewcut and horn-rimmed glasses, and once in awhile he glanced off to his right, nervously, as if someone were holding a gun on him. There was a clock on the wall behind him and a plant on the desk. It looked to be dead.

The news seemed to be about Truman and the Republicans in Congress and a steel strike and the crash of an Eastern Airlines plane in Washington, the President embroiled, people had been killed, but nothing in the news was half as interesting as the young man, not that he *was* interesting but that he was on television, and that was fascinating. Once he licked his lips, and Ray said, "Look. He's nervous." He licked them again.

His script lay on the desk and he took off the pages one by one with his right hand and then, suddenly, for no perceptible reason, *he used his left.* His eyes appeared dead: when he looked into the camera, he didn't look all the way in. When he came to the end and looked up and wished everyone a good day and smiled a grim smile, it was a little disappointing. *It would've been something if he'd knocked the plant off the table*, Frank thought.

A commercial for Chrysler was next, and it was good —a man in a tux walking from car to shining car and by each car a beautiful woman stood, in an evening gown with long white gloves, and she stroked the car a long loving caress and smiled a sexy smile as she stepped back and gestured down toward its underside. It would've been something if her dress had fallen off but you didn't really need it to, she was all right with it on. Another commercial, for a headache powder, and then a puppet show, a pig and a goose and a horse, and behind the backdrop, a man doing squeaky voices. "Oh boy!" cried the pig. "Heyyyyy!" whinnied the horse. The goose bit them both and they bit back. Then a clown came on and scolded the goose. "What do you say, boys and girls?" he cried. "Should we spank Goosey-Loosey?" There were forty children packed into a little grandstand and they looked wild, demented, they screamed "Yaaaaaay" so loud you could see their tonsils. They punched each other and jumped up and down and waved like maniacs when the camera came at them. Ray went out for a cup of coffee and when he came back, a western was on. "Turn it up," he said.

A posse rode through the woods and along the river, a long line of riders snaking through the trees. A lone rider raced far ahead, a man in a fringed buckskin jacket who kept looking over his shoulder and urging his horse on— but did not whip him or pull out his six-gun—just rode hell-for-leather and then stood in the saddle and leaped for a tree branch and hauled himself up into the foliage a moment before the posse swept beneath him. Then he jumped down, whistled, and his horse trotted out of the underbrush. He mounted and rode back toward town. There, at that moment, four masked men were tying a struggling woman to a chair. A gag was in her mouth but she tore it out and yelled "Lemme go!" The leader of the four laughed a rich, evil laugh. "Lucky'll be here, he's on his way, you just wait and see!" she said, fists clenched, fighting them off for a moment. The leader chortled. "Lucky cain't come. Lucky's goin' to a necktie party," he said. "And he's the honored guest!" The four of them laughed as if it were the funniest joke they'd ever heard in their lives. She slipped from their grasp and tore into the next room and barred the door. Lucky came galloping hard along the river, bent low, his head against the out-stretched neck of the big palomino. They hit the river full-speed and disappeared in the plume of water and bounded up the other shore and galloped away into the trees. The girl locked the door. The leader of the four stepped back and drew his revolver and blasted the lock.

"Have you seen Dad?" asked Dale Snelling in the doorway. "It's noon. We're starting the theme." Dad leaped up off the couch and careened off down the hall. Ray waved toward the radio—Frank switched it on—the voice of Reed saying, ". . . by Milton, King Seeds and as we join them today, the family is sitting around the kitchen table where Jo is fixing lunch . . ." and a soft clinking of utensils and Faith saying, "Well, I wonder where he is."

———

Up in Moorhead, Roy had looked at television too. He wrote to Ray: "Television offers the aural quality of a telephone and the video quality of a very poor snapshot, and to produce this requires an immense and unwieldy technologic apparatus, the equivalent of the brontosaurus. It will fall of its own weight. It simply will not work. It corrupts everything it touches, makes it flat and dull and empty. It is less than photography and less than radio and it combines the two to make something that is nothing but a minus. It is novelty, and it has its day, but when radio returns, when it comes for the second time, television will go the way of Smell-o-Rama. Perhaps it will have some use in hatcheries."

He is dead wrong, thought Frank when Ray showed him the letter, but Ray didn't ask him for an opinion, Ray wanted him to do a favor. "It's about my sister Lottie," he said. "You know. Lily Dale. It's her birthday. Buy her something."

Frank knew Lily Dale but not that she was Ray's sister Lottie. He only knew that when her fans showed up to visit with her, he had to make up excuses why they couldn't. She brought sunshine into their day and they wrote her faithfully and told her how wonderful her singing was, that when they heard her theme song, "Just a Little Street Where Old Friends Meet," they immediately started to feel cheerful, so they wanted to see her, of course, her oldest, dearest fans.

No, she was not able to visit. She was at the hairdresser, she was ill, she had gone shopping, she was resting. *Oh,* they said. *Well, tell her hello.*

Lily was young and lovely, coquettish, a true romantic, one of those gloriously cheerful young women who fly through life untouched by sorrow or dismay, but Lottie was fifty-four years old, big and squat, riding in a wheelchair, her face dark and bloated, her eyes black slits, her hair like wisps of moss. Cheerfulness was all she had left in the world. "Oh, don't look at me!" she cried to Frank, the first time he was assigned to help haul her upstairs. "I haven't done my hair or anything. Oh, you dear boy —what's your name? Frank White? Oh, I'll remember it. I'll remember it forever. It has the ring of true nobility. Oh, be true to me, Frank."

"Is she crippled?" he asked Gene later. "Polio," he said. "And weak ankles. One o' these days, we'll have to winch her in through the third-floor window."

And yet, she was a star, as much as anybody, and she knew it. Frank and two janitors lugged her out of the Antwerp every morning and onto the hotel loading dock in her heavy wooden caneback wheelchair and onto the freight elevator, and she smiled like it was the grand staircase of the Ritz. The thick wheels were too wide to go easily through doorways so there was plenty of grunting and janitors muttering, "Son of a bitch! This isn't going to work. Grab her leg and let's try it sideways," but she acted like the Queen of Sheba borne on the shoulders of Nubian slaves.

"What would I ever do without you, you darling darling gentlemen? My faithful, my gallant knights, O! I'll dedicate the first song to you. Oh, you are such darlings, and how can a lady repay such kindness except with a song?"

"Darling!" she cried to Gene. "Come and give us a kiss!" Gene rolled his eyes, but she paid no heed and took his jowly face in her hands and planted two soft sweet kisses on each cheek and said what a joy it was to see him. They might leave her parked in a dark corridor like a broken bicycle but the moment someone appeared around the corner, she smiled and held out her arms. "Oh darling, would you mind fetching a vase for these gardenias! Oh, that's a dear. How kind of you." She brought fresh flowers and dispensed them to those who shared her love of beauty, and she praised their new clothes, their hair, and especially their eyes. Eyes revealed the soul within, the longing for beauty. The janitors, Gene, Frank, their eyes spoke of nobility and compassion to her, they were the eyes of poets. Especially Frank.

"Oh, look at me," she cried. "Your beautiful beautiful blue eyes. I could gaze in them forever. Like mountain pools. Oh Frank, sometimes I wish you were all my own so I could look into those gorgeous blue eyes anytime I wanted to, which would be all the time, darling."

One day the chair lost a wheel and four of them had to carry her bodily upstairs to Studio A. One took her knees, one her shoulders, one her right haunch, and Frank took her left haunch. She was dead weight and slippery in her silk dress and his left hand slipped into her crotch and he said, "I'm sorry," but she said nothing, simply bore up with invincible good cheer, ever the duchess, ever regal, even with his hand between her legs and his sweaty face pressed against her immense breast, sobbing for breath, his back scraping the doorpost. He couldn't move his hand lest he lose his grip and drop her, so onward they struggled, through doors and around tight corners, and her blue dress hiked up above her fat knees, her calves in thick sleeves of fat, big blocks of blubber around her knees, her unspeakable thighs, and yet she smiled graciously, was a star. She acted like being hauled upstairs like a sack of potatoes was her biggest honor to date. If you dropped her in a pigpen, he thought, she'd hoist herself up and find something to admire in pigs.

Once she was planted in the studio, the other bearers left but Frank had to stay. He brought her a paper, candy bars, coffee, and dreaded the thought that he might have to take her to the bathroom.

"How can anyone sing in a world where such things happen? Look at this!" she cried, and thrust out a newspaper story about a herd of starving cattle in Montana, a terrible car crash and the stunned spectators looking at the overturned wreck in which three young people were killed by the westbound Empire Builder, a photo of a dead child in a foreign land, its dark eyes open—"What chance does music have in a world of such suffering, while the rest of us go about our business as if it never happened? It almost makes a person lose heart!" She cried a little, then apologized and dried her tears, and got ready to be Lily Dale.

She prepared by thinking of her mother, who died when Lottie was small, and trying to be exactly like her. Her mother, Helen, never said a bad word about anyone, always looked on the bright side, and accepted trouble and heartache and grievous pain as faint shadows in a world bathed in sunshine. Her mother died of appendicitis at the age of twenty-four. "Isn't it hard to always be cheerful?" Frank asked her. She said, "For me, yes, but, darling, my mother always wore a smile. She never let sorrow get a foothold."

John Tippy had been her accompanist since 1931, the year of her debut on WLT, and as closely as Frank could figure, the two of them had stopped talking in 1934. Tippy was a thin, pock-marked man with a blond wig that looked like a very bad hat. She brought the sheet music in a shopping bag, stacked it on the piano, Tippy arrived, took off his coat, and played it. They never looked at each other. She never mentioned having an accompanist or referred to him by name. That suited Tippy just fine. "My musicianship has deteriorated to the point where I couldn't play for a children's ballet class," he told Frank. "By accommodating myself to her voice, I lost all sense of musical phrase and rhythm. I used to be a pianist of some accomplishment, no Paderewski but I did perform the Blount Concerto No. 1 once with the Minneapolis Symphony under Oberhoffer, but I'm nothing but an old box-thumper now. A whorehouse piano-player. That's me."

Tippy was a chain-smoker and the old Steinway had a row of burn marks across the lid where he had parked his butts, and his smoking was ruining Lily's voice, according to her. "Almost twenty years I've been breathing his smoke and my voice gets croaky and by the end of the show I can hardly talk," she said, "so I gave him orders to stop, and he wouldn't, so I just don't care to have any more to do with him. Oh, Frank, I wish you played the piano. We'd make such a wonderful team."

Tippy smoked so much, he told Frank, to cover up the smell of Miss Dale's abdominal troubles. "I can tell the moment she gets cramps, she sort of grins, a death's-head grin, and she leans slightly to the left and out it comes, silent and deadly, smells like death on a bun. If you had to spend time with an old fartsack like her, you'd smoke too."

The two enemies met every morning, back to back, her

in the chair under the big boom microphone, and him sliding into the studio and onto the bench *at the last possible second,* and he played a few bars in F-major, switched suddenly to C-minor, jumped into A-flat, and she sang "Just a Street" in D-major, or sometimes in H-sharp, and chirruped "Hello, you dear dear people," and sang "The Baggage Coach Ahead," a request from the Barnums of Bigelow, and dedicated "Gently Bends the Willow" to the dear ones at the Ebenezer Home, and finally, a favorite of the Sorensens in Bagley and also for the Titteruds and the Wallace Petersons, "Backward, Turn Backward, O Time in Thy Flight." And then a "Bye everyone! Keep looking up! And remember: the way to feel happy is to *smile*. See you tomorrow!" as the evil pianist slithered at the keys, trying to throw her.

———

"It's my birthday!" she told Frank when he came through the studio door, a present from Ray in hand (a statue of a shepherdess). She wanted Frank to come for supper at her apartment at the Antwerp. She'd fix him meatloaf and potatoes, and play her Galli-Curci records. She wanted to tell Frank her life story so that when she died he could write a proper obituary. He lied and told her that he lived too far away.

"You could take a streetcar."

Well, he couldn't, not really, due to his sick mother who needed him. She invited him again the next day, and the next. He was sorry. He couldn't. Due to a friend who was in town. Due to a cold he could feel coming on. Due to tiredness. Due to a prior engagement.

And then she said, "I hear that you live in my building." So he had to go and eat dinner with her. Monday night, 7 p.m.

He asked Mr. Odom to be on the alert for sounds of struggle from Miss Soderbjerg's apartment.

"You think the lady is desperate? You could be right, Frank. I remember being in similar situations myself. You see, in a former life, I was a Lutheran pastor in North Dakota, and I—you seem taken aback, son."

"I'm flabbergasted. I thought of you as a janitor. And a caretaker."

"That's what a Lutheran pastor does, Frank. Lutherans don't require much theology, just caretaking. When God talked about believers as sheep, He was thinking of Lutherans. Anyway, I was out there on the windswept tundra, ministering to the lonesome and the outright desperate, and believe me, I was set upon by large women on a regular basis. These were farm women, big-boned, meaty women with sinewy arms and powerful haunches and quick on their feet, from years of herding animals, and something about me aroused them—I was younger then and had hair—and I'd be sitting in the kitchen drinking their coffee when suddenly they'd make a play for me. Brush against me, adjust my lapel, straighten my hair. Then they'd be leaning across me to reach for something—Oh, don't move, they'd say, and reach over for the salt and I'd feel a breast jab my arm, or they'd lean down to pour me coffee and there it is, the old mountain of love, pressed against my shoulder, and pretty soon she's all over me, arms akimbo, sitting on my lap. There's a women's trick from way back, the lap hold. Once I was saying goodbye to a woman who'd been edging around me for an hour, nudging, brushing, rubbing, and sliding, and she cries out, 'Oh, let me give you a big hug.' Well, I knew it was a hug I'd never get out of alive, and I took off running and she took off after me—around the chicken coop and the corn crib and into the barn and up to the haymow—and I was about to plunge out the haymow door and into the manure pile when I felt that hay hook grab my jacket and she hoisted me into the air and there I hung, my feet dangling down barely scraping the ground and my hands up over my head, tangled in the jacket that was hanging on the hook. I hung by my wrists for fifteen minutes while she had her way with me and it was ugly and shameful and I don't want you to ever ask me about it again, but just remember: don't let her sit on your lap. In a chase, however, I believe you have the advantage of her."

It was the most words Frank had ever heard Mr. Odom speak at once. He looked drained, as if he had used up a week's worth of language and here it was only Monday.

"Would you like to be addressed as Reverend Odom?" asked Frank.

"That would please me very much," he whispered.

Frank donned his blue jacket and a red tie and spritzed a whiff of Lilac Rémoulade behind each ear and walked down three floors. When Lily Dale opened the door, the apartment was ablaze with candles. He counted sixty. Dinner was on the table, lamb chops and tiny potatoes, and the Victrola was playing soft piano music. He bent down and kissed her on the cheek and she held on to him and gave him an embrace. "Oh, you darling," she whispered. "You beautiful darling. I do love you, and you know it, don't you."

She ate twelve lamb chops and three big helpings of potatoes and drank quite a bit of wine with dinner, which put her in a weepy mood. She sobbed into her chocolate cake and then had some cognac and brightened up a little. They sat on a green divan. She gave him a pad and a pencil to write the obituary with.

"My mother was named Helen Pointer and she was such a saint. She grew up in St. Louis, Missouri, in abject poverty, but nevertheless learned to cherish beautiful things, but I believe it was poverty that led her to marry my father, who was Norwegian. His name was Molde and it suited him well. My brothers take after him in certain ways. He was in the ice trade and it suited him well. He was a hard man. Nothing pleased him. He criticized and made fun of everything about me. *Nothing* was good enough. My only pleasure was when I sang in church. I was the alto soloist at Hennepin Avenue Methodist. It was my one moment of grace and beauty, Sunday morning, and I did that for years and then my brother Ray invited me to sing on the radio station. I remember that moment exactly. It was the moment that saved my life. Everything was so beautiful then, and people were so very kind to me, and so are you, Frank. Take me to bed."

"What?"

"I want you to take me to bed now."

And with pounding heart and panic in his brain, so that he could hardly think, he helped her into the wheelchair and pushed her through the hall toward the bedroom. He had waited so long for this moment, had rehearsed in his mind exactly how it should go, where to put his hands, what to whisper, the order of the removal of clothing, the rapid succession of thrilling moves and the seismic upheavals and the moaning and shouting, but he had never imagined that the woman would be as *big* as this. The thought of intimacy with this immense pile of flesh— where would a person begin? And who had enough lust in his heart to be able to get the job done? *Me*, he thought. But of course she had meant no such thing. "Help me up," she said, and he did, and she took a step toward the bed and folded up on it and a moment later she was snoring.

He put a comforter over her, turned out the light, cleared the table, washed and dried the dishes, and closed the door behind him, leaving behind the pad of paper on which he had written the names of her mother and father.

CHAPTER 29

Ballpark

"One of these days I'm going to tell Roy Jr. I want a real job, not just be his office boy, I'm sick of running errands," Frank announced to Maria, and that same morning, Roy Jr. asked him, "You like baseball, don't you? You got your evenings free, right?" And Frank, who thought baseball was slower than watching paint dry and who tried to spend every evening with Maria at the movies, said, "Sure."

Roy Jr. told him to go sit in the press box for a couple weeks with Buck Steller, The Voice of the Millers, and keep score for him and see how the games were broadcast. "Buck asked for someone to keep score and go for coffee, and you're him," said Roy Jr., "but as long as you're there, keep your eyes peeled and see how much the old weasel is betting on games. You ever hear about the Black Sox scandal? Good. We don't want that here. Buck came here from Chi Town, he was the Voice of something down there before we got him. So go see what he's doing."

So Frank had to tell Maria that he was off movies for awhile. "I have very cowardly tendencies," he said. "I've got to learn to speak up for myself."

She said it was all right, that she didn't mind if he worked at night.

"You mean you didn't enjoy going to movies with me?"

"We were going to the movies every night."

"I thought you wanted to."

"I did."

"You mean you don't anymore?"

She sighed. He took her hand and apologized. A little too fulsomely, because she put her hand over his mouth. Her little warm hand with its slender fingers. He was glad to shut up.

It wasn't that Frank loved movies so much as that he liked to sit as close to her as possible. After *Friendly Neighbor* they went to a matinee of "Up a Tree" with Marie Wilson, Harold Peary, and Henry Morgan, and he put his arm around her and she laid her head on his shoulder and fell asleep. She fit perfectly against his side. He put his face in her black hair and kissed her glorious shampoo and touched her perfect little ear and listened to her peaceful womanly snore. "I love you," he whispered into her hair. On the screen, the three comics were entangled in a love triangle at a lumber camp, complicated by a flapjack-flipping contest and a log-rolling and a small black bear, and in his arms lay the love of his life, except that she maybe had a boyfriend in Milwaukee named Merle.

"A *friend*," said Maria. "A very dear friend."

"How dear?" he asked.

"I'll tell you after I see him again. He's not a letter-writer."

"How long since you've seen him? Not that it's my business."

"It can be your business. I haven't seen him for more than a year. But what difference does it make?"

"You ready to make a change?"

"Change from what? He's a *friend*."

"Not a boyfriend?"

"We were very close at one time."

Merle was an actor too, that was where they met, she said. They went to acting school together. *Did you sleep together?* he wondered. Actors did, all the time. Look at Hollywood. But, being actors, they didn't know their true feelings as other people do. Look at all the divorces. Actors were gypsies, they never knew where the jobs would pop up or when, so they had to suck up to people all the time, grin and kiss and toss their handsome heads and flatter each other up one side and down the other, it was their job to, but actors were also down to earth and looked out for each other and they were free spirits. This one was. She was so different from other women, she was like a different gender. When you were with Maria, she was utterly *present*, alert, nose to the wind. When she looked at you, you were the only man in the world, bathed in blue light.

Outside the Bijou, he took her hand, and they waited for the Nicollet streetcar and when it hove into view over the hill and came screeching along, sparks flying from the trolley arm, he kissed her. And breathed, and kissed her again.

"I do love you in my own way," she said, and kissed him a third and sweeter time, and hopped aboard.

He rolled the sentence around in his mind as he walked to the ballpark. He didn't know how to read her kisses, she being an actress, a professional kisser, so to speak, and this made no sense either: how could you love somebody in your own way? Love isn't up to you. You don't decide it. Love is love.

Nicollet Field was an old green woodpile of a ballpark, one city block paved with grass, with the pavilion on the southeast corner and bleachers strung out north and west and the green board fence beyond, and in straightaway center field, a four-story apartment building where dim tiny figures moved through the rooms. Nobody stood at their windows and watched, but then the Millers were not a longball team. They were a foul ball team. Heavy chicken wire protected the press box high above home plate, and night after night, as Frank sat up there, wedged in tight between Buck Steller and his pal, The Pressbox Padre, Father John Ptashne, Frank looked beyond the bright green field toward the center-field apartments, the glow of windows, and wished he were in a dark room with Maria.

The press box perched atop the grandstand, a shack on a cliff, and the writers sat at a rickety plank table pockmarked with thousands of cigarette burns. Under the table were coffee cans where the men urinated during the game. The wall behind them was gouged and splintered and adorned with violent and disgusting writing, everything that a person could never put in a newspaper. Above them, on the roof, the purring of hundreds of pigeons. The ceiling was barely six feet high. Every so often a writer would stand up and pound on it with both fists and the pigeons would rise in a burst of pigeon hysteria, to return to the roost a minute or so later. There was room for twelve at the table, plus Sparks the Western Union man at the end, but because certain men refused to sit next to certain others, the seating was complicated. Buck, for example, insisted on keeping an empty chair to his right, and the *Star* man couldn't be near the *Tribune* man, who had once stolen his coffee can, and the man from the *Dispatch* was kept as far from everybody as humanly possible. He was a hard drinker and became elaborately ill.

Frank had never met people quite like sportswriters, not since he was a small boy; they were cruel as a matter of art—cruelty for its own sake—and they devised elaborate pranks, such as tying a rope to the *Dispatch* man's ankle and then throwing him out of the window, and simple ones, such as pouring urine in his beer cup. They gawked at women in the seats below and scanned the rows with their field glasses to pick out good specimens. They gabbed about pussy, pussy, pussy, but they never talked about any woman in particular or recalled good times with a woman. They were most passionate about distant tiny unknowable facts—questions such as "Against which pitcher did Heinie Spartz hit his inside-the-park homer when the ball got stuck in the outfielder's glove?" or "Which Miller did *not* pitch in the famous 32-inning Uncalled Rain Game of 1919?" could get them going for hours, and a question like "Who was better, Zez Hoover or Tooty Beck?" could touch off ferocious discussions for days. But none of them looked as if he had ever swung a bat himself. And none of them looked like a ladies' man.

When Frank met Buck, the old guy reached out for a handshake and missed—he was almost blind, Frank soon saw, and that was why he needed Frank, to venture out between innings and fetch the hot dogs to sustain him through nine innings of broadcasting. The steps down to the hot-dog stand were treacherous.

Buck smelled of powerful cologne—to keep the writers away, he explained. He was a dapper old guy in a plaid jacket and a green tie, which he tucked into his shirtfront, between the fourth and fifth buttons. He kept a cold cigar plugged into the left corner of his mouth, and talked around it, his gray brush moustache riding up and down under his hooked nose, hooded eyes, arched eyebrows, and gray snap-brim hat.

As near as Frank could piece together the story of Buck Steller over the next month, he came from Colorado, an old cowpuncher, who had arrived in Chi Town (via Nashville, where he had killed a bunco artist in a fistfight) aboard a B&O freight without a spare pair of underwear and walked straight west to Tony Studs's Bar in Cicero and shoved aside the gunsels at the door and sat down with the boys in the boiler room and eight hours later, $14,000 richer, he pushed back his chair and walked to the Palmer House. He slept for three days, and a week later was flat broke again—the best week of his life! Everything the best! Oysters and steaks, wine and whiskey, a penthouse suite, banks of fresh roses, and a tall dark lady named Pasqual who could turn a man inside out. Buck went through the simoleons like a hot knife through butter. Soon he headed back to Cicero to reload but a big genial fellow named Gino took hold of his elbow and said to lay off, that Tony Studs did not like to see greed on the part of newcomers. Gino spoke softly and carried a cannon on his hip, and as he spoke, he smoothed out Buck's lapels and straightened his tie. Buck said, "Fine. What Tony Studs wants, he's got. I'm gone." He headed for the North Side, won a little there, and finally talked his way into The Game at the Drake Hotel, in a room eighty feet long overlooking the Lake, though Buck didn't notice that until six hours later when "I was down so far that if I jumped out the window I'd fall up" but twenty hours later he had collected a pile of chits a yard high and that's how he came to become The Voice of the Cubs on WGN, because so many of those chits belonged to Mr. Phil Wrigley, who owned the club. He said, "Steller, here's my personal check for sixty-eight thousand dollars. When you're done spending it, come see me about a job," and two weeks later he made Buck his broadcaster, which lasted three years, until a chewing-gum underling who resented Buck's heavy fan mail and way with the ladies fired him.

That was Buck's version. Arnold Dingell of the *Star* said, "Buck Steller, a.k.a. Ernest Twiff, was an old cigar butt from the Chicago *Trib* copy desk who landed the WGN job when the able-bodied went off to the war. The Cubs fielded a team of gimps and cripples and dingleberries and they stuck Twiff behind the microphone. He was fired on V-E Day. Ask anybody on the Cubs."

But this was Minneapolis, a Triple-A town, and the Cubs didn't play here, so who could you ask? Buck never mentioned having worked at a paper. To him, newspapers were fish wrap, and the scribes and the Pharisees who sat poking at their typewriters in the press box were nothing but sore losers. Nobody cared what they wrote. The game was all over by the time the paper came out. Buck sat at the microphone, taking a paintbrush to the game, making the Millers into giants who waged war with blazing fastballs against an arsenal of bats, the merciless sun beating down or black storm clouds threatening. If Buck spotted a kid hanging over the railing by the dugout, he'd make the kid an orphan with a rare blood disease or a gimpy leg. The players looked at that kid, wiped the tears from their eyes, glared at the enemy, and vowed to decimate them. Hatred burned in the dugout. Old grudges flared up. Revenge was always uppermost in their minds. The Millers played for the love of the game and the good people of the Midwest, but they were human too, and not to be trifled with.

———

The writers snickered and hooted at him—it was pure green envy, he told Frank. He got one hundred letters a week, and they got none except for complaints that the paperboy was heaving the Daily Whosis up on the porch roof. By the time a writer got into print, the game was yesterday's mashed potatoes. No wonder they were so bitter and vengeful.

Blindness seemed to improve Buck's powers of narration. He could make out shapes and shadows, evidently, and follow the sound of the play, and was free to invent the rest, to elaborate and give it weight and color. "And Fisher leans back on the mound and he kicks toward the sky and reaches back and *hurls* the fastball. And Dusty *jumps* on it and sends a sizzling grounder *off* the lanky left-hander's glove—Ouch! that stung! Fisher drops to his knees! and the ball *shoots* up *through* the hole, Davis missing it by a half-inch as he *lunges* headlong in the grass, and out to left-centerfield it merrily rolls as Ginter comes charging around to third safely, and Dusty wisely holds up at first, though he made the big turn, challenging Barger's arm in center, trying to draw the throw—there's been bad blood between those two for *years* but I guess I don't need to tell you *that*," Buck hollered, taking a fairly routine single and making it into a Play that made the listener perk up his ears.

The writers thought this was one of the dizziest things they had heard. They cackled and wheezed and sometimes took a wire coat hanger and tried to hook Buck's microphone line with it and yank him off the air. Buck had no engineer, just himself and a microphone and a cord that he clipped onto a phone line. If a writer knocked him off the air, Buck bided his time, waiting for revenge, waiting for the enemy to let down his guard, waiting for a big inning below to distract him and then, bingo, the man had an earful of guano. Buck was blind but his aim was sure.

He looked forward to road games, when he had a chance

to shine—WLT couldn't afford the long-distance line charges so Buck did his play-by-play from the studio, reconstructing a big colorful game from the skinny little facts that came in over the tickertape. The tape might read: *Ball 3-2*—and Buck would say: "And McPherson is ready. He glares over at Reedy on third—oh, what history in that glance! what depths of frustration!—and now he winds up, and throws a high inside fastball that sends Husik sprawling in the dirt. He jumps up! It looks as if he may charge the mound! But he thinks better of it, and steps back into the box. Three balls, two strikes, and now McPherson is looking in for the sign, getting ready to deliver again."

The engineer supplied the sounds of booing, cheering, and crowd chatter, from transcriptions, and Buck made the crack of the bat or the smack of the ball in the catcher's glove, and at least once a game, when the tickertape read: *Foul—No play*—Buck would holler, "And Dandy sends a high high foul ball straight back—LOOK OUT BOYS!—into the press box!" And he'd pound on the table a few times and drop some tin cans and rattle a walnut in a popcorn box. "Oh boy! OH BOY! Wish you'd seen that one, folks! Ha-ha! All these old fat writers hitting the deck and diving under their typewriters—hee hee hee! Yes sir, you could hear the jowls flapping on that one! Oh boy! The fear etched on their faces! Oh, they look like they could use a clean pair of knickers now—ha ha ha! Yes sir! Smells like somebody dropped the whiskey bottle! Oh boy! That was worth coming all the way to Indianapolis for!"

The writers heard about the fouls Buck was banging their way and how they were diving for cover—"Oh boy! Old Man Dingell from the *Star* practically climbed into my lap on that one. Easy, Arnie!"—and they were laying for him when the Millers returned to Nicollet Field. They grabbed him during a fifth-inning Miller rally, with the bases loaded and nobody out, and stripped every stitch of clothing from him and threw them in the street and emptied a coffee can on his head. All the time, of course, Buck had to stay on the air, talking as if nothing was happening.

That was when he invited Fr. Ptashne from Our Lady of Mercy to join him on the broadcast. Father sat between Buck and the writers and offered comments on the game—he had a voice that could knock your hat off—and talked about his playing days at St. Lucy's back before they used gloves and about his brief career in the minors: "Yes, friends, I even had me a year of Class D ball, but then I got a better offer to catch in the Church, and that's the Big League, with Our Lord on the mound, shutting out Satan in the bottom of the 9th, score tied, bases loaded."

"You take Christ for your roommate, and you'll never regret it," said Father, looking over at the writers, and none of them cracked a smile. They looked straight ahead like they were in class. But none of them tried to pull anything with Father in the press box, and Father stayed nine innings. He had a bladder of steel.

Roy Jr. asked Frank if he had seen evidence of gambling, and Frank said, "No, I don't think Buck is a gambler. I'm sure he isn't. He's just a sharp-eyed old buzzard and we're lucky to have him." Frank brought Father John around to the Ogden to see the station—"lifelong dream of mine, radio," said Father—and to meet the boss. Father clapped Roy Jr. on the back with his big mitt. "Too much fornicating music in radio nowadays," he told Roy, "but otherwise, you run a good shop." They disappeared into the office.

Two weeks later, Father was broadcasting Mass on Sunday morning, in the dual role of celebrant and play-by-play announcer. "I now greet the congregation," he whispered into the microphone as if covering a tennis match, and then thundered, "*DOMINUS VOBISCUM.*" The microphone was mounted on a brace around his neck. "And now we're preparing the chalice, mingling a few drops of water with the wine," he confided a moment later. "And now I'm going back to the middle of the altar for the offering of the chalice. . . . and now I am blessing the incense. . . . and now I am incensing the offerings." And a few minutes later, the audience heard a couple hundred *Corpus Domini*s as he dispensed the sacraments.

━━━━━

A week after that, it was Frank's twenty-first birthday, and Buck took him to a whore. First, they went to a bar called The Backstop, around the corner from the left-field pole, and enjoyed a few boilermakers. Then Buck said, "I've got a surprise for you, a couple blocks from here, a birthday gift. From me to you, slugger." Frank thought it was a joke. He imagined that a naked girl would jump out of a cake. Buck pulled up in front of a grocery store. "Go to the side door and up the stairs and knock on Apartment B. She's expecting you," he said.

She was a skinny blonde lady named Dandy who lived in an apartment strewn with clothing in cardboard boxes. She wore a blue bathrobe and her hair was snarled. She laid him down on a tattered quilt on an Army cot and pulled his pants down. What in the world are you *doing?* he was going to ask, but by then he knew. "What a nice big guy you got here," she said in a sad voice. "Should I undress?" he said.

Nawww, takes too much time. She dropped her robe. Her skin was so pale and thin, her breasts like small turnips. She stepped out of her panties. My gosh. She squirted cream on him and lay down next to him and touched him. He kissed her and she pushed him away. She said to get on top. *You're awful big, sonny, and I ain't, so don't get too excited.* This was exciting and he pushed into her two, four, six times and groaned and out it came. *My, aren't we horny today? Was that nice?* Yes, it really was. Thank you very much. She wiped him off with a cold rag and went in the toilet. He guessed it was time to go. "How was it?" asked Buck, in the car, grinning. Frank looked away. *It coulda been worse.*

Back at the Antwerp he tumbled into bed and tossed like a boat and finally dropped off and woke and slept and then awoke. Downstairs, Patsy sat very still in a chair, sipping a glass of sherry, listening. He was alone, thank goodness. She was afraid, it being his birthday, that that Italian tramp would be climbing into Frank's bed, but it was just Frank, a little drunk, judging from his footsteps, and weary, but home safe. Then Frank groaned and sat bolt upright. "You pig," he said bitterly. "Oh what a pig you are. What an awful pig. How could you do that! That poor kid. You are such a pig."

So, she thought. The Italian tramp had come across, gave the birthday boy a roll in the hay, poor Frank. Those Catholic girls had a way of giving you what you wanted and making you sick with guilt at the same time. Patsy knew the type. Well, it was time to make her move, she thought. The emanations seemed quite clear. There were no intervening currents whatsoever, no shadow thoughts, no psychic hands reaching out of the bushes to draw her back. Her path was absolutely clear. She had never spoken to Frank face to face before but now she would offer herself to him.

She also thought she would get rid of Delores Du-Charme and Corinne Archer and place an embargo on any new young female characters until the tramp packed her bags for Milwaukee. Then she dozed off in the chair.

When Frank awoke, it was Sunday morning and Father John was proclaiming his own unworthiness. *Mea culpa, mea culpa, mea maxima culpa*, he intoned and struck himself on the breast three times, the breast where the microphone hung. It felt as if Father John were beating him on the head.

Debut

"Uncle Ray, did you ever meet a woman you didn't want to make love to?" Roy Jr. asked at lunch. Frank blushed, and looked at the waitress coming, butt first, through the kitchen door, hauling a tray.

"Well," said Ray, thinking carefully, "my mother, of course, died when I was young so I can't say about her, and my sister, I would say, I had no particular desire for after I was old enough to see what all was available. And there were aunts, I must say, who had lost most of their charm, such as it was, by the time I was of age. Other than them—I'd have to think—I suppose there must've been a few. Offhand, though, I can't think of them."

Frank had tuna stackups and the cherry cola Jell-O salad. He thought about Maria. The night before, they had gone to see Deanna Durbin, not their favorite star, in *How Bright the Morning*, and he had kissed Maria, or she had kissed him, one kiss so thrilling that she grabbed his leg and he slipped his hand into her blouse. Her bra unclasped in front! What an innovation! He unfastened it, expecting the theater lights to flash and sirens to wail, but instead her breast fell into his hand, a small, friendly breast. Then a man and his wife slipped into the row and sat next to Maria and the woman gave Frank a walleyed look and whispered to her husband. The man shook his head in disgust. Frank withdrew his hand. Deanna Durbin smiled onscreen like she didn't have a brain in her head. A man leaned across the table and took her hand. A close-up of their hands. Frank didn't know what the story was about, but there is only one story, he thought; the only difference is, who is the girl?

———

Dear Daddy, he wrote after lunch. *You said you wanted me to go to college but this is better, to be around smart people (some, not all) and listen to them without having to repeat everything back. My boss loves to talk. I sit and listen to him go on and on, and I wonder, "Why is he saying all this to me, I'm nobody, I don't know anything," but of course he isn't asking me to be anybody. He is a frustrated performer who had to become the manager because they didn't have one of those. He tells me things I know he wouldn't tell his own wife. He told me that he thought it must be happy to be on the air. Just for those minutes, then you might be very unhappy, but those few minutes would be like a dream. I wish I could get on the air myself one of these days. P.S. I am in love.*

———

Frank had asked Roy Jr. for a shot at announcing and Roy Jr. said he was too valuable to waste. "Announcers sit around, waiting. You'd never like it," he said. "You're a doer."

So Frank went to Reed Seymour, the Chief Announcer, and invited him to the Red Eye for a beer and by the second pitcher they were on the verge of friendship. Frank said he sure admired people in radio, people who could talk on the air, announcers, and Reed said, "I got into radio because I wanted to impress a girl I knew, a beautiful girl with red hair and green eyes and long legs. I met her at my brother's wedding. She asked me what I did, and I said, 'I'm in radio.' 'Oh really,' she said, 'my gosh that must be scary.' *Nawwww*, I said. So I had to get into radio. I knew how disappointed she'd be if she knew I was lying. It's true."

Frank said, "But the thought of talking to all those people at one time—even late at night, when nobody's listening, it's still eighty thousand people out there, *listening*. More than you could put in Memorial Stadium. Imagine standing in Memorial Stadium at midnight and reading the news to eighty thousand people."

Reed said modestly that it was nothing, anybody could do it if you worked at it and had concentration. "When I met her, I was washing dishes at the Curtis Hotel, except I had just been fired for coming to work a week late, so I came over to WLT and I wrote down a lot of experience on the application form—at WABC and KDEF and WGHI and KJKL—made it all up, and they needed somebody, so they took me. You could do it too. A lot of people could."

Frank said that, no, he didn't have Reed's voice. Reed rolled his eyes. "Oh please," he said. "You *could* do it." And pretty soon he talked himself into offering Frank an air shift. "Just a couple hours, on Tuesday, as a tryout, nothing permanent."

Frank tried not to think about Tuesday and it loomed as big as a mountain, but it wasn't scary, he told Maria. "What scares me is the thought that I might've stayed in Mindren and never got to do it." She told him he needed to relax and get a good night's sleep. "I know," he said, wishing she would say more about sleep. *Maybe you could come over tonight*, he wanted to say.

———

In the morning, he arrived at WLT an hour early. Ethel asked him to run over to Billy and Marty's and pick up a box of cigars, and he said, "Can't. I'm on the air today." He poured himself a cup of coffee in the Green Room, which was empty, and stood in the corner and practiced saying, "You're tuned to your Friendly Neighbor Station, WLT, 770 on your radio dial, from studios in downtown Minneapolis." He said it over and over, with his chin on his chest to make his voice deeper, trying to get just the right inflexion, smooth and clean. Then somebody cleared his throat, *ahem*. Gene the engineer, napping in the corner, said, "Hey, who put a nickel in *you?*" Frank went into Studio C to practice and there was Dad Benson, sorting out items for the *Almanac*. He looked up and smiled. "Big day, eh? Well, good luck."

Studio B was half-full of junk, like a basement, but it was more secret in there, nobody to stare at you through the glass, and it did have the good-luck painting of Donna LaDonna, who lay back and smiled, glad to see him, her two happy breasts, her handsome downstairs. "Good luck, big boy," she whispered.

His first line in the copybook was "You're listening to WLT, Your Home in the Air, studios in downtown Minneapolis. The time is 10:45." Then a couple of transcribed commercials, the second one for Grain Belt Beer and at the end of it he said: "Look for Grain Belt at your neighborhood grocery or liquor store." Then an organ theme, twenty seconds' worth, and then fade, and he said: "And now Sanitary Dairy brings you. . . . What's for Supper? . . . the popular recipe program devoted to quick and easy dishes that are sure to please the whole family. . . . And remember, when those recipes call for milk, look for the big red Sanitary Dairy label. It's your guarantee of quality. And now, from the WLT kitchen, here's LaWella Wells. LaWella—"

Waiting for 10:42 and then 10:43, his face got hot and his mouth was dry, as if encrusted with baked sand. The control room was crowded with engineers who were all chortling at something, possibly him, hard to say, and the sweep hand came around to the 12 as Alma Melting wound up *Community Calendar* and the engineer Gene gave him a baleful look and the red light flashed on and an awful silence filled the room. *He forgot to put on the headphones. Too late!* He said, "You're listening to WLT, Your Home in the Air," in his own voice, and then the rest of it, and Vesta Soderbjerg loomed above him through the window as he said, "The Classroom of the Air . . . Mid-America's oldest continuously running instructional program. Today Professor Ferguson resumes his study of world federalism . . ." and then he had forty-five minutes to relax, and then it was Irving James Knox, and when the red light went off, Gene said, in the intercom, "Scratch the Dairy Council spot and do a PSA," just like Frank was a regular staff announcer. So he hunted up a public service announcement in the big black copybook—found one for Library Week, and put on the headphones and read that during the break, poured his heart into it—sincerely urging people to *please*, support their public library. He did the livestock report (No. 1,2,3 220–240 lb. barrows and gilts, 17.75–18.25, canners and cutters 12.15–12.25)

268

and introduced *Dad's Almanac* ("And now, with the Almanac, here's Dad Benson . . .") and over the monitor came the familiar husky voice of Dad saying, "Thank you so much, Frank White, and now here's a look at this day in history. . . ."

Thank you so much, Frank White. He blushed for sheer pleasure. His own name, spoken out loud by Dad Benson. He was famous. His name now a known radio name. People in Mindren mentioning to their friends, "I was listening to Frank White on the radio today," not knowing it was Francis With, and people he had never seen before, thousands of them, saying, "I heard Frank White say on the radio today that barrows and gilts are selling about fifteen cents a hundredweight lower," and their friends saying, *Oh, is that right.* "Yes, that's what Frank White said." A good name, two short strokes: Frank White.

He almost didn't hear Dad's last line, "And now here's Frank again with the weather," and his brain lurched and there were a couple dead seconds while he formulated a sentence: "In the forecast for today, we find sunny skies . . ." and then he drew a blank—where to go next? Back for more livestock? Back to Dad? He looked up at Gene, who gestured as if breaking a stick. Station break. "WLT, Your Home in the Air, broadcasting from studios in the Hotel Ogden, 770 kc., Minneapolis." Then Gene's voice in the headphones: "Smelser copy." It was right there. He read: *If you've been thinking of adding on a porch, now's the time, say your friends at Smelser Construction. There's nothing like a porch—it lets the air in, keeps the bugs out—and you can put a bed out there and get the best sleep of your life. The folks at Smelser know porches because they've built so many of them. So choose experience and reliability. Choose Smelser.* Then Gene said: "Here she comes!" And the studio piano, with a modest flourish, rolled out, "A Little Street Where Old Friends Meet," and Frank said,

"Yes, wherever you are, it's time to smile. So sit back, relax, and listen as One Fella's Hardware presents our very own Miss Lily Dale," and from Studio A came her very own girlish voice: "Thank you so much, Frank White. You're very sweet. Doesn't he have a wonderful voice, folks? Oh, I can hear all of you out there say, Who *is* that young man? Well, his name is Frank White, and we're so extremely proud of him, and—awwww, look at him, I've made him blush."

But she was nowhere to be seen. Studio A was around the corner and down a long hall. She couldn't see him though, true, he was blushing. He turned in the chair and looked up at Donna. She seemed about to climb down off the wall, give him a big kiss, lay him on the floor, and pull down his pants. He stood up and patted her. "My, how the years fly by without our knowing it," Lily Dale was saying. "And I'd like to dedicate this song to that little boy who went around the corner, goodbye—this beautiful song, 'Memories of the Old Home Town.' "

———

Roy Jr. told him he had sounded quite smooth, very professional. "You have a natural voice. Don't screw it up by trying to make it sound like something. I don't think you ought to be an announcer, it's a dead end, but if you do it, just use your own voice." And then he said, "Did you get a look at my aunt today?" No, Frank hadn't, he had been off the wheelchair detail and on the air.

Roy Jr. stood up and walked to the window and peered out through the blinds. "She's a hophead," he said. "Cocaine and codeine and God knows what. Powder stuff. Tippy brought me a sack full of empties. She gets it from a drugstore and she uses fourteen different names. The druggist is a fan of hers from way back. His name is Oliver something. I've seen him around here, bringing her presents."

"Maybe she could give it up if we asked her to," said Frank. He felt itchy all over.

"People don't change, Frank," he said. "Not often, and never for long. Besides, she's a terrible singer, don't you think?"

"No. I think she's okay. People like her a lot."

"You're too kind."

"It could be a lie. Tippy is so bitter, you know. Maybe he made it all up."

"He showed me the goods. It's better to end it right now. Bring her up."

When he wheeled Lottie into Roy Jr.'s office, she said that it was the coziest, the most beautiful office in the building, and why not, it was Roy Jr. who kept WLT together, always had been, so why shouldn't he have the best? Of *course* he should.

He said, "Aunt Lottie, I've decided it's best that we terminate your employment here as of one week from today." He talked about her remarkable record of service, her loyalty, the old-timers from long ago, and then said, "I'll work out a pension arrangement myself."

"For heaven's sake, why?"

"I don't want Ray or my dad to have to do it."

"Ah, your father," she sighed. "I never hear his name but what I think of the beautiful radio he made for me. I still have it and it's never needed repair of any kind other than replacing the tubes. Oh he is a genius, your dad. What a lovely man. And your mother too. Please remember me to them. Will you? Oh I think of your mother and to me, she's like the first day of spring. Innocent and pure— Oh, there are cruel things done, child, and dark deeds and hearts are easily broken, but that sweet girl, she knew nothing of heartbreak or cruelty either."

"This isn't easy for me to do," he said, "but we have to face facts. Times change. Popularity changes. People like you for awhile and then they want something else. That's a hell of a hard fact for a performer to accept."

She cried. She knew he didn't mean it. WLT was her home. She couldn't leave it, even though she met a little discouragement along the way, she would remain true and do her duty and give people the old songs, the good old songs, they never fade away, people come to appreciate them more and more, especially as we get older. No, the old songs are the best songs, and though some might scorn them, she would not. And then, sitting in his office, she commenced to sing "O Danny Boy, the pipes, the pipes are calling, from glen to glen and up the mountainside."

He said, "Can you live on three hundred dollars a month, Aunt Lottie?"

"Oh I don't need much, child, my needs are few, all I need is a microphone." She said, "Money is the farthest thing from my mind. You don't owe me a thin dime. It was my boon and privilege, darling. All I ask is to keep on singing." But finally, it was agreed, she would retire. "Do you understand what I'm saying?" Roy Jr. asked. She said she had always understood him perfectly. "But about your retirement?" She said, "Whatever you say, I'll do." They shook hands on it, and Frank wheeled her out the door, and she looked up beaming and said, "Child, I feel my career is just beginning."

He ran upstairs to 4-C and called Maria. "You sounded so good!" she cried. "I listened to the whole two hours while I took a bath."

———

Patsy thought Frank sounded like a million dollars. She said so to Dad Benson. And to Ray and Roy Jr. "It's a shame we go looking for talent and we don't see what's right under our noses. Frank White is pure gold. There isn't a *thing* he can't do. You wait and see if you don't get some mail on him." That afternoon, she bought seventy-five postcards and notecards and an assortment of stationery, and sat down and wrote, in a variety of handwriting styles and on her four different typewriters, a variety of listeners' letters admiring WLT in general and then zeroing in on the tremendous young announcer ("White, I believe his name is") who had suddenly emerged in the ozone, so personable, so intelligent, so warm, a major talent who would bear watching.

Maria and Frank ate dinner at the Pot Pie and the waitress said, "You two look like you're sweet on each other"—Frank had his left hand on Maria's thigh, about halfway up her skirt, and he did not eat his meat loaf. They walked to his apartment, and sat on the sofa. He kissed her again and again, but she didn't grab his leg, and when he touched her breast, she shrank back. "I want you to hold me," she whispered.

"I'm trying to."

"No, you're grabbing at me."

"Well, I'm sorry."

"Would you like some coffee?"

She filled the kettle with water, lit the stove, and got down the coffee can. "I used to have to boil water for my father," she said.

"Oh?"

"I had to clean up after him. What a filthy brute he was."

She stood in the doorway. Frank wished she would come back to the sofa and congratulate him on his big debut.

"An awful thing for a daughter to say, but who would know better? My mother died when I was seven. She was in childbirth. I think the baby died too, but I don't know if anybody told me or not. My father was in a fog. My sister and I took care of him, and then she left, and I lived with him until I was seventeen. Do you know Milwaukee? We lived near St. Basil's, on the South Side. He was a streetcar conductor, and he'd come home at night and sit in his green uniform and hardly touch supper, just sit and drink beer. He gurgled like a pump. I would lie upstairs on the bed with my coat on and listen. Not move a muscle. I was afraid he would come up and get me. I was ready to go out the window."

Maria stood, her hand on the door, alert.

"He sat and drank and then his chair scraped and the icebox door opened and the beer bottle popped open and the icebox slammed shut and down he sat and swallowed that one and got up for another. After four or five, he climbed the stairs and went in the toilet. Didn't even close the door. Then came this *deluge* of water, and he *would not* flush, he just lumbered downstairs and repeated the whole process. Then after awhile, he didn't bother to climb upstairs, he made water in the kitchen sink, and when he was dead drunk, he wet his pants, and then he fell asleep on the sofa." Maria stopped. She was weeping and she put out her arms for Frank. He held her head against his shoulder and put his face in her hair.

"When I came down in the morning to go to school, there was Papa, red-eyed, and that terrible acrid smell, and he was crying, head in his hands, and yelling at me, *Why do you treat me like I was nothing to you? You're worse than your mother was.* I had a scholarship to the Milwaukee Academy of Dramatic Art. I went off to school with all the kids from nice homes and sometimes, if the classroom was warm, I could smell my father's urine: it was in my blouse, my skirt, my hair. I was sure that other girls could smell it, that they made faces at me behind my back and held their noses, that it was in my school file—'has poor personal habits and smells of body waste'—and that I would never get a job, and I'd have to live with Papa the rest of my life, wash his clothes, haul his beer bottles, pour Hilex down the sink. So I started using a strong perfume but then, on the streetcar home, these men would grin at me. They leaned against me, they leered at me. They looked down at my breasts like it was fruit on the counter. That's where I met Merle, at the Academy. He was my best friend, the only one who invited me home for dinner. His family was so good to me. I moved in with them a year later. You're different from other men, Frank."

Frank was not sure he wanted to be completely different, but anyway the coffee was ready. He got down the cups. He told her that he had now finally discovered his place in the world, radio. He didn't mention the birthday girl. He wanted to tell her exactly what happened, but now was not a good time. No need to beg comparison to other men.

A few feet below, Patsy Konopka smelled their coffee and put on water to make herself a pot. She had almost finished Frank's fan letters. "There is something in his voice that makes radio come alive," she began, with a fountain pen, soft loopy letters, on bluebell stationery. "I am going to be listening for him in the future, believe me."

CHAPTER 31

Gospel

No Sex On The Premises was Ray's rule, spelled out
to every man he hired, even the Rev. Irving James
Knox way back in 1927. Ray said: "Keep your
hands off the females, I don't care how you feel, or what
suddenly comes over you, or how her hand brushed your
lap and her left breast jumped out at you, I don't want to
hear it. No matter how sad and lonely your life is: don't
touch women around here. Keep your hands off them."

"I'm not sure I care to work for someone who addresses
a man of the cloth in those terms," said the pale Pres-
byterian, smiling faintly, peering over his wire rims.

"Suit yourself, but if you come to work here, remember:
no sex with a WLT employee, or anybody else you meet on
the premises. You can jump into the sack with your fans all
you like, but keep the fornication out of the station."

Rev. Knox decided he could join the staff on those
terms, but that summer, a few weeks after Frank's debut,
Knox was nabbed in Freddie's Cafe slipping his hand into
the blouse of a girl from the typing pool who was dizzy

from three vodka sours. "I've been working too hard," the minister explained. "My nerves are shot. I'm on the verge of a nervous breakdown." Roy Jr. told him to go south and have it. "No sex on the premises, that's Ray's rule," he said.

Rev. Knox wept. He told Roy Jr. that he was troubled by unnatural sexual urges and that he had tried to seduce the girl as a way of proving that he was normal. Roy Jr. wavered. He detested clergymen, but the station needed one, and Knox had the sort of chummy tone that people liked in a spiritual leader. In person he was a pill but on the air he shone as a beacon of manly Christianity, a light on life's dark paths, and Roy Jr. was loath to have to break in a new man. He gave Knox a dreadful, withering lecture that left the man pale and trembling and his hanky damp with tears. "I don't need a loose pecker around this place, believe me, and if I catch you trying to grab one of my girls again, I'll call up the bishop and have him trim your nuts for you. I'll throw you in the street and call the newspapers." But he let the man stay, a mistake.

"We are showing weakness. You should've kicked his skinny butt across the street," said Ray. "Now the word is out. Sex is okay, just don't do it on the desks. We are in for a storm."

But he agreed with Roy Jr. about the horror of replacing Knox: when you thought about all the clergymen you'd have to interview for the job—days and days of aimless uplifting conversation with flabby men in dowdy clothes, men with big watery eyes and trembling lips and a per-petual look of faint hope on their faces—plus the inevitable Bible-beaters and the whoopers and jumpers—who would you find in the end? At worst, some brilliant demagogue like Pastor Paul Anderson the Lutheran Lothario on WEVE ("A Man Named Paul"), who would draw an immense audience of peabrains and then you could never get rid of him, and at best, you'd find another sad sack like Knox.

But Ray was right about the storm. After Knox was not fired, WLT went through months of heavy erotic activity. John Tippy fell in love with the music librarian, a young pianist named Jeff, and they were said to spend weekends together in Duluth. The staff organist Miss Patrice had a fling with Phil Sax and for a whole week she showed up for the 7 a.m. Organ Prelude with an exhausted, moony look about her, smelling like a cigar. But the busy boy was Wendell Shepherd of *The Rise and Shine Show*. In his Milton, King Seeds pocket calendar, he drew in twenty-seven shining suns in one month, twenty-seven times with three different women, three *very* different women. Lottie Unger was a secretary in a pretty tweed suit that Wendell removed and hung up without a wrinkle, and Julia Jackson Butts was a fine young woman with long black hair piled on top of her head, the assistant editor of *Dial: The WLT Family Magazine*, whose hair Wendell unpiled, and Lacy Lovell was an actress on *Up in a Balloon* who mistook him for the producer of *The Hendersons*.

"The staff is acting just like the President," said Roy Jr. "And I don't mean Mr. Truman."

Ray bristled. "I do *not* run around here jumping secretaries," he said. "The women with whom I am acquainted are women of attainment—"

"Employees, nonetheless."

Ray stared him down. "Life is not always reasonable, or even logical," he said. "There are exceptions and anomalies. Consistency is the hobgoblin of little minds. I am extremely fond of a number of women who work for me. True. I wouldn't dream of lying to you about that. And yet I do not permit the men who work for me to run around here like animals. Do you understand?"

"Perfectly."

And now, on a warm October morning, there was a boxful of allegations about Knox himself that Roy Jr. had found locked up in Sloan's old file drawer (under "Knox: Testimony in re Patrimony: SAVE") that pointed unmistakably toward debauchery on a scale that would shame a goat.

"Frank! The man is crazed. He's besotted with lust. Look at this! Letters in his own hand, written to schoolgirls! Offers of private swimming lessons! Invitations to travel! Invitations to pose for photographs! Hikes in the woods! Rendezvouses in the library stacks! Romps in the hay! Fondue parties! Listen to this: 'My darling dearest Marjery, Yes, I do love you, deeply and absolutely, and it has taken me months to get up the courage to say so, and now, with a trembling hand and a heart full of profound feeling, I am asking you to—' Outrageous! The man seduced Little Becky! Look at this—" And he tossed Frank a packet of letters, from Marjery to the minister, whom she addressed as "Nervy Irvy" and "Snuggums" and "My Little Lemon Drop" and who, evidently, she accompanied to ministerial conferences in Seattle and Cleveland, in the role of his niece.

"Well," said Frank, "she's a grownup person. I suppose she knew what she was doing."

"So did he. He knew he was cutting his nuts around here." Roy Jr. picked up the phone. "*Damn.* And now I gotta go find another one."

"How about Reverand Odom?" said Frank.

"Who's he?"

"He works here. Harold Odom. He's a janitor. But he's also a Lutheran minister. He's a very sensible person."

"Odom. I know him. He's the guy who's in love with Patsy Konopka. How come he gave up the ministry? Is he some kind of nut?"

Frank sat down and leaned across the desk. "No. Not a nut. Just a very practical person. He had a church in North Dakota and he thought he wasn't doing any good, he was only being a minister. So he asked himself, What job can I find where I *know* I'll do some good? and he came up with janitor. But he'd make a great radio minister. You should try him out."

Frank stopped—he was trembling. He had never tried to tell Roy Jr. what to do before, and it felt as if he had walked up to the edge of a chasm.

"If he did a radio show every day, could he still continue as a janitor?"

Frank said he thought Mr. Odom would insist on retaining his janitorship.

"Good. So you tell him. Monday through Fridays, the 'Scripture Nuggets' segment of *The Rise and Shine Show*, and the five-minute meditation at ten-fifteen, and Sunday morning, the chapel at six a.m. and vespers at ten-thirty. Right? Good. Now I just have to fire Snuggums and then deal with Wendell Shepherd and his hormones."

Frank found Reverend Odom wet-mopping the lobby and when he told him about Roy Jr.'s offer, the man's eyes filled with tears. He put his arms around Frank and squeezed him so tight his back cracked. "I knew something good was going to happen to me today," he said.

And the next morning, he was on the air. He read from Ephesians on *Rise and Shine*—the Shepherd Boys were glad to see him, they knew him from way back, Elmer Shepherd said—and a few hours later the old minister did a nice meditation about leaving our burdens with the Lord. Roy Jr., on his way to lunch with Ray, gave Frank a thumbs-up and said, "Good man." And Ray said, "Frank, you're the first *smart* person I've met who hardly says anything. Come and have lunch with us."

Come and have lunch with us. What sweet music to his ears! He had raised up Reverend Odom—lifted him up from his mop and pail and put him on the Mountain of Radio—just like Dad Benson, who lifted up his brother and his friends. Dad had once said, "It takes genius to elevate the ordinary, a very ordinary genius," and that's exactly what I am, Frank thought, an ordinary genius. He had unlocked the secret of radio. The sport of the ordinary! Brilliant men like Reed Seymour couldn't figure this out for the life of them! Reed was ashamed of radio. Vesta was ashamed of it. Reed wanted to do something worthy with his life, like write books. He had part of a manuscript in his desk drawer. Frank had read it. Very intense, very poetic. *And very hard going.* Vesta wanted to bring in the treasures of the world and display them on the air, like opening a museum and showing postcards of the Venus de Milo. No, radio was a cinch if you kept reaching down and grabbing up handfuls of the ordinary. *Keep your feet on the ground.*

Tour

Ray was looking for Dad Benson. Frank said, "He's in the Green Room, but he's feeling a little sick." "I hope so," said Ray.

He walked up to Dad, who was lying on the couch, his face covered with the morning paper. "You in the sack with Faith?" Ray asked. Dad sat right up. "What does that mean?"

"It means are you humping her? Are you hiding the salami? Are you pearl diving?" Sometimes, Ray thought, Dad had the worldly sophistication of a Camp Fire Girl. Dad probably thought "Tobacco Road" was about the evils of smoking. Dad probably thought that prostitutes were women waiting for buses. He probably wished they would dress more warmly and not smoke so much.

"Are you balling Faith?" Ray asked.

Dad looked stunned. "Ray, don't try to go between the tree and the bark," he said.

"What in blazes is that supposed to mean?"

"Like my father said: don't say anything you wouldn't want somebody to know." Dad started to get up. Ray put a hand on his shoulder.

"So the answer is yes." Sweet little Faith, the radio housewife, turning tricks with her radio dad—it made a person blanch to think about it.

Ray let him stand up. The two men faced each other. Ray cleared his throat. "Dad, we have a long-standing rule here. Let me offer it to you as a recommendation: *no fornicating between employees.* Please."

"Ray, all I can say is that the big thieves hang the little ones."

"What does that mean?" But of course he knew what it meant. He blushed. He said, "Dad, I have just one thing to say about that, and that is: what's sauce for the goose is Greek to the gander," and he wheeled and marched out.

Soon after, Faith Snelling announced she was leaving the show. "You can't," said Roy Jr. She said she wanted to do other things. "You're doing this thing," he said. She wanted to act in plays.

"Be my guest," he said, "but you can't quit the show. You're Jo. Nobody else can *be* Jo. Everybody *knows* Jo. She's got to *be* there, on the radio. You can't just go and murder a friend of five-hundred-thousand people because you *feel* like it. If it's money we're talking about, let's talk. You don't even need to say anything. I'll offer you $300 a week. That's a 25-percent raise." Faith stayed and she did not act in plays after all. She and Dad remained close, so far as people could see. With her husband Dale playing the role of her husband Frank, Ray thought that might keep Dad in line, the old gander, but no such luck. Dale seemed to be running around with Laurel Larpenteur.

It was one thing after another. Sex was on the premises, and there was no way to get it out.

"What is that naked woman doing on the wall in Studio B?" Ray asked Roy Jr.

"You never saw that before?" Roy Jr. clapped his hands to his head. "That's been there since I was a child!"

Ray said meekly, "It must have slipped my mind."

———

Roy Jr. was not in a kidding mood when he found out that Wendell Shepherd of the Shepherd Boys, stars of *The Rise and Shine Show*, was seeing a secretary in Continuity named Hazel Park. He got so mad he changed the show from seven a.m. to six.

"She was a valuable employee, and you used her like you'd use a couch, and you broke her heart, you jerk," he told Wendell. "Yes, you. You're nothing but a gold-plated gospel jerk. So all right. Set your alarm an hour earlier."

Wendell pleaded for mercy. "The guys'll kill me," he moaned. Roy Jr. looked at him in disgust, splayed out on the sofa. Wendell was a tall slope-shouldered fellow with long hair oiled down and swept up high on his head in swoops, and he wore white shoes and pink socks and a glittery green suit that shone like seaweed in the moonlight. All the Shepherds were bold of dress and favored rare items such as checkered vests and brilliant ties with rural landscape scenes, but Wendell, the lead singer and the youngest, was the showboat. Wendell wore diamonds, a stickpin in the lapel and a tietack and diamond studs, and Wendell dyed his hair black. It had been mouse brown.

———

The Shepherds were four brothers, Elmer, Al, Rudy, and Wendell, and they had been a big crowd-pleaser on the *Barn Dance* since 1937, when they came down from North Dakota, winners of a gospel quartet contest. The gospel contest was the bright idea of a Program Director named Milford Scudder, and it was his last; Ray fired him. "I didn't get into radio to be in with a bunch of holy Joes with fancy clothes and brilliantined hair—gospel quartets! Holy cow, don't you know what these people are like?"

Scudder did not know. He was a Congregationalist. He imagined that gospel singers were like choir members, stolid, hearty, well-meaning folks, except fewer in number. He had no idea. Ray had to yell at him for awhile.

"Gospel singers are *nothing* like choir members. Nothing. This is the grass-eater element you're inviting in here, the Bible pounders, the snake handlers, the holy rollers. These are the people who run around church and howl like dogs and speak in tongues and faint in a heap and lie there and twitch like spastics, with foam dripping off their mouths. These people are faith healers, Scudder. And I will not allow that—I am not going to *tolerate* any faith healing around here. None! Nobody is going to write in to WLT for the holy hankies or the light-up crucifixes or the tiny New Testaments. Nobody is going to take a WLT microphone and speak in tongues into it. Never. We are not going to have snake handling here."

It was the grass-eater element that brought William Jennings Bryan down, those crazy fundamentalists who grabbed the old giant and flattered him and hoisted him up on their shoulders and hauled him down to Dayton, Tennessee, for the Monkey Trial. One of the most brilliant minds that ever graced the nation, one of the truest sons of the Middle West and a good heart and a great American, and the grass-eaters got him to shill for them against that cagey, money-grubbing appleknocker Clarence Darrow, a man who knew which way the wind blew and who blew with it, and Bryan was made the fool, the bear in the circus, and died, and all the greatness of his life would be forgotten, and his last dumb moments remembered, because he fell for the fundamentalists. Well, Ray would not.

"I'm sorry," said Scudder.

"You're exactly right you're sorry. You're fired," said Ray.

But the contest must go on, of course, and as winners, the Shepherd Boys had to sing on the *Barn Dance* and then, when they tore down the house with "My Lord Calls Me" and the crowd wouldn't let them go until they did it *three more times*, the only way Leo LaValley could restore order was to invite them back for next week. And then it happened again. The Shepherds were powerful. They were young and dark and when they got into the Spirit, they moaned and whooped in a way that Minnesotans do not generally do in public. When Wendell sang, "Please, Jesus, please—don't leave me here—the night so dark and cold—please Jesus, put your hand in mine—just like the Bible told," women in the audience leaned forward and put their hands to their faces and shuddered and whispered his name, *Wendell*.

So, on Monday morning, Ray called the Shepherds in, and the four boys sat politely, in dark plain slacks and black sweaters, as he told them he was offering them their own show, *The Rise and Shine Show*, five days a week at 7 a.m., to sing five songs, three of them requests, and to do birthday and anniversary greetings, the weather forecast, and a few jokes. Clean jokes. "You wouldn't happen to do an occasional non-sacred song, would you?" he inquired. Rudy said they did lots of them, like "Red River Valley" and "Long Long Ago," but that people preferred the gospel ones. Variety goes a long way, said Ray. Then he paused. "Boys?" he said. They smiled. *Yes?*

"Boys, if there's ever even so much as one tiny bit of faith healing on that show, one little smidgen of tongues, or one mention of snakes or hankies, I'll kick your ass out of here so fast, your heads'll spin. You hear me?" They heard.

"You are going to sing your songs, give the weather, sell the seed corn or whatever, and you're not going to cut loose and start whooping and crying and asking people to send their love offerings, right?"

Oh yes, they understood. But even with no healing, no praying, no tongues, no snakes or hankies, there was plenty to put up with. The loud clothes, the clouds of cologne, the pinky rings, Rudy's violet Pontiac ensconced in the parking lot like an ugly welt, the trail of empty vodka bottles, and the women, a constant parade of frowsy women.

━━━

But it was Hazel Park's fall that burned Roy Jr. She was a stocky girl with piano legs and a big cheerful grin and a ponytail that came out of the top of her head, and she sat by a radio and logged commercials in a big black ledger that she called Henry. She named other things around her desk. The typewriter was Vivian, for example. She kept four photographs on her desk and a great many little souvenirs, such as rocks she had garnered from her trips to the North Shore, and pine cones, a brass buffalohead coin bank, a cowgirl figurine, and a little plastic piano from Rapid City, S.D. Open the lid and there were souvenir matchbooks. The memorabilia came to form a sort of windbreak across the front of the desk, which faced the door to Studio B, where *The Rise and Shine Show* aired from.

Wendell had spotted Hazel one morning when he came rushing back from the Antwerp, having forgotten the little spiral notebook where he wrote down ideas for new songs, and she helped him look for it. The two of them rummaged around, and then she crawled on the floor looking under the record cabinets, and he got to look down the front of her blouse. She was awfully sorry about him losing all that hard work, she was terribly sorry, and so she went to dinner with him at The Forum. When he suggested that they get together at the hotel and try writing songs, she trotted right over the next day after work. They wrote a tearjerker called "Little Dan" ("When his daddy went away in a car crash one dark day, he became his mama's man, Little Dan") and then a gospel number, "One More Sinner," during which Wendell collapsed from the strain of creation. "Lie next to me," he moaned. She did. He told her that he had never met anyone with her raw song-writing talent. He would teach her everything he knew, and she would go on to write the songs he never could, not having her talent. She admitted that, yes, she did have quite a few creative ideas and notions—such as her idea of writing a tribute song to her mother, just to name one—and now that he had given her self-confidence, she could see that these ideas would make wonderful songs. She had been an odd duck in Mankato, never fitting in, always lonely, terribly shy—"a typical story for a creative person," Wendell noted. Nobody in Mankato had ever seen this talent in her because she had not seen it herself. It took Wendell, a fellow creator, to notice it and to bring it out. She kissed him in gratitude. He smiled. "You're going to be rich and famous and live in Chicago someday," he said, "and you'll forget all about your Wendell, but

I'll understand, and I'll just enjoy reading about you."
She protested his assessment of her character. She would
never forget him. He put his arms around her. He apologized. "Of course, you won't forget me," he said, "but
I do know that the currents of life will sweep us apart.
We are but islands in the sea of life, and seldom do our
peripheries touch. I want to touch you." He unbuttoned
her blouse and unclasped her brassiere and her perfect
generous breasts spilled out and lay beside him, magnificent twins breathing, sighing, happy, wanting only to be
cradled in his hands. "This is a moment we'll remember
for the remainder of our lives," he said, as he whipped
off his pants. "Let's make it the most memorable moment
it can be."

They had sex every business day for two weeks, plunging
in the percale like white whales, and when he got tired
of her and her passive manner, he told her he couldn't
anymore, on account of his conscience. The Lord was
telling him that this adultery would not go unpunished,
and Wendell was afraid that Miss Park might have to pay
the price—he had had a terrible dream in which he saw
her body, decapitated, lying beside the road—and so, for
her own protection, he had to stop their love-making, and
because he was so filled with desire for her, he could not
bear to ever see her or speak to her for awhile.

Thus it was that Hazel, a valued employee of WLT
despite her clutter of memorabilia (to which Wendell added
a photo of himself signed, "Best Wishes to a Real Big
Talent"), collapsed, emotionally shattered, and went home
to Mankato to walk around and weep for a month. When
she returned, she was a shadow of herself, a faint, tremulous, apologetic lady instead of the hearty office girl of
yore. One day she sobbed out the whole awful story to
Winifred Winter, the boss of Continuity, and Winifred

went to Roy Jr., and Roy Jr. hit the roof. He was still angry after he changed the time of the show and sent Wendell off to buy an extra alarm clock.

Roy Jr. paced around his office for a minute or two, kicking chairs and balling up paper and hurling it at the walls, and when Frank didn't hear any more kicking, he poked his head in.

Roy Jr. peered at him through narrowed slits. "I'm going to put him in your charge."

Frank eased into the room. "What do you want me to do?"

"Take him and his sorry brothers and their wretched band and take them out of here. Out of our lives. And take Slim Graves too. And take Barney, that whiny engineer. And that drummer, Red, the one who goes around here always tapping on things. Run the whole damn bunch out the door and take them on a three-week tour of Minnesota and let's get them out of the radio business once and for all. Except you. You come back."

"It's December," Frank pleaded. "Couldn't this wait until after Christmas?"

"I'm calling the Artists Bureau and I'm getting the whole bunch of them out of here and on the road starting tomorrow morning at 6 a.m."

Frank stood up, stunned. "Why me?" he asked.

Roy Jr. put his arm around Frank's shoulder. "I want them to suffer a little but I don't want them to die in a ditch and I don't want them going through Lyons County raping and pillaging. You're going to see to it. You're going to save them from themselves."

He sat down and pulled out a drawer and fetched a roll of cash out of a jar. "You're going to do this for me," he said, "and when you come back, I'm going to do something for you. Something wonderful. Meanwhile, here's $800 expense money. For emergencies. Let Elmer pay the day-to-day stuff. If you need more, wire for it."

Frank asked if Reverend Odom could come. Roy Jr. said, "Of course."

"Can Maria come?" asked Frank. "She can sing." Roy Jr. pursed his lips.

"It's a way of giving a little more variety to the show. She isn't a gospel singer. She could sing stuff like 'Sunny Side of the Street' and 'Pennies from Heaven.' "

"I don't know," said Roy Jr. and Frank grinned. "I don't know" was an affirmative, coming from Roy Jr. Now all he had to do was convince Maria.

CHAPTER 3 3

Big Chance

The first stop on the tour, said Harry of the Artists Bureau, would be Roseau, seven hours north of Minneapolis, at 6 a.m. the next morning. The Shepherd Boys were singing that night at a Baptist church in Roseville. Frank arranged with Red, the bus driver and drummer, to get the Shepherd Boys' old bus from the garage in Brooklyn Park where it sat rusting, to put two new tires on it and stock it with groceries, and to pick the Shepherds up at 9 p.m. Al Shepherd said that, with encores and offering and all, they might not be out before ten. So it might be a hard night of driving. And they had to pick up Slim at the Five Corners Bar on Cedar Avenue before 9, before he could do too much damage to himself.

———

Maria had gone straight home after *Golden Days*, said Ethel. "She said she was pooped and for nobody to call her." Frank dialed the number and after six rings Maria answered.

"I'll come right to the point," he said. "I'm in love with you and I want to marry you. But before you say yes—I'm taking a show on the road for a couple weeks or so, and I wish you'd come with me. I want to be with you more than anything else. It'd be a hard trip, not a vacation, two weeks, a lot of driving and bad hotels and bad food and the show isn't Duke Ellington. It isn't even the Norsky Orchestra. But it'd be the greatest two weeks if you were with me. Do you want more time to think about it?"

"Frank," she said, "you shouldn't ask a girl to marry you on the telephone. You're supposed to come over and kneel down and clutch at my ankles."

He let his breath out. "I don't have time to come over."

"What show is it? The *Barn Dance?*"

"The Rise and Shine Show."

She laughed. "With The Shepherd Boys? The jerks with the hair?"

"One and the same."

She screeched. "We'd go on a two-week honeymoon with a gospel quartet in a bus? And get up at six o'clock in the morning? I can't even *talk* that early. Honey, if you saw me at six o'clock in the morning for two weeks, you'd never want to see me again. Sweetie, I can't do it."

She was silent for a moment. He could hear her breathing. He wished she were breathing on his shoulder, her hair in his ear, kissing him on the neck. She said, "I meant to tell you this before but I only found out yesterday. Merle is coming up from Chicago. His sister lives here and he's going to stay with her and he asked me to go out with him a couple evenings and I said yes."

She said, "I know that hurts your feelings, and I'm sorry, Frank. You're the sweetest man who ever was and

I don't want to ever cause you an instant of pain, but I have to think about Merle too."

Now Frank had almost gotten his breath back after it was knocked out of him. Still, there was nothing to say, except *Please come with me, please, and I will make it be wonderful, oh yes, I will make your life happy forever and ever,* and he couldn't say it.

"Well, it's up to you," he said.

"I think you would *like* Merle if you ever met him," she said, vaguely. "He's smart. He's very funny."

I hope his train crashes and falls into Lake Pepin.

"Oh. What's he up to these days?"

"He's trying out for a road show called *Yippee-Ay* that he'd like me to try out for, too. A big musical revue with dancers and trapeze acts and elephants, and he said they have a small speaking role that'd be perfect for me, the part of a Chinese girl, but I'd have to ride an elephant and be in this number where you hang by your ankle fifty feet in the air and a guy twirls you for awhile. But I guess I could do it."

Frank was neatly tearing an envelope into squares and arranging them in facing rows, like houses. Why was she telling him this? The less he heard about Merle, the better. He wanted Merle to be swallowed up by the earth. On the other hand—maybe—she *had* to tell him because he was the only one who could talk her out of this Merle foolishness and get her to see what she already knew but couldn't bring herself to say, which was that she loved him. Loved Frank. *Listen.*

"How long would you be gone with this show?" he asked softly. The thought of Maria gone, his evenings vacant, his arms hanging by his sides.

"I don't know. Six months probably. I don't know if I can do it or not. It's so *long*. Of course it would be fun to see Merle again. He was the first person in theater who ever thought I was good. He helped me with *everything*. I have learned so much from him."

Frank's hand hung over the houses, the shadow of the tip of his index finger touching the exact center of the block, and then swept them off the table with one stroke and they fluttered down—the exquisite pain of those soft sentences! Hearing her speak warmly of Merle was a knife in his side, and he wanted to yell at her to get the hell out, go, find Merle, leave me alone, *Do what you wanted to do all along, You never fooled me for a minute, You were only playing me along, well, I was playing you too, you mean nothing to me, go,* but then the word rang like a gong in his head: *listen. Listen.*

She sighed. "I've never been this confused," she said. "I like you a lot, Frank. You're sweet and you're more level-headed than anybody I ever knew and you're gentle and *good* and I have tender feelings when we're together. Maybe that's the same as love, I don't know. But—" Another exquisite sigh.

And then, two sighs later, she said that her biggest dream was that the Majestic Theater in Chicago would call up and offer her a decent role in a real play. Ibsen or Shakespeare. She would give anything for that. "I'm twenty-one!" she moaned. "I haven't done anything yet!" Merle knew people at the Majestic.

Frank said, "I want to marry you, but there's no reason to rush into something you're not sure about."

"The first time I went to Chicago, I was seventeen, I ran away from my father," she said. "When I got off the train, I had two dollars and a suitcase with all my books in it. I walked west, away from the Loop, looking for a cheap hotel—but a really nice one, you know? I hiked for about eighteen miles down streets of pawnshops and bowling alleys and taverns, streets where I thought I might need to suddenly start running very fast, but I was tired from carrying those books. Finally, I put the suitcase down and sat on it. I couldn't take another step. I said, dear God, if you send me a policeman, I will never do another unkind thing the rest of my life. A man came out of a grocery store and locked the door and saw me and came over and asked what was wrong. He asked me if I was in trouble. Yes, I said, and he drove me to a home for unwed mothers. They gave me a bed and in the morning I went to a class on Bathing the Baby. So I know all about that."

"Well," Frank said, "it's good he wasn't a policeman."

"When will I see you?" she asked.

He said, "In two or three weeks."

When they said goodbye, Frank went to the bedroom and packed his grip. He squeezed in ten pairs of socks, six boxer shorts, six undershirts, three corduroy trousers, a wool shirt and three show shirts, a red plaid tie, and his shaving bag, and then the phone rang.

It was Maria, weeping. "Don't leave me," she said.

"I'm coming back."

"Please don't leave me." She said that no, she would not go tour America with Merle and ride elephants with hair like sewing needles and be twirled by the ankle by a roustabout and hang there with her breasts falling out of her bodice—no, she would stay at WLT and play small parts and hope for something good to come along. She would write to him. She would wait for him.

He would be back in a few weeks. Maybe he would come and live with her, or maybe she would go to Chicago with him. Maybe it would be a vacation. Maybe for good. That was how they left it.

CHAPTER 34

Drunks

R ed picked up Reverend Odom and Frank in the bus at the Antwerp at 7 p.m. and they swung up to the Baptist church to get the Shepherds' clothes out of Al's trunk, planning afterward to pick up Slim and then back to church at ten for the boys. But the boys didn't have their clothes packed. Al did but he'd left his at home. The boys were all sitting in Rudy's livid Pontiac, laughing and eating fried chicken out of a brown sack, and passing another brown sack around, a small one. When Rudy rolled the window down, his eyes didn't focus on Frank at all. "We'll be there when you need us!" he yelled. "Don' worry!" Wendell was sprawled on the passenger side with his head against the window; he looked as if someone had whacked him with a baseball bat. "Grab me some suits outta my closet, wouldja? You know where I live. 12-B. The back door's unlocked. Just don't let the dog out, okay? Grab me a couple of the show suits and some cowboy shirts and some string ties and underwear and—well, you know."

"We gotta be in Roseau at five tomorrow morning," Frank said, peering into the back seat.

"Never missed a show! Never! Ask Odom. He knows," said Elmer. "Nobody ever accused a Shepherd of blowing a gig! You get the clothes, we'll do the shows!" They all laughed.

———

"They're drunk!" said Frank, climbing back on the bus.

"Yes, I suppose so," said Reverend Odom.

"It doesn't bother you to see that?"

"See what?"

Frank scowled. "A bunch of gospel singers going into church fried out of their minds?"

Reverend Odom shook his head. "It takes more than a few Everclears to make a North Dakotan lose his mind, son. The Shepherd Boys always could hold their alcohol."

"What is an Everclear?" asked Frank.

"An Everclear is pure alcohol. So pure you feel it evaporating as it goes down. No frills, no coloring, no anise or juniper flavoring, no little olive or twist of lemon, no fruit. Everclear has but one purpose. It is the rocket ship of the barroom. Leaves no evidence on the breath. It's the preferred beverage of gospel singers."

The bus swung around the block and headed back to the Antwerp.

"You sure don't talk like a minister sometimes," said Frank.

The Reverend bristled. "As a minister, I resent the hell out of that. Just because I know something about the world doesn't mean I—I mean—you don't have to be dumb to be good, you know. It helps but it's not a requirement. Besides, I go way back with the Shepherd Boys. I know them too well to ever be disgusted with them. And there's nothing they could do that I haven't done twice myself."

"I'm sorry," said Frank. "But why do they have to drink?"

"They come from North Dakota, from a little town called Stacy," said the Reverend. "Out on the prairie, where the wind blows all the time and the trees grow up bent and the idea of civilization is a hundred years too late. Everybody who stays in Stacy winds up being exactly like their mother and dad except a little worse. From November to May you feel as if you're living on the moon, and in January, nature makes a serious attempt to kill you, so religion is sort of an occasional hobby compared to people's faith in gin and bourbon. I know. My brother used to pastor a church east of there, Zion Lutheran. The Shepherd boys attended their parents' church, known as The Church of the Perfect Gospel, a little fundamentalist bunch that believed that God tolerates no sin or error, so these people spent six years erecting a church edifice and then discovered the front door hung three-quarters of an inch off. This was due to wind, of course, but it was a test of faith for them, and some of them left to form a new church, based on the faith that God tolerates variation, a *rented* church, and some stayed to keep building the Perfect Church, and the Shepherd boys stayed but they also learned to like whiskey. And whiskey inspired them to sing gospel music.

"Forgive me if I am too frank. There were six of them then, the four Shepherds, Wendell Shepherd's girlfriend Alice Hammer, and her brother Raymond, and every Sunday night after church, they went to East Grand Forks and drove up and down Main Street, drinking whiskey and thinking about sex and singing gospel songs. The ratio was definitely against them. Raymond and Alice went to Zion Lutheran, my brother's church, and being fundamentalist, the Shepherds thought of Lutherans as morally

299

loose. So Wendell kept after Alice and they had a little bit of sex, or what seemed to them like sex, and the four boys in the front seat sang 'Almost Persuaded.' They got a good sound off the windshield, and sounded wonderful except that Raymond couldn't carry a tune in a paper sack. They needed Wendell in the front seat singing, but he was busy in the back with Alice, and besides it was Raymond's car."

Reverend Odom stopped. "This is too long a story," he said. He looked out the window at a factory cruising by. "Where are we?"

"Northeast Broadway," said Frank. "Continue."

"Then one day Elmer Shepherd heard about the WLT Golden Gospel Quartet Tournament taking place in a few weeks at Bathsheba Bible College in Minneapolis. Bathsheba was famous among church kids as the Bible school that put the fun into fundamentalism. Bathsheba believed that a Christian who married a non-believer was lost, so they did what they could to challenge Christian young people to mate. They put boys and girls in close proximity, put a wall between them to build up interest, locked the doors, installed chaperones, gave lectures on Sex—Lust —Concupiscence—Carnal Knowledge—the Desires of the Flesh. . . . After a few weeks of that, a boy could hardly bear to cross his legs.

"Winning the WLT Tournament was going to be the Shepherds' one-way ticket out of Stacy, but first they had to get rid of Raymond. They didn't know how to tell him. Raymond dearly loved to sing. You couldn't find anybody who sang worse and enjoyed it more. Then one Saturday night, a few miles west of town, his car missed a curve and crashed into a tree and he was killed. Only three curves in the county, and only one with a tree near it, so it seemed to be God's will, all right. He hit it dead center at 90 m.p.h. A few days later he was reconstructed and laid out in a $150 mahogany coffin dressed in a new blue suit and looking nicer than he ever looked in his life, his skin problem finally cleared up. I know, because I was visiting my brother, and he officiated at the funeral and I played the organ.

"So this was the Shepherds' debut as a quartet, with Wendell singing lead. They shuffled in, sniffling, and Wendell said to me, 'You know "Rock of Ages" in C?' and I didn't, so they did 'Just as I Am,' 'How Beautiful Heaven Must Be,' and 'The Land Where We'll Never Grow Old.' They were pretty broken up about Raymond, and yet—they sounded *good*. My brother said that Raymond's death left a hole in all their lives that could never be filled, which may have been true, but on the other hand, life is full of holes. At the end of 'The Land Where We'll Never Grow Old,' as my brother began the benediction, Al leaned over to Rudy and said, 'Shit, we're better'n ever.' "

———

"Raymond's death was awful for his girlfriend Pearl Pierce because she was waiting for him at the Clover Motel that night. He had dropped her there with her little pink ted-dybear negligee and he had gone to Grafton for a couple quarts of beer. Ordinarily Raymond was a cautious driver, like most good Lutherans, but here he was on his way back to the motel to find pure joy and his hormones stepped down on the gas and his member took hold of the wheel and he was a goner. Being Lutheran, he needed that beer to dull the pleasure of love, so you could say it was guilt that killed him, and poor Pearl lay there in her negligee, hair combed, teeth brushed, and her breasts lightly scented, lay for a couple hours, and by then was furious at being stood up and she called Raymond's house and said, 'I want to talk to that lying no-good rat's-ass son of yours,' and Raymond's mother had to give her the tragic news. Pearl was so broken up over this that she lost heart and married a minister—she is my wife—and our first child was named Raymond. We parted company five years ago, when I left the church. A sad story, son. A good woman.

"Meanwhile the Shepherds went for the championship. They found a gospel vocal coach, who gave them some good tips, such as: eliminate nervous habits like picking at sores or warts, always look happy when you sing, and if you hit a sour note, don't wince or turn red—close your eyes and hold out your hands, maybe they'll think you went sharp from the emotion. The coach—who was Baptist, by the way—also took Al aside and told him that if he wanted to be a *real* bass singer, he'd have to smoke Luckies and drink Jim Beam before every performance to tone up his voice. Al did as told and the others decided as a matter of loyalty to join him.

"Now, here I'm coming toward the answer to your question, son. The Shepherds knew it was wrong—to get drunk so you can sing gospel music better! It's terrible, of course it is—but some things that you know are wrong, you still do because you're curious to know how it'll turn out. And it turned out great. On a pack of Luckies and a pint of hooch, Al could sing down under the floorboards. And you know that the key to a good gospel quartet is the bass. So they sounded better. And the guilt for having done something wrong is not so terrible if it turns out well. And then, too, they were from Stacy. So that's why the Shepherds drink so much even though they sing gospel music."

"And then?" asked Frank.

"And then what?"

"What happened to them then?"

Reverend Odom's mind had drifted away for a moment.

"I always get thirsty when I think about North Dakota," he said softly. He looked out the window at Franklin Avenue drifting by.

"Do you want to stop for a beer?"

The man's face clouded. "No, I would like an Everclear. And then three beers. But I'm not going to do it." He smiled. "Praise God for the victory. I'm not going to do it." He glanced up at Frank. "*So*—what happened was that the Shepherds won first prize in the regional sing-off in Minnesota, beating out several quartets much better than them. I remember there was one from Park River, N.D., who came with a cheering section that waved pom-pons and screamed:

> Father Son and Holy Ghost,
> North Dakota is the most.
> Minnesota can't come near it.
> Father Son and Holy Spirit."

"Excuse me," said Frank, "but why were you there?"

"By then, I was their accompanist and their driver. So we headed to Minneapolis for the Golden Gospel finals, and Wendell fell asleep in the front seat and saw Raymond in a dream. Raymond was driving a white convertible and he looked blissful. He said, 'This is heaven. I really like it up here. It's neat. But you can't come unless I say so. Maybe I'll let you. I don't know. I gotta think about it. By the way, what were you doing dinking around with my sister, you jerk?' Wendell woke up and threw his arms around me and we almost went in the ditch.

"It scared the Shepherds silly. To this day they're terrified to death to be in a car. Like Wendell said, God loves symmetry and sometimes you can see too clearly what comes next. He was scared that if they won the tournament, then on the long drive home God would run their car into a tree and kill them. It bothered him so much he got the dry heaves backstage and then Rudy told him to straighten out. Rudy said, 'It's only if we lose that we have to drive home. If we win, we stay in Minneapolis and go on the radio, and down here you can walk or take the streetcar.' So they went out and sang their butts off.

"Their big opposition was a quartet called Prisoners of Christ from the State Reform School, with a bass so low he made your shoes shake and a high tenor who made your hair stand on end, and a cowgirls' quartet who sang 'Climb Climb Up Sunshine Mountain' with all the hand motions and who wore extremely short skirts so that when they reached high, high up for the *tippy-top* of Sunshine Mountain, the judges could see their pink undies. The pink looked so much like flesh tone, you had to look hard to see they weren't naked underneath. But the Shepherds beat them dead with their song, 'Crash on the Highway.' It was about Raymond. You can find a copy of it in the record library. But anyway they won. They attended Bathsheba for a year and fooled around with Christian girls—at least they were Christians when they met the Shepherds—and they settled down in Minneapolis, within walking distance of WLT, and they've been singing on the radio for ten years, and always expecting God would punish them, but He hasn't yet. So why should I?"

The bus pulled up in the alley behind the Antwerp. Frank thanked him for the story, and they took the elevator up to the twelfth floor and found Wendell's back door. A big dog was snarling on the other side. "Open it quick and I'll grab him," said the minister, and Frank yanked the door open and the dog leaped and Reverend Odom had him by the collar and twisted it and hauled the dog into the bathroom and locked him in. The apartment stank of garbage and cigarette smoke. Frank found the closet and a suitcase and packed some suits and then he heard the scratch of an old Victrola.

"Here it is," called the minister. " 'Crash on the Highway.' " Frank listened, and so did the dog. He stopped scratching on the bathroom wall. The record hissed and crackled like a bonfire and then an organ slithered in, slow and quivering like gelatin, and Wendell's high mournful voice.

> It was one a.m. when five of us
> Were heading toward the hop,
> Driving cross the barren plains
> So fast we could not stop.
> Raymond was a Christian boy
> And he avoided sin.
> He did not want to be with us,
> He would not taste the gin;
> He would not smoke a cigarette,
> Or neck like you and me.
> Then we swerved and missed the curve
> And crashed into a tree.

WENDELL: I don't know how it happened. I was on the floor of the backseat and the next thing I knew there were flames and broken glass and the smell of burnt rubber and I cried, "Where is everybody?"
ELMER: We were all there without a scratch on our bodies, standing in the road, not even our hair burned, and I was still holding a Dixie cup full of gin and not a drop of it spilled.
AL: Not a button was missing on my clothing, nothing was ripped or torn, I noticed as I hurriedly dressed, and then I thought, where's Raymond?
RUDY: The tree we crashed into was on fire, its branches blazing bright white against the starry western sky, and

there on a branch hung the poor broken bleeding body of Raymond.

WENDELL: We lifted him down and laid him on the ground and he was in pain but he looked up at us and smiled and tried to speak.

ELMER: We put our ears down close and we heard his last words. He said, "I want you guys to go on and sing. You're good. I never told you that before but you are. Music is hard work, you've got to practice and practice until you can't practice anymore and then you have to keep practicing, but you can do it, you can go all the way, and when you reach almost to the top and you need a little bit extra to put you over, then I want you to think of me, Raymond." And then he fell back in death.

> Teen Christian,
> Teen Christian
> Living in the sky.
> You didn't do nothing wrong,
> How come you had to die?
> Teen Christian,
> Teen Christian,
> We look up to you.
> We hope you're happy up above,
> We send you all our love,
> Cause now we're Teen Christians too.

Frank put the last slithery show suit in the suitcase, grabbed up a fistful of underwear and one of socks, and stuffed them in. Reverend Odom opened the bathroom door as they both headed out, and the dog hit the back door full-tilt just as they slammed it behind them.

CHAPTER 35

The Long
Night

S|lim was standing out in front of the Five Corners.
He did not appear to be sober, but he recognized
them and boarded the bus without assistance. "I need
some smokes," he said. "Anybody got a quarter?" They
got smokes and drove on to the church. Elmer was ready
and Rudy, but Wendell was camped in the vestibule signing autographs and cracking jokes and having his picture
taken and Frank had to pry him loose from a gaggle of
girls, who clung to his seaweed arms, and maneuver the
star through the ranks of the faithful and up the bus steps
where he turned and flung his arms open wide and yelled,
"I love ya! Every one of ya! Love ya!" He ducked into
the bus and pulled off his tie and said, "Holy shit, gimme
a beer." Then he peered out the window. "Didja guys
see that little brunette number with the blouse? Her nipples
were poking out so you coulda hung your coffee cup on
'em." Rudy hooted. "You sure bring out the best in 'em,
Brother! You had 'em creaming in their jeans! Not a dry
seat in the house tonight!" The bus pulled away from the

church at 11:07, by Frank's watch. "Hang on to your socks!" said Red. Elmer was lying in his bunk in back, smoking a cigar. Al was asleep already, butt out in a top bunk, snoring lightly. "I need a woman so bad I can taste her," said Wendell.

"In six hours," said Reverend Odom, "we'll be in Roseau, on the radio. Roseau is seven hours from here, I believe. God help us."

The bus was an old Hawkeye Custom Coach, with inboard toilet and kitchen, that slept eight, supposedly, and there were nine of them, the four Shepherds plus Slim, Reverend Odom, and Red Pfister the driver-drummer, and Barney Barnum the engineer, who also cooked, and Frank who would announce and sell the songbooks and 45s and pass the hat at their church gigs. The bus had belonged to The Rankins, another gospel family and the Shepherd Boys' hated rivals, who were now touring in a larger bus down South, where people loved them and where it was warm. "I hope snakes bite 'em," said Rudy. "I hope they catch hemorrhoids from each other, great big grapes the size o' lemons, hemmies so big they can't sit down, and then I hope God sends each one of 'em the biggest, hardest stool of their lives. That's what I wish for The Rankins."

This bus had seemed luxurious to Elmer when it was full of smiling Rankins in their white cowboy suits with the green and gold fringe. He bought it from them hoping some of their luck would come with it, and found out that the clutch was shot. Al nicknamed it Rankins' Revenge, but of course The Rankins were sitting pretty and had nothing to avenge. They were hot, burning up the charts, with a big cheesy photo of them on the cover of *Radio Romance* this month and a story, "The Christmas I Can't Forget," by that turd Ronnie Rankin describing the Christmas he spent visiting orphanages and handing out gifts to crippled kids—what a liar! No, it was the Shepherds who were dragging ass.

A 6 a.m. broadcast and a noon show just to pay over-head, and an evening concert to earn the salaries, and their profits (if any) had to come from songbook and record sales—WLT was paying them squat for the tour, and as for the sponsors, Home Salad and Prestige Tire & Muffler, their total contribution was thirty quarts of cole slaw and six tubeless tires for the tour, and the slaw was sour and the tires were the wrong size. The people at Home felt that the gospel audience probably was the sort that made its own salads. They told Elmer that they would not renew their sponsorship past January unless things picked up. Meanwhile, Rudy had heard a rumor that The Rankins were about to buy a *plane*.

"I pray to God they crash in flames and land right square on their hinders," he said.

But the bus was too small for nine, a fact that dawned on them as they sped through St. Cloud and started feeling sleepy. The four bunks were the Shepherds', of course, and Slim and the Reverend Odom, who were shorter, were supposed to share the table, which folded down to make a bed, and Frank and Barney would take turns sleeping in the hammock over the driver's seat, whichever one was not talking to Red and keeping him awake, but the motion of the hammock made a person sick to his stomach, and the table-bed was only four feet wide. A tight left-hand curve would dump the outside man (Slim, who had weak kidneys) into the aisle. He tried to rig up straps to keep himself in, but was afraid he might fall in his sleep and be strangled by them. So nobody slept at first except Al and Rudy and Wendell. And Reverend Odom, slumped in the seat behind the driver. Red was barrelling north at 90 m.p.h. and the Reverend's bald head rolled from side to side like a loose bowling ball. Barney sat at the table, staring out the window at the farms zooming by as they rocketed north on Highway 10, and Frank sat beside him, writing a letter to Maria, and Slim sat across the aisle, slumped down, playing his guitar and singing:

> There was an old bugger named Rudy
> Who cared not for youth or for beauty
> But for ignorant sluts
> With thunderous butts
> Whom he jumped as a matter of duty.

> Ay-yi-yi-yi.
> In China they never eat chili.
> So let's have another one just like the other one,
> And waltz me around again, Willie.

He was just beginning, "There was an old fairy named Elmer," when Elmer emerged from the back, sat down beside him, and sighed. "This is a hell of a way to start off a tour on such a low note," he said. Elmer had a slight lisp that got more pronounced when he was upset, and Frank could tell that he was a long way from being upset. Elmer was the oldest Shepherd and he had put up with so much from his brothers, he didn't upset easily.

"Slim," he said, "I wish you'd try to be a little more positive about the music business."

"Elmer," said Slim, "you're even crazier than I am and that's saying something."

"This band is right on the verge of a big, big success, Slim. You saw those folks tonight. They were crazy about us. We *entertained* those folks tonight. They loved us to death. We weren't like all those poosy-woosy gospel groups who stand around and hum with their hands folded and their eyes rolled up toward the ceiling—man, we did a *show* tonight. No, we're on the verge of success, Slim, and you oughta stick with us, but you get so negative sometimes, it's hard to put up with."

"Elmer," said Slim, "this tour is going to hell and it hasn't even started. I saw the itinerary. This show was put together by people who hate you, Elmer. Four and five shows a day, miles apart, in the dead of winter. It's a killer. They're trying to shove us off the end of the earth. This isn't for promotion—you're nuts if you think so. This is winter! It makes no sense. You don't want us down in the dumps? Fine. I'll grin till my teeth get a tan, but that doesn't change facts. We're going up north, the roads are glare ice, and Red is a drummer, not a driver, and one of these nights we skid off the road and into a tree, and we'll have to be buried in closed coffins. Those of us up in the front anyway. You princes back there in your warm beds, I suppose you'll wind up fine."

Hearing the remark about his driving, Red accelerated. Frank glanced at the speedometer. Ninety-five. "I figure that seventy should be good enough to get us there," he said, looking over Red's shoulder at the centerline stripes that whooshed underneath them, like solid white rail. Red liked to stay in the middle of the road and take the curves low. He sailed down into the left lane on a left-hand curve and let the force of the curve bring him back up. "You never know when you may lose time later," he said. "Might run into snow north of here. Gotta make time while the road is good."

> There was an old lecher named Wendell
> Whose cock was indeed monumental
> But so worn from abuse,
> He could only induce
> Orgasm by inserting a candle.
>
> Ay-yi-yi-yi.

"Candle doesn't rhyme with Wendell," Elmer pointed out. "I'm going to bed." He trundled back to his bunk and settled in as the bus went into a sharp curve. He added, "Better get your rest, boys. Big day tomorrow." A long honk went sailing past them on the left, and Red swore under his breath, *damn farmers*. He held to the middle of the road. Frank leaned around to look out the windshield and to check the speedometer. Back down to ninety, but the road was curvier and there were more dips and potholes. "Looks like the road's getting bad," he observed. "She'll get worse later on," said Red. And Slim sang another verse:

> There was an old fellow named Al
> Who wouldn't take any old gal.
> He preferred one with boobs
> And Fallopian tubes
> And perhaps a vaginal canal.

> Ay-yi-yi-yi.

He paused, hoping for a word from Al, but Al was out cold, and when Al was asleep, nothing could wake him up before he was ready to rise. The other Shepherds had carried him in and out of buses and hotels, they had parked him in taverns, they had leaned him against the walls and draped him over tables, and once they had floated him in a reflecting pool, to see if a sleeping man will float, and he never woke up once. You could use Al for a shelf, he slept so well. Once, on a *Barn Dance* tour years ago, Slim put the sleeping Al's hand in a bowl of warm water to see if he'd wet the bed. It took three bowls, but it worked, and Al still didn't wake up.

Slim sang a verse about the sailor named Tex who

avoided premarital sex by thinking of Jesus and penile diseases and beating his meat below decks.

"I bet you can't do a verse about Elmer," said Barney. Slim said that for ten dollars he would be glad to do Elmer too. "Ha," said Barney, "you wouldn't dare."

As they slowed down to go through Motley, Reverend Odom awoke and stumbled back to the toilet. It was hard to keep his balance, half-asleep, the bus careening from side to side. The toilet was a plywood closet, three feet square, that one of The Rankins had constructed, that sat over the left rear axle. The throne emptied through a large hole straight down onto the inside edge of the left rear tire, presumably so that the deposit would be dispersed. At least, that was the original idea.

The Rankins were famous in the gospel world for their fascination with the colon. Each Rankin had a different secret for regularity, a pill, a potion, a salve, and each of them was glad to talk about it. Sometimes they suffered from the runs and other times they were locked up like Fort Knox, but The Rankins always tried to execute a good bowel movement before each and every performance. They could not sing their best without it. And after years of touring, when The Rankins finally could afford to stay in hotel rooms, they found that they couldn't be sure of a good dump unless they were aboard a speeding bus. So, an hour before the show, the five Rankins would pile into the bus and drive back and forth, up and down the highway, for an hour if necessary, until they were done. No enema ever worked for them in the same way. You could run a hose up a Rankin and never get the results that a ride on the bus would give. But the bus had to be going fast. Right around eighty was where The Rankins got loosened up.

The bus toilet had the opposite effect on the Shepherds. With the toilet seat placed over the rear wheel, a person

313

was liable to get a volley of gravel from below, and the effect of getting a buttload of gravel was to clamp the boys up tight. Whenever a Shepherd disappeared into the john, some drivers liked to veer to the left and get that wheel onto the shoulder and hear the victim howl, but Red was not the sort who went in for jokes of the juvenile kind.

He told Frank this—and told him about The Rankins and their lower-tract peculiarities—a half-hour later as the bus sat parked outside the Milaca hospital. It was one-thirty in the morning and Reverend Odom was inside, having a small twig removed from his member. He had been half-asleep as he stood peeing and when he was impaled, he woke up immediately, but he was dignified about it. "I am bleeding and I need to have a splinter removed," he announced. "Kindly stop and find me a doctor. Either that or shoot me. It hurts."

By the time he got mended and had carefully eased himself back onto the bus, it was almost three-thirty. Two hours and twenty minutes to go two hundred miles. Red pulled out on the highway. "Hang on to your shorts," he said.

Frank had arranged seat cushions on the floor, back behind the luggage, for the old man to sleep on, and he covered him with an old quilt. "I will live, but barely," Reverend Odom whispered. "I am only grateful that I don't need to explain this to my wife." And he closed his eyes and began to snore. Barney was asleep on the table. Slim poured himself a cup of whiskey. He tried to pour quietly but Elmer heard it and woke up. "Put the bottle away," he said.

Slim pointed out the safety aspect of drinking: how so many drunks escape injury in terrible crashes that kill sober men instantly.

"I hate to think of what you're going to sound like in the morning," said Elmer.

Slim bristled. He stood up and lurched back and hung on to the bunk and informed Elmer that, with the Shepherd Boys, musicianship was a lost cause. The way Wendell hammed it up, you couldn't tell the difference between "Old Rugged Cross" and "Into a Tent Where a Gypsy Boy Lay," it was all the same to him, and since Wendell sang almost everything in the key of F, Slim used the same fingering and the same licks on every song—it was like cutting two-by-fours at the sawmill. Well, Elmer said, if that was how he felt, there were plenty of sawmills up around Roseau where he could get a job.

"That was not the remark of a true Christian," Slim said. Then he toppled over on top of Rudy, who was sleeping on his back and who doubled up in pain.

"Sing that verse about Elmer," muttered Barney, who was awake now.

Elmer got up and hauled Slim off Rudy, half-carried him up to the front, and planted him next to Frank in the seat behind Red. Red had the speedometer pinned at ninety-five, the needle wouldn't go any farther. They could have been going a hundred-fifty for all Frank knew. Elmer sat down in the opposite seat. "Slow down," he said. Red eased it down to ninety.

"Listen to me," Elmer said, draping an arm around Slim. "This is temporary. We're going to make it back to where we were and even better. The best is yet to be, Slim. You'll see."

———

Frank knew that the Shepherd Boys had once been, if not at the top, then headed that way. Their "He Gave Me a Crown" had been a big hit in 1942, and they toured nationally on The War Bonds Gospel Caravan, but then Rudy slugged a nosy reporter in St. Louis and Al was caught selling ration books and Wendell got involved with a woman in Seattle who turned out to be much younger than he imagined. They lost their record contract and went through a number of years subsisting on a WLT salary that Elmer felt the Lord intended to make them dependent on Him. Now he was optimistic again. If they could hold on at WLT for one more year, they'd have the money to bring out his new song, "My Mother's Bible," and it would be a hit and they'd enter a new phase of packed auditoriums and big money and a brand-new air-suspension bus with large bunks.

He whispered this into Slim's ear, patting him on the back, shaking him gently. "You have to have faith," he said. "It's about to get better. I know it. I can feel it coming."

Just then the bus hit a big dip and they all flew up in the air. Frank cracked his head hard on the ceiling. From in back came a muffled cry from Wendell, then a crash as he lumbered out of bed and was thrown against the toilet wall. Then, when Red braked, Wendell was flung forward and lost his balance and landed on Elmer and wound up head-first in the stairwell, where he lost his cookies. It took him a long time to lose them all. He lost most of them right away but then a few more cookies came up and then a few more and then another one.

"This is the longest night of my life, I swear," said Elmer.

Then some more cookies.

"Now you know how I feel when you sing 'Give Me the Roses While I Live,' " said Slim.

They flew on down the road. Red opened the front door and Elmer threw a bucket of water on the steps and that cleaned it out a little but not much. Rank odors filled the bus. Elmer helped Wendell back to bed.

"We're going to die tonight," Slim muttered. Frank

offered to heat up some milk for him, but Slim had lost his appetite for milk. His mind was on the crash ahead. He sat, stiff as a board, and stared ahead at the spot where they would meet their end. "You've been good to me for the most part," he said to Elmer, though Elmer had gone. He asked Frank to put his guitar under the seat and wrap it in a quilt. Then he took off his suspenders and tied one end around his neck and the other around the leg of the table behind him. He didn't want to be disfigured in a crash, he said, and this way his neck would be broken upon impact, and his family would have the comfort of knowing that he had died without prolonged suffering, and there would be reviewal. "When Coop Jackson was killed, it took them eight hours to put his head together, and they had to make one-half of his face out of latex rubber," he informed Frank.

"Shut up," said Red. "You give me the creeps."

"It's colder'n a well-digger's ass in here," said Slim.

Red told him to shut up.

"Okay," said Barney. "Here's ten dollars. Go on. Sing the one about Elmer." So Slim reached down and unwrapped the guitar and tuned it back up and sang:

> There was an old bastard named Shepherd
> With a big hairy ass like a leopard,
> Where all of the fairies
> Liked to pick dingleberries
> And fry them up, salted and peppered.

> Ay-yi-yi-yi.

"That didn't rhyme with Elmer at all and I'm not paying," said Barney. Slim reminded him that the verse was supposed to be *about* Elmer, that nothing had been promised as to rhymes. "You welsh on a bet, then go ahead, be a piker, I don't care. I forgive you for it. I forgive everybody. I don't want to go to my grave with any hard feelings toward anyone." He began to play "Nearer My God to Thee." Red turned on the radio, loud, to drown him out, and Slim put down the guitar, crawled under the table, and fell asleep. It was four in the morning.

"Can you keep awake?" asked Frank. Red snorted. "Swipe me some smokes out of Wendell's jacket. A pack of Luckies and two more Grain Belts and I'll have us in Roseau in no time."

They were in a dense forest now and Frank thought, "What if a deer runs out on the road?" Daddy had once told him about a man from Mindren who hit a deer and the deer flew up and its four feet came through the windshield and it kicked the man to shreds with its sharp little hooves. One minute he was barrelling along, listening to the radio, on top of things, and the next a deer was kicking him to death. His last thought was probably, *This is impossible*, just as Daddy must have thought. Daddy was steaming along, his hand on the throttle, hollering at Jack and A.P., and next thing the horizon fell over and No. 9 slipped off the tracks and Daddy thought, *This can't be*, and he was eaten alive by a blazing sun of pure pain.

Frank's head jerked—Red was reaching back and poking him. "Don't fall asleep on me, buddy. We got a hundred miles to Roseau. What do you want to talk about for a hundred miles? You want to hear how I started out in music?"

Red bounced in the seat to wake up. He slapped himself. He shook his head so hard his cheeks flapped. *Plip plip plip plip plip.*

"I learned to play drums by milking cows. That's the truth. I had ten cows to milk morning and evening and I learned a staggered five-teat rhythm, fast and steady, and kept varying it so my hands wouldn't stiffen up—and then I'd pour the milk into the milk cans and sit and go rap-a-taptap on the empty pails, copying the rhythms of the threshers and the mower and the corn planter and the auger, the beat of the big steam-powered combines in the fall, what a blast, the thump and the clatter and bang, the big flywheel going *whoopa-wocka-whoopa-wocka* and the big blades answering *shoop-shoop-shubidua-bop*, and when I was eighteen, I heard King Oliver on the radio and that was all I needed, I packed my bag, said goodbye to the cows, and went and told my dad.

" 'I'm going to Chicago to play in King Oliver's band,' I said.

" 'I can't allow you go, son,' my dad said to me, and he stood in the kitchen door. 'A man cannot make his way in the world playing music. You go out there and they'll lift you up and carry you around and then they'll drop you down so hard you'll never get off the ground again. No, sir. It's tempting, and I understand that, but I couldn't let you go and still call myself a Christian. Before you go, you'll have to knock me down.'

"Well, sir, my dad was a big man without a bit of flab on him, with fists as hard as horse's hooves, but I swung and hit him on the tip of his nose, and it drove the bone up into his brain and killed him. My dad lay dead in the doorway. He had felt no pain and he had died in a Christian moment and gone straight to heaven, but still it felt bad to kill my dad, and I thought to myself, 'Now everything he said will come true, as punishment.' But I went anyway. Might as well be punished for a musician as punished for a farmer. So I headed for Chicago but I wound up in Minneapolis, playing at a burlesque joint on Chicago Avenue called The Rapid Rose."

Frank lay down across the seat. Had he heard right?

Was he riding on a bus driven by a man who had killed his father with one punch? A murderer at the wheel. Nevertheless, the moment his head touched the cushion he was gone. Then it was light. The bus sat outside a church. Reverend Odom was shaking him. "Showtime," he said.

CHAPTER 3 6

Monday Morning

Patsy Konopka heard about the *Rise and Shine* tour from Art Finn when she called him Monday morning, worried about Frank. The silence upstairs had kept her awake half the night. Four or five times, she had gone to the hole in the kitchen ceiling and listened for his snore, thinking he might have come home while she dozed. She had keen ears from living alone for years, and had always been able to pick up the sound of his breathing. Now, nothing.

"They sent him up north with the Shepherds, poor kid," said Art. "Running around in a broken-down bus with that bunch of lowlifes and they're forecasting a blizzard for the weekend. Did you hear about Slim Graves?" No, she hadn't, and she didn't care to, it was Frank she wanted to hear about.

Roy Jr. had heard about the blizzard forecast, too, and thought of the *Rise and Shine Show*, and called up the Norsk Nightingale, and said, "Jens, we may have that morning show opening up for you that you wanted, I'll let you know next week." The Nightingale was stunned with joy, thinking he meant the 8 a.m. slot, and called Elsie and Johnny and asked them to be his band. "We're on our way, kiddoes!" he cried. "No more Jubilee!" He and Leo hadn't spoken for years, though working together on the noontime show, since the time the Nightingale accused Leo of not chipping in his fair share for gas for a fishing trip to Morain. Elsie said, "Did you hear about Slim Graves?" She had heard that he had died on the highway and all of his family with him. The Nightingale thought, "Well, that 6:30 Sunrise Waffle spot wouldn't be bad either."

———

Frank sounded exhausted on the radio from Roseau, Maria thought, hoarse and a little shrill, and when he talked about Home Salads and what a comfort they were to the Shepherd Boys when touring, there was a rasp in his voice like an old sideshow barker, but then he dedicated a song to her, "Traveling That Highway Home," and she sat up in bed, charmed. What a sweet guy he was.

Merle turned his head on the pillow next to her and muttered, "Hey, turn down the damn radio. Please." He squeezed his eyes shut and rolled over, his back to her, taking most of the blanket with him. She lay, naked, looking up at the ceiling. It seemed to her the most fascinating coincidence that she was listening to one boyfriend on the radio and lying in bed with another. Merle had arrived Saturday. They had dinner. He slept on her couch. They walked around the city lakes on Sunday—Nokomis, Harriet, Calhoun, Lake of the Isles, Cedar—and went to the radio station Sunday evening. She had gotten them parts in a play by Vesta called "Edison and the Magic Lantern"—Vesta felt that only radio could dramatize the invention of motion pictures—and afterward the two of them walked home, and she said, kidding him, "How are your ducks doing?" in reference to his pair of blue undershorts with yellow ducks that she had washed for him Saturday night. He took this line to be encouraging, and she didn't say otherwise, nor did she protest when he opened her blouse and covered her breasts with kisses. After all, she had invited him to stay. And here he was. It was nice. To think that such a dear old friend could be so intense in the dark, so urgent, and cry out, and do it again and again. It was nice. But she loved Frank. She knew that now. She said it softly to see if it were true. It was. Merle grunted.

"Honey," she said, "it's six-thirty. I've got to get somewhere." He grunted again. *Oh Frank*, she thought. *Please don't try to find out about this. Please just accept that I am yours.* And then she heard a man singing on the radio, a voice like syrup in a glove, "Hello, lovey honey lamb, I'm a lover man, I am, love to find you half-asleep and put my johnny way in deep. O yes yes yes, lift your pretty little dress. O well well well, sure do love that fishy smell. O my my my, sure is nice, that sugar pie. Well, hey hey hey, here comes johnny, on his way."

——————

Patsy had overslept and missed the Shepherd Boys broadcast that morning and not hearing Frank's voice struck her as an acute deprivation. He had a beautiful voice and she had meant to tell him so, but you had to be careful, look at Reed Seymour. She told *him* once what a nice voice he had and the boy went on the air and tried to be John Gielgud. All that tremulous fluting and whinnying and the shopgirl dips and quavers and the pale Anglican piety and the faint suggestion of pain and loss—while

323

reading a dogfood commercial!—no, you had to be careful telling a young midwestern man that he spoke well. Boys in the Midwest grow up without a word of praise, their parents fearful that a compliment might make them vain, and by the age of nineteen, they are riding so low their boat may be swamped by one small wave. A compliment may go to a young man's head and he may try to be as good as he thinks he is and from then on he won't be able to talk worth beans. No, you had to be careful praising a young man.

Patsy sat spooning her boiled egg out of the shell and thought that maybe she could write Frank into *The Hills of Home* as a young reporter from the Bigville *Beacon* come down from the big city to snoop around town—for what? he won't say, and rumors abound. Buried bodies from gangland slayings? a discrepancy in the bank's books?— and then Fritz and Frieda are sure they know why: *oil.* They begin quietly to buy up land and go deep in hock and accumulate a dozen small parcels around Happy Valley. Then Frank writes a front-page story about a strange bacterium in the drinking water that causes liver disease, and of course the value of real estate falls to nothing, Fritz and Frieda are ruined, and after all those years of drinking six glasses of water a day, their livers ache and their hands turn blotchy.

A good idea, and Frank would be perfect as a young reporter, keen but lovable. He could be a young reporter who arrives in Elmville to investigate something on *Friendly Neighbor*, she thought. Ha-*ha!* He could investigate Delores! The little Italian tramp.

Patsy paced as the ideas jumped into her head.

Delores could be a Mafia gun moll who calls Chicago late at night while the Bensons sleep and conducts mysterious business with a man named Gino, talking tough talk *sotto voce* with a cigarette dangling from her lip, which

Frank overhears, but she sees his shadow and slips him a Mickey Finn in his morning juice but Dad takes it instead and slips unconscious to the floor. In the uproar, she grabs the silverware and the taxi arrives and Frank offers to help with her suitcase and it falls open and bundles of fresh C-notes tumble out and she says, "Freeze, buster, I got two guns concealed in my blouse and they're both pointed at you right now!"

Well, maybe not her blouse.

Patsy rolled a page into the typewriter and as she did, she saw her reflection in the glass door of the highboy, her tangled black hair with swashes of gray, the bags under her eyes, the pouches under her chin, and then she held her head high, rose, and closed the door. Intelligence will triumph in the end, she thought. Brains over boobs.

It was a big morning for gossip at WLT, with a knot of people around Laurel at the front desk and more upstairs by Ethel's desk and other groups in the Green Room and the Women's Bureau, and messengers darting from one to the other with fresh bulletins, and the gist of it was that Slim was on the road with the Shepherd Boys and so The Blue Movers had done the Sunrise Waffle show in his place after spending the night around Seven Corners crawling from Larson's Bar to Koerner's Copenhagen Club to Palmer's to the Stockholm where they had had a skinful, whiskey and beer and brandy and peppermint schnapps, and had gotten plotzed, blotto, schnokkered, burned to the ground, so they wound up on the control room floor at 6:15 a.m., too drunk to know who they were or why. A musician friend of Slim's who had chauffeured them to WLT in his truck had picked up a guitar and done the Sunrise Waffle show alone under the name "Mr. Pokey" and had sung a song called, "Baby, I Got a Big Wiener for Your Bun," and that Ray Soderbjerg, on hearing it at home, had collapsed in the bathtub and died, either from the concussion or by drowning. That the station would be sold to the Wills radio chain, the cheapest SOBs in broadcasting, and that everybody would be fired in two weeks with only one week's worth of severance.

What was true was the part about Mr. Pokey. Itch had the proof, on tape, and the men of WLT—the stuff was too strong for women, Itch said—packed into the control room and they played the Waffle Show over and over. Not only did Mr. Pokey sing the hot dog song—

> Baby, I got a big wiener for your bun.
> Big and hot and sweet,
> Where you ever seen such meat?
> I got lots of mustard too—and (uh *uh*) onions . . .

but he also sang "Ram Rod Daddy" and "You Got Me Dancing in My Pants" and "I'm the Best Banana in the Bunch"—

> I'm the best banana in the bunch.
> Baby, don't you know
> I'm not for dessert, I am your dinner and your lunch.
> Peel me nice and slow,
> With just a gentle squeeze,
> And I don't mind to ask it—
> Please put me in your basket,
> That lovely little basket
> That you keep between your knees.

He sang one after the other, dedicating them to various WLT people—Ray, Patsy Konopka, Faith Snelling, Slim, Wendell Shepherd—"Here's one of Dad Benson's favorite songs"—and was smooth and professional—

326

paused for the commercial and said, "Now here's LaWella with a word from the Sunrise Waffle kitchen," and LaWella, stunned, came in with a recipe for pigs in blankets ("After the dough has risen, heat your oven to 325 and wrap each wiener in a little muffin of dough, making sure it fits nice and tight"), and then Mr. Pokey said, "Mmmmm-*mmm*, that sure sounds good, Miz LaWella, I hope you'll be making me up some of those little piggies *real* soon," and then he sang, "I'm your handyman, I do anything you want me to," and "Got so much lead in my pencil, I could write you a *book* tonight," and then poor LaWella returned ("LaWella Wells, tell these folks about your sweet li'l cakes, honey——") and had to do a commercial about how good Sunrise pancakes are if you spread jelly on them and roll them up tight ("You can use two if you like it thicker, but make sure to put enough jelly in so a little bit oozes out the end when the cakes are rolled"). Mr. Pokey thought those roll-ups sounded just right. Then he closed the show with "Baby, You're My Radio":

> Baby, you're my radio,
> I love the way you broadcast all your charms.
> Your lovely little knobs
> That do their special jobs——
> I'd love to hold your speakers in my arms.
> Your dial makes me smile,
> You're the star of every show.
> And I guess you know that when a
> Man extends his big antenna,
> Baby, you're my radio.

It was quite a morning. The phones rang and rang, and the switchboard lady had to be augmented by two others. "Thank you for calling," they said over and over, until they were hoarse. "We appreciate hearing your views on our WLT programs. Thank you, ma'am. Thank you." Quite a morning. Dad Benson fell into a hiccupping fit in the middle of the *Almanac* and Reed Seymour had to finish it for him, while the old veteran was hauled away to a doctor. And minutes later, while Roy Jr. was phoning around, trying to find Frank so he could fire Slim, Miss Lily Dale stopped in the middle of "Charlie Darling," and she was weeping. On the air. She sobbed, "Oh, my dears, I am so sorry, but this week will be my last here on the little street where old friends meet, unless you all write to WLT or give them a ring this morning and tell them how you feel." She sobbed. Then she laughed. "Oh, heavens, I know I'm nothing to look at, but how we need these old songs—I know I do—Oh, Mister Tippy, play 'Ave Maria' for me." And she sang the hymn to the Virgin, and at the end, after the last long lingering note, she whispered, "That's a song my mother used to sing, and though she's been dead these many years, she lives on in the songs she loved. Please call or write today. Thank you so very much. Goodbye! Goodbye!"

The moment the *On Air* light blinked off, Roy Jr. strolled into the studio and stood, hands on his hips. He shook his head. "Dear Aunt Lottie, what are we ever going to do with you?"

"Keep me and cherish me," she said. "Bring me flowers. And when I'm too old to sing anymore, have the kindness to shoot me like you would a horse."

He personally wheeled her to the back elevator and down to the loading dock, avoiding the crowd of forty foaming fans in the lobby, all in a lather that the Friendly Neighbor station could consider dumping a bosom friend after all

328

those years, passing around a petition that vowed that the undersigned would *never* eat Betty Brand Party Wafers again until WLT offered Lily Dale a lifetime contract, and hissing at poor Laurel who had to tell them that, no, they couldn't go upstairs and talk to Mr. Soderbjerg in person. No, he wouldn't come down and talk to them. "How can you work at a place like this and live with your conscience?" a woman screeched at her. Laurel said, "I sleep a lot."

Monday Afternoon

Ray was not dead, he had only gone to the dentist. His No. 4 upper tooth, to the left of the incisors, the tooth used to crunch a peppermint stick, had gotten infected around Thanksgiving and the gum swoll up, and he had dosed it for awhile with an elm compress soaked in whiskey, and reduced the pain to a steady throb, but then it got worse, about the time Vesta left for London. There was a meeting there of University Women for World Understanding, and a full bill of speeches by authors and mystics and such, but what sold Vesta on going was the thought that she would miss the WLT Christmas party. *No eggnog, no damp handshakes, no making small talk with people who weren't that smart sober.* So off she flew, and the same afternoon his cheek had ballooned out and the pain was insistent, so he dropped in at Dr. Nordstrom's office. The dentist was reading the paper. He was a stocky young man with thick glasses and his practice was slim because he perspired heavily and breathed hard while working on patients for fear that he might hurt them. Many people found this disconcerting.

The door jingled as Ray entered but the young man was absorbed in the news. "Morning, John!" said Ray. The young man leaped out of the chair, knocking a half dozen steel picks off the tray. He stood with the chair between him and the patient. "What is it?" he said, his eyes big. "An emergency," said Ray. "Why didn't you call?" the young man pleaded. "I hate to have things just *thrown* at me, with no warning."

He took an X-ray of the tooth, and then another, and poked at it timidly with a pick, and sprayed it with water, and put a cotton plug under Ray's lip, and looked at the X-rays, and announced that the tooth was infected. He thought about this for a minute. "Then let's pull it out," said Ray. "I don't have all day." The young man pondered this. Then he filled an immense syringe with anesthetic and, with a hand that was trembling, eased it into Ray's gum and uttered a soft murmur of pain, "Ohhh!" As he slowly pumped the liquid in, Ray felt the left side of his head go numb.

As the young man waited for the anesthetic to take hold, he read a book that appeared to Ray to be a textbook with diagrams of teeth. He jotted down a few notes. Then he glanced at the X-ray again, and let out a low gasp. "Oh no," he said. "I never noticed this. Oh my God. Oh, this is terrible."

"What is it?" asked Ray.

"I think you have cancer."

"In my tooth?"

"No. In your jaw. It looks like a terrible tumor or something up in the roof of your mouth and it's in the bone and it's—oh, this is an awful thing to have to tell somebody. I'm sorry! This is just terrible!" The young man's eyes were full of tears. "You woke up this morning and you thought it was just a tooth and you come down here and now I have to tell you that you have cancer. I'm sorry. Maybe I shouldn't have told you!"

He changed into a fresh white smock and he put Ray, who was now stunned and glassy-eyed as well as numb from the neck up, into his car and drove him to Abbott Hospital and delivered him to a doctor named Forbes who sat him down in a row of miserable people sitting in the hall. The young man squeezed Ray's hand and burst into tears and fled around the corner. Forbes disappeared into an inner office. The man next to Ray was slumped down as if shot and he stank of whiskey. Ray looked straight ahead at a water stain on the opposite wall, which somewhat resembled the state of Texas. A state he had never seen nor felt any desire to see. Texas nor most of the rest of the South, except maybe Nashville. He had known a Nashville girl once named Judy Jo who taught him a bedroom technique called The One-Man Band; Or, The Ballplayer's Friend. Now he was sick, maybe near the end, and he'd never see her again. How gladly would he trade this whole week for one minute alone with her!

The man next to him said, "The last days are here, the last days of the end of time, and when I was young I scorned the thought and now I see they are here. And God will come upon us with fire and a sword. And God will open the book. And our torment will be great."

"Shut up, ya old rum-dum," said a man down the line, and there were murmurs of agreement.

The man looked at the wall. "And there will be no escape from it. And they will cry out for comfort and there will be none. And they will cry out for the end to come, and the end will not come, only grief and pain. And their weeping and gnashing will rise up to the heavens, and there will be no answer, only fire and the sword."

Ray blinked. He was not sure if he wanted to go quick

or go slow. Quick, he thought, but how could a person want to cease to exist when the world was full of so many delights, such as the nurse who now came and helped him up. "Mr. Soderbjerg, we're ready for you now," she said. Such a sweet girl! She took his old hand in hers and he heaved himself up on his feet. "That's the way!" she exclaimed, as if he had leaped over a fence for her. She led him around the corner to the room where Forbes would see him. Ray took her arm and his hand brushed against her breast and he felt a quickening of the loins. *O love, dear love.* Even at the end of the last days, a strong persistent urge. Maybe he wasn't sick after all. Maybe a few days' rest and some little green pills and it'd all clear up. Maybe she'd like to go to New York in the spring.

———

Roy Jr. had no idea where Ray was until around five o'clock, and meanwhile Ethel had been dispatched to Ray's house to search for him and Laurel was sent to the police. The switchboard ladies had given up answering calls and gone home after lunch. Between Mr. Pokey's party songs and Lily Dale's tearful appeal for public support, WLT had managed to touch the folks in radioland all too deeply, and then, on *Friendly Neighbor*, Dad Benson, weak from his intestinal troubles, misread a line and instead of saying to Dale Snelling, "Well, Frank, did you send the seed all right?" (referring to a complicated order at Benson Feed & Seed that had to go out by parcel post), said, "Where did you spend your seed last night?"

FRANK: Where did I spend my *seed* last night?
DAD: I mean . . .
FRANK: You're one to talk, ya big letch—how about you keep your hands off my *wife!*

JO: (*Burst into tears*)
DAD: What?
(*Slap*)
TINY: Mornin', everybody! Howdy, Miz Jo! Lawd, but
them pancakes smells good! Hoo-eee! Whass dat you
sayin' 'bout dem seeds, Mista Dad—you means dem
seeds dat dey orders up to Hatchetville, you askin' if'n
I sent dem seeds, why sho, Mista Dad, why *sho!* you
knows I did! Yassuh! Yassuh!

Dale and Faith Snelling stalked out of the studio at the
end of the show, tight-lipped and green in the gills, and
a few hours later she phoned Roy Jr. to say that neither
of them would be returning to *Friendly Neighbor* again.
They planned to return to Bird Island and resume their
careers in secondary education. Dad, she said, had told
her he wouldn't continue the show without them, but she
couldn't think about that now, her marriage had to come
first.

"Are you sure about this?" A silence. "Faith?" And then
a click in her throat, and out came a river of remorse.

"How could I have done it! I feel so—stupid. I feel
like dirt. Why did I do it? I was *happy*. I didn't need
this—this *intrigue*. But I did it. And I'll have to live with
it for the rest of my life. And you know what? I won't
even have nice memories of it—because it *wasn't that much
fun.*" And at that thought, she was racked with sobs. To
have launched upon something so shameful and then have
nothing to show for it—to be no good at virtue and then
prove to be an artless sinner on top of it and *to have
no fun.*

"Well, I'm sure you're not the first or the last," said
Roy Jr.

He buzzed for Ethel. "Find Frank and tell him to come back, all is forgiven," he said. "I need him here. We're falling apart." Ethel thought the *Rise and Shine Show* was probably in St. Cloud at the moment, en route to Moorhead.

"But they were way up in Roseau this morning," he said. "How can they be down in St. Cloud?" But then he remembered what he told Harry in the Artists Bureau: *lose these guys.* He said, "Can you reach him, Ethel? It's important—"

And a minute later, she reported that she had raised the Shiners. Not Frank, but she had Slim Graves on the line.

"Is he drunk?"

"Worse than that," she said. "He's remorseful."

When Slim came on the phone, his sinuses were backing up on him.

He said, "Morning, boss," and turned away and hawked and cleared his head, and said, "Sorry. Kind of a rocky day today. Believe me, I feel real bad about that Pokey business. I knew I never shoulda left the Movers to do the show," and he turned and hawked again.

Roy Jr. didn't have the heart to fire him. He had already fired Itch the engineer, and one was enough for one day, and Itch was a better choice. Itch had been sober, mostly, and sat and listened to Mr. Pokey for half an hour without touching the switch.

"I'm an engineer," he muttered, standing on Roy Jr.'s rug. "I don't listen to all that shit. It isn't my job to decide what goes on the air."

"A song called, 'Baby I Got a Wiener for Your Bun'?"

Itch blushed. "How'm I supposed to know what it was about? It coulda been a commercial."

"You didn't know what 'Ram Rod Daddy' referred to?"

"It coulda been about a lot of things. I didn't know.

Maybe 'Jimmy Crack Corn' is a dirty song. I don't know. Maybe 'Baa Baa Black Sheep.' I don't study songs."

" 'You Got Me Dancing in My Pants'?"

"I donno. It isn't my job. You wanna fire me, fire me. But don't try to convince me that it's fair."

So he fired him. Itch took it well. He looked Roy Jr. in the eye and said, "I saw your wiener once in the men's room and it was the size of a Vienna sausage. Your wiener'd be *lost* in a bun. It wouldn't've filled a bon bon." And he turned and stalked out.

———

Still feeling shrivelled in the loins, Roy Jr. rang up the hospital and got hold of Dr. Forbes, who said that Ray was resting up from his tests and would be released in the morning.

"How is he?" asked Roy Jr.

The doctor lowered his voice. "Do you want to know the truth or do you want what I told him?"

Roy Jr. chose the truth. "A few weeks," said the doctor. "He's full of cancer. I don't know how the old bugger kept going this long. He's like Swiss cheese inside."

When Ray came on the phone, a minute later, he sounded weak but still game. "They skewered me like a pig," he said. "Stuck a tube down my throat, and rammed a rod up my ass, had me running around in a little cotton dress with my hinder hanging out, I tell you it's the last time I ever go to that dentist."

He would rest up at home for a day and be in the office on Wednesday. "Everything shipshape?" he asked. Roy Jr. assured him that WLT was running like a well-oiled machine.

Touching Bottom

On Wednesday, the Rise and Shiners did Cloquet, Staples, Bemidji, and International Falls, playing in church basements and school cafeterias, and then Grand Marais, Aitkin, Willmar, and Granite Falls on Thursday, and over to Pine City for the Friday morning broadcast in a back room of Russ's Short Stop Cafe, a small, squatty, cinderblock edifice next to the locker plant. No posters were in evidence, nobody seemed to expect them. On to Owatonna, Wadena, and Bagley, and by Friday the lack of sleep was making them jumpy. Friday night, they hit the Bagley High School auditorium, where a crowd of sixteen sat, widely scattered in the auditorium.

Reverend Odom suggested that they cancel. He had studied the audience through a hole in the curtain and they looked to him like people who might be just as glad to have their thirty-five cents refunded. He was sure that they were expecting a movie show. But Elmer said that if you start cancelling shows, you might not be able to stop, so out they went.

"Friends," said Frank, who was not applauded, "tonight is a great night for all of us from the Friendly Neighbor, WLT, to finally get a chance to meet and greet you, and in honor of the occasion, we have a special low price on all Shepherd Boys records, pictures, plaques, and souvenir plates!" But nobody raised their hands to buy a thing. Nobody waved dollar bills. They looked at Frank as if he were a fencepost.

On Friday, Slim had no feeling in his legs or his right arm or between his ears, a gray oily film covered his unshaven face, and his eyes were hot and red; he vibrated continuously, was too weak to walk and too exhausted to sleep. The others felt similarly, except Red who was alert and reasonably happy, thanks to pills, but who saw strange shapes, like bladders or intestines, slithering in the air. The bus rolled along the miles, and they stared out at the bare December fields, the gray treelines, flocks of black crows strolling through the corn stubble like undertakers. The Reverend sat and stared straight ahead. He had dreams in which he walked over the edge of the world and fell into the darkness. His sermonettes had gotten darker and darker, with no hope of redemption in them.

"Wish we could sleep in a motel tonight," Elmer told Frank, "but once they lie down, I don't think we'd ever roust them up." The gate was poor, a measly $31 *total* for Friday, and Wendell was sick from eating a bad hamburger. "Otherwise," said Elmer, "we're holding our own." He tried to keep up their spirits by sheer flattery —"You're the best announcer I ever heard," he told Frank—and by giving them the spotlight ("We're going to let the boys move out on a fast one now—stand back, children, here comes the Orange Blossom Special!"), but flattery wears off fast, and when you are worn-out and hungover, the spotlight is not what you want. What you want is the day off in bed, a warm quilt, heavy curtains.

It was snowing hard when Slim fell asleep at 2 a.m. Saturday morning, stretched out on the table, and when he woke up, it was four. The bus was parked in a snowdrift in front of the Baptist church in Baudette, and somebody was knocking on the window, shouting muffled words he couldn't make out. He waited but they wouldn't go away. Slim couldn't sit up. He rolled off the table and landed on Pastor Odom, who was sleeping on the floor, who rolled over and tried to kick him and connected with the table leg instead. Slim opened the door. A man in a parka, ice frozen to his face, said he was from the telephone company. The church breakfast for *The Rise and Shine Show* had been cancelled so he had installed the broadcast lines at a restaurant a few blocks away called Guy's Breakfast Shack, the only place open in town at that hour and he hoped it would be okay.

"Okay by me," said Slim. He scrawled "Show Not Here, Go to Guy's" on a lunch bag and stuck it under the sleeping Elmer's hand, then dropped off to sleep himself, only to be awakened by a frantic Barney, who had broken into the church and found no lines there and was now, with fifteen minutes to broadcast, on the verge of tears. The Shepherds were dressing swiftly in the back and Red was at the wheel. Frank had run off to the telephone office. "We're supposed to go to Guy's Breakfast Shack," said Slim. He had slept in his clothes. He was all ready to go.

Guy's was a small stucco cafe tucked in between a garage and a warehouse, two brightly-lit windows pale with frozen grease. Frank dashed up a moment after the bus pulled up and Barney flew out, the microphones in hand. The cafe was packed with hefty men in flannel shirts glumly chewing big forkloads of eggs and sausage, cooked up by the fattest man Frank had ever seen. Even for Minnesota, he was a fatty. His belly hung down over his pants, he walked side to side. "Where's Guy?" asked Frank. "That's me," wheezed the cook, "who in hell are you?"

"We're here to do the radio show."

"Don't know about any radio show."

"Well, it's on in ten minutes."

The cook snorted. "We'll see about that," he said. Elmer peeled off a twenty and laid it on the counter. The man's eyes softened. "Two more of those and I'll listen to any radio show you want," he said. Elmer laid down two more.

There was no piano and no room for drums, even when Frank persuaded two tables to slide over a few feet, which they took their time doing. No sooner did Barney get two microphones hooked up and all the plugs in than Wendell and Al and Rudy sailed in the door, and Frank said, "Good morning, neighbors, from the makers of delicious Home Salad and our good friends at Prestige Tire & Muffler, as they bring you the Shepherd Boys with another program of good old gospel music—yes, it's time to Rise and Shine!" and Slim kicked in with the guitar and Al blew the harmonica and Wendell sang the first verse of the theme song—

On that resurrection morning when the saved of earth
    shall rise
From the beds of earth and gather at that breakfast in
    the skies,
O how pleasant and delightful when He puts His hand
    in mine,
Then I will Rise and Shine!

Just when he came to the second stanza, about the morning glories in the arbors of heaven, a deep growly voice from the end of the counter said, "Shut your yap, ya stupid hayshaker." A thick bearlike man with a red beard and red hunting cap got up from his stool. "When I want you to sing, I'll stick a nickel in yer ass," he said. His voice was hard to miss, like a trombone. Wendell stopped singing and the man said, "And if I want you to fart, I'll take it out." He took a fried egg on his fork and flung it their way. It caught Al on the throat and stuck to his collar, where the bow tie would be, and the yolk ran down his shirt. "Get your fat farmer butts out of here, we're eating our breakfast," said the man.

Frank took a step toward him, to explain that they were in the middle of a live broadcast, but the man did not appear to be at all curious about them. "It's a radio show," Frank said, and he put his finger to his lips, *shhhhh*. An old geezer said over his shoulder, "That's Hard-Boiled Hansen down there, sonny, and he don't shhhh for anybody."

"Now, here's an old favorite of ours," said Elmer, "a good old gospel song that my mother dearly loved, called 'The Old Account Was Settled Long Ago.' And we'd like to send this out to all these friendly folks here in Baudette, at Guy's Breakfast Shack—oh boy, wish you folks at home could smell the sausage and the coffee—yessir, soon as we're done with the show, we're going to set down and have us the world's greatest breakfast, but first here's a song about the old account and how Jesus paid it all at Calvary—boys?" Al started playing it softly on the harp and Rudy and Wendell stepped up to sing, but their eyes were on Hard-Boiled Hansen, to see if the mention of Mother and Jesus and a plug for Baudette and Guy's sausage might have softened his heart. It had not.

He reached down and picked up his plate, which Frank saw was empty now. "I come in here to eat my breakfast and drink my coffee and not to listen to these yoohoos stand around and have prayer meeting," Hard-Boiled explained to a little man sitting on his right. And then he threw. The Rise and Shiners ducked and the plate shattered on the wall about a foot above their heads. A splinter caught Elmer in the eyeball, and he dropped to the floor, microphone in hand. Hard-Boiled was reaching for the saucer when Reverend Odom slipped through the back door with a cast-iron skillet in his hand and crowned him a good one, flat and hard on the cowlick. The skillet rang, and Hard-Boiled's saucer crashed to the floor. Instantly six men got up and paid and left.

A quizzical look came over Hard-Boiled Hansen's face, as if he had never been hit on the top of the head with a skillet before and was puzzled that someone would make the attempt. He turned toward the old man and smiled. "You hit me," he said.

"But not hard enough," said the minister, sadly. Hard-Boiled grasped him by the lapels. "You people come in here aggravatin' me," he said. "I'm a peaceful man. I didn't come lookin' for you to aggravate you—I don't give two hoots about you. You come in here to do your singin' and yammerin' and aggravatin'—well, what I'm sayin' is you can aggravate yourselves right outta here. Otherwise I'm going to plant your rear end on the griddle over there. You want that?"

The minister shook his head.

"And then I'll pitch you through that window. You want that?"

No, he didn't want that either.

"And then we'll take you down to the lake and cut a hole in the ice and dip you by your ankles. How does that sound?"

Reverend Odom shook his head and tried to smile.

"So don't aggravate me another minute. Take your friends and all of you shag your hairy butts outta here."

342

And Hard-Boiled hoisted him up by the lapels and threw him at the Rise and Shiners.

Al and Wendell ducked, and the Reverend landed on Rudy, who was bending over Elmer who had the sliver in his eye, and they both fell on top of him in a heap.

Frank, to his own amazement, suddenly had his hand on the front door—he didn't know how he had gotten there—and then he was out the door and in the snow, heading toward the bus. Red was asleep in the driver's seat. The motor was running. Frank turned to go back and Rudy ran into him. Al streaked past, guitar in hand, and Wendell, they had all broken for the door at the same time, and Reverend Odom hobbled out and Elmer, his hand over his eye. "Where's Barney?" he cried. "Where's Slim?"

Slim was already on the bus, they found out, but Barney was nowhere. "I think he snuck out the back," said Rudy.

"Did he think to take us off the air, I hope?" said Elmer.

"Lemme see that eye," said Rudy. He peered into his brother's weepy eye and peeled back the lids and spotted the sliver of dish deep down in the lower one. The puddle of tears in the lower lid was red with blood. Rudy dipped a corner of his hanky in, trying to raise up the sliver, a wicked little thing about a quarter-inch long, but it disappeared, and then they heard the radio as Red tuned it to WLT.

A wheezy old voice was saying, "—run so fast in my life, they were scared shitless, they had a look in their eyes like deer lookin' into a headlight. Heeheeheeheehee."

A deeper voice: "Look, there's one layin' in the back by the woodshed. Want me to chase him outta there, Guy? Heeheeheeheehee."

The wheezy voice: "I don't think that old booger could run if there was bears after him, Jimmy, he went pedalling

343

out the back door and he ran smack into the low post. He wasn't quite high enough, Jimmy. I believe that old booger has made himself a soprano—heeheeheeheehee. I think I see the family jewels layin' over by the tree. Yessir. I believe the women of Baudette are safe for tonight, my friend."

CHAPTER 39

Chicago

R ed pulled the bus around back of Guy's Breakfast Shack and sure enough, there was Barney, folded up in the snow, next to a fence post, holding his vitals. Frank and Wendell hopped out and helped him up and carried him on board and *still* the show was on the air—the guys in the cafe were telling sheep jokes now— and Rudy was still trying to fish out the sliver. "Hold still, willya," he said, but Elmer was upset about the engineer down in Minneapolis not cutting off the show: "What, is he taking a dump or what?"

Finally, Frank went to retrieve the equipment.

On the bus radio, they heard the back door open and the footsteps across the linoleum floor. Then there was a loud *thump* when he pulled the plug. Hard-Boiled drank his coffee and watched Frank collect the three microphone stands, the cord, and the mixer, and he watched Frank go out the back door, which whacked shut, like a slap in the chops. There was one full minute of silence on WLT, and then on came the recorded voice of Reed Seymour to say, "We are experiencing technical difficulties. Please stand by. We will return to our scheduled program as soon as possible."

Red switched it off. "Radio as we know it is dead, boys," he said. "So where do you want to go now?"

Barney said it was his fault for not hitting the switch. "A man who can't remember to turn off a microphone—I don't know if I'd trust myself to carry a sharp stick," he said.

"It was my fault. I should have yelled as soon as I saw him," Slim said. "I hope that sucker gets his hand cut off in a planing saw."

"I hit him good and then I forgot to hit him again," said Reverend Odom.

Frank said, "I should've come to help you. I don't know why I didn't. What a coward. I turned and ran." Rudy put his hand on Frank's shoulder. "We all ran," he said.

It was a brotherly moment. They sat in the dimness, waiting for their heads to clear, looking at each other, shaking their heads. They had never been attacked during a show before. That was a new one. Sure, there had been audiences who had given them the fish eye, but nobody had ever thrown objects at them before, not hard objects anyway, or if they had, they hadn't thrown them hard enough to hurt. Rudy recalled a man in Sioux Falls once who threw his shoes at them from the balcony (and missed). But not during a broadcast.

Reverend Odom chuckled. "I do remember whatsisname who did that *Farmyard Merry-Go-Round* show on KSTP from the South St. Paul stockyards—didn't he get pelted with cow chips once?"

"Hoyt Buford."

"The one with the two-tone shoes and the creamy cowboy suit."

"Oh, he was riding high," said the Reverend. "There

was a big story on Hoyt in the St. Paul *Dispatch* about what a phenomenon he was, what a specimen of manhood, a new planet in the cosmos of broadcasting, and how a million people in four states doted on him and talked about him and longed to know his opinions on a wide range of topics. Unfortunately, he had granted the paper an interview, and they did him the terrible disservice of printing many of his remarks, one of which was to the effect of: those folks would believe me if I said it was snowing in July, they'd believe it if I told them it was snowing *cow chips*.

"Well, he denied he said it, and maybe he hadn't, but it sounded exactly like something he *would've* said. He dressed like someone who would've said exactly that. And the next day, when Hoyt Buford climbed out of his cream-colored Buick to do the show from the rotunda of the auction barn, he saw that he had a bigger audience than usual. Much bigger. He also noticed that men were up on the roof. He was moved by the big turn-out and put on an even better show, though the *Merry-Go-Round*, of course, was only a half-hour, but he went all out, told a couple stories, mugged and pranced around as he read the livestock prices, got the audience to sing 'Let Me Call You Sweetheart'—which he seemed to accept as a personal tribute. He beamed and said that he had, as they could imagine, gotten offers to do other shows, but that he never wanted to be anyplace but where he was right now, among the greatest people in the world, the livestock growers of the Upper Midwest. And right then was when a gentle rain began to fall. Little flecks of manure descended through the barny air, with some larger lumps and an occasional four-pounder, and he danced around, trying to dodge the storm, but the microphone cord was not long enough. That was his downfall, boys. *His cord was not long enough*. Because, you see, he never did interviews with the audience. There was his problem, because—take my word for it—shit never falls on a farmer. Because a farmer does not allow shit to rise. Right there and then, old Hoyt discovered a basic secret of show business. You stick close to your audience and you'll be all right. Unfortunately, just as this fact dawned on him, so did a blockbuster cowflop—the sort of pie that cowmen call the Moneymaker—they'll pour coffee down those cows for days to stop them up and get a twenty-pound bolus sitting there inside her and *bang* goes the auction gavel and there's your profit margin. That's why at auctions they go around and smell the cattle's breath for coffee. Coffee or cigarettes. Cigarettes will do the same thing."

"So what happened to Hoyt Buford?"

Reverend Odom shrugged. "What happens to *anybody* when twenty pounds of cow manure falls on them from a height? It knocked the man down. He fell in a heap, covered with dung, and in blind rage and frustration he screamed, 'I hope you bastards die in hell,' and those were the last words he ever spoke on the radio. That was his swansong. The capstone of his broadcasting career. Crushed by the mob. He lost the suit, the Buick, the woman who loved him, everything.

"Of course it isn't true, what he said. Nobody dies in hell, they just wish they would. And though he lost what he had, he got some of it back later. Went to Pierre and became a late-night DJ. Played jazz and talked in a low voice and everything. What passes for a farm boy in Minneapolis is a real bohemian in Pierre. He got another car and another girlfriend. But the rule is true: stick close to your audience. Otherwise you are going to have to bang them over the head with skillets and you saw how well that worked."

Al put a pot of water on the stove to boil. "At least,

our clothes are reasonably clean," he said. "Except for this egg on my shirt."

"I almost got 'er," said Rudy, and Elmer shuddered, and the bloody sliver came out.

Elmer sat with a hanky over his weeping eye. He had a cup of coffee. He let Rudy put a snowball on his eye. "You want some breakfast?" asked Wendell. Red turned in the driver's seat and asked if Elmer felt up to him driving. They had a show in Bemidji in three hours. Elmer shook his head.

"I think this is the Lord's way of telling us to move on," said Elmer. "I never ran out on a show before and I hate to start now but maybe there's a reason. We have done all we could do in radio. The Lord has used radio to teach us, but now school is out. We have to move on." He said, "We are done with WLT as of six o'clock this morning." They all cheered and clapped. He had an old buddy from Fargo who ran a Bible camp in Eveleth and they could get there by lunchtime and stay for a couple days and rest up and decide what they were going to do. *Real beds.* The Rise and Shiners fell all over themselves with gratitude—Wendell wept and Rudy hugged him and Al cried, "Thank you, Jesus!" Even Slim was moved. They were getting out of hell and into a warm shower, and then they'd eat lunch, talk, take a nap, sit around, like human beings—Red put the bus in gear and they bumped along out of the backyard and pulled onto the highway and Red yelled, "Eveleth!" and they all cheered, except Frank.

My job, he thought. *I can't throw away my job. I lose this job and I have to go back to Mindren.* On the other hand, it was an impossible job. Roy Jr. had told him his job was to get the Rise and Shiners through the tour, but the purpose of the tour was to punish them and get rid of them, drive them from the radio—so Roy Jr. had accomplished what he wanted: the Tour of Hell had worked and the Shepherd Boys were leaving radio. But they were leaving too soon, before their suffering was complete. Frank's instructions were to make sure they did all the shows.

You gotta get off this bus, he thought. *Or else you've got to head them toward Bemidji.* But how? Slim had unpacked his mandolin and Al was playing the guitar and they were singing,

> Onward to Canaan we joyfully fly,
> Swifter than eagles that wing cross the sky.
> With sweet jubilation we go round the bend
> And there we see Jesus, our Saviour and Friend.
>
> Away! Away!
> Away from sorrows and strife!
> Rise up! Rise up!
> Rise up to the heavenly life!
> Farewell to misery, we cannot stay—
> We're going to Canaan today!

The Shepherds were laughing and singing and had their arms draped over each other and they weren't even drunk. This troupe would no more go to Bemidji than they'd take work in a lacquer factory. Red was happy, driving with one hand, beating time with the other. Reverend Odom sat next to Frank, and Wendell behind them was talking a blue streak about how this was the beginning of the good times. Television. A big touring bus, bigger than The Rankins'. A bigger TV show than theirs. Records. Maybe movies. "There never was a good movie with our kind of music in it," said Wendell. "But more people like our music than that Broadway crap and all that tinsel and showgirls—that's rich people's music. We could get rich playing poor people's music." He laughed at that.

"Gospel music?" asked the old minister, cranking his neck around.

"Naw. Cheatin' songs. That's real poor-man music. Rich guys don't even understand somebody like Hank Williams. A rich man hardly needs a woman at all. If she runs away, who cares? he'll go get another one. But when you've got *nothing* and not much to look forward to, then if your woman runs off and you lose the one good thing in your life, man, that just about kills you. Rich sonsabitches can't understand none of that shit. It's like they say, a song only gives you a taste of what you already know. We oughta get out of gospel and into cheatin' songs, cause that's what *we* know, right?" He clapped the Reverend on the back.

Maria is waiting for me, I can't let her down, Frank thought. He slouched down in the seat, his knees pressed up against the seat in front, and imagined her next to him, her hair, his hand in her lap, his other hand easing into her shirt the way she let him do and easing along her soft belly, touching her tiny crevasse of bellybutton, reaching, slowly reaching. Everything that made a difference in this world lay inside that shirt and down below—everything else was so weary and stale, men, dreary men, angry men, the bragging and strutting and the loud words like a whipsaw and the sharp blow, but she was so sweet and peaceful. His hand against her breast, resting. He cupped her in his hand and she seemed to swell with pleasure, he slipped his hand into the cup and curled around her skin and her delicate sharp nipple and she sighed and turned toward him, almost snapping off his wrist—he withdrew—his hand slipped around to her back and unclasped her bra, his hand slipped down into her pants and along her sweet butt, left and right—his hand slid up over her hipbone

351

and up the delicious ribs and up and freed the breasts from their hammocks, slipped them loose, like opening an ear of sweet corn—he weighed them in his hand—he slipped down front over her soft belly and felt the slope—his hand tiptoed down the beautiful hill and into her soft darkness, and up the sides of her thighs—

O Canaan our homeland we praise thee and bless
The day we arrive at our true happiness!
So perfect and pleasant, the day of the Bride.
The Bridegroom awaits thee, O fly to his side!

It was all so perfect, what else was there in the world but her? The rest was all paper and long dry afternoons of typewriters ticking far away and the clock stopped and men's voices yammering over the office transom—he would gladly stay in the hallway and never go inside that room! The vanity of men in suits is hard to bear. Ray was right. One could hardly regret being alone with a beautiful woman and, compared to the men in the room, what woman is not beautiful?

A cold chill on his face: he remembered the money. The $800 for expenses. He touched his wallet. It was thin. He snatched it out. The money was gone. *Stolen. He hadn't touched it the whole trip, hadn't seen it, hadn't thought about it. Somebody had filched the whole wad. Stupid, stupid.*

"What's wrong?" asked Reverend Odom.

"I think my money is missing."

"What money?"

"Some money. Seven hundred dollars."

The mention of $700 rang in the air like trumpets, and Slim and Al stopped singing. "What money is that?" asked Elmer, his right eye red and swollen.

Frank looked straight ahead down the highway. "Expense money from Roy Jr."

"Why'd he give it to you and not to Elmer?" asked Wendell.

"I donno. Ask him."

"That was our expense money. You shoulda handed it over."

Elmer was hurt. "Why didn't you even *tell* me about it? We coulda slept in some motels, we coulda eaten some dinners we didn't eat. That's not right, Frank."

"All I did was what Roy Jr. told me. It was for an emergency."

"That don't make it right. This whole *trip* has been an emergency."

They kept sniping at him all the way to Eveleth, everyone except Reverend Odom. Two minutes before they hadn't been aware of the money and now the loss of it weighed heavy on them. Money they hadn't even seen, but its loss was a grievous blow to them, almost worse than if it had been taken straight out of their pockets. "Seven hundred dollars," Wendell kept saying. "Seven hundred dollars." Frank tried to look them in the eye, looking for that flicker that would give the culprit away. The thief knew it was eight hundred not seven, and he must wonder why Frank lied. Frank looked for curious stares, but there were only accusing ones.

———

It was a tired owly bunch that pulled into The Nazarene Bible Camp around eleven, nobody singing and Wendell was hitting the bourbon and getting argumentative—"Sick of gospel! We come to the end of gospel! If you can't see that, then you're too dumb to deal with!"—and though Elmer's buddy, Fred Porch, and his wife Alma turned out to be wonderful people and anxious for the company and they hustled the Shiners right into the main lodge and sat them down to a ham dinner with fresh biscuits and redeye gravy with peach pie for dessert, everyone was still mourning the $700. "That was our start-up money," said Elmer. "That's what woulda gotten us to Chicago." Elmer had friends in Chicago, important friends in broadcasting. Chicago was a day and a half away. In a couple weeks, Elmer could get them a show. In a month or so, the money would start to come in. The $700 would get them over the hump. "I hope you didn't throw away our whole future," said Elmer gloomily.

It had begun to snow heavier, and Reverend Odom told about winter in North Dakota when he was a boy, sleeping in the attic and waking up to find a snowdrift on your covers in the morning. This story cheered them up somewhat, and then Slim told about a winter in New Guinea during the war when he was in the Navy playing for troop shows with Uncle Soddy Johnson and the Destroyers, playing two and three ships a day, and the men hanging from the davits and yelling and beating on the deck with hammers in time to the music and it was so loud that it killed fish and the Destroyers scooped them out of the water from their launch and ate them for supper. Of course, the Shiners had heard these stories before, but they were good stories, and so was Al's story about seeing Faron Young in a Nashville department store buying a pair of cotton socks, and then Alma left to go take a nap and Wendell told his story about their childhood church's custom of baptizing in the river and how he had been dipped with his head downstream so the current ran up his nose and he floundered in panic and tore himself loose from the preacher and was swept away and carried over a waterfall and almost drowned but grabbed a branch and hauled himself ashore and when he stood up, he had the biggest erection of his life, nine inches, and he had to run from the search party, and as he trotted along, his penis jumping, it got so big it broke out of the front of his pants. Meanwhile, he could hear his ma back at the baptismal site screaming that he was gone, dead, drowned. "I was the farthest thing from dead," he said. "I had reached the other shore from dead. I had crossed over into the land of love, boys." It was snowing so hard, they couldn't see from the lodge to the lake. "It looks like we're going to stay here for awhile," Elmer remarked happily. He said he was almost done writing a new song called "Waiting for Thee" (or "I Know He Is Coming") and was pretty sure it would be a big hit.

———

There were warm bunks waiting in a little log cabin under a tall pine, Fred said, and supper would be at six. The Shiners ambled up the path between the snowdrifts and into the cabin, where a fire blazed in a cast-iron stove. "I could stay here forever," said Rudy.

Al found a shelf of Harold Hand, Christian Detective novels under a window. He had enjoyed them as a boy and had not seen a copy in twenty years. Slim found a crack in his fiddle. "I wonder if there's any epoxy in Fred's shop?" The old man found a book of sermon outlines, including the themes of Christ the Refuge in time of trouble, the tribulations of the Tribes of Israel, and the perfection of love through testing and trial. And then all of them undressed and climbed into bed and drifted off to sleep, except Frank. He lay on his back so he wouldn't fall asleep and when he felt drowsy, he thought of Maria and he woke right up. He imagined her climbing the stairs with him and him unlocking a door, but it wasn't the door at the Antwerp. It was a nicer room than his, with windows that looked out on a park. It was dark. They didn't turn the lights on. She took him by the hand and led him to the bed and he sat down and she took his shoes off. He unbuttoned her shirt and it came off in his hands. All her clothing melted away and his too and they plunged into the bed together and dove below the surface, hand in hand, bubbles streaming from their mouths as they laughed and floated and dove and turned—beyond that, his imagination did not go.

He lay in his bunk and it seemed to be several hours later. There was general snoring. He eased his feet onto the floor and sat up. The springs creaked, loud. The snoring stopped—there were snorts, groans, a sigh or two—then the snoring started in again, scattered at first, then steady and orchestral. Frank stood up and tiptoed over to Wendell's bed, where Wendell's green pants hung on the post, and slowly he slid Wendell's wallet out and felt his pockets. One down, six to go.

His next guess was Rudy, and that was no luck either. He even rummaged in Rudy's grip and checked his coat.

Frank felt that he was being watched but he didn't see who, nobody's eyes were showing. He slipped over to Red's bed, but Red had his pants on. So did Al. He looked in their suitcases. He checked Slim's mandolin case. He even tried to pry Slim's shoes apart, in case he had a false sole. Time was running out. If one of them had swiped the money from him, he didn't care to stick around. He'd have stuck by the Shepherds if they had played fair with him, but a thief in the crowd—and then he found the money. It was where he had hoped not to find it, smoothed out, almost flat, tucked into the minister's Bible, between Revelation and the concordance, leaving a slight gap in the gold edge, a gap that caught his eye, and Frank was ashamed of what came to his mind, the suspicion, the minister was a friend, and he opened the Bible to clear Reverend Odom's name and there was the cash.

Not a bill was missing. Hundreds. Eight crisp ones.

Gone

Frank slipped the bankroll into his pocket, took his coat off the hook, picked up his valise, and left. As he opened the door and as he tromped down the steps and as he headed down the snowy path, he expected the Shepherds to come hurtling after him with sticks of kindling in their fists, but he got all the way to the lodge and found Fred and Alma in the kitchen, washing dishes, and he asked for directions to Eveleth.

"You're not staying? But there's a blizzard coming." Fred bent down and looked out the window up at the sky. It looked leaden all right. "Where you going to?"

"Minneapolis," said Frank. "I need to get to Minneapolis."

"You're not going to the Cities tonight," said Alma. "I don't think there's even any trains running. Oh, I do wish you'd stay." She gave him a pleading look. "I know your mother wouldn't want you to go out on a night like tonight."

But he knew that blizzards didn't stop the train, of

course. Fred gave him a lift into town and the southbound train to Duluth had just arrived from Ely and was sitting in the station, steaming, and Fred drove up to the platform and Frank had barely time to run and jump aboard before the conductor waved and there was a *whoosh* of steam and the train pulled away. "What are you in such a big rush for to get to Minneapolis anyway?" asked Fred, an instant before they spotted the train, and Frank had been going to say, "Got to get my job back," but he wasn't sure about that as he rode down to Duluth. Time to ponder, while the train swayed and bucked through the snowy night.

He could get on a train to Minneapolis and be at work in the morning and see Maria at noon, but it seemed like the short road to nowhere. He had lost all the Soderbjergs' trust the moment he ran away from the show. It would take too long to win it back again. Besides, radio was dead. How do you know? *You know*, that's how. The ones who were trying to keep it alive were dying themselves —Dad Benson, Slim Graves, Elmer, Ray, Patsy, Reed Seymour—all fading away, not much spunk or drive left there. The audience was leaving in droves.

Ten years before, they would have been a big hit in these little towns, big crowds, lots of noise, reporters from the paper nosing around, pretty girls standing out on the periphery blushing and trying to catch your eye. But here it was 1950 and every tavern had a television set and every tavern was packed with people. All of the *Rise and Shine* audience was staying up late at night with their eyes glued to Milton Berle as they sat guzzling beer at Bud's Dew Drop Inn. And old Bud was bitching that business was dropping off every week, as more and more people bought their own televisions.

The tavern guys wanted television to belong to them, and Frank wanted radio to go on and on, but like Dad said, yesterday's river doesn't turn the mill.

You've got to be smart, he thought. You don't want to get yourself into a line of work where two years from now, four years from now, six—you'll be sitting high and dry, the tide gone out, and you feeling like you are somebody else's mirage.

Like Vince Upton and Sheridan Thomas. *Up in a Balloon* was gone, crashed two weeks before—they quit radio and moved to St. Augustine and opened a seashell shop. They made their decision the day the two German cleaning ladies, Charlotte and Mathilda, came marching into Studio B, ignoring the *Quiet Please, on the Air* sign blazing red over the door, and walked smack into the middle of the show as Bud and Bessie were navigating their helium balloon, *The Minnesota Clipper*, at 6,000 feet over the Burma Pass in pursuit of the Pasha of Endur. Charlotte started vacuuming the carpet.

"Looks like a monsoon moving in from the East!" yelled Vince. "Hang onto the guy ropes, darlin'! We'll have to ride it out!"—where the script said:

BESSIE: I see elephants—a whole train of them! They're going to ford the Wasabi below Luala Pindi.
BUD: We better go down and have a look-see.

Sheridan shouted, "Okay! Whatever you think!" Mathilda brushed past her.

As he called out the monsoon warning, Vince edged toward the wall, microphone in hand, and leaned down and yanked out the vacuum cleaner plug, but it wasn't, it was the plug to the turntable and slowly the transcription of stratospheric winds and the *thubthubthub* of the engine ground to a halt.

"I don't like the looks of this! I think we've hit a pocket of dead air!" he yelled. "The equalizer broke! Those mountain peaks are coming closer! We may have to abandon ship!"

Smoke drifted up from the wax that Mathilda spritzed on the hot tubes in the turntable console. She waxed the turntable too and the needle slid off the disc *grrrrrrrr-eee* and she dusted the microphone. It sounded like thunder.

And that same afternoon Vince packed his traps and said goodbye. "When the *hausfrau*s walked in, I felt dumb, like my mother had come in the bedroom and caught me loping the mule," he told Leo. "I'm sixty. It's too old to be standing in a little room and pretending that you're flying a balloon. Sherry and I are going to Florida and get into the seashell business. There's no limit to what you can do with seashells, you know. Ashtrays, wall plaques, you name it."

———

With the train steaming slowly through the pine woods, the snow swirling up from the wheels, Frank curled up on the caneback seat and pulled his jacket around his ears. He fell asleep and then awoke with a jolt and felt for the billfold. Still there. He slipped it into the front of his pants. He thought, "I could go to Minneapolis, back to the radio mill, return the money, work my way up the ladder, and ask Maria to stick it out, or I go to Chicago and send for her and then something else could happen." He fell asleep again.

He awoke as the train pulled into Duluth, under the long shed and up to the stone palace, alongside a parade of wagons of mailsacks and baggage. "All out!" yelled the conductor.

Frank crossed the platform to where freight men were loading the baggage onto another train across the platform. He tapped a man on the shoulder: "Is this to Minneapolis?" he asked.

"Chicago."

"You sure?"

The man shrugged. "I've never missed one yet."

It was only a thought, but he could go to Chicago, get an apartment, let her know where he was, find a job, and by the time his Maria rolled in, he'd be sitting pretty. You've got to jump out front and surprise a woman before she'll pay you proper attention, maybe, he thought. But there wasn't time to think.

The train to Chicago whistled, and rather than miss it, he got on. Three old red passenger cars and a baggage car and Railway Mail Service and a coal tender and the locomotive. "Now boarding on track four. . . . The Superior . . . with intermediate stops . . . to *Chicago*," said the train announcer, but Frank was already on board, in a double-facing seat, his feet up, looking forward. The whistle blew twice more, and he thought, *Daddy, be careful*, but of course it was him who was in danger now.

Ray lay pale, damp, unshaven, shivering under the heavy quilt and a wool blanket, and rolled over on his other side and faced the table. The lamp had a towel over it, and there was a glass of water and eight bottles of pills, and his old Crosley bedside radio, the Aztec model, a golden temple with triangular tuning knobs.

"I knew what would happen if I lived long enough," he told Patsy, "but frankly, I would give anything to have one more year."

She had come to visit him on Tuesday and now it was Friday and she was still there, nursing him. Vesta was still in London, where she had discovered tape recorders. She was so happy on the telephone, Ray didn't have the heart to tell her how sick he was. "The tape recorder is going to change everything," she said. "We can harvest lectures and speeches from anywhere, use them anytime. I can travel the world with a tape recorder—it only weighs forty pounds—I can gather the wisdom of the nations and bring it back to the Midwest. Ray, this is going to finally make radio what it ought to be." She laughed at the joy of it. She was heading for Stockholm, she said, to interview Nobel Prize winners.

He hadn't listened to the radio for three weeks. He was dying, for pete's sake—should a man be ushered into Eternity directly from listening to a Lakers game or a North West Orient Airlines commercial? His chest felt caved-in, it was hard to breathe. His heart hurt—and the iodine on his forehead from when he had fallen, which he didn't recall, though he remembered getting up in the middle of the night and trying to use the bathroom.

One morning he woke up and felt better and went through his desk and threw out everything. All the letters, all the check stubs, all the pictures. Put your house in order: clear the decks and make room for the young, that was his philosophy. The old men die and the children forget. When your time comes to go, get out. Not like that fool Dad Benson. Seventy years old and still hanging on. Poor sister Lottie, coming in to screech a few more songs every morning, young people smirking behind her back. Why couldn't these people see the handwriting on the wall?

"Man is conceived in ignorance and born in doubt and his life goes downhill from there," he wrote to Dad. "He makes his way from pure foolishness to outright stupidity, stopping now and then to do something mean and ugly, and yet, to some lucky persons, the Lord has doled out a modicum of common sense, enough to enable us to know our butt from a hot rock, to not spend all our money or insult our friends, and to sit down and shut up when it's

time to. *Now is the time to sit down and shut up, Walter.*
The urge to perform is not a sign of talent. Greed is not
an indication of business acumen. Keep this in mind; it
may be helpful in the future. The beauty of retirement is
the way it raises your reputation. Keep plugging ahead
and you will soon become a ridiculous old relic and a
back number, but quit soon enough and live long enough
and you will come to be regarded as a genius and a pioneer. This is the truth, otherwise I wouldn't tell you. The
key to a person's reputation is *He knew when to quit.* A
word to the wise should be sufficient. Good luck, your
friend, Ray."

No response from Dad. No response from so many. He
couldn't blame them. Dying people aren't much fun to be
around. Dying was so tedious and such a miserable business, it made a man not want to live. Dying was so
discouraging. Here you are, spending your last days on this
green earth and they should be beautiful days, and instead
you drag around with your willie in the dirt.

———

Ray's letter didn't reach Dad for a week because Frank
wasn't there to see to it. When Dad got it, it rode around
in his jacket pocket for a few days and then, finishing up
his toast and chipped beef at the Pot Pie, Dad reached for
his wallet and found the envelope, read the letter, looked
up and said, "We're going back to the barn, Wilmer. We
came into radio with Ray and we're getting out with him.
Tomorrow's the last show."

"What's the big rush?"

"No point in postponing our obligations, Wilmer. It
takes us long enough to wake up to them."

Wilmer went home and cried. Tiny was all he was good
at. People had told him for years that Amos and Andy

were nowhere *near* as well done as Tiny, including a great many fine colored folks on the North Side had come up and told him that. "What do I do now?" he wondered. If his main talent in life was to be a colored man, there wasn't going to be much call for him outside of radio probably. Maybe Patsy Konopka could make him his own show. *Tiny and His Buddies. And now, Powers Dry Goods Company—when it comes to fashion, come to Powers—is proud to present . . . Wilmer Benson as—Tiny! "Yassuh, yassuh, yassuh, and how do, ladies and gentlemens, it sho is real to be heah!"* And on this sweet dream, he fell asleep.

Little Becky went back to her dad in Manhattan. He wrote her a nice letter saying that he woke up one morning and decided "I want my little girl." He had reformed. No more long trips to Rome and Morocco with strange women. It was going to be strictly home and hearth from now on. Jo and Frank weren't home—they were off to Michigan to see their aunt, whose house burned down when the hoboes got mad at her because she stopped making johnnycake. There was only Dad and Delores and Tiny. "Mornin', li'l miss. Ah 'spected yo' might be fixin' to de-part so I come round with Ole Henry to give yo' a lift to the de-po. Wheah is yo' valise?" asked the old colored man. Delores the exotic dancer was leaving Elmville and going to Chicago to work with polio victims; life with Dad had lifted her aim in life, and now she hoped to trade her G-string for a nurse's cap. She thanked Dad for his goodness, and then Becky said her goodbyes and "Oh how can I ever thank you?" and Dad made his "We show our gratitude by doing good for others" speech and Little Becky cried, "Goodbye, Elmville! Goodbye, trees and houses and yards! Goodbye, church and school! Goodbye, seeds and dirt! Goodbye, snowstorms and thunderstorms and hot July days and Christmases and birthdays! Goodbye, everybody! Goodbye, Uncle Dad!" and a transcribed bus carried the child away. Dad said, "All good things must come to an end but God never closes one door but what He opens another. It is never a bad day that has a good evening." And that was the end of *Friendly Neighbor*, except for when Dad knocked over the stand, which hit the microphone, making a *bwaannngggg*, and Tiny laughed a loud white-man laugh.

That was all there was time for. "Whispering Hope" came in and Reed Seymour said *Friendly Neighbor* was brought to you by the friendly folks at Milton, King Seeds, and Dad said goodbye to Marjery, who was all torn up by the suddenness of the end.

"What's going to happen to *me?*" she cried. "You bring me in here to play a *child* and I spend half my life on it and now you throw me over the *cliff* like I was a piece of garbage."

Dad said that all good things must come to an end.

"But what am I supposed to *do?*" she cried.

Dad smiled. "Each man to his work. Find a job. There's work for all hands in life, Becky. Or go back to school. Learning, you know, is what makes a man fit company for himself." He patted her shoulder and turned away and a second later let out a shriek and hopped twice, sideways, trying to escape from her hand in the seat of his pants. Her sharp fingers dug into his wounded rear end, like someone sticking a hot poker in him, a hot green wave of pain, and he had to twirl around twice to get her out. "It hurts!" he said. She bared her teeth: *hee hee hee hee hee.*

"How evil you are," he said.

"Yes!" she cried. "Yes! I am evil. And I hate your ass!"

Dad lay on the Green Room sofa, recuperating. "Twenty-three years," said Wilmer. Dad corrected him: *twenty-four*. Or was it twenty-two? Anyway, nobody had been waiting in the Green Room to congratulate them. No cake or cookies. Roy Jr. was gone to see Ray, and Roy was on the farm. Leo was on the air. Everybody was somewhere else. "We should've remembered to have a party, but maybe nobody would've come," said Dad. "Like they say: In time of prosperity, friends there are plenty; in time of adversity, not one in twenty."

"It *is* lonely around here," said Wilmer. "Especially with Faith gone." He paused a beat. "Too bad about her." He waited. Dad said nothing. Wilmer said, "You never told me about you and her."

"Well, an open door could tempt a saint," said Dad. "And she was pretty wonderful. She kept me going. There's that to be said about it. It was wrong, but without her, I would've quit ten years ago, so maybe there's some good there somewhere. Let's go get a drink next door. No fans down in the lobby, are there? Good. Let's go."

The two old veterans came out the front door of the Ogden and stood on the corner in the bright sunshine. Across the street, at the MacPhail School of Music, a woman struggled to get her cello through the door. A man darted out of a roadster parked at the curb to hold the door open for her. She turned and blushed, and he tipped his hat.

"Isn't that Irtie Lybarger?" asked Dad. "The young fellow who used to work in the newsroom? That's him."

"Naw, he's too old to be Irtie. That guy's almost as old as us."

"Irtie was a long time ago, Wilmer. He worked for Phil Sax, and Saxy went out to San Diego in thirty-nine."

Wilmer suggested the Pot Pie, and Dad said, sure, but

they stood on the spot, under the WLT sign, reluctant to move.

"Look," said Wilmer. "You can't even *buy* a radio around here anymore." It was true. The Bush & Lane Radio Co., a fine outfit, was gone from across the street at 1200 LaSalle—moved or gone out of business, who knew which—and Lew Bonn Radios was gone from 1211, replaced by General Nut Sales Co., and Eckberg Radio was gone, and Mpls. Radio Sales, replaced by the Northwestern Casket Co. showroom. Four great radio shops within a block of WLT, all gone now. Actually, thought Wilmer, the big Zeniths that Lew Bonn used to sell, the big floor consoles, looked somewhat like those oak caskets, same sort of fluted molding, like the proscenium of a theater.

Once, the WLT signal was received all the way to the Alleghenies and west to the Rockies, but that was when radio amounted to something and radios were built to pull in signals. The Zenith had a tuning knob as big as a grapefruit. You'd spin that and bring in Nashville and Cincinnati and Detroit and Little Rock and Salt Lake City, but the plastic pisspot radios you bought nowadays wouldn't get a signal from thirty miles away. The industry figured, why build radios that can bring in the world when the listener lives in Minneapolis and we want him to shop in Minneapolis? So you sell dinky radios and fill them up with twenty-four hours of orange peels, cigarette butts, and coffee grounds, and it sells the beer, Jack, but gosh, what a comedown. *All the shows are gone that let people sing on the radio who were not famous*, thought Wilmer. They were chewed up and digested and shat out by big money, and soon the radio stations will be gone too, only their signals remaining, cranking out nasty songs by savage young capitalists. Radio was a dream and now it's a jukebox. It's as if planes stopped flying and sat on the runway showing travelogues. But of course if you climb on your high horse and talk about radio when it amounted to something, people mark you down as an old fart, the sort who grumbles about the decline of railroad travel and circuses and the 4th of July and the death of the six-day bicycle race.

"Well, I always knew that the end would come some-day," said Dad, "and now here it is."

CHAPTER 41

The End

Away from the office, sick, out of touch, Ray wondered about Frank, worried that he had been lost in the North Woods, left in a snowbank to die. Ray woke up at 2 a.m. with visions of Frank weeping in a forest, bruised, bleeding from the forehead, and called Roy Jr. at home. "What are we doing about Frank?" he cried.

"Hoping to catch the bastard," said Roy Jr. "He stole $800 from me. He abandoned ship in the middle of the hurricane. If he calls you, have him call me. I'd like to strangle him."

"But the boy is in trouble."

"You're damn right he is."

The Rise and Shiners had no idea what had happened to him; he had wandered off, that was all, Rudy told Roy Jr. Frank was an oddball and not one of *them*, they had no idea how his mind worked. Probably he had gone back to Maria. Slim came home, quit music, and became a janitor at a junior high school. The Shepherds returned to WLT, apologized, and Roy Jr. let them have a Sunday morning spot, 8:20–8:35, the former *Reflections* spot. "Suits us fine," said Elmer. "I always thought Sunday was the best time for us." He and Rudy and Al got jobs at the post office, and Wendell went to work laying concrete driveways, but it was only a temporary setback, they were sure. Maria left WLT when *Friendly Neighbor* ended; somebody said she was selling candy at Woolworth's. Roy Jr. tried to call her at home, but an old lady answered and said, "I don't care for your products, and if you don't stop harassing me, I'll have you arrested." Slim thought Frank had gone on to better things. "I don't know what his talent is," he told Patsy Konopka, "but he is sure good at it." She thought Frank'd go to Chicago. "If radio is going to be saved, Chicago is where they'll save it." She imagined Frank shooting to the top at a big Chicago station, WLS or WGN, and sending for her to write him a show. He'd have to shoot fast, though—Roy Jr. was killing off *Love's Old Sweet Song* and *Golden Years* and *The Hills of Home*. Chop, chop, chop, and down they came, the tall trees. She had written them out in style: the Hollisters got an amicable divorce—"We'll still get together for Christmas!" said Jane—and Elmer and Edna sold the Golden Rule Cafe in Nowthen and returned to the big city to jump back into the giddy social whirl of the smart and privileged, and Babs got on a bus to Los Angeles. "What do I have to lose?" she told Fritz. One, two, three, the stories collapsed, and only a pitiful handful of letters from fans asking where they had gone. Lily Dale was gone, too. Mr. Tippy went in the hospital with leukemia, and Lottie tried out other accompanists and discovered that her voice was wedded to Mr. Tippy, that despicable pansy, and she couldn't sing without him. She told Ray that Frank hadn't stolen the money, he had more than earned it. "Three weeks with the Rise and Shiners—I'd say $800 was cheap at the price. What a beautiful boy he was. He was a prince of the airwaves, our Frank. He used to carry me up and down the stairs in his two arms, like I was a little girl. He came to my apartment for dinner on many occasions and told me all about his poor sad mother. What a tender heart he is. I wish him every happiness and grace."

Ray tried to think about his own mother and about the Resurrection, but his mind drifted toward the problem of storm windows and the furnace, which gasped and wheezed and needed replacing. There was no sense patching it up again and running the risk of a breakdown and frozen waterpipes bursting and all the aggravation—no, a person shouldn't take half-measures, and he knew that now, having wasted so much of his life hemming and hawing, hedging his bets on the furnace, modifying it from coal to gas-burning: no, it had to be ripped out and a new electric one put in. But a new furnace would survive him. He would be cold and in the ground and turning to mold before the new furnace had come to the end of its warranty.

He thought of the radio he didn't listen to and had no idea what they might be doing, but who cared now, they could whoop and curse and screech filth on the air, it was no reflection on him, he was out of it now—the good part about dying: *I am not responsible anymore. Death pays all debts. Fix the damn furnace yourself.*

Time flew backwards. Pictures of Moorhead and Lottie on the farm, gathering eggs in her apron before she got crippled, and Vesta when she was young and full of ginger. Going to work for his father, working an ice route in northeast Minneapolis. Boy, there was a way to build muscles! Those hundred-pound blocks in the wagon, under the gunnysacks. You'd chip them with a pick and split them in two and haul them with ice tongs up to the customer's back door while the horse plodded ahead, old Prince, who knew the route better than anybody. A gang of kids following along, grabbing chips off the wagon. One house after another, up Buchanan Street and down Lincoln and up Johnson and down Grant. There was a job that made a young man look forward to Friday night! Take off your ice apron and it was holy shit, get out of the way, Jim, time to go to the moon. Go to Marklund's Moonlite Ballroom and throw yourself at the young women in the lemonade section and see who picks you up. Drink gin from a jellyglass and drive fast at night with your headlights out. Once his pal Duke told him it took two days to drive to Chicago and Ray drove there in ten hours, careening through Wisconsin. He sideswiped a coal truck and skidded three hundred feet and into a ditch and bounced out and fifty miles later fell asleep and almost collided with the North Coast Limited. And all to make a point. Twice he saw Eternity beckon, but he was young and got away, and now the Time had come, and there were all those Other Women to think about, some of them deceased by now, others long in the tooth, all of them disappointed, and WLT lay on his conscience like a brick.

Women and Radio. His life in a nutshell.

An earnest young Methodist minister named Joe Simpson, the son of a former WLT program director, came around to sit and read from First Corinthians. As he saw it, spiritually speaking, it was the bottom of the ninth with Ray sitting on a five-run lead, and the Lord waiting for him in the dugout, hands outstretched, *well done, thou good and faithful pitcher*. The old man closed his eyes. "I don't think God is going to be that glad to see me," Ray whispered.

"But God's promise of eternal happiness to those who love Him—"

"I didn't love Him that much, if the truth be told."

"You don't mean that. You're not feeling so good, that's all."

"Damn right I'm not. I'm dying."

"Is there anything you want to get off your conscience?"

"Yes. Women and radio. My big sins."

"I'm praying for you, Mr. Soderbjerg. The Lord's will be done."

"I just wish he'd do it and get it over with."

━━━━

Roy visited him, though Ray had sent him a note saying not to come.

I am over here dying, and before I am done I want to say goodbye to you.

Goodbye.

Also I want to forgive you for anything you did, whatsoever, no matter what. All of it. It doesn't matter anymore.

I am sorry that we didn't sell the station in 1937 as we could have. The Denhams would have bought out 51% for $100,000 which was quite a chunk of change then as you know, but that is all water under the dam. A person has to live one day at a time and not look back. That is my principle. My will, if you are interested, leaves everything to the University.

There is no need for you to come over here at all, and in fact I don't want you to. Death is private. I am very well cared for and don't wish to have spectators. So don't visit. We have had thousands of visits and lunches, and that is enough. I am no fun to visit anymore. This is the disadvantage of dying, that you *feel so bad* while you're doing it, and though it's sad to think "I'll never see them again," it's much worse to see them again and get no pleasure from it.

Roy read this and went straight over to Ray's house, and Ray was feeling good enough to get dressed and sit in the solarium. A big white wicker chair was pulled up next to the windows, between the potted hydrangeas. The waterfall was turned off. Ray sat in the chair, in a black sweater and slacks, under a blue comforter, smoking a cigar, looking out across the snowy lawn, toward the garage. "I oughta get out the Buick and drive her, she's been sitting there for two months," he said. "Good car. You want it?"

"You said not to come, but I came anyway, because I have to tell you something. You don't want to hear it, but I have to say it, otherwise I wouldn't be your brother, I'd just be a false friend."

"I don't want to see you," said Ray.

"That's okay. It'll only take a minute."

"I don't feel good."

"You shouldn't. You're a cheater and a jerk. You ought to stop and consider that."

"That's what you had to tell me——?"

"If we had bought that land and built that building like I told you, the family would've earned millions plus the profits from the station. But no, you sign us up with the Ogden instead, and we pay rent through the nose, and you keep paying and paying and paying and paying, more and more and more, so who gets rich off this? Not your family, not the people who are loyal to you and work for you, but your landlord! Pillsbury! The rich guys walked away with the money, Ray. And the rest of us got chickenfeed. You know that's right. You screwed all those women and you screwed us too. We worked our butts off and made the business go, and you hurt us. You did dirt to the people who loved you. That's all I've got to say. I'm sorry you're dying."

"Is that all?"

"Yes."

"Then get out of here. And don't show your ugly face at my funeral."

"I'll come if I feel like it, and I'll sit in the front row and look at your big nose sticking up out of the coffin. And I'll listen to the minister who never met you in his life tell what a wonderful person you were, and I'll follow your coffin out to Lakewood Cemetery and see you lowered into the ground and I'll toss in a handful of dirt *but it'll have a stone in it.* When you hear a big thunk on the lid, know that that's from *me.* And afterwards I'll go to Charley's Cafe Exceptionale and have oysters and a martini and a prime rib and a bottle of the best red wine and I'll have a beautiful woman sitting across the table from me holding my hand and laughing at my jokes even if I have to pay her to do it."

Ray laughed. "I hope you do," he said. "Take Patsy Konopka. She's good to take to restaurants. Has the appetite of a horse and she can talk half the night. Loved every minute I spent with her. I remember we talked for two hours once and ate tiny lamb chops and drank a bottle of wine. We told each other everything. I told her I wanted to sleep with her. She said, 'I know.' We had coffee and for dessert we had ice cream wrapped in ice cream. I walked her back home. It was one o'clock in the morning. We stood in the doorway of the Antwerp and we kissed for half an hour. What wonderful kisses! I hope you come to my funeral with a woman as beautiful as her and I wish you the best of luck afterward."

A week before he died, he had climbed out of bed to go downstairs and sit in a chair while twelve big fellows in red plaid shirts from the Order of Woodmen presented him with a brass plaque that made him an honorary Boomer and gave him six big whoops and a zinc pickaroon. "You Have Enriched the Lives of Countless Thousands Through Your Contributions to Broadcasting," said the plaque, among other things. Roy Jr., a former Chief Whoopdepoop of the Woodmen, had arranged the ceremony, but the fellows had no idea who the sleepy old man in the blue bathrobe was.

The $800 bought Frank a whole three months. He lived in a dark room above a cigar store, his room smelled of smoke from below, like the essence of Ray ascending. Ten dollars a week for an army cot and a bureau dresser with the mirror gone and no shade on the window and the toilet down the hall filthy, the bathtub unspeakable. He bathed standing up, pouring water on himself with a Mason jar. He walked the streets and haunted the public library and lived on hot dogs. His biggest expense was talking to Maria in Minneapolis. He got a fistful of quarters and called her up almost every night. "Is Merle there?" he asked. She said no. She told him Ray was dying and Dad had retired and Roy Jr. had killed off the old shows. She was working at the perfume counter at Young-Quinlan, a nice job except that her boss kept asking her to the movies. Frank asked her to come and marry him. She said, "Get a job."

The cigar dealer lent him a typewriter, and Frank sat and typed his job resume, smoking a Cuban panatela, thinking of Ray. Ray would have some good advice for him, but who would want to talk to a thief? The resume was triple-spaced, four sentences, and offered no personal references. He typed fourteen copies and took them around to fourteen radio stations, but radio was firing, not hiring. He considered going to commercial school and training to become an office manager: $90 for a three-month course, and they guaranteed a job afterward. He thought about becoming a streetcar motorman. One night he rode the Western Avenue streetcar out to Riverview Amusement Park, rode the Silver Flash and the Blue Streak, the Boomerang and Aero-Stat and the Fireball and the Pair-O-Chutes, saw the freak show where Popeye popped his eyes and the hootchie-kootchie dancers and the African Dip where men threw baseballs at a target to dump a black man into a tank of water—a gaudy evening under the blazing lights, the girls in summer dresses brushing against his arms, and then a fortune teller on the midway looked at his palm and told him, "You have the soul of a waiter," and he recognized the truth of it. Why wait and wait for something wonderful to come along? Why not get a job? He walked three miles home to save a dime.

Ray Soderbjerg died on a Tuesday, the morning of the Big March Blizzard of 1951, and his obituary ("Radio Pioneer Succumbs at 73") was buried under news about rural families marooned in cars a few hundred yards from their homes. Even on *The Noontime News* on WLT, his passing was noted deep into the broadcast, after the school closings and before the basketball scores. The *Tribune* said that he was instrumental in the development of radio as a tool of education and a forum for debate on important public issues, listed some awards won by WLT, said he had died at home, that Vesta was returning from Sweden, that the burial would take place from Mount Olivet and interment in Lakewood Cemetery, noted Ray's membership in the Sons of Knute and Masons and the Brighten the Corner Club, and did not mention a fact dear to Ray's heart: that, for the last week of his life, Patsy Konopka lay next to him in his bed, holding his hand, smoothing his hair.

When she awoke at six that morning, his eyes were open and he spoke to her. He whispered (she thought), "Me today and you tomorrow." He was having difficulty swallowing so she gave him a few spoonfuls of whiskey, which helped, and she went to make him a poached egg for breakfast. Even if Ray didn't eat, he still enjoyed looking at a meal. She put the egg on a slice of toast, garnished with parsley, on a china plate covered with a bowl, on a tray with a white linen and a single rose in a silver vase, just like at a swank hotel, and as she fixed the tray, she heard him call, and came in to find him gone. She closed his eyes and straightened his covers and called up Roy Jr. She put on her coat and tiptoed out the back door, as if not to wake him, leaving the breakfast by his bed, and drove downtown to the Ogden.

It was not quite 7 a.m. She carried two shopping bags down the hall past the Green Room, where Leo LaValley was trying to clear his throat, and into Studio B.

The poor old jinxed studio had become a glorified closet, full of boxes of old *Friendly Neighbor* scripts and boxes of *Love's Old Sweet Song* scripts (marked LOSS), and hats and banjos and brass plaques, an empty trumpet case, stacks of newscasts, Leo's file of gags, old banners and placards and posters, unclaimed prizes, lost coats heaped on the piano, and underneath it was the gravel box Shirley had walked on towards the deserted farmhouse where the murderer lurked on *Arthur Fox, Detective* and the framed door Arthur had opened slowly, and the padded box the murderer fired the pistol into, and the box of broken glass Arthur had thrown him through, and around the room were strewn Gene's many notices and bulletins warning people to clean up: "Kindly remove all personal belongings from this room immediately" and "Disorder will not be tolerated in this area. This rule is in effect immediately" and "ALL PERSONAL EFFECTS not claimed by NOON FRIDAY will be disposed of. No exceptions" and Gene's final *cri de coeur*:

THIS IS A PIGSTY. IT WILL NOT BE TOLERATED.
NO SMOKING, NO ALCOHOL, NO LUNCHING
IN THIS ROOM.
THIS MEANS YOU.
I HAVE ATTEMPTED REASON, I HAVE OFFERED COMPROMISE, AND NEITHER HAVE GOTTEN US ANYWHERE. ANY NORMAL PERSON WOULD BE DISGUSTED. THIS ROOM WILL BE PUT BACK INTO WORKING ORDER IMMEDIATELY OR I WILL BE FORCED TO TAKE STERN MEASURES.

Rubbery grayish mold grew in the dusty coffee cups on the floor, next to ashtrays full of historic butts, and there, his head on the carpet spotted with black burn holes, lay Buck Steller, on his back, asleep, in a brown suit and a gold vest, his snap-brim hat under his poor old head, his mouth ajar and arms flung out as if he were singing at the Ritz, his sportscast in his hand. His snoring sounded like he might be saying, "Noooooo, not Massachusetts." Patsy stepped over him and set down her shopping bags.

Ray had packed them a week before, his eyes shining with exquisite pain, all his treasures. "Someday this stuff will be worth something. I want you to have it," he said. Old 78s of Jimmy Noone and Bix and the Lunceford band and Johnny and Baby Dodds and J. P. O'Blennis & His Evening Creepers and a signed portrait of Bryan and a bottle of 1928 Château Morton and a gold watch and chain and fourteen morocco-bound volumes of Mark Twain and a jar of rare coins and a china teapot and a small carved ivory figure of a naked woman brushing her long hair, her eyes closed, her face turned up toward the sun.

Patsy set the bags in the corner and laid a coat over them. It crossed her mind to take the bottle of wine, or the watch, and then she thought, No, they belong here, and she turned and stepped over Buck and slipped out of WLT and into the cold starry morning.

Maria called Frank to tell him that Ray was dead, and the cigar dealer downstairs answered and said, "He's gone, toots. Got his own apartment. No phone there but he said to tell you to call him at work. He's at WGN. Nice, huh? I think Frankie caught the brass ring. Good luck, toots."

———

Frank told her the whole story. "I walked into WGN and asked if they had had time to look at my resume yet, and I sat in the lobby for two hours before the receptionist sent me upstairs. By then it was five o'clock, the woman at the personnel desk was ready to go home. She already had her hat on, a large woman in a pinchback suit and tiny wire-rim glasses. She shook her head and waved me toward a door at the end of the room. 'Go downstairs and talk to Dave,' she said. 'I don't have time to deal with this.' So I went downstairs."

He went down three flights and through a glass door, into a long hall, one wall covered with photographs of burning buildings and famous people shaking hands. He heard voices through a door held slightly ajar by a block of two-by-four. Frank walked in. The room was thirty feet high, the walls covered with green acoustic tile, a radio studio apparently except that a thin blue curtain hung from ceiling to floor, wall to wall, and he was behind it, and the voices and the bright lights were on the other side. "Fifteen minutes!" a man shouted. "He told me fifteen minutes! Where is he?"

"Screw 'm!" said an older man.

"He should be so lucky."

They were wheeling large machines into position. A circle of light ten feet wide hit the blue curtain, shrank to six, grew back to ten. "If it stays there, I'm going through," thought Frank.

He opened the curtain. The light blazed in his eyes, but he saw a desk in front of him, a chair, a microphone, a script. In front of the desk were two television cameras. The men were pacing in front of a glass control-room window, but they stopped when Frank appeared.

One of them said, "You're not Ingram."

Frank said, "I'm White. Ingram isn't coming. I'm ready to go."

"Who are you?"

"Frank White."

The older man studied him. He said, "You couldn't have worn a cleaner shirt?"

Frank said, "Gray looks better on television anyway."

He sat down in the chair. (Nobody had told him not to sit in it.) An engineer adjusted the microphone and Frank looked through the script. News. Nothing tricky about it. The clock moved toward six and he kept expecting Ingram to come in or somebody to ask him if he had any television experience, but then it dawned on him: he didn't and neither did Ingram or anybody else.

A girl in a dark green dress stood beside the camera, perusing him, and he smiled. *Hi.* She had a magnificent head of waving black hair and such a sweet smile, she looked like Donna LaDonna dressed as a Girl Scout. She stepped up to the desk and patted his forehead with a powderpuff and stroked his cheeks. She smoothed his hair.

"Do you perspire heavily?" she whispered.

"I don't know."

"Well, you look real nice."

"Thank you, Donna."

She stepped back behind the camera. Frank smiled at the thought of what he was thinking, and the red light flashed and Frank looked into the black lens like it was her own dark eyes. "Good evening, ladies and gentlemen, I'm Frank White, and here is the news."

———

WGN hired him, he told Maria, and maybe it hadn't been necessary but he had lied and told them he had been the news director at WLT for six years. "Why?" she asked. Because he had told them that he was thirty years old and he needed to account for the time. "And I gave you as a character reference," he said.

"How can I be your character reference? I'm going to marry you."

"Once you marry me, I'm on my own, but until then, if anyone asks, tell them I'm a great man," he said, and then the beauty of it dawned on him, that the voice on the line was her, that she loved him and chose to live with him, and that was that, as clear as a bell. The end of the old days, the beginning of the new.

C H A P T E R   4 2

Epilogue

A few weeks before Easter, 1991, a few days after President Bush launched the ground war against Iraq, Frank White's biographer Richard Shell read in *People* that White was in Manhattan for a few weeks to see his friends and look at art. Shell had been writing the book for almost two years—it was now called *Frank White: The Untold Story* and was due out in the fall from Furness Press—working weekends and summers in a spare office at the junior college in New Hampshire where he taught mass communication. You didn't often see White's name in public print anymore, and Shell was thrilled to catch a glimpse. He clipped out the story, put it under his desk lamp, and studied the photograph.

The old bastard looked remarkably well-preserved. In fact, he looked younger than he had the year before in *Us*. There was a suspicious smoothness under the eyes, a slight ridge below the mouth that might, Shell thought, be a scar from cosmetic surgery. Why not? He had always wondered if cosmetic surgery wasn't the secret reason for

White's move to Paris, a city where a famous American could walk around unnoticed and let his face heal up. A facelift would certainly tie in with the theme of White's self-revulsion that ran through the book, the famous self-hatred of the famous. Shell made a photocopy on the office machine, enlarged it, examined it closely. Now the ridge looked more like a scratch, a wound that one might get from an enraged woman. "You miserable bastard, Frank!" she cried, and he ducked as she swung and her long lacquered nails raked the Paris night air and left a thin red gash across his chin. But who was she? Probably not White's wife, Maria. After forty years, does a wife take a swing at her husband? Shell, though unmarried, thought not. Probably it was a mistress. A Parisian mistress. Or a male lover—impossible? Hardly. AIDS? He did not rule it out. In a year, the man could be dead from it.

It was only a hunch, of course, but Shell took a few days' leave from his classes and drove down to New York and staked out the Sherry Netherland Hotel. Probably there wasn't time to check out the facelift, the mistress, the AIDS, but at least he could lay eyes on the bastard and cop a description of him in real life. *Weary, stooped, shivering, the naked newscaster trudged down the street—* something like that. The *People* story, "Frank White's Moveable Feast," didn't specify the Sherry, only "a suite on the fourth floor of a gracious old hotel overlooking Central Park," but the Sherry was where the Whites always stayed in New York, according to Wendell Shepherd, a good source. Shepherd was remarkably unbitter toward White, though White had stolen a chunk of money from him to bankroll his jump to TV. "I'd've done the same if it was me," said the old gospel star.

The biographer parked his old green Rambler on Fifth Avenue, about fifty feet north of the entrance, and loaded his camera and sat and waited. The Sherry had no lobby, which was why big stars liked to stay there: the doormen could keep out the curious. He spread his lunch on the seat, a Big Mac and a carton of fries and a vanilla shake, and waited for a lean white-haired man with a famous face to emerge.

The book was mostly finished: White's grim North Dakota childhood, his early years in Minneapolis at WLT, the move to Chicago and then, his lucky jump into television—imagine somebody walking into a station looking for a job and ten minutes later he is in front of the cameras!—and then, of course, New York and the *News Tonight* and the famous part of his life. Now Shell was hurrying to finish the manuscript before June and collect the second half of the $50,000 advance. It had been grinding hard work, poring through newspaper clippings, hunting down White's children, interviewing the veterans of radio's Golden Days—what a bunch of tiresome old windbags *they* were!

He tracked down Marjery Moore in Orlando, working as a hostess at a Toddle House restaurant, a big red-faced lady in a muu-muu. She showed him to a table but when he asked about White, she walked away. He got some things from Marjery's neighbors at the trailer court though—information about her love for White, and his punching her in the mouth—and snapped a photo of her looking stunned, like a load of dirt had been dumped on her.

He found Roy Soderbjerg, Jr., in San Diego, wheeling around on a bicycle, lean and cheery at 92. White was a thief, he said, but he, Roy Jr., bore him no ill will. "Calm as they come, that Frank. Got the nerves of a burglar." He would say no more. "Live for today. That's my philosophy. Leave history to the losers." And pedalled away. Reverend Odom was dead. Ditto Roy Soderbjerg Sr. and Lottie Soderbjerg. Vesta was dead, the victim of a hit-

and-run driver who clipped her in St. Paul one evening as she walked to a lecture by Harold Stassen. Slim Graves was dead, shot in a robbery, a clerk in a convenience store, gunned down for $14 and a loaf of Wonder bread—but Buddy Graves lived in Shreveport, an engineer at a TV station. He had not opened his mouth to sing in forty years. He barely remembered Frank at all or anybody else. Buddy seemed to be deeply involved in bourbon. Jodie With, Frank's sister, lived in Sausalito and was pleasant but vague. "Francis and I were birthed in one family, but we weren't spiritually related," she explained. "A coincidence of incarnation doesn't mean a lot, frankly." She gave Shell a picture of Francis, taken in Mindren. A skinny kid, his billowy mom draped around him, but the kid looking straight ahead, *intense*, not smiling, *watching*. She didn't want it back.

The Shepherds were in Minneapolis, doing various things unconnected to music or the church, but were unwilling to talk for publication without a cash advance and a contract. Al hinted that they knew quite a bit and that the right offer would shake loose a wealth of stories with rich details, conversations, names and places. Wendell said he had the lowdown on White's violent temper—how White had almost killed a man in a cafe in Baudette in 1950.

Dad Benson was dead, after many years at the Ebenezer Home, eight of them almost unconscious, but Patsy Konopka was still in Minneapolis, 89, a poet now and a grand exalted feminist poobah, a mountain of a woman, her white mane pulled back and tied with a turquoise clasp, a red Mexican serape over her voluminous blue Chilean dress. She remembered Frank only faintly as "very ambitious, looking for his chance, but not particularly aware. I had great hopes for him and then he turned out to have a mindset more or less like every other man at that time."

She had attended the big WLT Old-Timers dinner in 1984 and stood up and denounced the Soderbjergs as "boring, treacherous men" and said, "I would rather have known *one woman* than all the men of WLT," and that was the big story in the *Tribune* the next morning, the old-timers were a footnote. Roy Jr. was still steamed about it five years afterward, though he had donated sixty-five file drawers of Patsy's scripts to the Minnesota Women's Circle. It tickled him to think of feminist scholars poring over the stuff, page after deadly page, trying to find its importance as women's literature, and that their eyeballs must be getting pretty tired.

White's children, two boys and a girl, were a dead end, even the son who was on the outs with White, Marco, who ran a canoe resort on the Gunflint Trail in northern Minnesota. None of the children answered Shell's letters, and the daughter, Sally, who was an editor of interactive computer fiction in Santa Monica, went so far as to sic her lawyer on him. She had had an affair with a violinist, Shell found out, while the oldest son, Benjamin, had been treated for alcohol abuse, but there did not appear to be major tragedy glittering in their lives. Benjamin was a counselor at a college in California. He told Shell on the telephone that White had been an absentee father, but that he, Benjamin, had always known that his father loved him, and he told about long hikes through the Met to look at the Cézannes and going to Knicks games and ice-skating in Central Park and family boat trips up the coast of Maine and roasting clams on the shore and the birthday poems his father wrote for them all and how he made them learn five new words a day and Christmases in their vast, decrepit apartment on Riverside Drive with the high-ceilinged rooms that Maria sprayed white every year and the commanding view of the Hudson from the ancient dining table where they did their homework, and Shell set down his pencil and let the man wind down. "I hate to bring it up but there are ugly rumors that your father has a closetful of black cocktail dresses," said Shell. The man hung up.

Shell had talked to everyone he could find, and now all he needed was an opening for the book, a preface, a thousand words or so with Frank White in it: "The familiar white-haired figure who hurried across Fifth Avenue into the Sherry Netherland Hotel one raw day last spring was a face that passers-by recognized instantly but how well did they know the man behind that face and the heartbreak and ruin he had brought to his children and old colleagues and all who had loved him? Did the man himself, as he paused at the newsstand and picked up a copy of *Women's Wear Daily*, feel any remorse for the lives he had ruined or was he only thinking about the $175 lunch he had enjoyed minutes before at Le Cirque?" That sort of thing.

He had written to White a year before, asking for an interview, and White declined, a typewritten note from Paris. "I appreciate your request but I have to say no, for many reasons, one being that I don't talk very well about myself. And the other is, too much knowledge is an awful burden for journalists like us. That was the genius of the News Tonight: we were fresh and enthusiastic because we never knew too much. Your book will be better without my help. Good luck."

Easy for *him* to say, "Good luck," but okay, the book was almost done now, and just a glimpse of White was all he needed, to trail him for a few blocks, pick up some color ("As he stood on the corner of Fifth Avenue and 59th, White unknowingly stood at the center of a world he once dominated. Not a mile away was the old Palladium Theater where, in a makeshift studio, White pioneered the early morning news-and-interview show. To the west stood the old 68th Street Studios where his *News Tonight* was the cornerstone of a broadcasting empire for two decades. So on, so on, so on. Yowsa yowsa yowsa." But as he sat around that day, and the next, studying the processions of tourists, the Plaza, the gold statue of Sherman on his horse, the carriages parked along the boulevard, waiting for White, Shell started to think that what the book *really* needed was an ending.

When you pick up a biography, he thought, you always flip to the last chapter first and enjoy the great man's demise. That's what he always did. The last ride, the Big Drop—*He smiled his big toothy smile, waved gaily, turned away, and then, as she watched in horror, sank to his knees and collapsed on the sidewalk. A dentist who was on his way to lunch in the Acme Building tried to give artificial respiration, but it was too late. Wilfred Burris was gone*—people like to have a death at the end, though if the great man lingers on too long, senile, speechless—*In 1972, when his heart finally stopped beating, nobody was present, not Gwen, nor Rick, nor Mr. Bibb, nor even the faithful Bubbles, and when Simone got the phone call from Blessed Shepherd and heard the news, she felt nothing, no sorrow, no remorse, only a dim thought that she must now buy a new pair of shoes*—it's hard for the biographer to make it vivid. And some subjects simply refuse to expire at the end—*As of this writing, Phelps is still alive somewhere in southern California.* But so many others—actors, writers, painters, musicians—make terrific deaths, violent or abject, and there, Shell thought, is where the money is made in biography.

The hours passed. Death, he thought: death is what gives a biography real weight.

Having suffered through almost five-hundred pages of

Bunny Bigelow's messy life, his lying to friends, his endless self-pity and raging narcissism, his infantile sexuality, his relentless search for punishment, the reader savors the approach of the logical conclusion. *Alone in room 1421, the livid wallpaper of the Hotel Seymour swarming at him like a phalanx of carnivorous fish, tanked up on gin and barbiturates and the Big Reds he had come to love in the months since Alice left and the Yellowstone property was repossessed and* O Youth! O Golden Days! *had been greeted with shrieks of derision, his head down in the sink, his small puffy yellowish hand grasping the dime-store journal filled with dismal little revelations including the admission of his latent Republicanism, his filthy clothing strewn across the gray vomit-stained carpet, he choked to death on the cold pork chop. His body was not found until Wednesday, when the rent was due.* Or perhaps he dies in a car crash, at the age of 28, two weeks after his stunning triumph, his desk piled high with ecstatic reviews, letters begging him to come and speak and be interviewed, his body lying in a ditch, burned beyond recognition, decapitated in the red Ferrari, the beautiful calf's-leather seats smeared with blood. Unfortunate, in a way, to write about a distinguished old broadcasting fart, Shell thought. Maybe he would be stabbed to death late one night by an inept burglar, or he could drink himself to death, of course, but chances were he was not going to go down in flames. The *People* story made it sound like White was in good shape and eating his bran flakes.

"Ensconced in the red drawing-room in a suite on the fourth floor of a gracious old hotel overlooking Central Park, a chipper, clear-eyed Frank White sat, at sixty-two, in jeans, moccasins, and a tan suede shirt, and talked glowingly about his move last year to Paris. 'We live near the Bois de Malène, in a building that Czar Nicholas owned and where tattered remnants of the Russian aristocracy lived in faded splendor and supported themselves by teaching ballroom dancing to teenage boys and lonely old ladies. It tells you something about the fragility of things. Maria and I live there with our two dogs and our books and our paintings and that's all we need.' White, a serious art collector since 1954, has six rooms of American paintings, including a Hassam, two Hoppers, a Sloan, and three Levines, that any museum in the world would feel lucky to own. Art, however, is a subject White shies away from. 'I love to look at them and the moment I open my mouth to say something about them, I remember to close it,' he says."

Shell sat in his car and read the story again.

"The Whites came to Paris en route to Norway to spend a month at a mountain spa where you sit in a warm plankton gel on the edge of the fjord and absorb pure life through your pores, and they stopped in the city to see a journalist friend from the old days in New York, and the grandeur and good humor and the *calm* of the French seemed to him a purer bath than plankton, and they stayed.

" 'We Americans worry about the big things, like the future of civilization, and the French don't. They figure they can't do anything about it, so they concentrate on having a very good life today. They want the next loaf of bread to be the best, the wine to be good, the conversation good. They love good things: a perfect fish stew is a joy to them, but so is a fresh pear, or an old book. They fashion a civilized life out of what's at hand. Civilization doesn't come easy for an American. For one thing, we want to tear it all down and start over all the time. We're fatally ambitious people. And we work far too much. This is the American tragedy today: we work harder than our pioneer ancestors did and see less return for our labor and have to work even harder to stay even. Somehow, a hundred years after the slaves were freed, the American corporation has managed to bring it all back. The bottom line has become everything, the unions that spoke up for the employees are broken, corporate life is in a vicious frenzy, work is everything, and the victim is the American family and the American child. Family life in America, compared to Europe, is starved and frantic and laced with injury and bitterness. We're pushing, pushing, pushing to make our kids happy and we don't have time to show them how to live. In France, I see grownups enjoying their life, and children watching and learning, and in America, I see parents too exhausted from work to do much with their kids except give them expensive toys and sit and study them and feel guilty. That wasn't so true thirty years ago, and you could change it by introducing a National Vacation Law, like they have in Europe: five paid weeks a year, for everybody, even the unemployed, as a tribute to the family.'

"But White said he went to France, not for the culture but for the freedom.

" 'A face like mine is a pain in the ass to haul around the United States. After a thousand people have told you that television hasn't been the same since you left, you are ready to either ship out or buy a new face. When I strolled down the Rue Saint-Honoré and into the Place Vendôme one afternoon and realized that nobody had the faintest idea who I was and didn't care, I felt like breaking into a song and dance, but nobody ever wrote a song about that feeling. It's like a paraplegic who goes to a paraplegic convention and, *voilà*, becomes a man among men, suddenly free of the obligation of receiving other people's pity.'

The Whites sublet an apartment and a year later they bought it. 'We both feel tremendously lucky and full of health,' he said. 'And my wife is dancing again.' "

The rest was about Maria. Shell shoved the magazine back in his briefcase. He was a little dazed by the traffic, the boredom—two days and no sight of the bastard—and he was also stunned by what he was thinking. He climbed out of the car and crossed the street and looked at the used-book stalls along the stone wall beside Central Park. He picked through the stacks.

The timely death of a famous man can mean *a million dollars* to his lucky biographer, Shell thought. The famous man conks out in his relative prime, while his name is fresh and his admirers and the people who hate him are still in their prime book-purchasing years, and the biographer, who has gotten the Life in order, wakes up one morning, picks up the newspaper, and sees he has won the jackpot. He pens the final chapter, and the book is in the stores two months after the body is in the ground. But the violent death of a famous man can mean vastly more, mucho millions, depending on movie deals, television rights, so on. It could mean *three million dollars*. Maybe more. If Frank White were to put a shotgun in his mouth and pull the trigger, Shell was all ready to go to press. He had months of work locked up, ready to go. If White killed himself, it would multiply the value of the book fifty times, a hundred times, who knows?

This is only a wild idea, he thought to himself. This is not a plan. *But*—he could offer White a ride—pretend to be a young TV reporter and corner the man on the street and fawn over him ("I know all about your life, I've read everything you ever wrote or said, you are— there's no other way to say this—you are my hero") and then: "Mr. White, I'm going to ask you a fantastic favor. I have my car *right here*. I'd like you to hop in and point out to me where you walked when you left the Palladium Theater that night in—what was it? 1953? when Roy Cohn had threatened your sponsor, Sport-Tex, and they told you to cool it and you took that long walk about 2 a.m. and finally decided to take a stand? I would like to know where that took place. It's the only thing I want to know. Then I'll bring you right back here or wherever you want to go."

The old fart'd be flattered out of his pants. He'd make a little flutter of modesty but he'd climb in and start gassing about the McCarthy era and Shell'd drive down Fifth Avenue and then hang a left into a side street and then suddenly clap the chloroform to Frank White's nose and shove him down on the floor and hold him until he went limp and haul him to the Brooklyn Bridge and throw him over. Then he'd go back to New Hampshire and write the last chapter.

"Sunk in a deep depression since his impulsive move to Paris, White came to New York for psychiatric treatment. Much as he talked up France and its superior civilization, White was miserable there. He missed the limelight. Once adored by millions as a fount of wisdom, now he was alone, barely able to converse with the newsboy, unable to explain to a plumber that the toilet leaked. Dejected, he and Maria took the $200/day suite at the Sherry Netherland, the same gilded suite where they had shacked up so often in the past, but the memories only aroused Frank's black guilt for what he had done to those who had helped him. Eating a $30 room-service breakfast, he was haunted by visions of (name), the first woman he loved, the one who stood by him in poverty and anonymity, who lived in squalor in (town) while he was ensconced in a red drawing room in a fourth-floor suite in a gracious hotel overlooking Central Park.

"A few days after their arrival, Frank was unable to

leave the suite, unable to talk on the phone or eat a sandwich or look in a mirror without weeping. He lay in a bed for three weeks, too infirm to hold a book or a copy of the *Times* and thus, the man *TV Guide* once called 'The Father of Anchors' was forced to pass the time watching television. He was struck by its unspeakable shallowness and brutality. After a few days, he saw that his life had been wasted and that his so-called talent had been a depraved and vicious one. He tried twice to hang himself with a leather belt, and to throw himself from the window, and to drop an electrical fan into the bathwater, but Maria intervened. Finally he gathered up all his willpower, and he forced himself to appear to improve. He made himself accompany her to dinners and movies. He made himself laugh and carry on conversations. Inside, his guts were busted, but he kept dancing, kept smiling, kept shaking hands, until finally she relaxed her guard, and that night he took a cab to the Manhattan end of the Brooklyn Bridge. The legendary abutments and harp-like suspension cables immortalized by the poet Hart Crane were wreathed in fog, as he walked to the midpoint, tied his Medicare card to his left ankle for identification, gave $200 from his wallet to a passing tramp and climbed up the rigging and over to the edge. Perhaps he paused a moment, looking down at the roiled waters, and thought of the day, etc. Perhaps he remembered (fill in details)——Did he perhaps feel a twinge of regret for the people he had hurt and the damage he had caused? (Etc.) If so, it lasted only a few seconds, and then his body hurtled down in the darkness. According to the coroner, he died immediately on impact from a broken neck."

Shell thought this passage, like a dream, in one smooth flash. And he remembered the line from William Safire —he had clipped it out of the *Times* and taped it to his refrigerator—"The inconceivable becomes the inevitable: that's leadership." The line referred to Bush's war, but it was so *true*, it applied here, too. One man can take things into his own hands. The unthinkable becomes unavoidable.

He had worked hard on Frank White. He had earned some property rights there and now he owed it to himself to kill him. He crossed 59th Street and looked at the Corvettes in the showroom window. Where could he obtain chloroform? Perhaps from a pet store. Tell them he had an old mutt he had to put away. They'd stock chloroform or something like it, and a bottle big enough to kill a big dog would be sure to knock out Frank White for an hour. He didn't think chloroform could be traced in the blood. Maybe they wouldn't even perform an autopsy, especially if there was a suicide note. Which would be a nice touch for the book.

All this brilliance was making him hungry. The hotdog wagon was right there, ten feet away; he got an Italian sausage on pita bread, onions, peppers, tomato, hot sauce, the works, two bucks, and ate it as he crossed Fifth Avenue.

He could get Frank White to write his own suicide note in the form of an autograph.

Simple. It'd go like this. *Before* the business about Roy Cohn, he'd say, "Mr. White, my mom is your biggest fan and I wonder if you'd write a note to her. She always loved your sign-off on the News Tonight. Could you write: *Dear Mother, Good night and good luck. Frank White?* Gosh thanks. She's going to be thrilled."

Or maybe in the car, parked on the side street, prior to the chloroform.

White's mother had killed herself in 1956. She was living alone in a rooming house in Duluth, and one warm spring day she came down to the harbor and jumped off the Lift Bridge. She had to wait for an hour for an ore boat to come steaming in off Lake Superior and the Lift Bridge to lift—in its normal *down* position, it was too low to permit suicide—and then she waited too long to jump, and jumped onto the upper deck of the boat as it passed beneath, a fall of twenty feet. She landed without a scratch. The crew had been at sea for more than a month and Mrs. White, though despondent, was attractive to them. They took her out for an evening on the town, carousing, dancing, moving from bar to bar along Superior Avenue, and after she had downed a snootful of gin rickeys, she dropped dead on the barroom floor. A leap from the Brooklyn Bridge would be, in a sense, the son's attempt to finish what the mother had set out to do—a sort of bridge between them (though one needn't lay that on too heavily)—the last chapter could be entitled "Mother and Son Reunion" and the famous sign-off seen nightly on national television could be seen now as White's lifelong suicide note, his secret pact with his mother, his covenant with death—Shell crossed 59th, eating the last inch of the sausage, thinking he might need another one. *This had been the theme of the book all the way and he had never recognized it before.* Suicide. It was written all over White's life. How had he missed it? The steadiness of the man, what was it but the certainty of one who has Already Made Up His Mind—that Olympian baritone voice, so reassuring to millions, was the voice of a man who knew his own end. He had risen to the heights to please the mother and now he would fall from the heights and rejoin her.

It was all there. A book that would earn him three million dollars *and* would be admired, really admired, held up on the front page of the *Times Book Review* as a work that blazes a new trail in the misty thickets of biography —*perhaps the best book on an American life since Henry*

Adams—he looked up at Sherman, blazing gold on his pedestal, the Sherry Netherland beyond—

———

According to witnesses, he never saw the yellow truck. It clipped him on the right side and flung him thirty feet through the air and he landed hard against a lamppost. Witnesses standing across the street heard bones snap when he hit. He lay on the sidewalk for ten minutes, bleeding from his mouth, his ears, his body crumpled like a pile of used clothing, and then an ambulance took him to Lenox Hill Hospital. He had broken his right arm, a collarbone, eleven ribs, his pelvis, his right leg, and crunched two vertebrae, but the cruelest injury, they found, after they had screwed his bones together, was to his brain. When they reduced the Demerol and he was fully awake, the patient had no memory at all and very little intellectual function. The brain CT scan and magnetic resonance imaging showed no lesions, no hematoma. Weeks passed, the patient seemed comfortable and in no distress, but he could not speak, though he was able, gradually, to learn a few words again: *Hello. Water. Toilet. Food. Pill. Thank you*, though he could not distinguish between *Yes* and *No*.

When he was brought in, he appeared to be about fifty, white, well-nourished, well-kept, and from his clothing, the corduroy jacket, blue button-down shirt, pre-faded jeans, Hush Puppies, the police assumed he was an academic. His billfold, if he had one, had disappeared before the ambulance arrived. Two detectives roamed along 59th Street for an afternoon and part of the next day, inquiring at hotels about missing guests, showing a photo of the man to bartenders and carriage drivers. The doorman at the Sherry Netherland said, "It's about time you guys show up." He had seen two young men hotwire a green Rambler—on Fifth Avenue! in the middle of the afternoon!—and he had called 911 and here it was a day later before the cops arrive. They gave him a number to call for auto theft—911 was only for emergencies, they explained.

The only clue—and it was a slim one—was a page of yellow legal-size paper, folded three times, on which somebody—presumably the unknown man—had written notes that referred, apparently, to the television-news celebrity Frank White. The notes did not make sense, being all about White's suicide, and White was very much alive. In fact, he was staying nearby at the St. Moritz. The detectives went up to see him. They apologized. They were sorry to bother him, extremely sorry, but he invited them in, sat them down, set out a couple glasses of Evian and a fruit plate, chatted with them. Their names were Vince and Sean. They asked him to look at the notes.

White took the folded yellow sheet. They were sorry, it was an unpleasant business, but could he think of anybody who might write such things about him? Anybody? White read the notes—about his mother, the old sign-off, his depression, his death wish—and looked up and grinned. "There's been a lot of negative stuff written about me," he said, "and this is the first I've read that didn't have some truth to it." He had no idea who could've written it.

They heard a key in the lock and the door opened and a woman appeared, lugging a trunk. "It was only forty dollars, it's built like a safe, you could ship rocks in it," she said. She was out of breath. She was tall, rangy like a runner, with cropped gray hair and bright green eyes, and she wore a black ribbed sweater and blue jeans and hiking shoes. Dark glasses propped on top of her head. "My wife Maria," he said. The detectives stood up to go. They apologized again for bothering him. The man had been struck by a truck, was incoherent, the paper was the only clue to who he was.

"What paper?" asked Maria. Vince showed her the paper and she read it. "It's got to be that man who's writing the book about you," she said. "Who else would care about this nonsense? It's that poor man Shell."

And so Richard Shell was identified. Lenox Hill was paid $220,000 by his health insurance company, and he was returned to New Hampshire, to a nursing home a few miles from the college, where, after his savings were used up, the state and the county paid for him to be fed and bathed and walked every day. His students looked high and low for the book manuscript, and found it on a disc in his desk at home, and there was talk of editing it for publication, as a memorial to him, but then school let out and everybody went home.